Summit
Books

ALSO BY DANIEL KEHLMANN

Tyll

You Should Have Left

F

Fame: A Novel in Nine Stories

Measuring the World

Me and Kaminski

THE DIRECTOR

A NOVEL

DANIEL KEHLMANN

Translated from the German by Ross Benjamin

SUMMIT BOOKS

New York Amsterdam/Antwerp London
Sydney/Melbourne Toronto New Delhi

Summit Books
An Imprint of Simon & Schuster, LLC
1230 Avenue of the Americas
New York, NY 10020

Originally published in Germany in 2023 by Rowohlt Verlag as *Lichtspiel*

First Summit Books hardcover edition May 2025

Interior design by Carly Loman

Manufactured in the United States of America

1 3 5 7 9 10 8 6 4 2

Library of Congress Cataloging-in-Publication Data is available.

ISBN 978-1-6680-8779-4
ISBN 978-1-6680-8781-7 (ebook)

For Anne and for Thomas Buergenthal (†)

How did anyone even manage back then to keep getting out of bed in the morning, day after day? Heaved up and drifting along on a broad wave of absurdity, although we knew and saw it, which made it all the worse! But in the end this very knowledge was what kept us alive, while others far better than we were swallowed up.

—HEIMITO VON DODERER, "Under Black Stars"

CONTENTS

OUTSIDE

What's New on Sunday?

Why am I in this car?

I'll sit still. Sometimes, if you don't move, your memory comes back.

But it's not working. One thing is certain, the driver is smoking. The vehicle is filled with heavy smoke. My eyes are burning. I feel sick. The man has gray hair, dandruff on his shoulders. On the rearview mirror a small cross is swinging on a string of pearls.

One thing at a time. The driver picked me up, held the door open for me, and the others looked on open-mouthed, scrawny Franz Krahler, stupid Frau Einzinger, and also the small man whose name I can never remember.

Because actually, at the Abendruh Sanatorium, every day is the same as the next. At breakfast the radio is on, you go to the park, your back hurts, there's lunch, you look at the newspaper and get annoyed, while the TV is on; some are watching, others are sleeping, someone is always coughing pitifully. Then it's already half-past three and dinner is served, and then you lie awake and have to go to the bathroom every half an hour. Sometimes there are visitors, but never for me. Sometimes someone dies and is taken away. But those who are still alive are not usually picked up by a black car with a chauffeur.

We stop at an intersection, where three teenagers with long hair are crossing the street very slowly. The driver rolls down the window and yells that another war would do young punks like them some good, and when they ignore him, he only gets angrier. He drives off, still ranting.

And now it comes back to me: to the television studio.

"But which program?" I ask, leaning forward.

The driver turns around and looks at me through the clouds of smoke, not understanding.

I repeat the question.

"I don't care!" he shouts. "Why should I give a damn?"

So I don't say anything else.

But he's getting worked up. "I want to be left alone, just left alone! Is that too much to ask?"

When we stop in front of the broadcasting studio, he has just pulled himself together. He gets out, walks around the car, opens the door for me. He grabs me by the elbow, pulls me up. This is rude, but it actually helps me get on the street without falling.

The facade of the broadcasting studio is even grayer than the surrounding facades. All the buildings in Vienna are gray now, except for a few that are dark brown. The whole city seems covered with dirt. In winter the sky is stony and low, in summer yellowishly damp. Even that was different once. If you're old enough, you know that in this city of garbage, coal smoke, and dog shit, even the weather is no longer what it was.

The revolving door rotates haltingly, and for a moment I'm afraid that my journey will end here, but I get through, and in the lobby someone is actually waiting for me: a very thin young man with a clever face and round glasses, who shakes my hand and introduces himself as Rosenzweig, the editor in charge.

"Very good," I say. I'm always pleased when young people are polite. It doesn't happen often these days. "In charge of what?"

"Of the program."

"What program?"

He looks at me for a few seconds before he says: "What's new on Sunday?"

"I don't know."

"The program!"

"What?"

"That's the name of the program. *What's New on Sunday.*"

What is this person talking about?

"This way please!" He points to a door at the other end of the lobby. I follow him down a short corridor; then we're standing—and this isn't good at all—in front of a paternoster elevator.

The first compartment passes by, followed by a second. I suppose I have to step into the third, I'm frightened, it passes by too. Come on, I tell myself, you've experienced worse. As the fourth compartment rises in front of me, I close my eyes and stagger forward. I make it inside, but would have fallen down if he hadn't held me by the shoulder. It's a good thing he reacted so quickly.

"Let go of me," I say sharply.

Getting out is even harder, of course. But he sees it coming, places his hand on my back, and gives me a little push. I stagger out, he holds me steady again, thank God.

"Stop that!" I say.

It smells of plastic; from somewhere comes the hum of large machines. We walk down a corridor with signed photos of grinning people hanging to the left and right. A few of them I recognize: Paul Hörbiger, Maxi Böhm, Johanna Matz, and there's Peter Alexander, who for some reason has scrawled *With great thanks to my dear, dear audience* under his signature.

The young man opens a door with the word MAKEUP on it. A fat fellow with a full beard is sitting in front of a mirror, with a makeup artist standing behind him, working on his face with a brush. When she steps back, he leaps up so suddenly that I flinch, and he hugs me. He smells of aftershave and beer. In a voice quivering with happiness, he asks: "How are you, Franzl?"

I mumble that I'm doing fine, which is actually never true, least of all right now. I'm trying not to inhale. His beard is tickling my cheek.

"And you?" I gasp.

"Oh Franzl, what can I say? Liesl died two years ago, and the thing with Wurmitzer didn't end well. And I even say to him: Ferdl, you have to do it now because of the old friendship, but did he want to listen? And, as you know, then I preferred to stay with Stenger, but he wasn't honest."

I can't breathe. Who the hell is this? Who are the people he's talking about? At last he lets go of me, takes a loden jacket with staghorn buttons from the coat hook, big as a tent, throws it on, and walks out.

I sit down. The makeup artist starts working on my face, and asks the same questions makeup artists always ask, what it is I do and what brings me to the program. They never know beforehand, they never recognize anyone, they've never looked it up, they always ask.

"Herr Wilzek is a director," says the young man who brought me here. I wish he'd told me his name, but young people these days don't know how to conduct themselves.

Of course she now asks what movies I've made, and with the same discomfort as always I list my three measly titles: *Peter Dances with Everyone* with Peter Alexander, *Gustav and the Soldiers*, also with Peter Alexander and with Gunther Philipp, and *Schlück Is the Last to Go Home* with people I don't remember.

And now, of course, she asks about Peter Alexander: "What's he really like? He's never been to me for makeup, surprisingly. I'd love to meet him one day."

I tell the anecdote that I always tell: "On the very first day of filming *Peter Dances with Everyone*, he knew all his lines by heart. Then the shooting schedule had to be changed on short notice, and a young actress, whose name I'd rather not mention, because in the meantime she's become quite well known, had only learned the lines for that day, and then Peter looked at her and said: 'Dear Fräulein, learning lines is like riding horses, do you want to know why?'"

God, my reflection! At the Abendruh Sanatorium we don't have mirrors, because no one shaves themselves; Zdenek, the caregiver, does it every morning. And so the sight comes unexpectedly: my eyes deep in their sockets, the sagging bags of skin, the cracked lips, the wrinkled gray skin on my bald head. My jacket sits askew, because my shoulders no longer fill it. My tie is not only stained but also badly tied, which isn't my fault, because it's been a long time since I've been able to tie a tie; Zdenek did that too. Can't he make an effort? How often does it happen that one of us is put on television? I close my eyes so that I don't have to see myself anymore. There's a hissing sound; cold wind from the hair spray can blows over my scalp. But why? I have hardly any hair.

"Yes, why?" asks the makeup artist.

What's going on?

"'Like riding horses,' he said, why?"

What does she want from me?

"All right," she says after a pause. "Done."

I stand up, my knees buckle, the makeup artist and the young man support me.

"Don't worry," he says, leading me out into the corridor. Hanging on the walls are signed photos of Paul Hörbiger, Johanna Matz, Peter Alexander. I once worked with him.

"Herr Conrads will ask only the questions we discussed beforehand. Just tell a few of those wonderful old stories of yours—nothing can go wrong. Herr Conrads never deviates from the script; he only asks questions prepared by the editorial team. And in this case, that's me. He never improvises."

"I have to go to the bathroom."

He looks at his watch. Rosenblatt! I don't know how I know it, but that's his name. Something about it worries me, but at the moment I can't say what.

He points to a door. "But please hurry."

I go in. Everything is complicated: my fingers are numb and can't properly feel the belt buckle and pants buttons, so it's not exactly easy to pull my pants down, and on top of that the toilet seat is set too low. Then the roll of paper falls to the floor. I bend down, but when I try to pull it back, it unrolls further, and disappears through the gap under the stall wall.

I hear footsteps, someone pacing back and forth, calling my name: "Herr Wilzek, we have to go to the studio!"

"Yes, yes!" I shout.

"It's a live broadcast!"

"Yes, just a moment. Just a moment."

Now there are several people. I hear agitated voices. And I've finished, actually, but standing up is fiendishly difficult, because the seat is too low, and now it's time for the pants buttons and the belt buckle. I do everything as slowly as necessary. Rushing only makes it harder.

I step out of the stall. Five men and three women are standing there, apparently all waiting for me. How can it be that women are allowed in here? Is this what we've come to, is nothing sacred anymore? But before I can even complain, they've surrounded me—one supports me from the right, another from the left, a third pushes; they don't even let me wash my hands.

"The program has already started," says one.

"We've moved the second guest up," says another.

"You have to go in. You'll be live immediately," says a third.

A steel door opens, we are in a studio. Two cameras glide soundlessly through the room, I hear the high-pitched whistle of the spotlights, microphones hang on wires from the ceiling. In the middle a small living room is set up: flowered wallpaper with little landscape pictures in golden frames nailed to it, a sofa, an armchair, a table with coffee cups. Sitting on the sofa is a huge man with a beard, wearing a loden jacket. Standing next to him is a man I recognize; he's always on the television in the Abendruh Sanatorium, but I can't remember his name. At the moment he is singing to tinny music from the loudspeaker, kissing his fingertips again and again. Someone is pushing me forward, I almost trip over a cable, I'm maneuvered past the camera, now I'm sitting next to the bearded man on the sofa.

The presenter is no longer singing, he's talking about me. "A special pleasure," he says in a peculiar singsong, "to have Franz Wilzek here with me, my dear old friend!"

And I don't even know him. I know I'm a little forgetful, but really, I've never met this person before.

He turns around and approaches me with his hand outstretched. "Dear Franzl!" The first camera circles around him, while the second turns to my face; the red light jumps from one to the other, and on a monitor I see myself, forcing a smile, with big bags under my eyes.

His name is Conrads! Suddenly it came to me, Heinz Conrads—my memory isn't that bad. But I've really never met him before. I shake his hand without getting up. He is visibly displeased that he has to bend down.

He turns to the camera and continues talking about me. He is reading from a stack of cards, but stretching the words in such a surprised, confusedly thoughtful way that no one would suspect he isn't coming up with everything he says on the spot. Director, he says, wonderful funny movies, brought us all much joy, *Gustav and the Soldiers*, *Peter Dances with Everyone*, worked with all the best-loved stars! The monitor shows a clip: Peter Alexander singing, leaping, and grinning. I give a friendly nod, even though I can see that I'm not on-screen; the red light is glowing on the camera filming Heinz Conrads, and the monitor again shows his doughy face under the concrete-hard white helmet of hair.

And now it has happened. He falls silent and looks at me. The light jumps; my face appears on the monitor. Did he ask me something? I was inattentive for just one moment, and that's when it happened!

I listen to the whistling, electrically crackling silence. Then I tell an anecdote chosen at random about the actor Schlück Battenberg. It's halfway funny, and it works too: Heinz Conrads kisses his fingertips and exclaims: "Delightful!" The bearded man next to me also laughs, pounding his chest.

"Have you two known each other long?" asks Heinz Conrads.

"All our lives," says the man I don't know.

They both laugh again. All in all, it seems to be going well. My head doesn't work like it used to, but a program like this is something I can still manage.

So I don't even wait for the next question, but tell the anecdote about how Gunther Philipp fell into the water during the filming of *Gustav and the Soldiers*. Actually a weak story, there's no punch line, the stupid fellow just fell into the water, and then they pulled him out, but the two of them laugh again, and so I also tell my best story, the showpiece: the young actress who only learned the lines for the first day. And how Peter Alexander looked at her and said, "Dear Fräulein, learning lines is like riding horses! Do you want to know why?"

"Yes, Peter!" cries the idiot next to me. "He is really one of the greats!"

I give him a sharp look to show him that he should be quiet.

"Why?" asks the presenter.

"Why—what?"

"Riding horses?"

The whistle of the spotlights is so shrill and yet so soft that you can't be sure whether you're really hearing it. The red light jumps from one camera to the other. I follow it with my gaze and see my head jerking back and forth on the monitor.

"Oh, like riding horses!" I take a breath to finish my story.

But something has been thrown out of rhythm, the story has become tangled, the next sentence won't come. The one after the next is ready, so I skip ahead, but just at that moment it too dissolves—I still sense its outline, and I can almost feel it with my tongue. But when the words don't form, I make the mistake of looking at the screen. There I am, my face confused and my mouth open. And sitting opposite yourself like this, split in two, and knowing that everyone at the Abendruh Sanatorium is watching, you really can no longer remember anything.

The presenter nods, folds his hands with the cards, looks up at the ceiling as if in prayer, and exclaims: "Delightful! Horses!"

The man next to me laughs.

"Marvelous!" the presenter exclaims.

They must be sick with envy at the home right now, especially Franz Krahler and the stupid Frau Einzinger. And because I can't push the image aside—I see Krahler sitting pale in his chair and Einzinger open-mouthed next to him—it happens once again, and I miss the next question.

"Excuse me?"

Heinz Conrads turns his eyes to the ceiling, sighs, and reads from his card: "Franz Wilzek became a director only late in life. Before that he was the assistant of G. W. Pabst."

Why is he suddenly talking about me in the third person?

"G. W. Pabst," he declares. "One of the great directors. A master, a legend. I knew him too, but no one knew him like you did!"

Images flicker on the monitor: Greta Garbo in *The Joyless Street*, Louise Brooks in *Pandora's Box*, Mack the Knife twirling his cane. I clear my throat and explain: "That's Garbo. He discovered her for the movie. I only joined later—in 1941 with *The Comedians*. We met on the set of . . . A year earlier. On another movie. I was actually a camera assistant."

Now Heinz Conrads's face fills the screen again. "He had just come back," he reads from the next card. "From exile. To make films in German again. You became his new assistant."

I nod. Apparently I'm supposed to say more, but what? Behind the camera a young man with round glasses has stepped out of the darkness. I've seen him before, but I can't remember where. All I know is that his name is Rosenkranz.

"Did he tell you why he came back?" Heinz Conrads reads out.

"He had already been in America. And then he was back here making movies for . . . " He falls silent and holds his card as if something is wrong. It only lasts a moment, then he gains control of his features, twists his mouth into his doughy smile, slides the card to the back of the stack.

"And after *The Comedians* the two of you made *Paracelcus*," he reads. "With the great Werner Krauss, a great film, a classic."

"A masterpiece!" I say.

"What was he like, G. W. Pabst—he did always have his name spelled with the two initials, G. W., didn't he? He was usually addressed that way too. So what was he like, how would you describe him?"

"A bit too fat."

Heinz Conrads laughs. "That's Franzl! Always joking!"

"He always wanted to lose weight. He wasn't very tall, but somewhat round, and on set he laughed a lot, but when the lights went out, he often looked emptied out. Like a costume that no one is wearing."

The whistle has grown louder and shriller, and the brightness is suddenly almost unbearable. I can barely see the presenter anymore, I'm so blinded.

"But when he gave an order, everyone obeyed. It didn't even occur to anyone to do otherwise. Except when his mother was there. I saw her only once, she came to visit when we were filming *The Comedians*, he immediately looked like a child. A few months later she died." I have to swallow; my throat is dry. The couch under me seems to be slowly floating across the room. "He had his own theory of film editing. That a cut must always be based on a movement, creating an unbroken flow from the first shot to the last. Later, when I was directing myself, I realized that in practice it's hardly . . . " No, I've gone too far, you can't talk like that here. "He often talked about Greta Garbo!" I exclaim. "Such a beautiful woman! And Louise Brooks, who is hardly known today, but back then she was almost as big a star as Garbo. He discovered her too."

"Ah yes! The beautiful women!" Heinz Conrads laughs with relief. He moves another card to the back and reads: "And in your next film, *The Molander Case*, the great Paul Wegener played the lead role?"

"Which film?"

"Your next film," he reads off the card. "*The Molander Case*. Paul Wegener played the lead role."

"Doesn't exist."

"Paul Wegener?"

"That film. It doesn't exist; it was planned, but never shot."

For a few seconds it's silent, then Heinz Conrads says: "No, no, it says here . . . It was shot. It's just that no one has seen it, it was then lost."

"It wasn't shot."

Heinz Conrads looks somewhere behind the camera. "Well, I was told you finished filming it, in early forty-five in Prague. Under difficult conditions, in the last weeks of the war, but then the footage just disappeared." He squints at his card. It's evidently the last one. He flips it over, looks helplessly at the back.

"It wasn't shot!" I shout. "It isn't true, goddamnit, it doesn't exist! It's a mistake! A lie."

"Excuse me?"

"A lie!"

Heinz Conrads looks at his last card, then at the young man with glasses, then at the card again. "Franzl, you must remember your film, don't you?"

"It was never shot!"

Heinz Conrads frowns so hard that his face seems to be imploding. At that moment my eyes meet those of the young man with glasses. He isn't looking at his boss but at me, intently and directly, with a thin, frozen smile.

I look at the screen. See myself looking off somewhere—of course, the monitor isn't the camera, you have to look into the camera to see yourself looking out from the monitor, except then you obviously can't see yourself because you're looking into the camera, not at the monitor. And now the monitor, even though it's showing me, is showing something else at the same time, and to avoid seeing it, I close my eyes, but that doesn't help, and I still see them: black-and-white people in a concert hall. From high above I'm looking down on them, as if I were flying, a crystal chandelier is shining brightly, I'm sitting next to the camera on the arm of a long crane. They're all facing forward, because they're not allowed to look up.

I open my eyes, but I still see it, as clear as ever, just as we saw it on the small screen back when Pabst was editing the film beside me. And at the same time I see it from above, from the sweeping crane on which I'm perched, while down below Pabst directs through the megaphone, farther forward, now pan to the right, to the stage, farther, where the actor is standing and playing violin!

"It wasn't shot! Your team did a bad job! You're wrong! It never came to be!"

The people below me. They're not allowed to look up. If anyone looked up, it would ruin everything. It is crucial that the soldiers stay out of the field of view, because the shot must be finished today, and now Heinz Conrads is coming up to me: "Dear Franzl, such a pleasure having you here, but unfortunately we're out of time!" I think he's about to take a swing at me, and I raise my hands in front of my face, but he turns to the camera, the red light flashes, the monitor shows his face so large that his nostrils look like craters. "Goodbye, dear friends," he says in a singsong, "thanks for tuning in, and wishing you all the best until we meet again!" Tinnily tinkling piano music from the loudspeakers, the red light goes out, on the monitor swirling letters form the words *What's New on Sunday with Heinz Conrads*.

Evidently it's over. The young man with glasses whose eyes have been fixed on me the whole time is approaching me. "The credits will now run three times in their entirety. We had to bail out early. That has never happened before. You can be proud."

"I hope you feel better soon," says the bearded man in the loden jacket next to me. "Nice to see you again, Franzl."

"You too," I say, because I can't think of anything else.

"Did you really not shoot *Molander*? I always thought it had been finished, but then, when the uprising began in Prague—"

I turn away and reach out my arm to indicate to the young man, whose name suddenly comes to me, it's Rosenkranz, and for some reason this bothers me, to help me up. He does so. We take small steps toward the door.

But Heinz Conrads is blocking our way. His face is contorted with rage.

"Goodbye, dear Heinzi," I say.

"Crawl into your shithole and die."

I stare at him. For a moment I think I've misheard him.

"And you?" he says to the young man. "How dare you bring this ancient shithead on my show? Here he is with half his marbles, and you stick me with these questions. You pack your things and get the fuck out of here, I never want to see you again!"

"Very gladly," says Rosenkranz.

"Shut up. I don't want to hear it, fuck off!"

"Gladly," Rosenkranz says again. We walk around Heinz Conrads, who is pale with rage. Walking with my eyes half shut, I hear a heavy door open and close.

"For months I've wanted to quit," says Rosenkranz. "But anyone can just give notice, I thought. You have to come up with something better."

I feel weak. The program really exhausted me; not only my hands but also my arms and shoulders are shaking. What happened anyway? My memory is already blurring. At first I was telling stories, everything was going well, then Pabst came up, of course, I'm always asked about him, and then everything fell apart. I got angry, perhaps even shouted, and I remembered the filming of *Molander*, but that's not actually possible, because we never filmed *Molander*.

"And then the boss said, all right, let's go ahead and invite him, and then I wrote the questions, as always." He falls silent for a moment, then he says: "My father was there."

"Your father?"

"He was an extra. In the concert hall . . . In hall seven, in the studio in Barrandov, when you were shooting *The Molander Case*."

"Where's the bathroom?"

I have to stop. The floor is swaying; I think I'm going to fall. But he's wrong, the film was never shot. I know because I was there. I was there when we didn't shoot the film. I remember it not happening. I clear my throat, I want to explain.

"I've searched everywhere," he says. "There's no copy. The negative is lost. You're probably the only person who saw the dailies. Besides Pabst, of course. But Pabst is dead."

I push on the handle of the bathroom door and go inside. For a moment I'm afraid that he'll follow me, but fortunately he stays put.

The door closes. Everything is difficult, my clothing resists. My numb fingers can't manage the pants buttons, the toilet bowl is too low. Only when I'm sitting down do I notice that the toilet paper roll is on the floor—I pull on it, but it only unrolls further, everything is so laborious. My elbow hurts, my back is stiff, my knees are so weak and wobbly that I can hardly stand up. One should die young. When I was a child, Dr. Sämann always came when I was sick. His cool hand on my forehead. "Are we sick?" he always said. "Do we have a fever?" And I thought, why is he saying "we," he doesn't have a fever at all, only I have a fever. I don't know why he comes to my mind now, I haven't thought of him for decades.

When I come out, a young man with glasses is waiting. His hair is untidy, his eyes are bloodshot, as if he's been crying. Probably an alcoholic. Young people these days have no self-control.

"What's the matter?"

"I was thinking about my father."

"Will you take me to the tram?"

He removes his glasses, puts them back on, and says softly, no, not a tram, a car will take me.

We walk down a long corridor. Actors' faces grin from the walls. I've made movies with some of them. There, for example, is Peter Alexander.

"That's a pro," I say. "Peter! You can't even imagine. On the very first day of filming knows all his lines. A young actress, I won't say her name now, because in the meantime she—"

"All right, all right!" he says sharply.

I fall silent, offended.

And here, to top it all, a paternoster elevator! Somehow I stagger into the compartment; I almost fall, but he holds me. The presenter—that much I still remember—was the famous Heinz Conrads. They'll be pretty annoyed at the Abendruh Sanatorium that I was with Heinz Conrads, while for everyone else it was just another endless Sunday morning with a lousy breakfast.

Can it be that the program didn't go well? I remember agitation, stupid questions, there was trouble, someone insulted me—or I insulted someone, one of the two. Pabst was brought up, of course, that goes without saying, everyone asks about him, my own career as a director was ludicrous, not to put too fine a point on it. The only thing that's important about me is that I used to be his assistant.

The young man pushes me out of the paternoster elevator, holding me again. We cross the lobby. There's a revolving door here too. The glass walls rotate, reflections interpenetrate, I shuffle forward and stand on the street. Soon I'd better lie down.

There are three cars parked on the side of the road, each of them labeled AUSTRIAN BROADCASTING CORPORATION. The young man—what's his name again?—opens the door of the front seat and helps me get in.

"My father survived," he says. "In case you want to know."

"I'm glad to hear it." What's this about his father now?

He looks strange, his eyes are wide, wild, and at the same time somehow full of pity. He looks almost crazy. He opens his mouth, but then he shakes his head and simply slams the door. Young people these days have no manners.

The car starts. On the back seat is someone's newspaper: The chancellor stands behind a lectern looking sternly and threateningly at a group of men in suits. "Death Blow for Zwentendorf Power Plant," says the headline.

"What program were you on?" asks the driver.

"Heinz Conrads."

"My wife likes to watch him. He's a gentleman, she says. One of those men from the old days. When Vienna was still Vienna!"

"And what is Vienna now?"

He doesn't answer.

I try to remember. Something happened, but what? It begins to rain, drops of water drawing curved lines across the glass.

"Were you watching?" I ask.

"Well, how am I supposed to do that!" he says in the singsong people use when they talk to children and old people. "I sit in the car all day. Either I'm driving, or I'm waiting for someone to get in. I can't watch TV until evening. But my wife must have seen it."

Outside, people are opening umbrellas. I lean my head against the cool window. I can hardly wait to get back. At the home everyone must be sick with envy.

Modern Hero

Not a breath of wind, the palms unstirred around the swimming pool. Pabst felt as if he had stepped into a colorized photo. A bird hovered motionless above them. The sun was reflected in the water as glaring and round as children draw it. The cigarette tasted of cold ash. He sucked; no smoke rose. The man on the deck chair whose name he hadn't caught earlier, and whom now it was too late to ask, looked at him without taking off his orange-tinted glasses.

Then the man spoke, and Pabst didn't understand a word.

He nodded. What else was he supposed to do? Ever since he had arrived in Hollywood, he had been struggling to hide how bad his English was.

Encouraged by Pabst's nod, the man said something else, and now Pabst at least understood that he was praising a film, which was either about cowboys or about a woman in love. The man had, as Pabst also understood, either just seen the film or not yet seen it. Either he had produced it himself, or he wanted to produce it.

"Great," said Pabst. He knew you could never go wrong using this word with Americans, just as it was always safe to compliment their shoes.

The man expressed his pleasure at meeting Pabst, declaring himself a huge admirer of his work. Pabst understood this, because everyone said it to him. At first it had filled him with pride and made him excited to work here, but by now he knew that it meant nothing.

Pabst's presence, the man enthused, was a colossal stroke of luck and a golden opportunity for the Warner brothers.

Pabst fiddled with his collar and loosened his tie. He had made a mistake: because of the air-conditioning, his hotel room had been so cold that he had put on a thick linen shirt and his warm jacket. He felt drops of sweat running down his face.

"I am very pleased about this meeting," said Pabst, adding that he'd done quite a bit since he'd been obliged to leave his country, had made movies in France, including *Don Quixote* with the singer Chaliapin—

"Yes, yes, yes, yes," the man interjected, "a great picture, just great!"

Because there was no ashtray, Pabst laid his cigarette butt in the grass. It was impossible that the man had seen *Don Quixote*; there were only half a dozen copies, none of them in America.

The man said the picture was a knockout. No longer content to lounge, he sat bolt upright, clapping his hands. The picture had knocked his socks off! It had thrown him for a loop, it was absolutely terrific!

Pabst nodded gratefully and fiddled with his tie to get more air.

"But my favorite," said the man, "is *Metropolis*."

"This one is not by me," said Pabst.

The man praised him for his humility. He couldn't be older than thirty, and he was so thin that the sight of him filled Pabst, who had felt overweight since he was ten years old, with envy.

It took Pabst a moment to realize that this was his cue: humility. He focused all his attention on the shimmering orange round glasses, which reflected the pool and his own sweating face. Suddenly he noticed that the bird was still stuck to the sky above them. He took a deep breath.

But before he could speak, a servant interrupted. He wore a livery, smiled fixedly, and asked what he could bring them.

"Water, please." Pabst would have preferred a drink, but he couldn't come up with the right words.

His host said something incomprehensible. The servant bowed and disappeared without anyone seeing him leave.

All right, said Pabst, taking a drag on his cigarette, he had an idea, it was great. A ship, luxury, on the high seas. Suddenly: War declared! Conflict, passengers everywhere, violence too. Tension high! He closed his eyes for a moment. He had hoped his English would improve once he started speaking, but it didn't happen. And yet *War Has Been Declared* was really a good idea, the breakdown of a civilization could be shown on a small scale: elegant people from all over the world, just a moment ago still in distinguished harmony, but all of a sudden mistrust creeps in, conflict breaks out, factions form, people succumb to delusional rage. He saw a man with a knife running through the ship's corridor, blood dripping from his sleeves; he saw a cracked porthole; he saw two women in ball gowns trembling as they cowered behind an overturned table in a once elegant parlor. And he saw the climax: a small man with a half-bald head, ashen faced, played by Peter Lorre, hanging from a chandelier with bound hands, surrounded by a bloodthirsty mob, and just as they are about to tear him to pieces, the door flies open. A radio operator comes in, bringing the news that no war has broken out, it was a false alarm, civilization endures! Pabst envisioned them exchanging horrified glances, not knowing how to go on after exposing themselves to each other so thoroughly. Quickly someone climbs onto the table and unties Lorre, and even he acts as if nothing had happened. And then the long tracking shot through the dining hall, where they've set up the tables again and are sitting down to eat. Many still have wounds on their faces, and their clothes are torn, but hesitantly the pianist, or no, better: a band once more begins to play "In the Prater the Trees Bloom Again," and for the majority of the audience in the cinema it is indeed a happy ending, but for the small minority who understand everything it is sheer horror.

"A big ship," Pabst heard himself saying. "Rich people. There is war! Everyone is angry. The glass breaks, and the mirrors, and there is Peter Lorre. But it is not true! There is no war! Is it funny, serious, you do not know! The band plays!" He made motions as if playing a violin, then he hummed the old Viennese tune, because that much, at least, he could do; that could be done in any language.

The servant placed two martinis on a small garden table. So his request for water had been misunderstood. Pabst took one of the glasses and drank. The cold, slightly greasy olive flavor of the alcohol did him good.

"Great," said the man. "Absolutely great." He sipped his drink and smiled thinly. All the same, the man continued, the clarity on the scope was not at issue, was it, for the time being?

Pabst leaned forward as if that might help him understand better.

And the second thing, said his host, placing the martini glass carefully on the grass, but that wasn't the crucial point, because the first thing came first, right?

Pabst also placed his drink on the grass in front of him and took off his glasses to rub his eyes and clean the lenses on his tie. Only once he had put his glasses back on did he see that his drink had fallen over, the bone-dry ground absorbing the moisture.

Pabst asked him to please repeat that.

But instead of replying, his host pointed at the house. From there came a man, thin, in a silk shirt without a jacket, bounding toward them.

"Jake," the host called out.

"Bob," said the newcomer.

Both declared that it was great to see each other. They shook hands with the enthusiasm of brothers reunited for the first time since fate had separated them amid a distant, difficult childhood.

"And this here," said his host, who Pabst now at least knew was named Bob, "is Will Pabst. Europe's greatest director."

"Will," said Jake. He professed his utmost delight. His handshake was warm and firm.

"I am very pleased too," said Pabst.

Jake said he knew Will's work. Such an overwhelming joy, you couldn't even begin to describe it! He hadn't slept for weeks after the Dracula film. Movies from Germany were the greatest of all, even if the day there sometimes began with the moon.

Especially at night, said Bob.

They both laughed. Pabst wondered what he had just misunderstood.

"So we're agreed now," said Jake. "*A Modern Hero* will be filmed?"

"No, no," said Pabst. In agitation he stubbed out his cigarette on his shoe. It was a terrible script, he protested, a completely dreadful melodrama. He couldn't do it.

The two men looked at him for a few seconds with expressionless faces.

"But there's a circus in the movie," Jake then said.

"And immigrants," said Bob.

"Heartbreaking," said Jake. To emphasize the point, he put both hands on his chest.

"Jean Muir and Richard Barthelmess," said Bob.

"The best of the best," said Jake.

"And both of them want to do it," said Bob. "They're all in!"

"But only with Will Pabst," said Jake.

"Because G. W. Pabst is simply the best," said Bob.

Pabst cleared his throat. But if that was the case, he then said, if he was really the best . . . Well, if that was true, then they could trust him, couldn't they? Then his judgment on a script would carry weight, wouldn't it?

Bob sipped his martini. Pabst saw himself in the lenses of his glasses.

They had full confidence, Jake assured him. Great, warm, sincere confidence. But first things still had to come first.

A Modern Hero was ready, Bob said. The actors were ready, the script and the dog were ready, they had a green light, even the camera-person had been hired.

"Why the dog?" asked Pabst. "What dog?"

Now it was Bob who leaned forward and tilted his head as if there were background noise preventing them from understanding each other.

Jake inquired what it was he needed a dog for.

No, said Pabst, he hadn't been asking for a dog, he had only mentioned the dog because Bob had spoken of one, but never mind that. He had to clear his throat again, his mouth was dry, now he would have liked a sip of water. Was the bird still hanging up there, in the same spot? He didn't dare look up.

"Well then, great," said Bob, "terrific meeting, let's go ahead!"

Jake clapped his hands, his enthusiasm seemed irrepressible—his whole body trembled with it. "*Terrific* meeting," he exclaimed. "Just the best!"

"No," said Pabst.

They both looked at him, not indignantly, but uncomprehendingly, as if something inexplicable had occurred before their eyes, a wonder of nature, a mystery such as the world had never seen.

A Modern Hero was a fundamentally bad script, said Pabst. None of it made sense! The hero was stupid, the girl was stupid, the story was complicated but still stupid! It was all senseless! Please, they had to believe him!

He waited. Both of them remained silent.

In Germany was Hitler, said Pabst. That was why he had come here. That was why they were all here, the refugees. People were afraid of a new war. That was exactly what *War Has Been Declared* was about, he said: "You have a small ship with the entire world inside. A microcosmos! Everyone understands it, this I promise you!"

The two of them nodded, and for a dizzying second Pabst thought it possible that he had convinced them. It wouldn't have been the first time. Back when he had filmed *The Joyless Street*, everyone had told him that you couldn't make a movie out of mere everyday life. German films were about dragons and vampires and ghosts and romantic shadows, not about girls driven by hunger to sell their bodies, not about inflation, not about desperate people on a Vienna street, but he had done it anyway, and when he had wanted to hire a young Swedish actress for the second lead, everyone had advised him against that too, but he had insisted on his choice, and the film had been a success, even though the censors had thoroughly bowdlerized it and no one had seen it as it actually should have been. Even here in America the movie was famous, in Hollywood, where he was now sitting in front of two demonic idiots to whom he couldn't make himself understood. And after *The Joyless Street* he had turned Wedekind's *Lulu* into a film, and again found a young woman no one had heard of yet, an American actress with a charisma such as he had never witnessed before, and the film had conquered the world. Did all this count for nothing?

"Everyone at the studio," said Jake, "everyone at Warner loves *A Modern Hero*."

"Trust us, Will," said Bob.

"After that we can see," said Jake.

When he had come to Hollywood, Pabst declared, everyone had said to him: Do what you want! Do what you did in Germany, only even better! Everyone had said that!

And now it had happened: He had raised his voice. And yet everyone had warned him that this was the one thing that wasn't allowed to happen in America. Here there was no such thing as no, Lubitsch had explained to him; even if you wanted to tell someone he wasn't right, you first had to tell him how right he was.

"We hear you," said Jake.

"We understand," said Bob.

"But this is how it is," said Jake.

"*A Modern Hero* will really be a great, extraordinarily wonderful picture," said Bob. "We all think so."

"Everyone," said Jake.

"And that's why," said Bob, "George Will Pabst has to make the picture. Because George Will Pabst is the best. In Germany, in Europe, everywhere!"

And because he was the best, Pabst said, they wanted to give him an old, bad script and actors from the second floor.

"Floor?" Bob repeated.

"Yes, however you say it!" Pabst shouted. "Second level. Tier!"

Jake and Bob nodded thoughtfully. And now the servant was back too, leaning forward and asking with the same sparkling mechanical smile whether he could bring them anything else.

"That's all right," said Bob. "But thanks, Jim! Nice of you to ask!"

"I'm so glad you get it," said Jake. "I'm so glad we see eye to eye. That's just terrific."

"Really great," said Bob.

"We're going to do so much together," said Jake. "First *A Modern Hero*. I have to tell you, I'm really excited!"

And afterward, Bob added, when *A Modern Hero* was a big hit, which it would be, he could feel it, then they would almost definitely want to discuss the great idea with the ship!

Both of them stood up. And Pabst, not knowing what else to do, followed their lead. Bob put his arm around his shoulder, and off they went, in perfect harmony, toward the street.

Now that they were in agreement, they could take care of the details, said Bob. His people would send Pabst's people what they needed.

Pabst nodded, without understanding what that was supposed to mean. Because they weren't in agreement, and besides, he didn't know which people Bob was referring to—he was an emigrant; apart from his wife and his small son he had no people! In Germany he had been surrounded by colleagues, in France he at least still had producers and agents, but here he had no one.

He stopped. This took some effort of will, because Bob was pushing him forward with his arm around him.

"No," said Pabst.

Behind them Jake asked whether everything was all right.

The sun was so bright. Pabst heard a mosquito buzzing. It went silent; a moment later he felt its bite on his cheek. He slapped it, now it was stuck to his fingers.

"No," he repeated.

The two men smiled fixedly.

"Nothing is all right," said Pabst. "Nothing."

Peacocks

She had kept him waiting for forty-five minutes—not because she had been busy, but because she treated every visitor that way. The whole time she had stood by the window, watching the colorful birds as they stalked and strutted back and forth. The gardener had once listed the names of all the species for her, but her memory had never been good; usually while filming, someone stood next to the camera holding a card with her lines written in large letters. That was why she had developed a certain restlessly searching gaze, which appeared very mysterious on-screen.

The reason she enjoyed watching ornamental birds so much was that she actually should have been reading scripts. New ones came every day, they came with recommendations, with pleas, with prayers. No one in this town wrote a script without hoping that against all odds she would read it and accept the lead role.

To her surprise she was looking forward to seeing him again. She briefly looked at herself in the mirror: She was wearing a simple brown silk dress and no shoes. Her face wasn't made up, her hair fell straight to her shoulders. She examined her expression; her features were as motionless and unreadable as they ought to be. She exhaled and opened the door to the sitting room.

As always, this room lay in cool semidarkness. It contained only a sofa, a small marble table on which the same never-opened book by an English comic novelist had been sitting for over a year, and a low armchair with a very straight backrest. The chair was, of course, for her. Almost all her visitors understood this instinctively; only very rarely did anyone sit down on the chair instead of the sofa. When it happened, she quickly excused herself with a headache and never let the idiot in question back into the house.

Pabst, of course, was sitting on the sofa. He was leaning forward, elbows resting on his knees, glasses perched on the tip of his nose. A cigarette was tucked into the corner of his mouth, unlit, because her butler asked every visitor not to smoke.

He looked up. Since the curtains were closed and the room behind her was brightly lit, he could see only her silhouette. This was how she always arranged it: The guests' eyes had to adjust before they could make her out.

He looked at her, and there it was, the broad but cool smile she remembered so well, the Pabst smile. At the same time, his body moved back, and his eyes narrowed for a moment, as if he were looking into too strong a light. Then he stood up.

"*Mon pape*," she said, extending her arm. With a perfect gesture, practiced in a Viennese dancing school at a time when a Kaiser still ruled, he took her hand and bent down to give it the hint of a kiss, his lips not touching her skin. Smiling, she gave a slight curtsy.

"Greta," he said, "to another woman . . . to *any* other woman, I would say, 'You are more beautiful every time I see you.' But not to you."

"Not to me?"

"It's too obvious. It would be the tritest statement. Like calling the rain wet or the North Sea cold."

She bowed her head as if in gratitude, for which there was, of course, no reason, because he was right, she was the most beautiful woman in the world, and everyone knew it. It was also this that made her life so difficult. Everyone acted skittish in her presence, anxious and confused, women no less than men. Excessive beauty was hard to bear, it burned something in the people around it, it was like a curse. Sometimes it seemed to her that she would soon have to hide from the world. Then she would do nothing but sit by the window and look at her birds.

"I hear you've made a picture?"

"*A Modern Hero*," he said softly.

"Who plays the lead?" She settled into her chair. He sat back down on the sofa, so carefully that despite his weight the springs didn't make a sound. This heavy man had always possessed grace.

"Jean Muir," he said, and his eyes flashed, because he had of course understood that she didn't mean the male lead.

"Why didn't you ask me, *mon pape*?"

"Would you have considered it?"

"You know I can't refuse you anything."

Both of them knew that it was a lie. But he inclined his head and pretended he believed it. "I would never have dared offer you something like that. A wretched script, a paltry budget, and the producer constantly interfering. Can you believe it, he dictated shots to me! I helped . . . You know I'm not exaggerating when I say I helped invent the art of the moving camera. And then he even meddled in the editing. At least I ruined their happy ending. Now the modern hero's wife leaves him, and he returns to his mother."

She laughed.

"And Richard Barthelmess. Why does someone like that become an actor! You know that I can guide actors to greatness, Greta! But not him."

"Did you crank faster with him too?"

Back then, during the first days of filming in Berlin, she had felt paralyzed with anxiety. Everything had seemed so foreign to her—the zeppelin hangar in Berlin ice cold under the klieg lights, the director and cameraman wearing thick coats, while she had frozen in her low-cut georgette dress; but even worse than the cold had been her stage fright, her nerves, her discomfort with her thin, freezing body. And that was when he came up with the idea of having the cameraman crank faster whenever her face was in view. It was a real magic trick: each of those slow-motion close-ups showed a play of expressions so enigmatic and impenetrably ambiguous that you couldn't look away. She had it done the same way in her subsequent films.

"With Barthelmess that doesn't help, believe me. Neither emotional work nor crank. I never raise my voice on set, but there were times I was on the verge of shouting."

"Why does Pabst lower himself to make such a film?"

"Because Pabst is a refugee. Homeless and helpless."

"Homeless Pabst may be," she said, "but I've known him for a long time now, and he is never helpless."

"Not as long as he has friends."

"Among whom I may count myself?"

"Greta, that I am yours is something you can hardly doubt. Is it too much to hope that you are well disposed toward me too?"

She nodded with a smile—proud that her German was good enough to have understood that sentence. Yes, of course he was there because he wanted something from her. That didn't surprise her. Everyone wanted something, all the time. People couldn't help it.

"I have an idea," he said. "Rich and poor people on an ocean liner, a parlor, an orchestra, grand manners, tea and cake, liqueur glasses, but suddenly a radio alert comes through: war has been declared!"

"You want to make another war movie?"

"No. And yes. But not really. Because the alert is false. And yet war breaks out on the ship. The passengers fight, form groups, and arm themselves, maybe there are even deaths, although that might be too much, maybe not. We'd have to think about it. But then it turns out it was all just a mistake. An illusion. And then—Greta, this is the most important part!—they all have to carry on with the farce of civilization. As if nothing had happened."

She was silent for a moment before saying, "That's good."

"So, would you do it?"

"This is not a picture for me."

"If I make it, it will be for you."

"This is an ensemble picture. A Pabst picture. Not a Garbo picture."

"Don't you trust the man who discovered you?"

She looked at him with curiosity. Now his nervousness was visible after all. He picked up the novel from the table, leafed through it carelessly, put it down.

"It's true that you discovered me, but that discovery also made you great. And then you discovered Louise Brooks, who made you even greater. Why don't you ask her?"

He bowed his head, adjusted his glasses, took the unlit cigarette out of his mouth, and shoved it in his breast pocket. She was sorry to have to talk to him like that, but there was one thing experience had taught her: directors didn't accept a gentle no, for the simple reason that people who accepted a gentle no never could have become directors.

"I'm writing a part for you. An elegant lady who during the supposed war on the ship turns out to be mad, to be bloodthirsty and extremely dangerous. You'd be good at playing mad, Greta, you have the nervous temperament. Together we'll create something unforgettable. For the second time."

She stood up and went to the window. Through the gap in the curtain she saw a palm tree trembling in the wind. The sea must be magnificent now. And theoretically she could do it—drive to the beach, jump into the surf, let the waves toss her around. But in reality it was, of course, impossible: people would gather, reporters would show up with cameras, the newspapers would write about it: "Garbo spotted on the beach."

Perhaps you should actually do it. Perhaps you should say yes to his film. He probably still had it in him, he was older, but he wasn't yet old. And it was true, of course, that she owed him her fame.

Back then he had taught her how to work on a role. No gestures, he had said, don't move your face much, don't *act*. This girl's suffering is not something you feel, it's not even something you know about, it is the substance of your being, the air you breathe, and yet you resist, the suffering doesn't swallow you up, you're still looking around for ways out, you want to escape. Once life has broken you, you'll give up, but things haven't reached that point. He had explained this to her with a seriousness she had never known people making moving pictures could possess. Movies—until recently that had been spectacle and eye-rolling, cowboys with pistols, duels between knights, ghosts in the night, and clowns fleeing from policemen. But when he spoke, it suddenly sounded like theater, like a novel, like true art. Don't think about the camera—ideally, don't think at all. I've already done everything necessary when I cast you.

When he had explained that to her, on her second day of filming, they had been standing in front of her dressing room, and because she was shivering with cold in her thin dress, he had put his arm around her shoulders. It was a paternal gesture, even though he was only in his midthirties himself, and yet she had immediately thought about how it was customary: when you got a lead role, you had an affair with the director. On the other hand, she had known for a long time that there was little about men she found attractive. Men were broad and loud, they rarely smelled good, their faces were prickly, and when they'd had too much to drink, which was almost always the case, they turned red and sweated.

With his arm around her shoulder he had led her over to the other end of the hangar, where the Vienna street Melchiorgasse had been re-created house by house, and in a soft voice he had invited her to dinner at his house, and she had nodded without a word. In the evening he had sent a chauffeur. Before she had stepped into the car, she had had to excuse herself, go back inside, and throw up.

But when she climbed the stairs of the cold Charlottenburg house to the fourth floor, his young wife had opened the door, and she greeted Greta with an embrace, saying, "It's true, what Wilhelm claims, you're really the most beautiful woman in the world!"

A Bohemian cook had served dumplings, and half an hour later his brother-in-law and his wife had arrived, and all the while a governess had been rocking a baby on the sofa, who sometimes moved his lips in his sleep and with his bald head looked like an old man. After the dumplings there had been apple strudel with vanilla sauce and sweet dessert wine, and in parting he had kissed her hand and told her that one day she would be called "the Divine One." And that was exactly what happened.

But that wasn't important now. Fate had placed her in a position where she couldn't afford sentimental gestures.

"This is not a picture for me," she repeated.

He remained silent for a few seconds before saying: "I hope you understand that I had to ask."

"Of course."

"In my country, hell reigns. And my mother is still there. I have to work here, but *A Modern Hero* is coming out next month and will be a flop."

"Not necessarily."

"Yes it will. I know it. And after that I won't be able to get back on my feet."

And there, she thought, he was unfortunately right. No emigrant survived a flop.

"You're far too pessimistic. If it's not a success, just make a new picture. The cards are constantly being reshuffled. You're the great Pabst. People will always count themselves lucky to hire you."

He looked down at his shoes for a moment before replying: "I wish I could believe that."

She suppressed a sigh. For all her affection, this visit had already lasted too long. "At least you escaped. That's the most important thing."

He stood up. "Thank you for your time. You have given so much to the world as a whole that no individual should have any further claims on you."

He stretched out his arms. Slightly confused, unsure whether he had just complimented or reprimanded her, she took his hands. He bowed again to give her a perfect kiss on the hand. She couldn't help thinking of the first time she had seen *The Joyless Street* and realized once again that this politely distant man was an artist through and through. The scene where the pushy butcher demanded sexual services from the young girl played by her in exchange for food—she had known immediately that she would never be able to forget it: the innocence, the realization, the mute despair on one side, the cold, mean greed on the other. That was what evil looked like, that was its face; it was no longer the actor Werner Krauss, it was meanness itself staring into the camera. She had indeed never forgotten the scene, and it was just as well, for no one had seen it since—the censors had cut it out, and all the copies in circulation were bowdlerized.

He walked out silently. Softly he closed the door.

She opened the curtains. A minute passed, then she saw him crossing the garden, accompanied by the butler. As he walked, he took the same already-crushed cigarette from his breast pocket, stuck it between his lips, pulled out a lighter, and lit it. The two men respectfully made a wide detour around a peacock fanning its tail. Its feathers shimmered in the sun, senseless and glorious.

She sat down and closed her eyes. In the past, situations like this had agitated her greatly. She could imagine what it must be like to be God or an archangel and constantly feel the prayers rising from the depths. Each one by itself could be fulfilled, but precisely because there were so many, there was nothing to do but ignore them all.

She wished she could simply disappear. Slowly step back into the shadows, becoming invisible there. Sometimes in her dreams she was actually walking on the street and no one turned to look at her. Often she imagined entering an ordinary place, like a laundry. She imagined what it might feel like to drop off clothes there, as completely ordinary people did.

"Please clean carefully, the fabric is delicate!" Or whatever it was you said in a laundry.

And the clerk, whom she imagined to be small and round and friendly, would moisten a pencil with her lips to fill out some form, for surely forms were filled out, though she wasn't certain since she had never been to a laundry. And then she pictured the clerk—and the thought nearly took her breath away—looking her in the face without confusion and asking what her name was.

By the Pool

Kuno Krämer walked gingerly across the lawn. Fred Zinnemann's party was in full swing. Two waitresses carried trays. Krämer took a glass and immediately felt less shy and not quite so out of place.

He saw several faces he recognized from the movies. Apart from the host there was no one there he had met before. So he pretended to admire the colorful flowers and the cacti. He heard snatches of conversation in English: *Acapulco*, said a woman; *over budget*, a man said, *it's curtains*. Another man was describing crossing on a ship, *seasick all the time, but Myrtle did much better*, another: *They start shooting next week*, and someone else said in German: "She was supposed to send me the recipe for apple strudel, but it's been two months and no letter!"

He stopped. "You speak German?"

An older couple, dressed too warmly for the California afternoon. She wore a wool jacket and boots, he a rumpled coat. Both had haggard, pale faces.

"Yes, we speak German. Unfortunately only German. Elsa and Karl Schneider. From Salzburg."

"Pleased to meet you," he said. "Kuno Krämer. From Bremen."

"Are you a refugee too?"

"A garden-variety emigrant. I've been living in Los Angeles for ten years."

"You're in film?"

"God, no. Engineer. GE." He saw their uncomprehending faces. "General Electric. I'm in the same golf club as Fred. And you?"

"Our son works in film. He's standing over there. He brought us over, somehow raised the money, got the affidavit, secured the visas. He's a cameraman."

"You mean the man who stands behind the camera and turns the crank?"

"They haven't cranked in ages," the old lady said. "It's been electric for ten years! What kind of engineer are you?"

"A different kind of engineer," said Krämer. "How are things in Germany now? My father writes to me that the Nazis are marching in the streets, and if you don't watch out, you'll get beaten up."

"If you're a Jew, that happens quickly. And worse. Are you a Jew?"

Krämer shook his head.

"Then you'd be safe. You could go back!"

Krämer shrugged, as if the suggestion was so absurd that it didn't even warrant a response. A waitress stopped beside them, he put his empty glass back and took a new one. The waitress moved on, balancing the tray, past the sparkling pool, then stepped over an orchid bed in her high heels.

A beautiful, dark-haired woman of about thirty-five reached for the glasses. The waitress stopped.

"Are you a dancer?" the woman asked. Her English had a slight German accent.

"Oh yes," replied the waitress. "Can you tell? And you?"

"I once wanted to be an actress. And many other things. Then I got married. To a director."

"A famous one?"

"Famous over there, yes."

"What movies has he made?" the waitress asked, not wanting to be impolite. The information that the man was famous only in Europe had dampened her interest significantly.

"Have you seen *A Modern Hero*?"

"No."

"It was in theaters here. For a weekend."

"Stars?"

"Richard Barthelmess."

"Who?"

"Exactly."

The women laughed together.

A very thin man came up to them. "Thelma," he said with a heavy Viennese accent. "It's nice that you're enjoying yourself, but my guests won't get drunk on their own."

"Mr. Zinnemann, I'm not Thelma. My name is Dory. The other waitress over there, that's Thelma."

"Interesting," said Fred Zinnemann. "But then again, not that interesting. My guests have nothing to drink!"

Dory rolled her eyes and carried her tray onward.

"*Modern Hero* wasn't bad," Zinnemann said in German. "You could see the mastery again and again. For moments."

"Yes, but what good does that do?"

"Look, Trude, this is a different world. Palm trees standing around, no good coffee anywhere, but the fruit juices are astonishing! Do you know what mango is? You wouldn't even believe how good a mango tastes. Who needs Sachertorte, I always say, when you can have mango every day!"

"What do you mean by that?"

"That life here is very good if you learn the game. We escaped hell, we ought to be rejoicing all day long. But instead we feel sorry for ourselves because we have to make westerns, even though we're allergic to horses." He paused for a moment and said as if to himself: "It's not easy either. You're sneezing all the time, and at night you huff and puff like you're a horse yourself. But I tell you, even a western can be something great! And you have to help G. W. so he learns the rules!"

"Me?"

"You're the practical one. He carries all the baggage of the Old World with him. But that's a misunderstanding. Hollywood isn't them anymore, it's us! Siodmak, Preminger, Lubitsch, Joe May, me. And Pabst too, if he does it right."

"You're younger than he is."

"No younger than you, Trude! You look scarcely older than a schoolgirl! And you know what else I wanted to tell you?"

But at that moment a man with a small mustache came up to them, and Zinnemann fell silent. His thin body seemed to grow even narrower, his knees buckled, his head sank to his chest, a tight smile appeared on his face.

"David!" Zinnemann exclaimed in English. "Great to have you! This is Gertrude Pabst, the wife of my great colleague. This is David Samuelson, until recently Paramount, now MGM. How's Betty?"

"She's fine," said Samuelson. "You're Pabst's wife? Is he here too? We're all great admirers, ever since *Metropolis*."

"God knows!" Zinnemann exclaimed before Trude could say anything. "A picture for the ages!"

"I read your script, Fred! I love it. Red loves it too. And Dan absolutely loves it!"

Zinnemann's body straightened, his smile broadened, his shoulders lifted to his ears. "Dave, that makes me happy! That makes me very happy! That's—"

"It's too serious, and the main character isn't likable enough, but we really, really enjoyed it!"

For just a moment Zinnemann's smile disappeared, then it was back. "Thank you, Dave! You are too kind!"

Trude Pabst looked intently at Zinnemann, but his eyes were fastened on Samuelson's face. He seemed not to notice her anymore. So she turned away.

She walked past the groups of party guests. She saw Billy Wilder wearing a cowboy hat, talking animatedly to a beautiful woman. She decided not to interrupt him. She would have liked to continue speaking with the waitress, but now two young men, strong and tanned, stepped into her path.

"I'm Ron," said one. "This is Zacharias."

"People call me Zach," said the other. "We were just wondering, Ron and I, whether you're an actress."

Trude laughed. "No, but I once wanted to be one." She liked how the two of them were looking at her. Apparently she really wasn't old yet.

"How come your English is so good?"

"I had an English nanny. And when my husband was filming *Pandora's Box*, I translated for"—she couldn't bring herself to utter the name—"the lead actress. And I've always read English writers . . . E. M. Forster, Dickens, Kipling."

"I'm a cameraman," Zacharias said in German. "From Salzburg."

"Do you hear anything from Austria? Ever since the annexation, one can't find out anything at all."

"My parents just got here, you can ask them!" He pointed to an older couple, much too warmly dressed, standing forlornly beside the swimming pool. "They talk about mobs in the streets, Jews being beaten up, shops looted. Our furniture is gone. The police help the looters carry things." He looked down and said in a suddenly thin voice: "My grandpa is still there."

"What did he say?" Ron asked in English.

"He's worried about his grandfather in Salzburg," she said.

"I have an aunt in Munich," said Ron. "She's trying to get a visa to England. No chance. Only Nobel Prize winners and trained butlers get one. And Sigmund Freud."

"Soon there will be war," Zacharias said to her in German. "Then no one else will get out. France will lose, then England will be conquered too. America won't get involved."

"How can France lose!" cried Trude. "That huge army. We were just living in Paris, and I can tell you . . . "

They spoke German excitedly to each other, and Ron, who no

longer understood anything, looked around. There were some pretty women, and they couldn't all be married. He sauntered toward the house. A waitress held out a tray, he put down his empty glass, took a full one, and felt the pleasant mellowness of intoxication slowly setting in. The waitress looked good. He noticed her shoes, which had very high heels, probably making it difficult to walk in the grass.

"Actress?" he asked. This was what he always did, it never failed: in this town the answer was usually yes, and there was already something to talk about; but if the answer was no, the women were all the more flattered.

"Dancer. But I wouldn't turn down a speaking part."

"I have no parts to offer. I'm just a lighting technician."

"Who have you worked with?"

"Lewis Milestone."

"Really? Was the job hard to get?"

"A lighting technician has it easy. I don't have to audition. Hardly anyone notices I'm there. I always find work." He extended his hand and realized only after a second that it was a stupid gesture, since she had to hold the tray. "I'm Ron."

"I'm Dory. But I'm not allowed to talk with the guests or I'll get in trouble."

And just at that moment, as he was about to say that it was really no problem, they could meet up again later, in a more comfortable place, a short man with a half-bald head approached, sweating heavily. Dory held out the tray, he took a glass, turned to Ron, and said, "Hot enough for you?" When Ron didn't reply, he added: "I mean the weather." And when Ron, watching Dory walk away, still didn't say a word, he extended his hand and said: "Kuno Krämer."

Ron shook his hand. It was soft and damp.

"Are you in pictures?" asked Krämer. "It does seem everyone here is in pictures. I'm with General Electric."

"That's nice," said Ron, just to say something. "I need your electricity for my lights."

Kuno Krämer looked at him blankly.

Ron briefly thought about how much he hated parties and small talk and above all people who interrupted conversations with beautiful women. Then he explained: "I'm a lighting technician."

The sweaty runt looked at him, still blank.

"I've always wondered," said Ron, "how it actually works: You rotate two magnets, one in the field of the other, why does that generate electricity?"

"I don't know. I'm in material procurement. I'm not a physicist."

Now Ron couldn't think of anything to say. Both were silent.

"How do you know Fred?" Ron finally asked.

"From golf. And you?"

"We filmed *Rhodes of Africa* together. He was Berthold Viertel's assistant director."

"Did you film that in Africa?"

"Of course not!" Ron could barely contain himself. "In the studio! No one films in Africa. Why would anyone do such a thing?" And then, because he could already feel the next long silence rolling in: "Excuse me, I have to . . . Over there . . . I have to talk to him, be right back!" He shot the sweating man, whom he now almost felt sorry for, a broad smile. Krämer smiled back uneasily, but too late for Ron to see it.

Kuno Krämer watched the lighting technician stop on the other side of the garden beside a man in a cowboy hat and a beautiful woman, who looked vaguely familiar. Krämer sighed. He longed to be back in his own house, not so far from there, where his friendly poodle, Harro, was waiting. Krämer drained his glass. The champagne had grown warm and lost its fizz. Where on earth should he put it? He heaved a sigh. The air tasted of eternal spring. He took out a rumpled handkerchief and dabbed his forehead. Then he slowly approached Fred Zinnemann, who was conversing with a round, clever-looking man with glasses.

" . . . just be persistent," Zinnemann was saying in German.

Krämer cleared his throat.

"And don't give up," said Zinnemann.

"Easy for you to say with your Oscar on the shelf!"

"A short film Oscar! Does no good at all!"

Krämer felt invisible. He cleared his throat. Then he said: "Fred?"

"You're younger than me!" said the man with glasses. "I can't start over. Not after everything I've accomplished."

"Start over, nonsense! Everyone knows who you are!"

"They pulled *A Modern Hero* from the theaters after one weekend!"

"That can always happen. To any film."

"To any film! When you have a flop of that magnitude, there's only one. You don't get a second chance! And I told them from the beginning that the script was no good, and they forced me, and now it's still supposed to be my fault?"

"Fred!" shouted Krämer.

The two men fell silent.

"I wanted to say goodbye," said Krämer.

Zinnemann looked at him with a furrowed brow.

"Kuno Krämer. We know each other from the golf club!"

"Oh yes," said Zinnemann, who clearly did not remember.

"Do you hear anything from Austria?" Krämer asked, not so much because he cared but because he knew it was a question that always got an answer.

"Not much." Everything about Zinnemann radiated impatience.

"You're Herr Pabst, aren't you?" said Krämer. "Your film *The Treasure* gave me sleepless nights. Such a rich work. A German fairy tale. You are a master."

"Thank you," said Pabst, seeming only now to really take notice of Krämer's existence. "Thank you very much!"

"You're a dark painter, a true artist of dreams."

"Oh, that was the old Expressionism. After that I did quite different work."

"I know. I've seen all your films. Are you going to make movies here now?"

"I don't know. I have another offer from France. I might go back. In these times no one knows what lies ahead, right?"

"That's how it is," said Krämer. "But if you—"

"Unbelievable!" exclaimed Zinnemann. "She's chatting with the guests again! She just isn't serving!" He hurried over to the waitress with the high heels, who had set her tray down on a small table near the entrance to the house and was laughing and talking to two young men.

"You've really seen all my films?" asked Pabst. He put his hands in his pockets, blew smoke into the air, and gave Krämer a friendly look.

"But don't stay here!" said Krämer. "You see how it is. What can you achieve in Hollywood?"

Pabst laughed. "What do you suggest? That I go back to the Reich?"

"You would be welcomed with open arms. You could do whatever you want. Make any film."

"As long as it was Nazi propaganda."

"Not at all. You're mistaken."

"God are you naive. Do you have any idea what's going on in Germany?"

"I do. And I repeat. With open arms."

Pabst took a breath, but then said nothing and looked Krämer in the face. "I'm not sure I understand you correctly."

Krämer took out his handkerchief and wiped his bald head. "It's not easy to get used to the heat. Snow on cobblestones. I'd like to see that again. You would too, wouldn't you?"

"I can't go back. Even if I wanted to, I can't."

"Germany needs you. Our government is more pragmatic than people often think. You're a great artist. And you're not a Jew. And you have not always . . . Forgive me, maestro, but I must speak plainly. You have not shown yourself to be entirely uncompromising in your previous work."

"What?"

"*Scandalous Eva* or *The Mistress of Atlantis*—were those films truly worthy of you? You wouldn't have to make such compromises if you returned."

Pabst was silent for a moment, then asked: "Is that just your opinion?"

"It is not just my opinion."

For a while the two of them looked at each other. The hubbub of voices rippled around them.

"How dare you?" Pabst asked softly.

"Dare what?"

"Come here like this."

"I'm an acquaintance of Fred's. We play golf. He invited me."

"Get out of here! Or I'll scream, I'll call everyone over!"

"And what will you tell everyone? That I said how much I'd like to see another German film from you?"

"I'll smash your face in, you swine!"

"There's no need for that, it's not necessary, because everything has been said. I'm already on my way."

Krämer swallowed, his hands were shaking, his throat was raw. What should he do if this man really attacked him? But luckily it didn't seem like it would come to that; Pabst seemed even more agitated than he was. Krämer turned away and quickly walked off. He heard Pabst saying something else, but he didn't stop. The message had been delivered, the mission fulfilled.

Suddenly two shoes hovered in front of his face—startled, he recoiled and bumped into a woman, causing her to spill her drink. She began to scold him—though in the way Americans did, that is, softly, with a fixed smile and clenched jaw, and only after he had apologized did he realize that someone was walking on his hands in front of him. But already the acrobat had flipped back over with a somersault, stood on his feet, and bowed. A few people clapped. Krämer took advantage of the moment to leave the property discreetly. Only when he could no longer hear the noise of the party did he breathe a sigh of relief.

The acrobat, encouraged by the applause, did a cartwheel. People moved out of the way. He landed on his feet, but this time he had overdone it, and no one clapped.

"Who's that?" Trude asked Billy Wilder.

"I think he's an actor who knows that movie producers are here."

"That's how you get a part?"

"He probably thinks if it doesn't help, it won't hurt. But he's wrong."

The young acrobat had a smooth, angular, utterly stupid face. Now he stood on one leg, stretched the other leg out at a right angle, spread his arms, and balanced on his tiptoes. Trude couldn't help yawning. The alcohol was taking effect; for the first time in a long while she felt cheerful and light. Above them hung the dome of the California sky, cloudlessly fiery, unreachably high.

Her husband came up beside her. "You won't believe what just happened."

She leaned her head against his chest. The ground swayed a little when she turned her neck.

"What?"

He didn't answer.

"Shall we go?" she asked. The air was so warm; it smelled of freshly mown grass. Suddenly she wished to be alone with him.

"Yes," he said. "Let's go."

But he didn't move.

Pandora

"Have you been waiting long?"

"Five minutes."

"That's not true, Mr. Pabst. I know you. You're always on time, except when you meet me, because then you're early. And since I'm an hour late, and you were at least ten minutes early, you must have been sitting in this coffee shop for seventy minutes by now. That's math."

"Possibly," he said softly. She's here, said a voice inside him, she came, she's in this room, she's sitting there, she's really here, at this table, on the banquette, across from me.

"Poor Mr. Pabst. You don't have it easy."

"Do you have it easy?"

"Depends how you look at it. Everyone's nice, everyone wants to sleep with me, no one gives me a part!"

"I told you not to go back."

"And you were right, and I went anyway. 'Louise Brooks Is Back,' writes the *Times*, and then absolutely nothing happens. They offered me a Wodehouse play, in Milwaukee, but then that didn't work out either. Nothing worked out. And now you're here too."

"I'm here because I have to be. My country has disappeared."

"Are you working? Making a film, Mr. Pabst? Do you have a part for me?"

"Louise, I would do anything for you."

"But no one is giving you work either."

The waitress came over and asked for their order with that slightly offended look Americans often get when French is spoken in front of them.

"Just coffee for me," said Pabst.

"Coffee and pancakes. Lots of maple syrup. The gentleman is paying."

"Are you . . . " asked the waitress. "You are . . . ?"

"Yes."

" . . . the actress?"

"Sometimes."

"Can I have an autograph?" The waitress tore a piece of paper from her pad, Louise took it, scribbled on it, handed it back. The waitress thanked her and moved on.

"I wrote 'Greta Garbo.'"

"You're better than she is."

"No one is better. You must have gone to her before you came to me."

"That's different."

"Sure, she's the biggest star in the world, and I'm just your last hope. If anything else had worked, you wouldn't have called me, Mr. Pabst. We both know that."

"Why not?"

"Because you're afraid. First of all, that I could ruin your life. That I'd stand up and say: 'Come, we're leaving, from now on you live with me and do as I command!' Because you would do it. Admit it!"

"What's the second thing, Louise? What else am I afraid of?"

"You're afraid that I won't say that. That you'll never see me again. My poor Mr. Pabst, I've already ruined your life. In a single night I crushed it underfoot, your beautiful, orderly life, your entire equilibrium, I'm sorry! I wasn't thinking. It was just so amusing."

He rested his head in his hands and remained silent. Even without looking at her, he knew where her hands were, how her shoulders were moving, and where her eyes were looking. A magnetic force emanated from her. It had been like that from day one. And every day on set he had told himself once again that he had to ignore it, it had nothing to do with him, his task was to capture her magic on celluloid, she wasn't here for him, but for the world.

"When I came back from Europe, there were no more parts for me here, and I spent my money right away."

"But you always have rich men."

"Only until the rich men find out what a handful I am. And that I talk back all the time. But I can't help it—when they spout nonsense, I have to laugh. Then they usually say, 'What am I rich for anyway? I don't have to put up with this!' Soon only well-off men came along, but they found me too expensive; to live in the way to which I've grown accustomed, you have to be really rich. And then came men who not only had no money, but also wanted my money. What was I supposed to do? They were the best looking and were funny, and I had the most splendid time, and then my money was gone too!"

"Was it worth it?"

"Oh yes! If I had the chance, I'd do it all again."

"Listen, back then . . . "

"Yes?"

"Back then, when . . . "

"Mr. Pabst is blushing!"

"Back then, when . . . "

"You mean Paris? Our night? Actually it wasn't even a night. People always say 'a night,' but it was more like an hour, wasn't it? Forty minutes or so."

"Everything could have changed."

"But Mr. Pabst . . . "

"Do you have to call me that?"

"To me you'll always be Mr. Pabst. And yes, everything could have changed, but I didn't want to change anything! I was content. I still am. Do you really think I longed for Mr. Pabst to leave his poor Trudy and move into an apartment with me in Charlottenburg?"

"Or in Montmartre, or Chelsea."

"Yes, but you would have always been around, right?"

They were silent for a while. The waitress came over, set down cups, poured from a large pot, and left again.

"Oh, Mr. Pabst. I don't mean to hurt you. But think, what would we do together? You couldn't bear me. Not for long. First of all, I'm not faithful; secondly, I have no interest in the great man and his great art. I'm not a muse. I'm Lulu. That's why you gave me the role. You understood me completely, and then you wanted me to be someone else?"

"The day after . . . you went away, I moved up our next film, just to see you again that much sooner, and when you got off the train, that man was with you."

"The albino!"

"Did you love him?"

"Love him? The albino? I didn't even sleep with him."

"What?"

"He stayed in my room, but only on the sofa. He was completely impotent, or I don't know what his problem was. But he was all right. Still, what did you actually want? Admit it, at first you just wanted to continue the little affair. A few more nights . . . a few hours . . . Yes, let's say hours. It's always hard for men to bear when it only happens once. The first time is the confirmation. The first time, that's: 'It's happening, she's really saying yes, I'm not dreaming, it's happening.' But then it's over before you believe it yourself. That's why it has to happen again. Only the second time is really the first. And yes, I brought the albino along so you wouldn't get any ideas."

"Ideas? You were the one who—"

"Yes, that's right, I seduced you, you were a perfect gentleman. But you know, that was exactly why. Who can stand a perfect gentleman?

Especially one who is always making disparaging remarks about the way I live. It's enough to make you wonder what you'd have to do to knock the gentleman down. And it wasn't hard. You took me to the hotel, bowed, and gave me your usual stupid kiss on the hand, and then you wanted to leave, but all I had to say was: 'Come, don't be a fool!' You didn't even hesitate."

"How could you—"

"Do that to you? Ha! So much for gallantry. One must take life lightly, Mr. Pabst. It doesn't last long, and if it goes wrong, not so much is lost. And every bit of fun one has, every beautiful day, every—"

"Every man."

"Yes, every man, Mr. Pabst! And every woman! Everyone who gets naked and lies under a blanket with you and gives you pleasure and likes you for a little while is a stroke of luck to be celebrated. And then you move on. Otherwise it gets boring."

"You really are—"

"Careful! Remember the last time you insulted me."

"I just wanted to say, you really are Wedekind's Lulu."

"I'd have liked to meet him, the old fellow. Such a shame he was dead. For him, I mean."

"It was better that way."

"Do you remember how Kortner hated me? That was because he found me so attractive and didn't want to and I told him, 'Not in your wildest dreams!'"

"I knew that. I only gave him the part because he would hate you and because that would be so plain to see in the film. He had to play love, and he would have preferred to kill you—it's apparent in every frame. I don't know much, but I know how to make films."

"And now you want to make another one with me?"

"Ideally with you *and* Garbo. I have an idea for a film set on a steamer. A voyage. Suddenly they learn that war—"

"Ugh, I'm through with the movies. You have to get up so early, your makeup takes hours, then you say the same line over and over again, then you wait three hours in some trailer, then you say another line over and over. What sort of a life is that?"

"I thought you needed money!"

"Oh, I do."

"So you need work!"

"I need work, but it certainly won't come from you. I've learned how Hollywood works. Your picture was a flop. *If* they give you another one, you won't get to choose the script. And you'll have to take the actors they offer you. And I'm not in demand at the moment. And if the next one flops, it's over. The American dream, baby."

"Baby?"

"That's what they say here. Do learn some English. Your beautiful French is no help to you here." She leaned forward and took his right hand between both of hers. "Just look at you, with the face of a lovesick horse. You wouldn't be able to handle it. In the end you'd leave your poor Trudy and your poor child, just hoping I'd feel guilty and take you because I wouldn't have a choice. But I do. I will." She leaned back with half-closed eyes. "And now he looks so poetic. That's what I mean, how can anyone live with a man who stares at you like that? Also, you're on the fat side. You should see what the others look like, I can't help it, I just . . . need men to be more attractive."

She slid out of the banquette and stood up.

"The pancakes are taking too long. Eat my portion, it will make you feel better. People always think despair will kill them, but a little maple syrup, and life looks different." She looked down at him for a few seconds, then leaned forward and placed her hand, her soft, warm hand, her firm hand, the hand he incessantly thought about touching, on his cheek. "You have such a lovely wife. She adores you. She's there just for you. What more could anyone want!"

"Would you want a man who adores you and is there just for you?"

"God, no! But then, I'm a living flame. That's what you called me once, a living flame. In other words, a catastrophe. You don't need a catastrophe like me. I'm doing you a favor. Imagine if I ruined your life now like Marlene did to the poor teacher in that picture."

"So I can't count on you? Not even for my film?"

"No, Mr. Pabst. First of all, no one can count on me. You know that better than anyone. Secondly, you'd go crazy working with me. You can hardly sit calmly across from me. How would you give me direction?" Already walking away, she blew him a kiss.

For a long time he sat motionless. Would he ever see her again? The mere question was almost unbearable. The waitress brought the pancakes and the glass bottle of syrup. He began to eat. And once again she had been right. He would never get over the despair, but the pancakes tasted excellent, and the syrup was sweet and robust.

Sea Voyage

He had to make films. There was nothing else he wanted, nothing was more important. But whatever happened, Pabst thought, lying in a lounge chair on the first-class deck with a cigarette in his mouth, he would never make a film on a glacier again.

Seven years had passed, but it still happened that he jerked out of a half sleep, feeling the abyss open under him. Then he was back there, tied to the steep slope, wind whipping his face while Fräulein Riefenstahl attempted to be an actress. At least he had managed to teach her a little. Listen inward, keep your hands steady; the bigger the emotion, the less you *do*. But her abilities had been limited. She was clever and eager to learn, but whatever she did, her lack of talent was a heavy impediment.

He should have seen it all coming when Arnold Fanck had suggested that they codirect. "I'll do the mountains, you do the faces," and after some hesitation—because he did, after all, have two apartments and a castle and a beautiful young wife and a son and a taste for expensive hotels—he had agreed.

Fanck had invented a new kind of film. People climbed mountains, had accidents, were rescued. Nothing else ever happened. No one quite knew why this man had turned to filmmaking, but now he shot one film after another with a group of dedicated collaborators, all as athletic as monkeys, and since every critic noted that Fanck's actors, though terrific at climbing, unfortunately couldn't act, in stubborn humility he had asked his famous colleague for help.

"We'll split the fee, you'll get half of everything that comes in, and a lot will come in, I promise, because Udet has signed on!"

Indeed, the great ace from the Flying Circus wanted to be in the film too, so financially nothing could go wrong, and after a long night Pabst had decided to accept the offer—and not just for the money, but also because of Fritz Lang.

In Babelsberg, Lang was preparing the most expensive film of all time. He had given Pabst a personal tour through the artificial city: huge buildings towered over them and were enlarged even further by mirrors. With his somewhat silly monocle clenched in his eye, Lang had spoken of effects such as no one had ever seen, cars of the future, trains on absurdly high bridges, crowd scenes with thousands of people, a machine-person who turned into a woman. Even if he realized only half of it—which was highly unlikely, he'd probably realize it all, for whatever Lang wanted, happened—it would be a long time before anyone could rival him.

Except for mountains. No matter how high Lang built, he would not achieve anything higher than the Alps. So Pabst had no choice but to go to the glacier.

He had hoped they'd let him shoot part of the film in the studio, but there he hadn't reckoned with Fanck. Studios, Fanck was convinced, were a font of deceit and lies—even dialogue and close-ups, loving gazes, fear, doubt, and worriedly furrowed brows had to be captured up there, on the mountain, in the deep snow.

Pabst sighed and blew smoke into the air. The sky had darkened: wispy clouds gathered, gray on one side, still bright white on the other, illuminated by the setting sun. A fine layer of haze veiled the horizon. A steward passed by, carrying pitchers, coffee in his right hand, tea in his left. Pabst signaled, the steward stopped and asked: "Cake? Sandwich? Fruit salad?"

"You have everything?"

"The ship is empty. It will be full on the way back. Everyone wants to go to America. No one wants to come back. You're filming in France again, Monsieur Pabst?"

Pabst remained silent for a moment, pleased to be recognized on a French ship. As soon as he was among Europeans, he was someone again.

"The film is called *Mademoiselle Docteur.*"

"Who's in it?"

"Dita Parlo and Pierre Blanchar." The steward pondered, wished him a nice day, and moved on.

Well, all right, thought Pabst, so the man had never heard of them, neither Parlo nor the other one. But he would teach them the craft; after all, he'd almost made even Fräulein Riefenstahl into an actress.

She really had wanted to learn, she was constantly asking about focal lengths and when the camera should move and when it should stand still. When he had composed the best shot of the film, a view upward into the sun through a melting icicle, she had been the only person on that wretched peak besides him who was genuinely interested.

And how cold it had been! He had worn two thick jackets, one on top of the other, and even then, after three hours of work, he had hardly been able to move. His chest had felt clamped in a vise. There had been no feeling left in his fingers and toes, but far worse was the realization that no effort of will could do anything about his fear of heights. Don't look down, he had told himself, over and over: Don't look, don't look now, don't look under any circumstances, don't look down, just don't look!

And then, of course, you did. You looked down. And the depths gripped your heart with strange force. The word "vertigo" didn't quite capture it: it was more of a horror, an utter revulsion that such a thing existed on God's earth and that only your own will, which suddenly you no longer fully trusted, kept you from throwing yourself down. Then your heart pounded and the gray sky tilted so that the snowflakes rose from the depths and nothing seemed in its place anymore.

At night they had lain in the specially built hut, lined up in their sleeping bags. Next to him Fanck had snored like a threshing machine, and on the other side the athletic cameraman—whose name, to top it all off, was Schneeberger—had made the strangest sounds in his sleep, sometimes a whistle, sometimes a murmur, and someone else had spoken in a language Pabst had never heard before, from a deep sleep. The hours had been endless, the floor hard, every minute he became more acutely aware of the stench: three dozen men, no shower, and no window could be opened for fear of the icy wind. Only Fräulein Riefenstahl got to sleep on a mattress in a room of her own. Every night Pabst considered asking for the same thing, but then he was too afraid of being mocked by Fanck and his men. He knew that they smiled behind his back, that they found it amusing how much he feared falling, and he knew they secretly imitated how he helplessly cried "Stop" whenever his glasses fogged up, for what good was a director who couldn't see? No, he had to stick it out in the large dormitory, listen to their night sounds, and console himself with the thought that the movie would undoubtedly be a success.

And so it came to pass. The premiere audience cheered. Fanck and he and the pilot Udet were called to the stage two, three, four times, Fräulein Riefenstahl curtsied, her cheeks flushing despite her makeup, her ambition seeming to radiate from her in hot waves. The first-night critics were effusive, not only in the Social Democratic but also in the Nationalist and Communist newspapers, and the following day *The White Hell of Pitz Palu* was already showing in 259 cinemas. The agonies had paid off.

Just two weeks later, there was another premiere. In front of the Zoopalast lay the same red carpet, and the same gentlemen in the same tailcoats were there, as well as the ladies, albeit wearing different gowns.

Pabst sat in the ninth row. To his left sat Trude, to his right the bald-headed illustrator Gulbransson. With anxious curiosity, Pabst watched Fritz Lang standing at the front, his monocle flashing, next to his wife, Thea von Harbou, who had written the screenplay, dressed all in white, her face marble-pale; both of them shaking hands, nodding to the people streaming in, greeting them majestically. Once everyone was seated, the curtain opened. The conductor gave the cue. On the screen, in strangely angular lettering, appeared the word "Metropolis."

Pabst sat rigid. He watched. He listened. At some point Trude spoke into his ear, but he didn't understand her. He felt as if he were dreaming. He wasn't sure whether he was really seeing what he was seeing.

The lights came back on. Pabst sat motionless. Strangely, he saw himself from the outside, as if someone had pointed a camera at him, filming him slowly taking off his glasses and cleaning them with the handkerchief from his tailcoat pocket, while the audience remained silent. No one clapped. But Pabst knew what was going to happen.

And it continued, the silence, and then it continued longer. And then longer, and the silence was absolute. No one coughed. No one stirred.

Only then, as if someone had given a signal, did the cheering break out, clapping, shouting, hurrahs, seeming to swell ever louder, while Lang, all alone, dragging his feet, and stooped, sauntered as if absent-mindedly onto the stage and stared into the auditorium and then finally, with defiant nonchalance, bowed. Then he left, and then he had to come back, and he left again, and had to come back, and ultimately he called out his wife and the set designer and the cameraman, and they bowed and left and had to come back, and so it went on for over half an hour. Pabst stood and clapped along. Now and then Trude cast him a worried sidelong glance. Gulbransson on his other side said at some point that he'd had enough, a film was a film, even if it was colossal, he was going home!

Even at the reception afterward Pabst couldn't speak. People spoke to him, but he barely heard them, until Trude finally took him gently by the elbow and led him to the exit. And there stood Lang.

"Congratulations!" Pabst said hoarsely.

"The same to you. *Palu*—fantastic, and my God, those must have been tough shoots!"

Pabst nodded. Nothing else occurred to him. He thought about mentioning the stench in the hut and his fear of heights. But he found it difficult to speak.

"It will be a great success," said Lang. "I saw the actors hanging there, on their ropes in the rock face, and I thought: God, am I glad I didn't have to shoot that. Unlike you, I'm not immune to vertigo! Outside the studio I'm completely useless."

"*Metropolis* is the best film ever made," said Pabst.

"I know," said Lang.

Both were silent.

"You're leaving already?" Lang finally asked. Behind him, his wife's stony face loomed. And Pabst mumbled that unfortunately he did indeed have to leave, pushed his way to the exit, and breathed in the cold night air as deeply as he could.

And now, he thought, lying on the deck chair and blowing gray smoke into the gray sky while the sea rocked him, Thea von Harbou was with the Nazis, and Lang, long divorced from her, was on his way to America. It was possible that their two ships would pass in the darkness of night, heading in opposite directions. Lang wouldn't make any of the mistakes he had made. He wouldn't let a bad script or a Richard Barthelmess be foisted on him, and if he was determined to cast Greta Garbo, she wouldn't turn him away.

Director was, all in all, a strange profession. One was an artist, but created nothing, instead directing those who created something, arranging the work of others who, viewed in the cold light of day, were more capable than oneself. That was why so much was required before one could even start to work: writers, artists, composers needed only paper, at most paint, sculptors needed marble and a few tools, but a director needed a hundred people and a studio and machines and a great deal of electricity. All this had to be paid for, so he always also needed someone to entrust him with a lot of money. And that was why one only rarely made films, the rest of the time one talked to people and went out to lunch and wrote letters and gave lectures and tried to convince someone. And again and again one secretly wondered when all the people working on a film together would realize that they could do it without a director too, if only they agreed. Because the actors could certainly act on their own, the camera operator could easily film them, the architect could build a stage for them, and the editor could select and assemble the best footage afterward. But because everyone simply believed that a director was necessary, the whole thing was not undertaken without a director.

Moving pictures had once been a fairground attraction: bouncing balls, boxing kangaroos, dancing couples, cane-swinging men. A dirty screen at the Kutschkermarkt in the eighteenth district, a man named Zacharias Molander shouting, "Step right up, ladies and gentlemen, ladies and gentlemen, come and see for yourselves!" while his wife played the accordion and images they had recorded on their homemade cameras jerked overhead. It had made a deep impression on Pabst, he never forgot the fighting kangaroos, never the men with their twirling canes and never the name Molander.

A little later, by which time he was a big boy, the movies had begun telling short stories. Two knights dueled, a gangster with a pistol robbed a bank, a little man with a hat and cane was chased by a policeman. As he fled, the camera followed him down the street, so that while watching you had to hold on to something to avoid being swept away and losing your balance.

His father was an official. He had his office in the Eastern Railroad station, up under the roof, a portrait of the Kaiser looking down in weary majesty at his desk; he was the stationmaster. Down below trains arrived and departed, on their way to distant cities in Galicia and Bukovina and even farther away, as far as Moscow—and over all this, over the hissing locomotives, the steel wheels, the people in their uniforms, and even the passengers streaming in and out, his father ruled from that desk. On his twenty-fifth anniversary of service, not the Kaiser, but still an archduke, who also managed to look very weary and majestic, had shaken his hand and wished him a long life. Every evening their maid Milena cooked a dinner, including appetizer and dessert, together with his mother, which wasn't easy since Mama refused to learn Czech, and over the years Milena's German kept getting worse. Back then, almost everyone who wasn't in service themselves had servants, because the country was so large and the poverty even greater; they were paid almost nothing. His mother suffered from having only one maid. Her parents had been wealthy, they had not wanted her to marry an official, it was not a good match, which was why her only son had to address her as "Frau Mama," making sure to stress the second syllable, *Mamá*.

Why had he wanted to become an actor? Later he didn't understand it himself, it wasn't due to his talent, but rather a longing for the dusty smell of backstage, the women in makeup, the tenderly soft light of the stage lamps, not yet electric at the time. Mama had wept bitterly, and Father had summoned him to his office in the station to declare in a quiet voice that he would not support him—not a heller for a son in the theater. Georg Wilhelm was a kind, even then somewhat round boy, he didn't want to hurt his parents, but he also didn't want to study law, and so he had negotiated a year from his father, just one year, to see whether he could make it as an actor. His father had silently shaken his head, and yet he had gone to Graz and played minor roles there until the director of the Irving Place Theater in New York cast him.

"But I can't speak English!"

"That's perfectly fine," the director had said, "because we're a German theater."

He sighed, stood up, and stepped to the railing. The sun had sunk even lower, its rays slanting onto the waves, here and there and even farther away. How far could you see if there was no obstruction? The horizon was now blurred, just a bright zone, no longer sky, not yet sea, and above it the fine veil that would turn into clouds once the evening cooled the water.

He leaned forward. Far below him the ship's keel plowed through the spray. He thought of the other ship, on which he had traveled to America back then, not in first class like this, but in the confines of third, while on land war had suddenly been declared.

A French armored ship had captured his steamer, just like that. Back then no one had imagined such a thing was possible—to be traveling through a world that had been peaceful for decades, having done nothing to anyone, innocent and unsuspecting, and suddenly to be arrested. Yes, such things were common today, but at the end of the long peace no one was prepared for it.

And so it was mainly a boundless surprise. He had been surprised amid the bellowing of the French soldiers, who stood lined up with their rifles upright, as he went from one ship to the other, surprised as he spent the next weeks huddled below deck without seeing the sun, surprised as he disembarked in chains on a prison island near Brest, and still utterly bewildered as he moved into his camp barracks.

Only later did he realize how lucky he had been. While the bone mills were grinding at the front, while his schoolmates were being slaughtered by a killing machinery the likes of which the world had never seen, for him it was all already over. Of course he had suffered hunger; of course the guards were brutal, beating some of the men into the infirmary with their iron rods; and of course the forced labor was so hard that it sometimes seemed his back would break—but all this was better than the existence in the trenches that the new prisoners described. After a year the camp authorities even approved a drama club.

He had only wanted to act, but it suddenly seemed obvious to everyone that he knew better than anyone where people should stand, from which side they should enter, how the lines should be delivered. At first, he took on minor roles, but it soon became clear that this was a waste of time and effort, so he gave it up. He realized he was a born theater director. When he read a play, he knew how it had to look onstage. When he watched actors at work, he could tell them what they were doing wrong.

So he had directed plays in the camp until the war ended. Then he had gone back to Vienna. The best thing about a lost world war: afterward there were few people and many opportunities. Wherever you looked, someone was missing, and wherever you wanted to go, there was room. He wandered through the empty streets and saw a small theater. He went in and asked two men reading newspapers in the foyer whether he could direct there.

One was the janitor, whose opinion didn't count, but the other was the manager. Pabst directed Schnitzler and Bahr and Hofmannsthal and Arnold Zweig, and because one did have to make a living, he took a job as an assistant director for a film, *Good-for-Nothing*, based on Eichendorff's novella.

The studio was a huge hall under arc lamps that filled the space with absurd brightness. Even when you closed your eyes, your eyelids couldn't block out the light: the air itself seemed to glow. The actors wandered up and down, performing aimlessly, while the camera operator was the only one who knew how to hold the device, how fast to crank the handle, and how to change the film canister. The director gave occasional instructions, which no one heeded.

The end result looked terrible. Since the light had come only from above, the things and people looked completely flat. The actors, all from the theater, didn't know how to behave in front of a camera. But the close-ups had astonished Pabst: you saw faces from a proximity that at first seemed preposterous. Only people you kissed did you usually see so close. And the painted backgrounds looked real and unreal at the same time, like something out of the strangest dreams.

Soon he was hired for other films. An assistant director had little to do, because the director did little himself. It was actually the camera operator who determined everything. Operators came alone and kept their secrets, each had his own camera, and among themselves they were enemies, who didn't help each other or exchange ideas. The actors, on the other hand, didn't take filming seriously, they came from theater rehearsal, shot for a few hours, collected their fee, and went to the evening performance. The films were then cut up with scissors and glued together so that, more or less, a story emerged.

Some rules evolved: if someone went off to the right, he had to enter from the left in the next shot, or else he appeared to be going back, and if two people were talking to each other, neither of them should look into the camera, but one to the right and the other to the left past it; if they did it differently, it didn't seem like they were looking at each other. And if something happened, and then *immediately* something else, the first event always seemed to cause the second: show a dog barking, followed immediately by a man falling down dead, and the dog killed the man with its yapping. Let four seconds pass, and the dog is merely an ominous foreshadowing. Show a tree for a second in between, and the events have nothing to do with each other. The film, assembled in this way, was copied four or five times in a small workshop on the outskirts of the city, no copy looking like the other because each had a different color, brightness, and contrast.

These copies were no longer shown on market squares but in taverns and sometimes in variety theaters. Film was a new and disorderly medium, but that didn't bother anyone—after all, the whole world lay in pieces. Only the future was bright. Once the turmoil of the present was overcome, there would never be war again, technology would develop, and everything that film wasn't yet, it would become. And so Pabst convinced the Anglo-Austrian Bank to finance his first feature film, and he persuaded the famous Werner Krauss to take the lead role. He shot in the Expressionist style that was already going out of fashion. The story was gothic, the sets wildly unreal, the result grand and a little boring.

His second film, however, would be even more gothic, even wilder: Ansky's ghost play *The Dybbuk*. For five months he had worked on a script, and the sugar manufacturer Mehlson had promised him forty thousand dollars. But in Mehlson's office, just before signing, something had suddenly possessed him, and he had said: "Forty thousand is not enough. At that price the film won't be any good, and can't succeed. Give me forty, and you're throwing money away. Give me sixty, you'll end up with a hundred and twenty."

He had expected Mehlson to throw him out. Instead, he thought about it and said: "I can give sixty thousand. But not right away. I don't have that much money lying around. In the summer there's a Jewish congress in Basel, I'll collect twenty thousand there. After all, this is Ansky's *Dybbuk*!"

"But I have to shoot now. I need the money. We're having a baby!"

"Well, then just make another movie. One that will also be good for forty thousand, and so good that it will bring in two hundred thousand."

"I don't know a movie like that."

"Dear sir, that's not my problem."

Pabst realized that his existence was on the line. One was offered only so many chances, and so often they went to waste.

"It doesn't have to be right away," said Mehlson. "We can meet again sometime, dear Herr Pabst."

"*The Joyless Street*."

"Pardon me?"

"The novel by Bettauer. About poor people, about inflation, about hardship. No ghosts, no painted sets, no gothic romance. I'll make it for forty thousand, and it will bring in ten times that."

"You can promise that?"

And Pabst, who knew that you could never promise such a thing, but who also knew that chances were rare and had to be seized, didn't hesitate a second, stretched out his hand and told Mehlson he could promise it, on his life and his honor and on his mother's life and that of his unborn child.

The Joyless Street ended up costing a lot more than forty thousand. But the film brought in ten times what it cost.

He tossed his cigarette into the water. Slowly, with his hand on the railing, he climbed a swaying staircase and walked down a sluggishly rolling corridor. And there was his cabin.

Trude and Jakob were sitting on the sofa. The child's head rested on her shoulder, his eyes closed, as she read aloud: "'The sight was indeed great and magnificent. A bright spot appeared on the horizon between the dark water and the blue of the sky. "A telescope, here!" cried John.'"

"I always used to think about making a Schlemihl film," he said. "But then Expressionism went out of fashion. Now it might be possible again."

Trude raised her finger to her lips, he fell silent.

"'The telescope passed from hand to hand, and not back to that of the owner; but I looked at the man in amazement, not knowing how the large machine had come out of the tiny pocket; but no one seemed to have noticed it.'"

Pabst looked at her and was almost happy. He would have left her immediately if Louise had taken him, but since Louise didn't want him, he stayed and loved her very much, knowing it was for the best.

He had met Trude thirteen years earlier at the house of his friend Fritz Henning, the lousy scriptwriter. He had come for dinner, then still an assistant director. Fritz's cousin Gertrude had come with her husband, a tall, side-whiskered, friendly man. At dinner Pabst had stared at her, not intentionally, for he was shy around women, but because he couldn't help himself. Everyone had noticed, but they pretended not to, even her husband, for what else could he do; the days of challenging each other to duels were over. Trude, however, had met his gaze with her clear dark eyes. He felt as if he were dreaming.

They hadn't spoken. In parting he had kissed her hand without his lips touching her skin, just as he had been taught in dancing school. On the way home through dark Berlin, he had convinced himself that he must have been mistaken, she couldn't have looked at him that way, it was impossible, such things didn't happen. Although he smoked some opium and then drank cognac too, his sleep was restless and flickering.

The next morning a messenger brought a letter: Trude asked whether he wanted to meet her for a walk in the Tiergarten.

Then his life had accelerated: for several months it had been breathless and full of heated energy. She had visited him in his apartment, he had booked hotel rooms in the Uckermark and on the Baltic Sea, they had run out of lies, and in the end everything had resolved itself with surprising ease: the side-whiskered husband had let her go without resistance and signed the divorce papers; as it turned out, he had his own plans and had long hoped for just such an eventuality.

Trude carefully put the book aside. Jakob was breathing peacefully and deeply; he had fallen asleep.

Kneeling down, Pabst carefully slid his arms under his son's body, and heaved him up. He was actually already too heavy for this, but if you mustered all your strength, it was just manageable. Pabst felt the child's breath in the crook of his neck. At that very moment the ship's hull rose and sank, making him almost lose his balance; but Jakob didn't wake, and he laid him down on the soft bed. Inappropriately and for no reason at all, he found himself thinking of Louise, so he smiled that same big, cheerful smile he used at work to calm the mood and ensure that everyone did their utmost not to disappoint him.

Trude stood up. They kissed. How fortunate, he thought, that even the person closest to you couldn't see what was going on inside you.

"What is it?" she asked. "You looked as if . . . "

She fell silent and scrutinized him.

Luckily, there was a knock at the door.

She opened it. A steward handed her two folded pieces of paper on a silver plate. It was not uncommon for several telegrams to arrive at the same time, since the onboard radio operator was allowed to receive private messages for the passengers only one hour a day, so there was always a backlog.

She unfolded the first one and read.

He watched her with a mixture of dread, worry, and calm. After all, the three of them were all there and alive, so how bad could it be! Unless, of course, it was about his mother's health back home in Austria.

Trude lowered the paper and laughed.

"So not Mama?"

She shook her head and handed it to him. In the telegram, one of the two French producers informed him that the other producer had backed out, there was no money, the film could not be made.

He went to the cabinet with the bottles and poured vodka. He had misunderstood her reaction. Trude hadn't laughed. Tears were running down her face.

"But that's not so bad," he said softly. "It might even be good. There are so many opportunities in France. They want me to make *Le Drame de Shanghai*, now I have time, with this silly comedy out of the way. It might be a stroke of luck!"

"Unless there's a war."

"Even if there is, do you think they'll overrun France?" He drank the glass and poured another. She held out her hand, he passed it, she drank.

For a few seconds they were silent. The floor of their cabin rose and fell. Jakob sighed in his sleep.

"God," said Trude. "Where's the other one?"

They stared at the carpet. There it was. Again she was faster, picked it up, opened it, and read.

"And?"

"It's from your mother."

At Alain's

Adam Grosz and Maria Cornetti were already there when Ilse came in. There were lively greetings, hugs, slaps on the back. At home she had never been able to stand Grosz, he was unbearably pretentious onstage, always spreading his hands and widening his eyes. He could also be scheming: nine years ago in *Tasso* at the Deutsches Theater, he had refused to exchange a single word with his colleague Maria Ehrlich, looking right through her as if she were air. But now, with all of them stuck in Paris and only Ehrlich performing in a Nazi play by Arnolt Bronnen at the Schiller Theater, things looked quite different, and Ilse was surprised to feel her heart pound with joy when Grosz jumped up, embraced her, and cried, "Oh, Ilse, you're alive," even though they had never been on a first-name basis before.

In her joy Ilse even hugged Cornetti, who had become even bonier. The poor woman surely wasn't living in luxury. Who in this city needed an old Hamburg film critic who didn't even speak French?

Neither could Ilse, unfortunately. Not well enough, at least, to deliver even a single line without an accent. So, although she sometimes got small roles, they were always silent or required her to stammer curses and threats in broken French. Last week she had played a Chinese contract killer in a René Castain picture, with heavy makeup and taped-back eyelids. In one scene she had to hiss and bare her teeth, in another she had to quarrel in invented Chinese with Fred Kanzler from the Aachen municipal theater, also made up as an Asian, and thanks to this engagement she at least didn't need to worry about this month's rent. The rent was always a problem, especially since Ilse also had to help her ex-husband. He was stuck in Rouen with his new wife without an exit visa, neither of them earning a sou.

"I've just had some luck," Cornetti recounted, puffing on her cigar with relish. "A fine lady in the third arrondissement has hired me for German lessons, which covers the most essential expenses. The woman is constantly asking about Goethe, of whom I myself have no knowledge—it's remarkable how inventive one can be in a pinch, all the things one can come up with about Goethe when one's livelihood is at stake."

The writer Carl Zuckmayer came in, accompanied by a gaunt little man and a tall woman. He introduced them as his colleagues Walter Mehring and Hertha Pauli. All three were in transit and looked around with the typically absent-minded glances of refugees: you are never quite where you happen to find yourself; all that surrounds you seems like a sloppily constructed set, not worth remembering.

And really there wasn't much to see at the Bois de la Bière. The dark room with puddles on the floor, the bar with the engraved notches, which the proprietor, Alain, claimed were made by none other than Rimbaud—after midnight you even believed him—the three tables, two of which wobbled slightly less than the one in the back where they were sitting. They often came there, Alain kept a tab, you didn't need to feel alone, you always found someone.

Zuckmayer, whom everyone called Zuck, spoke loudly as always, slapped Grosz on the back, placed a paw on Ilse's skinny forearm, and bellowed for wine, saying the first round was on him.

"I have a chance to get into Switzerland," said Mehring.

"But they don't like Jews there," said Grosz. "German refugees aren't allowed to publish in Switzerland. The reason is that they write better than the Swiss. The government considers this a fact."

"Not without reason."

"Unless their name is Thomas Mann. For him an exception was made."

"I thought Mann was in America."

"No, he's in southern France. Werfel, who's in the same village, wrote to me."

"But if there's a war—"

"There will be!"

"There won't be!"

"—Switzerland will be overrun immediately or will surrender. Only France is safe!"

"I don't believe that anymore," said Zuck. "Alice and I, we're going to America."

"Do you have visas?"

"Yes. It was incredibly hard to get the affidavit. But now we can get out."

The proprietor came, Mehring spoke French, Alain replied, Mehring and Hertha Pauli laughed, and the others looked at each other in perplexity, having understood nothing. Then Zuck asked the group whether they'd heard any news about this person or that, and for a while they spoke about friends scattered across the world, and only then, having drunk enough to bear it, did they speak of the dead: Mühsam and Ossietzky, beaten to death in camps; Tucholsky, who had drunk poison in Sweden; Kästner, who was still alive but for some reason had stayed in Berlin, hopefully still free, no one knew. He had written him a strange letter, said Grosz, full of odd circumlocutions to evade the censors, and it was impossible to make out what he had been trying to say.

A man and a woman came in: he was round, wore glasses and had a warm, cordial smile. Immediately everyone patted him on the arms and shoulders, and Zuck tenderly stroked his hair. The woman who had come with him, however, did not seem at ease.

"Who's that?" Ilse whispered to Maria Cornetti.

"That's Pabst, the director." She turned to him. "G. W., this is Ilse Hochfeld from the Schiller Theater."

"But of course I know you!" Pabst exclaimed as chairs were pulled up. "I've admired you for years."

That was flattering, but also strange. If he really admired her, why had he never cast her?

"I saw you in *Criminals*," said Pabst. "Do you happen to know where Ferdinand Bruckner is now?"

"In America. He made it."

For some reason this answer seemed to displease Pabst, who turned away abruptly and began talking to Zuck about some movie idea they'd once had, which had apparently come to nothing, as most movie ideas do. Since this wasn't very interesting, Ilse asked Cornetti how it could be that the man who had brought Wedekind and Brecht to the screen was just sitting here in the Bois de la Bière. Why was he still here and not making films in Hollywood?

"I wouldn't mention Brecht. He sued the production company because they didn't want to use his screenplay."

"Brecht wrote a screenplay?"

"No, he didn't, which is why they couldn't use it."

"He didn't write a screenplay, but he sued them because they didn't use the screenplay?"

"That's right."

"Did he win?"

"He didn't—go figure!" With her most malicious smile Cornetti lit a new cigar from the stub of the last one. "By the way, the film is better than the play. Didn't you know any of this? Haven't you read my articles?"

"Now and then."

"You must read every article I write, otherwise you'll drown in ignorance."

"It was just a joke," said Ilse, taking her wrinkled hand and kissing it. "We all read everything you write."

"That's true," said Hertha Pauli. "Even when we disagree."

"But what's that supposed to mean? That's nonsense. Anyone who doesn't agree with me is wrong!"

"Well, for example, your accusation against Fritz Lang that *M* is a fascist film. You can't possibly—"

"Of course I can!"

"What's that about Lang?" asked Pabst, who had suddenly turned back to them.

"Degenerate criminals stalking young German girls," said Cornetti, "the police of the democratic state helpless, paralyzed by their adherence to the law, and then who can get something done? Tough men in leather coats. And when they finally have him, he isn't handed over to the police, but summarily 'exterminated.' The word is used. 'Exterminated.'"

"But it's a critical vision," said Ilse.

"Not very critical. You know that his devoted wife and screenwriter is now a member of the party?"

"Not very devoted," said Grosz.

"We don't know that for sure," said Zuck. "About the party, I mean. That she slept around we all know. But the party, those are rumors. We mustn't be too quick to suspect each other. We who escaped owe it to those still living in hell—"

"In the dark of night," said Mehring.

"In our wretched, rotting Fatherland," said Hertha Pauli.

"—not to assume the worst. That much we owe them."

"Attention!" said Mehring. "Quiet. Listen closely." And he recited in his high, metallic voice: "Compatriots and compeers: Cast your hope across new frontiers! Like a hollow tooth, yank out the old. Where uniforms glitter, all is not gold. Let them spew slander and rage with glee. They spit hate into a sea! The emigrant carries his home from place to place, on his soles and in his suitcase."

He fell silent. Everyone clapped. Mehring gave a hint of a bow.

"What does 'compeer' mean?" Maria Cornetti asked.

"It's archaic."

"Yeah, that's what they always say when they invent a word for the rhyme. That it's archaic."

"Look it up!"

"Where?"

"What can I do if you don't carry a dictionary of archaisms!"

"And you, Herr Pabst?" asked Ilse. "Are you also trying to get to the US?"

"We were there already," said Pabst's wife.

Everyone stared at her in surprise.

"That's a joke," said Maria Cornetti. "Right? It must be a joke!"

Pabst's wife looked at her husband, who cast her a brief glance; she looked down at the tabletop and silently tugged at the ends of her hair.

"It was very difficult over there," said Pabst. "I got the worst script. I couldn't choose the actors. During the filming a man from the studio was always interfering. He even wanted to decide where the camera should be, and the cameraman obeyed him, not me! And then I didn't even have the right to the final cut! And you probably know my work, editing is my strength, I can save almost anything if only . . . And then the film came out and was, of course, a flop, and then it was supposed to be my fault, because there you're only as good as your last film, and they wouldn't have let me make another. But I might be allowed to assist, they said. You must understand, I can't go back to being an assistant director, in all modesty. I'm simply not quite ready to forget who I am."

"And then the offer came from France," said his wife.

"When are you shooting?"

"The film didn't happen."

For a moment there was silence.

"You can always become a farmer," said Zuck. "You rent a cabin, grow corn or oats, survive somehow. How hard can it be?"

"I'm a rootless cosmopolitan," said Mehring. "I don't grow anything!"

"We're going back to America," said Pabst. "What else can one do? Greta Garbo or . . . Louise Brooks will help. I have projects they can't turn down. For example: A ship on the high seas, suddenly a radio alert comes in . . . "

But as he described his idea, Ilse had already stopped listening. It was always boring when directors described their projects. Instead, she observed his wife, who had turned pale and was sitting there as if thrust back into herself. Her lips moved silently, for a moment she smiled, but not cheerfully, rather sadly and uncertainly, as if trying to put a good face on something terrible.

"But it was a mistake," said Pabst. "A false alarm, and now they have to carry on as if nothing happened. That's good, isn't it?"

Everyone nodded and made approving sounds, because when the evening is late and someone tells an idea, you have to find it good, that's common courtesy.

Ilse thought of all the things she had heard about Pabst: that he hardly paid attention to the script, instead improvising on set, making up scenes, changing plans like a child at play. That the actors liked him because he guided them to their best performances without ever raising his voice. She had heard the same about Lubitsch, and once or twice about Murnau, but of course never about Lang, who everyone knew spread fear and terror during filming, which Ilse could confirm from her own experience, since she had a small role in *Woman in the Moon*. It had been one of the worst days of her life.

When she started listening again, Mehring, Zuck, and Cornetti had begun a discussion about the danger of war. Someone had ordered another round—was it the fifth?—and although they were speaking louder and louder, it was becoming increasingly difficult to follow them. One said Maginot, another Pétain, another Briand, and Maria Cornetti had the complicated theory that France would sacrifice Czechoslovakia, but that Hitler would understand because of this very sacrifice that he could not go any farther. She kept tapping on the table with one hand and gesticulating with the other, and the gray smoke of her cigar mingled with the greenish smoke of Mehring's cigarette.

Then it was time. The proprietor stood there once again, and since it was her turn, Ilse ordered wine for everyone. Since nothing seemed to matter anyway, she asked Pabst why he had never given her a role.

He looked at her for a long while before saying that he had never had anything suitable for her specific talent, and besides, he saw her more on the stage, where true art was more at home anyway than in the industrial disorder of film.

Now Ilse didn't know whether he had just insulted or complimented her. To change the subject, she asked when his passage to New York was booked, and he mumbled something she couldn't understand, most likely because he suddenly spoke so indistinctly. His wife, however, said they still had a few things to take care of first, including withdrawing money in Basel for the trip, and visiting her mother-in-law, who was not doing well at all, in Styria, probably to say goodbye forever.

"Every day," interrupted Mehring, who had also had quite a lot to drink, "is now a goodbye, and every goodbye is forever—that's the nature of time once you're over thirty." Maria Cornetti said that she spoke with people who used phrases like "the nature of time" only when it couldn't be avoided, and Mehring asked whether time had no nature, and she said time was an illusion, and Hertha Pauli said, "But that's Buddhism," and Zuck pounded on the table several times, which could express either agreement or just general verve and élan, and Maria Cornetti said that if something was true, you didn't have to call it Buddhism just because the Buddha had also said it; only false beliefs needed a name. And all this happened so quickly and was so distracting that Ilse had completely forgotten the question she had just been about to ask. She felt dizzy, the whole room was swaying, which was probably also due to the fact that Zuck was drumming on the table once again.

"Excuse me," said Adam Grosz. He hadn't spoken loudly, but

something in his voice made everyone fall silent. "Excuse me, did you say Styria?"

She nodded.

"Styria is in Austria."

"Yes."

"You're going to the Ostmark?"

"The place is called Tillmitsch. A small village. We have a house there, a sort of house, an estate. That's where Wilhelm's mother is."

And then Ilse remembered what she had wanted to ask Pabst. "I was wondering, when you mentioned my 'specific talent,' what exactly—"

"But you can't go to Austria!" Zuck shouted. "Are you crazy?"

"My mother sent a telegram. She wrote that I should come right away. What would you do?"

"I'll tell you what I would do," said Mehring. "Not go back to the Nazis once you've managed to escape the Nazis. Not at any price. Your mother wouldn't want that either."

"How do you know what my mother wants? She does want it. She telegraphed 'Come quickly,' that's not ambiguous!"

"But you're Jewish!"

"No, I'm not. We don't even have any Jews in the family. Those thugs have nothing on me."

"As if they needed an excuse!"

"We're going in and right back out, we'll be on the next ship to New York, we'll see you there."

The conversation came to a halt. It was one of those moments when everything seems to have been said, when it suddenly feels like the present has been used up and nothing is left but a threatening future. The clock showed half-past one, and all that lay before them were the pale hours of early morning. And they knew that they, who barely knew each other and whom chance had thrown together, would never again come together in this group; some of them would be lucky, and the others would perish.

And so it came to pass. Zuck became a farmer in Vermont, Wilhelm and Gertrude Pabst went to the Reich, Walter Mehring and Hertha Pauli made it to America, and Adam Grosz shot himself in Marseille when his transit visa expired, while Ilse Hochfeld, together with her ex-husband and his new wife, managed the march over the Pyrenees and remained interned in a Spanish camp until the end of the war, after which she went back and played minor roles at Bremen's municipal theater. Maria Cornetti, thinner than ever and no longer smoking because she had run out of cigars, was apprehended while hiding in a hayloft near Cabriès. She was taken in a cattle car to the East and gassed in Majdanek.

They looked at each other in silence, in the Bois de la Bière in the predawn hours, and listened to the noise from the other tables. And then, as if someone had given a command, they all stood up at the same moment to go to their small rooms with the squeaky chairs and bad mattresses.

As Ilse climbed the three well-trodden steps to the street behind Pabst, she gathered her courage one last time and asked him what exactly he had meant when he had mentioned her specific talent. But she never learned the answer, for he was apparently too absent-minded or perhaps had simply had too much to drink.

INSIDE

Border

The wire swings up and down, flees, and is pulled back, again and again and again, tears come to your eyes, everything blurs from yawning. It's always like this on the train, you're too tired to sleep and too bored to read, even though Papa always says, read, take a book, at least look at the landscape. But something strange happens to books when you read them on the train: they become empty. The words lose their meaning.

And the landscape does something similar. The hills and forests and castles and clouds and donkey carts are there, but everything seems flat, translucent to the yellowish-gray boredom of the train, so you end up watching the wire and its up and down and up and down again. Sometimes Mama gives you a sandwich and a hard-boiled egg, but they taste boring too, and the worst is when Papa remembers the drawing pad and pencils, because how can you draw when you're so bored? The most you can do is draw the thin black line of the wire, but that's finished quickly, and then what?

"How much longer?" Jakob asks in the rhythm of the rattling wheels. "How much, how much, how much longer? How much longer, how much?"

But because he asked the same thing just a few minutes ago and because his parents are very distracted and nervous, no one answers.

They are alone in their first-class compartment with its flowered seat cushions and striped curtains and small golden ceiling lamp. Until a short while ago an elderly lady with a hat was sitting with them. When she got off, Papa lifted her handbag off the luggage rack and helped her into her coat.

"You're traveling on?" she asked with a heavy Swiss accent. And when Papa nodded, she said: "Then keep safe!"

And now the train is moving again, and aside from the clatter of the wheels, which sounds like a conversation between two confused people—why do you think, I don't know, why do you think, I don't know—there's nothing to be heard, no voices from the other compartments, as if everyone had gotten off or fallen silent, and his parents are no longer talking either, but looking out in silence. Mama is very pale, Papa is silently dragging on his cigarette.

"How much longer?" Jakob asks again.

This time Mama answers: "It depends."

"On what?"

Just then the train brakes and slows down, squealing, groaning, and huffing. His parents stare out the window as if something important is happening there. A station rolls up, slows down, stops. A sign reads: FELDKIRCH.

A church in a field, thinks Jakob. A field around a church. The church field. And he can already see it before his eyes, the church with the cross on the tower, casting a long shadow on the grass, on the field, which, strangely, is blue in his imagination.

Mama moves to the seat next to Papa and takes his hand. He whispers something in her ear that Jakob can't understand.

The platform is almost empty. A man behind a small stand is selling sausage sandwiches. A gentleman with a hat is sitting on a bench reading a book. A poster is stuck to a piece of wall, *Holeczek shoes, good and waterproof, last a lifetime, only at Holeczek's.* Above it a swastika.

Jakob has never known his parents to be so silent. Papa stubs out his cigarette in the ashtray.

On the other side of the platform, a train approaches from the opposite direction—braking, slowing down, braking harder. It is packed with people. As far as Jakob can make out through the fogged-up windows, all the seats are occupied, and people are standing in the aisles, and the luggage nets are bulging under the weight of all the suitcases.

And now the train has stopped. But the doors don't open.

"Why isn't anyone getting off?" asks Jakob.

Papa doesn't answer.

Then people come onto the platform: four, six, eight, more and more, all in uniforms, always in pairs side by side, some with rifles strapped on. Jakob has seen rifles before; two years ago in France Papa took him hunting and he could hardly believe that real bullets flew out of them, little powder clouds glistening in the sun. But these rifles look different, they have broader butts and longer barrels, probably making them more accurate.

The men in uniform are not marching, they are strolling, each at his own pace. They walk around the man selling sandwiches, and around the man reading on his bench. The two barely look up, as if it were the most normal thing in the world. More uniformed men keep coming onto the platform, and still more—Jakob counts thirty, thirty-five, thirty-eight, thirty-nine, forty-two. Now no more are coming. There are exactly forty-two. They line up alongside the opposite train, the full length of the platform, from the locomotive to the last car.

And so they stand and wait. Not stiffly, but casually, bored, talking to each other. One of them is eating a pear.

And the people on the train stare out. A woman presses her nose against the glass, something you usually see only children do. The man next to her is crying, but that could be for any number of reasons, Jakob knows by now that people also cry when chopping onions or sometimes just looking into the sun.

"That's passport control," says Papa. "That's normal."

But Jakob can tell that it's not normal from Papa's voice, which suddenly sounds like he has a cold.

"Why are they all standing by the other train? And none by ours?"

"Well, what do you think?" Mama asks with strange sharpness.

At that moment a new group comes onto the platform. There are only eight men, not wearing uniforms, but ordinary clothes. Three have coats, seven have hats, all have ties, four have beards, one is fat.

"Because the other one is going out of the country?" asks Jakob.

Mama nods.

"Is that why it's so full? Because everyone wants out and no one wants in?"

"You can't say things like that anymore. Once we're out again ourselves, you can, but not until then. Do you understand?"

And the eight men split up. Two get into the first car, two farther back, two even farther back, two in the second to last, each followed by one of the men in uniform. Jakob can see that the people on the train are pulling out passports, slips of paper, thick and thin folders of documents.

"And when?" asks Jakob. "When will we leave Austria again?"

"You can't say that word anymore either."

"Which word?"

"Austria."

"I can't say 'Austria' anymore?"

"The country is called something else now."

"And when will we leave?" Jakob asks again, watching one of the men on the other side take the papers from the hand of a gentleman with a fur collar.

"We're just going to look after your grandmother," said Mama. "In the castle!"

"You like the castle," says Papa.

"You remember the castle?" asks Mama.

Jakob nods, but it's not really true. A long corridor, strips of light under the doors, a howling draft at night, the smell of mothballs, and a lone earthworm crawling across a carpet—that's all he remembers.

What he does remember clearly is his parents arguing in the hotel room yesterday. They were whispering so loudly that he couldn't sleep. "But she's my mother!" he said, and she said: "It's too dangerous!" and he said: "It's just a visit, we'll find a sanatorium, then we'll be off," and it went on like that for half the night, until outside the sky brightened and the morning crept over the rooftops.

The man on the opposite train lowers the passport and shakes his head. The uniformed man behind him immediately steps forward. The man with the fur collar gesticulates excitedly, but the inspector shakes his head and gives back his passport—or rather, he doesn't give it back, but tosses it to him with a disparaging gesture before turning away. The uniformed man pulls the man to his feet, forcing him to stand.

The door of their compartment is opened. A completely ordinary policeman stands in front of them. He is alone, no soldier is with him.

"Heil Hitler," he says wearily.

Papa hands him their passports. Quietly wheezing, he opens the first one.

Jakob looks out the window again. On the other side the man with the fur collar gets off the train, followed by a woman and two girls. The man is carrying two large suitcases. He talks urgently to the soldier, who shakes his head and points across to the train where they're sitting. The man seems to sink into himself. He grabs the suitcases. Slowly they cross the platform.

More people are getting off the train, many of them crying. A man shakes his fist, shouting something that Jakob can't make out. Farther back, at the end of the platform, a woman collapses and lies down right there on the concrete. A man and a boy try to pull her to her feet, but she seems to be struggling, resisting, refusing to stand.

The policeman in their compartment closes the first passport and opens the next. His breath comes in whistling bursts, he must have asthma.

"What's the matter with that woman?" asks Jakob.

His mother makes a gesture to show him to be quiet.

"They have to go back," the inspector says in the soft Austrian rural accent that Jakob hasn't heard in a long time. "They just don't have their papers in order."

Jakob would like to ask what that means, having their papers in order, but he has understood Mama and remains silent.

"We can't let them Jew their way out of it," says the policeman. He looks at Jakob kindly. "Anyone whose papers are not in order goes back."

Indeed, all the people who have to get off on the other side are now coming across to their train. And where else are they supposed to go—the soldiers are blocking the exits. Now three men are lifting the woman together; as if in her sleep, she moves her feet and walks.

"So many stamps," says the policeman. "You've been to America, France, Switzerland?"

"For work," says Papa.

"What do you do?"

"I direct films."

The policeman lets out a grunt.

"Mostly thrillers," says Papa.

"Have I seen any of your movies?"

"Have you seen *The Mistress of Atlantis*?"

When Papa is asked about his films, he usually mentions *The Joyless Street* and *Pandora's Box*. Sometimes also *The Threepenny Opera*. But never, really never has Jakob heard him mention *The Mistress of Atlantis*.

The policeman shakes his head.

"An adventure movie. I shot it in France a few years ago."

"Why in France?"

"You have to make the movies where they're financed. Where you get the money. Where someone pays for it."

"So in France someone wanted to pay you and not in Germany?"

"That's how it was, but now we're on our way home. My wife, my son, and I. At last. On the way home."

Papa is speaking in the quiet, almost purring voice that Jakob has heard only a few times, always when he visited him with Mama on the film set. When things get difficult, when spotlights explode or scaffolding collapses or actors argue, Papa uses this voice, which soothes everyone and gets them to do what he wants. At home Jakob has never heard it.

"So you've been abroad for some years?"

"And now we're on our way home."

"How do you feel about the regime?"

"Which one?"

"Ours!"

"I'm not a political person. I make films. Exciting films. Thrillers, adventures."

"But surely you're not indifferent to it either, the national awakening."

Papa is silent for a moment, then he says: "You can see that I'm coming back."

Apparently that was the right answer. The policeman gives the passports back. "Heil Hitler," he says, pulling the door shut and moving on.

Mama is about to say something, but Papa shakes his head, and she remains silent. They both sit motionless and listen. The train is rocking because so many people are getting on; voices can be heard from the corridor. Across the platform in the other train an inspector in civilian clothes is rummaging through a duffel bag. In the next compartment a uniformed man is pulling a woman's necklace roughly over her head. It catches on her hair, he yanks it loose, and puts it in his jacket pocket. Jakob is curious as to whether the woman will now have to get off too. But the man moves on, she is allowed to remain where she is.

And suddenly, even though countless people are changing trains and others across the platform are still being inspected, a jolt runs through their train, and it starts moving—slowly, then faster and faster. The platform rolls past and is pushed away by small houses, these by trees, fields, hills; and soon a wet, green, somewhat untidy landscape is rushing by.

"Why didn't they wait?" asks Mama.

"The timetable," says Papa, tucking the passports into his jacket pocket. Then he takes out a new cigarette. Mama stretches out her hand. He gives her a cigarette too and lights both. That's unusual; Mama hardly ever smokes.

The door is pulled open, and a man with a mustache asks whether he can sit in the empty seat, the train is full.

Mama and Papa exchange a glance. "Yes, of course," says Papa.

The man slumps down on the seat. The springs groan. Then he takes out a completely crumpled handkerchief, wipes his face, and immediately starts talking. Papa hands him a cigarette too, and he takes frantic drags, telling how he left his family behind to find work in Switzerland and bring them over later. "I paid the Reich Flight Tax and everything else, down to the last pfennig, but one form was missing a stamp," he says. "The border guard said he could turn a blind eye, but not for free; how much money did I have on me? So I pulled out the five hundred reichsmarks I had hidden behind my belt, and the border guard said carrying cash was forbidden and he had to confiscate it. Then he said that unfortunately the stamp was still missing, so what could be done about that? And when I told him that now I had nothing left, he laughed and said: 'Then please get off!'"

The man with the mustache keeps wiping his face and shaking his head as if he himself were more surprised than horrified, as if his strongest feeling were still astonishment that such a thing is possible. "Even after all these years in the Reich," he says, "after all the humiliations and persecutions, even after they took my house away from me and beat me up in the street and threw my two children out of school—after all that I still didn't expect something like this!"

Again he wipes his face and starts telling the story from the beginning, and Papa, who actually hates it when people repeat themselves, doesn't interrupt him.

The wires fly up and down and up again. On the train everything simply becomes boring; even the story of this man, whose presence bothers Jakob greatly because it just isn't right for adults to be so confused and upset, becomes monotonous over the rattling and rattling and rattling of the wheels. If only sleep were possible. He closes his eyes. But the train with its rattling doesn't permit sleep; nor do the wires, which want to be seen beating their rhythm.

So he opens his eyes again, and to think about anything, he thinks about the many schools he has attended in recent years. There's the Paris school with the serious teacher, Mademoiselle Grecque, in her strangely becoming sorrow. Her round glasses, the hard ruler in her hand that can suddenly strike inattentive pupils on the back of the head. Next to him sits Maurice, who has taught him the card game rummy, here you put down the spades, *les piques*, and here the numbers, now you've lost again, Jacques, slide the coins over! And on the other side Charles Salomon, whom he sometimes visits at home, where there are thick carpets and wallpaper made of silk, and in the garden you can play hide-and-seek for hours; it's so big that you never find each other.

He was at the school in Los Angeles for only a few months. Every teacher has her own classroom, you go from one to the other, and in the hallway you have your locker, where you keep your books and notebooks, it's a terrible mess, you never find anything, and everything smells like chewing gum, trade Babe Ruth for six packs, and on the field you race, and Bob Jenkins with the freckles wins every time. The language is blurredly broad, you sing rather than speak, while French consists of little needles, tiny stitches in silk fabric, none of which is allowed to miss.

Then the school in Basel. The peculiar German, why do you speak like that, you foreigner, but actually they are kind, and their math teacher, Herr Urs Bissler, manages to make him understand for the first time what numbers are, but the very next day Mama explains to him that they won't be staying: Papa makes movies, after all, and they don't make movies in Switzerland. We're going to visit Oma, we're saying goodbye to her, she is very ill, we won't see her again afterward. Your papa is as attached to his mother as you are to me. Then we'll go to Marseille and take a ship to New York, you already know the city, and you speak the language too.

And now he hasn't been to any school at all for weeks. Being with his parents all the time is not easy. While watching the wires rise and fall and rise again and listening to Papa soothe the agitated man, Jakob notices that the train is now no longer running on tracks but swimming through water. A large octopus is wriggling down there, causing the sand to rise in small eddies around it; and just before his consciousness completely dissolves, he realizes that he must be falling asleep here on the seat, with his head leaning against the window, even though he knows that this is impossible, because he can never sleep on the train.

Jerzabek

Despite its name, Dreiturm Castle in the village of Tillmitsch didn't have three towers. It didn't even have one. It had seven damp and hard-to-heat rooms at ground level and nine cold and damp rooms on the second floor as well as three bathrooms, two of which had running water. The floors were covered with old carpets, thick and dusty, but not as dusty as the even thicker curtains on the windows, whose panes were so old that they had flowed downward under the pressure of the years and were now several centimeters thick along the bottom edge and thin as fingernails along the top. From the ceilings hung old but at least electric lamps. The oldest things, however, seemed to be the paintings on the walls: thickly painted farmers plowing lumpy fields under heavy skies, a fat nobleman staring stupidly over his twirled mustache, a landscape with gray hills, green cottages, trees, heavy clouds. In the largest room stood a four-meter-long and two-meter-wide oak table, so heavy that supposedly eight men were needed to move it, though probably no one had ever tried. Hanging on the wall above it was the head of a stag, furry and with blackly staring glass eyes. Its antlers were huge and branched.

Dreiturm had once been the hunting lodge of the bishops of Salzburg. After the war it had come into the hands of the real estate speculator Wornizek, from whom it was purchased by the manufacturer Stelzhamer, who had made his fortune producing well-sprung horse-drawn carriages and then had been driven into bankruptcy by automobiles; thus the famous director Pabst had been able to acquire the estate cheaply, along with the surrounding land and a small forest unfortunately plagued by bark beetles. For the previous eight years, his mother had lived on the upper floor. On the ground floor lived the caretaker, Jerzabek, with his wife, Liesl, and their daughters, Gerti and Mitzi.

Karl Jerzabek was known far beyond the borders of the village of Tillmitsch as a good soul. His agreement, first with Wornizek, then with Stelzhamer, and finally with Pabst stipulated that he could cultivate the two small fields for his own profit and keep everything the small forest yielded. Additionally, he had free lodging in the castle. In return, he had to maintain the building, repair the roof, clean the gutters, mow the lawn, drive away the martens, and set mousetraps. In recent years his wife had taken care of Erika Pabst. She had made the bed for the old and already somewhat confused woman, washed her clothes, and cooked for her once a day in the oversize castle kitchen.

Jerzabek helped the farmers of Tillmitsch whenever they needed anything. He was there to repair Farmer Stingler's plow, he came when Farmer Schrader's horse went lame, he brought food to Farmer Mauler when he was sick, for his wife had died the previous year, and he was on hand to shoot the rabid dog that roamed the fields at night, working together with Farmer Rescheck. He could be counted on when there was something to do in the church; he repaired the dilapidated confessional and, together with the priest, bailed out the water that collected in the cellar during the snowmelt.

He was gaunt and usually red-faced. Due to a war injury, his left hand had only a thumb and index finger, and because this made shaving difficult for him, there were always a few hairy patches on his neck. Unlike him, whose parents had come from eastern Austria—a subject he didn't like to talk about—his wife, Liesl, born Stingler, was from Tillmitsch. She was originally supposed to marry Farmer Schrader, but he ultimately decided he didn't want her, and because she was the youngest of three daughters, her father had given her to Jerzabek. So they lived together and raised their two daughters.

Since the previous year, when Austria had ceased to exist, Erika Pabst's meals were only rarely warm. Her rooms on the second floor were no longer cleaned; only the sheets were changed by Liesl Jerzabek once a month. And if she was in a good mood and Erika asked really nicely, she would sometimes still wash the old lady's clothes, although not without bending over the tub and ranting about people who thought they were better than others, even though their sons were abroad with the Jews.

Since the annexation of Austria to the Reich, the two girls played all over the building. They hid behind Erika's curtains or under her bed, they rolled their marbles in the upstairs corridor—they couldn't do it anywhere else because of the carpets—and they enjoyed scaring the old woman: they would jump out screaming from behind a curtain or wait a long time in the wardrobe to rush at her when Erika finally opened the door. Once she actually fell on her back in fright, so the girls had to fetch their mother. She lifted Erika up, maneuvered her into the armchair, scolded the children, and spoon-fed Erika chicken soup. While doing so, however, she soon grew tired of the situation and began to talk herself into a rage about how her good heart was being exploited in this house. After a while she had worked herself up into such a fury that she banged the bowl of soup down on the table, went out, slammed the door behind her, and didn't come back to the old woman for two days.

Shortly thereafter, the telegram arrived. Erika wept with joy for over an hour, though she did so secretly in her bedroom with the windows closed so that the Jerzabeks wouldn't notice. She didn't know that the caretaker's family was, of course, nonetheless aware of everything: they opened all the mail, nothing was too trivial, Liesl Jerzabek even read the long and deeply incoherent epistles that Erika's cousin wrote from the Steinhof mental hospital, and when Erika received her monthly issue of the *New Garden Arbor* magazine, Liesl had long since tried to solve the crossword puzzle, which was all the more remarkable since she could barely read and write, and therefore scattered block letters at random across the pages softened at the edges by her damp fingerprints. Sometimes the Jerzabeks also wrote letters in Erika's name, which they then presented to her for signing. When they had sent the telegram to Erika's son—COME QUICKLY STOP SERIOUS ILLNESS STOP HELP NEEDED STOP—and Erika had said that she wasn't ill at all, Liesl had replied that it wasn't about that; it was about finally getting her son to come back. And by the time an answer came from somewhere in the world—ARRIVAL AUGUST 30—Liesl Jerzabek had already changed her mind: What did the master and mistress want here, it would all only mean more work, they should have stayed abroad!

On August 30 Karl Jerzabek was waiting outside the Leibnitz station next to the wagon he had borrowed from his father-in-law, Stingler. There was an old truck in the castle courtyard, but it was broken and gasoline was expensive.

The local train from Salzburg was on time. As the family stepped out of the station building, blinking and travel weary, Jerzabek sprang toward them and exclaimed in a broad dialect how joyful it was, welcome home, kiss your hand, madam, and what a fine young gentleman! Greedily, he grabbed the suitcases and threw them into the back of the wagon with a strength it was hard to believe his crooked body possessed. He was wearing his brown party uniform—for Karl Jerzabek had recently become the leader of the local group of the Nazi Party in Tillmitsch.

On the way he spoke about the Jews. The Führer was now driving out the vermin, making them crawl away all over the world. Here in the Ostmark too, decency had finally prevailed since the Führer had brought his homeland into the Reich. And now the Jews who were still here were finally keeping their mouths shut, just like the Communists and the Catholics, they all were afraid because none would be forgotten! And he repeated: *None!* and let the whip whistle over the horse's back.

So they rolled into the village of Tillmitsch, where half of the three hundred and twelve inhabitants stood at the windows of their houses and watched as the lord of the castle returned. A thin drizzle filled the air. They rolled past the fountain and past the oak tree towering askew over the village square and then past the whitewashed church, then past Fraunzler's farmhouse, and finally they were approaching the castle.

Erika Pabst stood outside the front door. Bent over, leaning on two canes, in her best silk dress, a string of pearls around her neck, and a woven scarf over her head to protect her from the rain. She had waited for an hour, despite the wetness and her aching legs, and even before the wagon had stopped rolling, her son jumped off, ran to her, hugged her, kissed her on her forehead where her hair was thinning, lifted her up and set her down again so that she could greet her grandson; Jakob and his grandmother had not seen each other for so long that they no longer knew each other. The old woman wept with happiness. Pabst stroked her head.

"Go to bed," he said softly. "Lie down, Mama!" And of course he put the emphasis on the second syllable, just the way she wanted.

Step by step, he led her back into the building, up the stairs, into her bedroom. Meanwhile she talked to herself and spoke about her son's childhood: What a clever boy he had been, always reading books, he had ruined his eyes, but got the best marks in school! It had been such a shock when he had suddenly wanted to become an actor! "I'll have to provide for that good-for-nothing," his father had always said, and then he had died and fortunately never had to see the film his son had made about that indecent woman, that Lulu, who consorted with men. Pabst supported her as she settled onto her bed. She had heard the worst about the film, felt deeply ashamed, a disgrace to the family, and then, as Pabst gently covered her up, she wept a little with joy that her son and her grandson had come, because she had asked them to, from distant, dirty America. About Trude she said nothing, and the next moment she had fallen asleep.

Pabst stepped to the window. Down on the lawn, neatly lined up in the rain by Jerzabek, stood their suitcases.

They all had heavy, bad dreams: Trude had been lying in a coffin, it had been dark and cold, and from a distance she had heard her son screaming for help. Pabst had been on the set of a movie, in the director's chair, next to the camera, under a pale white sky with no moon, clouds, or sun. In front of him a medieval town had been built out of plywood and cardboard: pointed roofs, gables, a tower. He hesitated. He knew he shouldn't give the command, but then he did, and when he shouted "Roll film!" an army of the dead began to march past. Empty eyes looked at him, ready to follow his instructions, but when he tried to speak, his tongue felt like a stone in his mouth, and he had no voice. At that moment he heard his son. From far away he heard him screaming, but he was powerless, he couldn't go to him, because he had an obligation, he had to shoot this movie, and then he woke up with his heart pounding, it was morning.

Jakob had dreamed of a forest. But it wasn't a beautiful one; it was an old, gray, sinister forest, and cobwebs hung from the trees, and when he looked at the gnarled trunks, insects with long antennae were moving on them. When he realized he was lost, it wasn't he who screamed for his parents, but someone else. This other person looked like him and even had his voice, but was still a stranger, and for some reason this was so horrible that he was seized by a fear he had never felt before, and now he himself screamed so loudly that he could still hear it even after he had been awake for a while, staring at the cracks running across the ceiling of his nursery, where there were no longer any toys, because the Jerzabeks had sold all the old things—the tin soldiers and train cars and teddy bears—and burned the rest out in the field.

At breakfast in the cold parlor Erika told her son what she had endured from the Jerzabeks. Trude sat silently next to him; Jakob had fallen asleep again upstairs. Unfortunately, Erika's mind did not gain clarity, and so she alternately confused Karl Jerzabek with her deceased husband and her father. The existence of his wife, Liesl, however, she had completely forgotten, while she took the two daughters for her own granddaughters.

"They're always hiding. And when I fall down, they laugh, one of them especially, but the other one too, and once there was a needle!"

"For God's sake, did they prick you?"

"No, I pricked myself."

"Where was the needle, then?"

"Well, where I pricked myself."

"But where was that?"

"On my arm." She rolled up her sleeve. "Look!"

"No, I mean—where was the needle?"

"Hidden."

"But where?"

"Where you couldn't see it."

"But where was that, Mama?"

"You have to call me Mamá. You were such a well-behaved boy. It's all changed since you got married."

"We just want to understand what happened!" said Trude. "What they did to you!"

But Erika, as always when Trude spoke to her, acted as if she hadn't heard anything. The wind rattled the shutters. They all clasped their steaming cups to warm their hands. The stag's head stared from the wall.

"Well, now we're here," Pabst finally said.

And what a joy it was, a dialect-heavy voice said from the doorway, that the gracious master and mistress were here, such a great, great joy! Jerzabek was wearing his party uniform again.

Pabst thanked him and tried to look like a lord of the castle. That was why he had bought the estate: he had envisioned a delicate watercolor image of himself calmly and contentedly looking down from a high window onto a leafy courtyard and walls and golden ears of corn. Above all he had hoped a castle would convince his mother that he had amounted to something. In truth, however, he had only ever felt like a visitor to Dreiturm—one who had no business there. Nor had he been prepared for how much it rained in the countryside. If there was a similar amount of precipitation in the city, he had never noticed: the beautiful forest paths were in reality always sodden, and heavy drops fell unrelentingly over the meadows, as if the heavens wanted to punish them. Everything had been different from what he had imagined, and so he had always made an effort to spend as little time there as possible.

What a joy, repeated Jerzabek, and if one had only heard his voice and not seen his face and his smile made up of yellow teeth, one might have believed he really meant it.

"I had to bring the suitcases in myself yesterday," said Pabst. "The rain got in, the clothes are soaked, the tobacco is ruined."

"Coming back from abroad and making a fuss," said Jerzabek. "Coming back and playing the great lord as if nothing has happened. But a lot has happened, and you don't take that tone with Local Group Leader Jerzabek, or you'll quickly find yourself somewhere else."

The pendulum clock on the wall filled the silence with its sluggish ticking. The stag's head stared.

After a while Jerzabek asked what the gracious master and mistress intended to do today. He could fix the car. An excursion to Grössing perhaps, a picnic at the beautiful Schleinzbrunnen? His wife would make sandwiches!

Pabst remained silent, confused. For a moment he wondered whether he was still dreaming. But a glance at Trude's face showed him that she had heard the same thing.

Near the Schleinzbrunnen was also the local jail, said Jerzabek. That was where the people who would soon be sent on to the concentration camp were held. They were being taken care of now. His dialect distorted the words so much that it took Pabst a moment to understand them.

"I have no time for an excursion," said Pabst. "I have to work. I have to write."

Jerzabek asked whether he was writing a movie.

Pabst nodded, stood up, and walked out.

"It'll probably be another Jew movie," Jerzabek said to Trude. Trude stood up quickly, wanting to leave. Jerzabek stood in her way and asked, "Is there anything else I can do for you, madam?" His words ran together, becoming indistinguishable from each other.

"Nothing," she said.

"But if you need anything, madam," said Jerzabek, "you'll let me know, won't you? It's important that I can rely on you to inform me if you need anything!"

Trude promised.

"My wife and I," said Jerzabek, "are so happy that you're back, we want to make it as pleasant as possible for you, as comfortable as it can possibly be on God's green earth."

Trude wanted to get past him. He took a prancing side step and blocked her path.

"After all, I don't want the master and mistress to end up like the scum in the concentration camp," he said. "My wife and I will make sure of that. We want to take good care of you, just like we take good care of the old lady, even if she's weak in the head like a dairy cow and never knows what's going on—isn't that right, madam?" He directed the question toward the kitchen table, where Erika Pabst was trying with little success to spread hard-frozen butter on a soft piece of bread. "Never! Right?"

"Yes," replied Erika.

Jerzabek asked whether Gertrude had ever been an actress.

"Excuse me?"

"You're a beautiful woman, madam, is all I wanted to say, so one might wonder whether you've ever been an actress. Because, after all, the gracious master is known to have a fondness for actresses due to their beauty and their loose way of life."

Trude looked over his shoulder. Pabst was nowhere to be seen. There was a clatter. She wheeled around. Erika's plate had fallen to the floor and broken to pieces.

"Such a beautiful plate," cried Jerzabek. "Such a cow, something always happens!"

"Excuse me?" Trude asked again. Her heart was pounding; she could feel herself turning red. In her agitation she couldn't think of anything else.

"Oh no no no," cried Jerzabek, "that wasn't aimed at the old lady! Around here 'cow' is simply what you exclaim when an accident happens! Even if she's very stupid, the old woman, and has gotten ugly to boot, my natural reverence for the mother of the gracious master"—his words were running together again—"is far too great to ever utter such a thing when the master and mistress can hear me."

Then he abruptly stepped aside to let Trude pass. She had to restrain herself from running, instead walking past him step by step, feeling his vinegary breath for a moment on her cheek. She walked through the hall, up the creaking stairs, along the corridor, into the room they called the library, where Pabst, surrounded by the gray spines of hundreds of books, all of which he had taken over from the previous owner, sat with pencil in hand over a blank sheet of paper. It was obvious that he wanted to write. It was also obvious that he wasn't writing.

He saw her face. "Yes, I know."

"As soon as possible," she said.

"But first we have to get Mama settled. I have to get her into a sanatorium. There's supposed to be a good one near Giesshübl. Or on the Semmering. It would be best if I go to Vienna and look around, and then I'll come back and—"

"Are you crazy?" Trude closed her eyes for a moment. Then she opened them again, squatted down next to his chair, and said softly:

"You're not leaving us here alone! We're going to Vienna together and from there back to Switzerland."

"But that's an overreaction. Yes, he's strange, but that doesn't mean . . . "

Trude shot up, turned around, and opened the door. There, smiling rosy-cheeked under her headscarf, in the smock apron she always wore, stood Liesl Jerzabek.

She had, she said, been listening to the master and mistress.

They stared at her.

She inquired whether the master and mistress needed anything, whether she could bring them anything.

When they didn't answer, she turned around and walked away with pattering footsteps. Trude closed the door.

"All right," said Pabst. "Then that's how we'll do it."

"Right away?"

"We have to take care of a few things beforehand. First of all—"

But then they had both jumped up even before they grasped what it was they were hearing: a scream suspended in the air. It still hadn't stopped, and now still hadn't stopped, and now, as they were already running, they could still hear it, and it led them up the stairs and through another creaking corridor, whose existence Pabst hadn't even known about until now. At its end was a ladder leading to a ceiling hatch—he climbed, slipped, held on, climbed farther, heaved himself up, and fell belly-first onto floorboards covered in dust as thick as snow. He sneezed and pushed himself up, blinking. It took a few seconds for his eyes to adjust to the darkness and for him to recognize his son.

Jakob stood on tiptoe pressed against a wooden post. He was tied up. Thin straps cut into his neck, his bare arms, his bare belly, his exposed calves; he was wearing nothing but underpants.

On the floor of the attic sat the two girls, each with a bird feather in her hair. Their faces were painted with reddish chalk. One of them was holding an ax, the other a gleaming kitchen knife.

"What's going on here?" shouted Pabst.

Soundlessly, like cats, the two retreated into the darkness. "We're playing Indians," said the bigger one.

"We're Apaches," said the other. "Jakob is Comanche. I'm Winnetou. A redskin, brave like a German."

"Give me the knife please," Trude said gently.

Something fell to the floor with a clatter. Trude stepped into the darkness, groped, picked up the knife, and cut the straps.

"You two go back down now," she said.

"Say please," said a girl's voice.

"What?"

"You have to say please, or else it's not polite. I mean, you have to say please, ma'am."

"One must be polite," said the other voice.

Trude was silent for a moment before she said, "Please." A floorboard groaned, two shadows slid toward the hatch, rungs creaked, and then quick footsteps receded below.

Jakob pressed his head against his father's chest and wept.

"It's not so bad," Pabst murmured, "it's all right, everything's all right."

"They had an ax," Jakob sobbed. "They were playing scalping." He pointed to his forehead, across which a thin cut, more like a scratch, ran from his hairline to just above his eyebrow. A little blood was running down his face.

Pabst was silent for a moment, then he said: "We're leaving."

"Immediately?" asked Trude.

"We'll take Mama to Vienna, find a sanatorium, then from there straight to Switzerland. But not a word to anyone!"

"You're not going to complain to their parents?" asked Jakob.

"When we're out of the country, I'll explain it to you."

"But we're packing only one suitcase," he said to Trude. "They have to think we're coming back."

* * *

Pabst took a walk through the surrounding fields. He breathed deeply, squinting into the drizzle. When he thought about leaving, ideas suddenly came to him again—a man in flight, hunted by the whole country. He envisioned quick cuts, a camera moving at a low height, images of running feet. It's never revealed what he's done wrong. It would work out, Pabst thought, he would make movies again, he still had plenty of inspiration. As soon as he was back in Hollywood, he would convince them, the way he had always convinced everyone in the end.

They gathered around the long table for dinner. Next door the Jerzabeks' radio was blaring. Liesl Jerzabek was standing in the kitchen, stirring pots and talking to herself softly and incomprehensibly, as if she were casting spells.

"Can't you sit up straight?" Erika asked Jakob.

Jakob tried, stretching his back.

"Straighter," said Erika.

Liesl Jerzabek brought plates. Dumplings swam in brownish soup. When you pressed on them with a spoon, they made little bubbles.

"What is this?" asked Pabst.

Liesl Jerzabek answered, but they couldn't understand her. Her dialect was too strong. As she walked out, a man's voice could be heard on the radio saying: " . . . all assembled before our Führer!"

"I don't want to eat this," said Jakob.

"Pull yourself together!" said Erika. "A young man has to eat up, or else he won't get strong."

"You don't need to eat that," said Trude. "Just take some bread."

"He has to eat!" cried Erika.

"He's eating," said Pabst. "Don't worry!"

"You were such a good boy," said Erika, "before you got married."

Liesl Jerzabek came back. Voices on the radio shouted "Heil!" The door closed again. She was carrying a large loaf of bread; groaning, she sawed it in half, then into four almost equal pieces. Everyone got one. Jakob took his, carefully tried to bite into it, tapped on it, put it down. It was as hard as stone.

"How old is this bread?" asked Pabst.

"Completely fresh," she replied. "From Zantzner."

For a while they silently spooned their soup. Liesl stood at the door, watching them.

"Please tell your husband to borrow the wagon again," said Pabst. "Tomorrow morning we're heading to the Leibnitz station."

The door flew open. Jerzabek stood there, the din of the radio surging around him. Red-faced, in what sounded almost like High German, he asked whether the master and mistress really wanted to leave.

"Just for a few days."

"Your mother is going with you?"

"Yes."

"I'm not going anywhere!" cried Erika.

"Mama," said Pabst. "Please not now."

"There's no way I'm leaving."

"Tomorrow morning at eight," Pabst said to Jerzabek. "You can get a wagon, can't you?"

Jerzabek rubbed his bald head so hard that his skin made a crackling sound. Then he went out. The door closed and stifled the radio shouts.

"And now we're going to bed," said Pabst.

"But I'm hungry," said Jakob.

"I'm not going anywhere," said Erika. "This is my home."

That night Jakob didn't dream at all. Trude dreamed she was invited to an evening party at Max Reinhardt's castle in Salzburg. Liveried servants carried champagne bottles through a room flickering in candlelight, but next to her sat someone whose face she couldn't see: she knew she needed only to turn her head and direct her gaze at him, but she also knew that she'd better not, and so she looked at his hands; he had a gold ring on his pinkie and an ugly scar on the back of his hand, and she felt his eyes on her, but she resisted, looked down, ate a delicious trout with calm movements, and when she woke up, she realized that it was most likely hunger that had given rise to the dream.

The morning pressed palely against the window. Somewhere outside a small animal hissed. The rain drummed against the pane. She lay still. She knew they wouldn't be leaving. Not that day, not the next, not anytime soon.

Next to her the bed was empty.

She knew that Wilhelm was somewhere, probably in the library, packing the essentials. He was so full of confidence, so certain and convincing, and she would have liked to put her trust in him.

But she knew they wouldn't be leaving. She was as sure as she was that two times two was four. She closed her eyes, listened to the rain, and waited for the inevitable.

Pabst was indeed in the library, where years earlier he had hidden a cardboard box at the top of one of the shelves. It contained his old notebooks, the script of *The Joyless Street* with handwritten notes, a silver cigarette case that D. W. Griffith had given him in Paris fifteen years earlier, as well as letters from Chaplin, Abel Gance, and Schnitzler. But what meant the most to him was the cigarette case. "You are a true colleague," Griffith had said. "Take this!"

Actually nothing could go wrong, thought Pabst, looking around the library. They had everything they needed: Swiss entry visas, French transit visas, an open-booked first-class passage across the Atlantic, a valid affidavit and visas to enter the United States. He still had almost ten thousand marks in his German account; that would be enough to pay for six months at a good sanatorium in advance, plus four thousand francs in Switzerland, which would allow them to live there for a few weeks. Then he would probably have to work as an assistant director.

On the shelves stood hundreds of gray books from the middle of the previous century: *Debit and Credit*, *A Struggle for Rome*, *Ekkehard*. In the corner was a ladder: on top it was hooked into a metal track; on the bottom it rolled on two wheels. Pabst pulled it to the right spot. On the side of the ladder was a small lever with which the wheels could be locked. Pabst lowered it, then began to climb up carefully. All the agony back then on the glacier, and still his acrophobia was so bad that he couldn't even climb a ladder without fear.

The rungs creaked. The room seemed to grow higher above him, the floor descended faster than he was climbing. Don't look down, he thought. The same rules that applied on the mountain applied here—only look up or straight ahead.

He hesitated. Leave it, he told himself, forget the stupid thing, climb back down. But another voice said: It's only a few rungs. He had already reached the upper edge of the shelf. Three more steps, don't look down, two more, one more, and now he was at the top. And the cardboard box was actually there—exactly where he had left it. He wanted to reach out for it, but suddenly he was afraid to let go of the ladder.

"Gracious master?"

That was what was meant, anyway, even if the voice hadn't actually said it, instead uttering two sounds that merged into a single word. Pabst recognized it, of course, and he had to summon all his willpower to turn his head and do what he had sworn all this time he wouldn't do—he looked down.

And again his mind played a trick on him. Because when he saw Karl Jerzabek looking up at him, it seemed to him, quite naturally and out of old habit, as if he were at work and filming. It was a perfect shot: straight down with a short focal length and side lighting, so that the perspective shrunk the figure and seemingly increased the height at which Pabst was standing. Now for this, of course, the camera needed to be mounted on a crane. Handheld, it would shake. Pabst tried to cast off the vision. This was no film, Jerzabek was really standing down there and really looking up and repeating: "Gracious master?"

"Is the wagon ready?"

Jerzabek replied, but Pabst didn't understand. It was as if the man had now completely switched languages: A mash of sounds came out of his mouth, an *A*, an *O*, a *U*, another *A*, a long rolled *R*, and then a sound that, endlessly drawn out, went back and forth between *A* and *O* and *U* and *A* again.

"Pardon me?" asked Pabst.

And then, as he stared down in horror, he suddenly felt like he was in a film after all. Because what was happening couldn't really be happening: Jerzabek bent down and raised the lever that locked the wheels. Then he grabbed the ladder and began to rock it back and forth.

At first Pabst took it as a silly joke, but then Jerzabek rocked harder, and now he began to shake with all his might.

"Stop!" cried Pabst.

Jerzabek rolled the ladder to the right, then to the left, then farther to the right, then farther to the left. Pabst could no longer hold on to the shelf, he clung to the ladder and shouted: "Stop it!"

Jerzabek actually stopped. Pabst turned around again and could see Jerzabek standing close to the ladder, clutching it with his arms, and groaning with exertion as he lifted it a few centimeters, causing the hooks to come off their metal track before Pabst's eyes.

Jerzabek pulled the ladder toward him. Pabst saw the shelf swing away from him. The ladder stood free in the room. The caretaker was holding it.

"Stop it!" shouted Pabst.

Later he wasn't sure whether Jerzabek had actually said "Yes, sir!" or whether he had imagined it. Then Jerzabek looked up with an obsequious smile, let go of the ladder, and stepped aside.

The room leaped, Pabst saw the shelf dart away, he saw the ceiling swing into the depths. He felt himself falling.

As the world pieced itself together from fragmented dreams and pain and dizziness, he lay in bed. He was wearing striped silk pajamas.

Under his neck was a wet canvas pouch of melting ice. On his belly was a hot rubber bottle. He sat up; his back felt like something in it was broken. He sank back again.

He carefully turned his head. He was lying in a dark room with stained wallpaper. A slanted wooden table stood forlornly, with a candle burning on it. Shadows danced on the walls. This was not his bedroom. Outside the window it was dark. Neither his clothes nor his shoes were anywhere to be seen.

He listened. It was completely silent. A hum hung in the air, but he didn't know whether it was the blood in his ears, the rain outside, or the sound of the silence itself. He opened his mouth, but then closed it again because he suddenly no longer knew whom he had wanted to call.

Once again he tried to straighten up. But his back wouldn't allow it. He thought for a little while, then remembered his wife's name and called out to her.

No one answered. He cleared his throat and called out again. His voice had no strength. For a moment he thought he heard footsteps, but then it was silent again. He must have been mistaken. And now the memory came back with full force: the moment the caretaker had seized the ladder below him, his squirrel face furrowed with malice, his narrow eyes and the sharp little teeth between his lips.

When Trude entered, he cried out in fright. He hadn't heard her coming. Perhaps he had fallen asleep again.

And when he looked at her face, guilt washed over him like a heavy wave, because he realized he had actually been asleep for a little while and had been dreaming of Louise. She had embraced him and looked him in the face with love. I'll never go away again, she had said.

"You have to call the police," said Pabst.

Trude placed a hand on his forehead. It felt very cool.

"He knocked me over," he said in a hoarse voice.

"Wilhelm," she said, "you fell over with the ladder."

"Not fell over," he croaked. "Not fell . . ."

"You were dreaming."

"No! He knocked me . . . " But his voice failed him. He had to speak more clearly, everything depended on her understanding him.

"I was on the ladder," he tried again. "The cigarette case. In the library. The box. Griffith. Then he came in, Jerzabek, and then—"

"I have to tell you something."

"No, me first!" He couldn't let himself be interrupted now, he had to explain it to her; the danger of forgetting was too great, his head wasn't working properly. "I was on the ladder. Then he came in, and then—"

"Wilhelm!"

"—he knocked it over, like it was nothing! I mean the ladder. Just took it and knocked it over!"

"Wilhelm!"

"Listen to me! We have to call the police! I was on the ladder, he just took it—"

"Wilhelm, there are no police anymore."

"What do you mean?"

"There are people in uniform, but they're not the police you can call if someone threatens you or robs you. Everything's different now. Besides, you imagined it."

"Imagined?"

"I was there. I saw what happened."

"Where?"

"In the library."

"No. I was on the ladder, he just took it and—"

"I was there too. You were on the ladder. He was next to me."

"Who?"

"That horrible man. Jerzabek. But the ladder was positioned wrong. It was standing straight up and down. I was about to say it didn't look safe. Then you turned around, and suddenly it tipped, and he ran over to hold it, but he got there too late. Then he carried you here, and he helped me change your clothes and put you in the bed."

The bedroom had begun to spin; as if he were on a ship again, it slowly rose and fell. He was overcome by the peculiar feeling, familiar from fever dreams, that a huge mass, weighing tons, was resting on a blade of grass, and this was, in a way that could not be put into words, indescribably unpleasant.

"You're mistaken! I was on the ladder, and he just—"

"Wilhelm, it's war."

"He just knocked it over. He wants to keep us here so we—"

"Germany has invaded Poland. The borders are closed."

He stared at her.

"It came on the radio this morning. I heard it myself, down in the Jerzabeks' quarters, we all heard it together! There's shooting. The trains are stopped. The borders are closed."

Pabst felt a knot in the pit of his stomach, his breath was coming faster and faster, and there was nothing he could do about it. He squinted, for the light was suddenly gone, he could see nothing, his eyes were blind.

Then he must have passed out, for when the room around him became clear again, filled with objects that had no names, he could sense that time had passed. A person he didn't know was leaning over him, it was a woman, he didn't know her, he didn't recognize her, now he recognized her. He wanted to speak to her, but it took a moment for her name to come back, along with the memory that in his unconsciousness Louise had been with him once again. But now the memory of what Trude—yes, that was it, that was her name, which didn't actually suit her at all: Trude—now the memory of what she had said came back, and when his voice somewhat obeyed him again, he whispered: "Closed?"

"Yes," she said, "we can't get out anymore."

"War," he repeated. There was something abstract about the word, which didn't evoke any emotion. He had experienced war once before, it had taken him to a prison camp, where he had become a movie director, but what did it mean this time? "The visas are no longer valid?"

"I don't know. But what good are visas if there are no trains?"

They couldn't go to Vienna either. Too many people knew him there. And certainly not to Berlin. They couldn't go anywhere.

He closed his eyes. He felt like he was lying on the bottom of a deep ocean. The open air, the light, the sun—all that was now so far away that you could spend a lifetime struggling upward without ever reaching it.

When he tried to breathe in, there was only icy water, and in the distance, he knew, monsters were moving, even though they were already visible: black and many-armed, at home in the darkness. And before he could dispel these visions, before he could free himself and sit up and look his wife in the face, his senses faded.

Citadels of the People

Jakob likes art class. He has always enjoyed drawing, but recently he has become good at it too. The trick is to look at a thing as if it weren't a thing and as if you didn't know what it was. Then it turns into a collection of surfaces, some dark, others light, a pattern of shadow and light, or actually not even that, but just white and black, and when you put that on the sheet of paper, the thing appears there again as if by magic: a jug, a leaf, a hand, a dog's head.

The same goes for colors: Look closely, and the world recedes, becoming a mixture in which nothing is clean and everything runs together. If you manage to capture this on paper, you get a picture. It works quite well with crayons, better with watercolors. If you really look, you will notice that shadows have not only the colors of the background on which they fall, but at the same time those of the body that casts them. Or you will notice that the world is full of reflections: almost every object holds the world that surrounds it on its surface, points of light, outlines, and glimmers—all images contain other images. To recognize this, you must in a sense become stupid. You must stop thinking.

In art class he always sits in the last row, where he can concentrate. He squints his eyes, looks at the paper, and paints: the narrow rectangle with the heavy shape of the roof above it, the tiny windows, the vast blue with patches of white that once, before you forgot all names to be able to paint, was the sky. For reasons that seem compelling to him, even if he could not have explained them, he has placed the angular shapes not in the middle of the page but at the left edge, slightly below the center.

"Farmhouses are the citadels of our people" is the assignment. Their art teacher is Herr Kail, he wears a party uniform, just like the caretaker Jerzabek in the castle, and he speaks in short sentences that Jakob now understands because he has grown accustomed to the dialect.

Herr Kail would like to be feared, but he's not that bad: when you look at his face, you find restless eyes above his constantly twitching mustache, you find fear, worry, and a nervous sniffle. Truly dangerous, however, is Frau Klinzer, the math teacher; she immigrated from distant Dortmund, for some reason married a blacksmith in Ragnitz, and is not happy in the Ostmark. She enjoys meting out punishments: whoever speaks in class has to stand in the corridor and copy the four typewritten pages of the school rules, without a table, pressing the paper against the wall. The rules are short and easy to understand: "The pupil of Seyss-Inquart Middle School must conduct himself with courtesy, propriety, and honor. He obeys the teachers in everything and does not talk back," or "The pupil of Seyss-Inquart Middle School takes care to dress well and tidily, he does not wear short pants, and his shoelaces are always tightly tied and do not drag while walking," or "The pupils of Seyss-Inquart Middle School do not make noise in the corridors of the school building and move forward in an orderly column on the right side of the corridor." There are a lot of them. The stupid thing is that Frau Klinzer often sends you to write the school rules when you haven't even been talking—sometimes she imagines it, other times she's just in a bad mood, but what are you supposed to do about it, since paragraph one of the school rules forbids you to talk back to the teachers. When someone chained up her bicycle the other day, she got so angry that you would have thought her heart would stop. Fortunately, she never found out that it was Jakob.

He did it because he realized that it's dangerous to be unpopular in class. But you become popular by playing pranks. So he put a new chain with a very strong padlock on Frau Klinzer's Steyer bicycle, on the very day the school janitor was visiting his sister in Graz, so that no one far and wide could saw through the chain for her. She stood there, not knowing what to do and screaming, and even her fellow teachers Kail, Witschnick, Schleinzer, and Reib walked past with suppressed smiles. Of course, no one knows who it was, but at the same time Jakob made sure that everyone knew, and the reputation this earned him has almost made them forget that he was recently abroad.

It also helped that the German teacher Witschnick praised his father right on the first day of school: "*Westfront 1918* is a great film about the war, about German people, a film about what we suffered back then!"

Herr Witschnick is popular. He is a good teacher. He reads them poems by Eichendorff, Goethe, and Hölderlin, his delivery is melodious, afterward they have to write essays and explain what they have heard. Jakob likes that too: German is the language whose words flow most smoothly, whose sentences fit together of their own accord. In French he always had to stop and think and sometimes change his mind to finish a sentence. In German that doesn't happen: When he says something, he can say exactly what he would like to say, and when he writes, it turns out that what he really wanted to express is there. Only the spelling still gives him trouble; there are so many silent *H*'s and long *I*'s in German, and when you least expect it, a *Th* suddenly jumps out at you—but he knows he will learn it. His memory has never let him down. In history, for example, where he has to memorize so many dates connected with events that are completely new to him, it works well: the Battle of the Teutoburg Forest, the Goths in Rome, the Turkish siege of Vienna, the shameful dictated peace in the Forest of Compiègne. He has memorized it so well that Jürgen Peltz, who sits next to him on the right, is starting to copy from him.

But here you have to be careful: on the one hand, it's obviously good if others copy, you're helping them, they need you. On the other hand, you quickly gain a reputation as a teacher's pet and a bookworm this way, and to make up for that—there's no avoiding it—you have to hurt someone.

Jakob has thought a lot about this, for there must be a way to solve the problem with reflection. And he has to hurry—this morning, for example, the boy on his left just took his history notebook and copied from it, then threw it back on his desk without even saying thank you; and as if that weren't bad enough, Herr Reib praised him in Latin class for a good translation, a very unfortunate combination of circumstances. He really has to do something.

They always walk the first stretch of the way home together: Peltz, Perzinek, Wurfitz, Krauber, and little Frummel—first along Grazergasse, then Wiesbergstrasse past Grottendorf, then through the open meadows to the junction where Peltz, Wurfitz, Krauber, and Frummel turn left toward Altenberg, while Perzinek and he continue on to Tillmitsch.

It's about forty-five minutes to the junction. So he knows how much time he has. He also knows that Krauber will stand up for little red-haired Frummel whenever someone says something disparaging about his village of Altenberg, because these farm kids are predictable. What he doesn't know, however, is how he can hurt the big, broad Hans Krauber in a quick, effective manner that is safe for himself.

The whole way, while he hears them behind him making jokes about the teachers and spitting—children here spit a lot; it seems to be a custom—he racks his brain. It has to be something clever that no one notices; he can't just pick up a stone, hide it in his hand, and strike—that's far too simple . . . Thoughtfully, he bends down, picks up a flat stone, playfully passes it from one hand to the other, is about to toss it away but keeps it after all, weighs it, finds it surprisingly smooth, heavy, and usable, and thinks: Why not, actually? And he thinks, Nonsense, that's too easy, and what if it goes wrong? And he thinks: Then it just mustn't go wrong. Sometimes something works precisely because it's so simple.

Casually, he asks whether it's true that it rains more in Altenberg than in Tillmitsch, and although this is really a harmless question, he sees that Krauber is frowning and Frummel is turning red, and indeed Frummel immediately says that it *definitely* doesn't rain more in Altenberg than in Tillmitsch.

"But I've heard that more than once," says Jakob.

"Complete nonsense," says Frummel, "why should it rain more in one village than in the neighboring village, the clouds move freely from one place to the other—usually, by the way, from Tillmitsch to Altenberg. By the way, in Tillmitsch the roads are always dirty and the baker is a Yid."

Jakob knows nothing about the Tillmitsch baker, but he knows by now how to respond to insults, and so he says that the baker in Tillmitsch may be a Yid, but in Altenberg even the mayor is one, adding, "Altenberg is so Judaized that you can't go there at all!"

Little Frummel suddenly has the face of a forest animal, ears folded back, eyebrows bristling, teeth pressed to his lips. Jakob would almost have had to laugh if big Krauber hadn't clenched his fists next to the little one and said, "You take that back." And then it suddenly comes to Jakob what he has to do, because, after all, they always emphasize fairness, that's what the teachers teach them, that's what they constantly tell each other: Fight like a man!

But at the French school he learned that Genghis Khan's army won all its battles by shooting the Christian knights from afar with well-aimed arrows, without ever fighting like a man. Had the knights survived, they would surely have complained bitterly about such underhandedness, but none of them survived, nor was there anyone to whom they could have complained about the lack of chivalry, and so the Mongols had been the victors every time, and if the Khan hadn't fallen ill, Europe's lands would have long since been part of Mongolia.

Jakob is about to make another witty remark about the people of

Altenberg intermarrying with Jews, but Krauber is already coming toward him, fists clenched, the left in front of the right, head bowed to his chest, just as you apparently do when you're going to box, and Jakob holds his breath and commands himself to stay calm, and when Krauber is just three steps away from him, he kicks him with all his might in the kneecap.

It works. Krauber bends over, whimpering. Jakob drops to his knees and, taking a wide swing, hits him on the nose with the stone in his hand—instinctively he doesn't do it very hard, it's surprisingly difficult to hit a person on the nose, everything in your body resists it, you don't want to, you almost can't do it, but when it has to be done and you know things will go badly for you otherwise, you manage to do it after all.

Krauber, however, doesn't go down as hoped. He just staggers. Jakob understands he has to act very quickly—he has to overcome his hesitation, because of course he's afraid of making everything even worse. If his attack goes wrong, Krauber will only hurt him even more; on the other hand, everything will certainly go wrong if he does nothing now. He manages to strike again, on the same spot, from the same angle, only this time harder, sending a sharp pain through his fist and elbow, and because he realizes that his hand will soon no longer be usable for blows, he strikes a third time, although blood is suddenly running down Krauber's face and it is no longer clear exactly where his nose is. He hits and hears something crack, without knowing whether it was Krauber's nose or his knuckle, and now he has obviously succeeded: Krauber is lying on the ground, blood running down his face. Holding his hands in front of his eyes, he is suddenly no longer a strong German boy at all, but a sobbing child.

Jakob leans over him as if he wanted to check on his opponent. In reality, however, he does it to make the stone disappear inconspicuously into his pants pocket. He doesn't drop it on the ground, because that would be seen, but no one pays attention when your hand slips into your pocket—that looks perfectly natural. The magician Dai Vernon, a kind and elegant gentleman, once explained it to him when they were invited to lunch at the home of Papa's friend Fred Zinnemann, on a bright day under the palm trees: The oldest rule of the art of deception: a large movement makes a small movement invisible.

Jakob steps back. He looks at Peltz, Perzinek, Wurfitz, and little Frummel, they all look at him—but not from the front, rather in a strange way from below. Wurfitz has interlaced his fingers in a pleading gesture, and little Frummel now no longer looks like a squirrel, his teeth have disappeared, his bitten lips are twisted into an almost friendly smile.

Jakob approaches Perzinek, who immediately steps back, despite being a head taller. But Krauber still hasn't gotten up, and his face is a smeared mass; the sight has its effect.

Jakob says he's sorry that it's so bad, and the others say things like: "It'll be okay," and "Don't worry, when you hit the nose, it just bleeds." So he has achieved what he wanted. They always side with the winner. He knew it beforehand, but when it actually happens, it's still a surprise.

He feels dizzy, his ears are buzzing, the colors have drained out of things, which must be due to the excitement and also the injury to his hand. But he knows he can't let it show. He manages to stretch out his aching hand and help his opponent up.

Krauber stumbles to his feet. Blood drips to the ground, his nose still looks normal, but Jakob knows it will soon swell and discolor, and this nose will quite certainly never look the same as before. He now has to take all necessary precautions to ensure that there are no repercussions for him, that Krauber doesn't ambush him next month, that no one complains to the teachers or the principal.

So he puts his arm around Krauber, exactly as he has observed in the schoolyard. He pats him appreciatively on the chest. The gesture feels idiotic to him, but if it works for others, why not for him? Softly he asks whether this will stay between them. Whether he can count on it. Because only cowards go out and snitch.

He looks first at Krauber and then at the others, and sure enough, they all nod.

They move on. Krauber presses a thick cloth he found in his satchel to his face. Because of the kick to his knee, he is limping. Jakob feels a sense of guilt rising hot and throbbing inside him, ebbing and returning. He has the urge to cry, but he knows he must not. He wants to apologize. Yet that would be even worse than crying.

At the crossroads they promise each other once again not to say anything. They certainly won't snitch, they'll definitely keep quiet! It's amazing, Jakob thinks, you can be as underhanded as you like—if you demand chivalry afterward, nothing will happen to you.

Half an hour later he reaches the castle.

He steps softly into the hall. The girls are more dangerous than his classmates, because they're not bound by the snares of fairness. But lately they've been leaving him alone. They no longer ambush him, they now only rarely lock him in the closet, they no longer beat him up, and thankfully, they've now stopped hiding needles in his food. He has managed to become boring to them.

He tiptoes through the hall. The day before yesterday he disturbed the caretaker, who got angry and slapped him so hard that his ear is still ringing. But with Jerzabek too it was more difficult at first; by now they've all gotten used to each other. The caretaker scolds less now, and he hardly ever threatens them with the Gestapo anymore. Even Oma no longer complains so much about having to sleep with Jakob in the former bedroom of the caretaker's daughters; and now Jakob himself hardly notices how loudly his grandmother snores or how often she talks in her sleep—besides, it's good that he no longer sleeps alone. Even a snoring, confused grandmother is better than the empty darkness where ghosts, vampires, and large spiders hide. Unchanged, however, is Oma's firm conviction that this deterioration in living conditions is her daughter-in-law's fault: "She came," she says again and again. "It was so nice before. Ever since she's been here, I'm not allowed upstairs anymore."

But none of them are allowed upstairs anymore. The Jerzabeks are now up in the living quarters, and the Pabsts are downstairs in the caretaker's apartment, which Papa hardly ever leaves. He stays in bed for a long time, staring out the window for hours and only sometimes leafing through the newspaper that Mama brings from Tillmitsch. If he does get up for a short walk, he limps and has to lean on a cane, since he has not yet recovered from the accident.

And so Mama has to take care of everything. She washes the clothes in a tub of hot water on the stove, and not only theirs but also the Jerzabeks'. She irons, she cooks—not only for her own family, but also for the caretaker's. Mama also has to look after Erika—changing her clothes, helping her eat, giving her something to drink, getting up at night to help her to the toilet.

All this is much harder for her than it is for Jakob. He has adapted well at school, has quickly understood what to say and to whom and how to behave, so that the mistrust of the others has soon diminished. And after what he managed to do to Krauber today, he shouldn't expect any more problems.

He sits down at the kitchen table. He's allowed to, the Jerzabeks don't mind. He opens the math exercise book: *Two Hitler Youths are collecting money for a Horst Wessel memorial stone, the grateful people give them 743 Reichsmarks, the stone costs 104 Reichsmarks per kilogram of marble, the engraving costs 9 marks per letter.* Yawning, Jakob does the arithmetic. The solution is quickly found, but he's having trouble holding the pencil: his right hand is warm and swollen, the knuckles bluish. Still, he draws the stone for Horst Wessel under the calculation, with elegantly curved edges, finely hatched grain, and the swastika slightly tilted to the side, balancing on one of its corners. He then has to write a short essay: "Why Our Wehrmacht Will Win," which is of course easy to answer, because the Wehrmacht is stronger, more determined, braver, and above all free of Jews, while the armies of Germany's enemies are riddled with the most impure elements and also led by people who cannot be trusted and who fail to arouse enthusiasm in any breast. He is proud of this last phrase. His handwriting, however, is becoming more and more scrawly; if his hand swells a little more, he'll no longer be able to write at all.

Mama comes in. She has carelessly pinned up her hair and is wearing a blue smock apron. This is how she usually looks now. When she sees him, she lets out a scream and asks what happened to his hand.

Fell down, he says, knowing she will believe it because she wants to believe it. She would never think him capable of intentionally hurting someone. And she's actually right, he really did it only because it was unavoidable. Otherwise he would have become like little Frummel, someone whose money and lunch are taken, someone who is mocked and whose schoolbag is emptied over the garbage can whenever the others are bored. But Jakob's advantage is that he has seen so many countries and so many other schools that he can quickly grasp how things work. The children here know only their village. That puts them at a disadvantage.

Mama fetches a piece of meat from the pantry and wraps it around his hand. She still smells of her expensive perfume, but when he sees the fine lines around her eyes, he realizes for the first time that his beautiful mother is getting older too. He leans forward and gives her a kiss on the cheek. She strokes his head.

It does worry him a little that she took the meat, because he knows she should have asked Liesl Jerzabek for permission.

"We won't stay long," she says. "Don't worry. We'll leave soon."

He knows she's trying to reassure him. But he would have preferred to tell her that there's no hurry. It's very hard for his parents here, but as for him, they don't need to worry. He's getting along fine.

Hamlet

Kuno Krämer got out of the car. The driver said something he didn't understand, but by then he had already slammed the door. He hesitated, then decided it would be silly to open the door again and ask. After all, he was the boss and didn't have to be polite.

During the night it had rained, the ground was muddy, he had to step over puddles. But the sky was bright and the air smelled of spring. Here and there small blossoms sprouted in the greenery, a cloud frayed above, and the leaves on two trees trembled in the wind. He was surprised that Dreiturm Castle didn't have even a single tower. He looked up at the facade, then yanked on the bellpull. Somewhere inside a bell rang.

For a long time nothing happened.

He was about to turn away and walk around the building when he heard footsteps. A shuffling and clattering, then a bolt was pushed back, and a disheveled, poorly shaved, and on the whole quite untidy-looking man opened the door.

"I want to see Professor Pabst," said Krämer, using an inappropriate academic title in the Ostmark manner.

"Why?"

"On an important matter," said Krämer.

The man asked the nature of the matter. He was hard to understand; he spoke a very coarse dialect.

"I want to tell Herr Pabst myself," replied Krämer.

The man in the doorway stood and stared, clearly not knowing how to handle the situation.

"Immediately," said Krämer, without raising his voice. There was no need to speak loudly; it was enough not to sound polite. Politeness was interpreted as weakness; he had been back in Germany long enough now to know that. "I've come from Berlin," he said brusquely, "and don't have much time."

That did the trick. The man let him in. As Krämer passed by, he noticed that the man was missing three fingers on his left hand.

"It's not a good time. The master is busy."

"Nonsense," said Krämer.

The man asked him to wait a moment while he informed the master.

"Wait?" Krämer repeated it in such an incredulous tone that the man just mumbled, "Very well, this way, please." They walked down a low-ceilinged corridor. It smelled of cabbage and onions. They passed an open door behind which a red-faced woman stood at a stove.

"From Berlin!" the man shouted, as if anticipating her question.

She backed away, and then she seemed to dissolve into the shadows in a corner of the kitchen: one moment her face, an arm, a shoulder were still visible, the next nothing. At the same time children's voices could be heard from somewhere, laughter and a clatter, something rolled down the stairs, but when Krämer stopped and listened, it was silent again.

"Please continue this way," said the man. "This way, please. Here!" He opened a door, and they stepped into a cramped, stuffy room. In an armchair turned toward the window so that only the back of a head rose above the worn backrest, sat Georg Wilhelm Pabst.

He turned around. On a small table lay a clothbound edition of *Hamlet*, but it didn't look as if he had been reading it. His face was pale, his hair hadn't been cut in a long time, he wasn't well shaven either, and as he stood up, he had to support himself with his left hand on the backrest. Then he stood crookedly, one shoulder higher than the other; probably his hip was hurting. Krämer knew this posture from his father, who was in a nursing home in Oldenburg patiently waiting to die. Pabst, however, was not yet an old man, he was even younger than Krämer. Running across the right lens of his glasses was a thin crack.

"Heil Hitler," Krämer said in a friendly voice. "Remember? We talked on another continent. It was quite hot."

Pabst didn't respond. Krämer turned to the disheveled man and pointed unmistakably to the door.

The man asked, "May I bring you something? Water or beer or a tipple of wine?"

"No, thank you," said Krämer, momentarily disgusted by the word "tipple." How did people go through life speaking like that?

The man shuffled backward, pausing for a moment and looking back and forth between them. No one moved. Finally he went out and closed the door. But no footsteps receded. Well, he should go ahead and eavesdrop! You have to readjust, Krämer thought, we don't need to be afraid of listeners, we are the listeners; we don't fear informers, because the informers work for us!

"What do you want?" asked Pabst.

"May I sit down?" Krämer asked. Pabst didn't answer. Krämer pulled up a chair. It was hard and wobbly, he would have preferred to remain standing, but precisely because Pabst had not invited him to sit down, he had to sit down, so that he wasn't standing in front of the director like a schoolboy. He crossed his legs, took out his pack of cigarettes, and offered it to Pabst.

Pabst shook his head. Krämer sighed, because that meant he had to smoke now, even though he still felt sick from the car ride. He took out a cigarette, flicked open his lighter, and lit it.

"How did you know I was here?" asked Pabst.

"You think we don't know that the greatest German director is back in the country? My dear fellow, I certainly understand the wish to live inconspicuously, *lathe biosas*, the beautiful ideal of Epicurus, but at some point you have to work again, don't you? I mean, is this really a coincidence? I say to you: Please come back. I say: All the doors are open. I say we would consider ourselves lucky. And here you are! Has anyone forced you to return? I don't think so. Were you abducted? Not that I know of."

"My mother," said Pabst.

"Ah."

"She wasn't well. We had to come to her, and then the war broke out, and the border—"

"You're making a lot of work for us, by the way. You have no idea how many letters we get because of you. From the neighbors. 'The Communist is back, arrest him,' from the baker in your lovely village, 'Every day the Jew whore comes to buy bread, do something,' and also a great many anonymous ones, always in the same handwriting, apparently from someone who knows your daily routine at home very well. I'd rather not quote those. Since we are an orderly state, the process always follows its bureaucratic course, from the Gestapo in Graz to the Gestapo in Berlin, from there to the ministry's Film Department, from there to the office of the Minister, who, however, is very well disposed toward you. By the way, how is she, your mother?"

"Fine, thank you."

"Yes, but is this"—Krämer made a hand gesture indicating the low ceiling, the dirty carpet, the small table, and the damp patches on the ceiling—"really the right place for an elderly lady in poor health? Don't you at least want to go up to the second floor?"

"We were on the second floor."

"And what happened?"

Pabst didn't answer. Krämer pointed questioningly at the door, behind which they both knew the man was pressing his ear to the wood. Pabst nodded.

"Well, fortunately something can be done about that. And your mother—do you need a sanatorium? We can arrange a nice room.

Wherever you want. With a view. And you don't have to worry about the costs."

Pabst remained silent.

"Do you want to direct that?" Krämer pointed to the copy of *Hamlet*. "Stage or film? Just say the word. I could imagine that the material suits you well. A highly talented man, capable of anything, but he has such a hard time deciding!"

"But Shakespeare is English."

"On paper. He's German at heart. All our theaters put on his plays. If you weren't hiding from the world like a mole, you would have noticed that by now. Our best actors embody his characters so truthfully, so . . . profoundly that it should make England blush with shame."

"Can a country blush?"

Krämer's throat tightened. He felt hot. Once again he had said something that wouldn't pass muster among educated people, once again the wrong word, the wrong nuance, the wrong allusion. Once again he had proved that he didn't belong.

But it didn't matter anymore. Everything was different now. He could say what he wanted, when and how he wanted. No one would mock him anymore, and whatever he said, people would listen, and if they still didn't respect him, at least they wouldn't show it.

"I suggest we talk about the next step," said Krämer. "You're here. Back home. That's good. Because at a time like this people belong in their homeland. We rally around the flag, everyone does his part—everyone except those rootless men we saw over there trying to offer their services to new masters." Pabst's expression darkened, and Krämer realized he had gone too far. Of course, it wasn't a good idea to remind him of Hollywood, of the bright sky and the palm trees, of all the clever and cheerful people. Krämer too longed for Los Angeles; in his dreams he still regularly found himself on the Santa Monica Pier, feeling the sun warm on his scalp and the sand beneath his feet. How much more must Pabst miss that place. He actually had friends there, whereas Krämer had only become more closely acquainted with a single employee of the Consulate General, a certain Eggebrechter from Münster. Every Monday they had met in Krämer's bare house to play cards, and both had carefully weighed their words, each knowing, of course, that the other was sending reports home. But what Krämer missed most was his poodle, Harro, whom he'd had put to sleep because he couldn't take him along.

"You're here," said Krämer. "That's the most important thing. We see it, we understand."

"You understand nothing!"

"I understand that things have to go on somehow. You're probably telling yourself it won't last. You'll wait until the war is over, then you'll take your family and go to France or straight back across the sea, and there your life will go on."

Krämer paused for a moment. But Pabst, who had slumped just a little bit during these remarks, resisted the provocation and remained silent. From outside they heard a crack, then something that sounded like a groan: the man at the door was apparently finding it difficult to stand still.

"The Minister would like to speak to you," said Krämer. He crossed his arms, looking at Pabst intently. This sentence was his trump card, his sword, his arrow. A famous actor had jumped for joy. The editor in chief of a left-wing newspaper had wet his pants in fear. Krämer scrutinized Pabst's lap, then looked back into his glasses, where the bright rectangle of the window was reflected twice, crossed by the crack on the right side. Nothing discernible. No joy, no terror. Too bad.

"Thank you," said Pabst. "I'll present myself in Berlin soon."

"When?"

"I don't know yet. My health is compromised. I had an accident. I can't leave so quickly. My mother needs care."

"As I said, we can take care of your mother. I can make arrangements immediately."

Behind the door a cough could clearly be heard. Krämer stood up and opened the door in one swift movement. "The Pabst family is to be housed on the second floor again!" Without waiting for an answer, he closed the door and sat down. That's it, he thought, that's how it's done, short and sharp. He had come a long way since his days as a mailman!

"Would the day after tomorrow work for you?" he asked. "That way you have tomorrow to pack."

"That's not convenient. I urgently need to recover. Last year I fell off a ladder, I seriously injured myself, a hip fracture and a concussion, at the moment I simply can't—"

"As you wish. You're not under arrest."

Krämer fell silent—first of all, to let the pause take effect, and second, because the thought of his job as a mailman back then had reminded him of his boss, a Socialist named Hungermann, a mustachioed dirty swine who had bullied him from morning to evening. Was Hungermann still with the postal service? He must have been promoted several times by now. But that won't do you any good, thought Krämer. I'll find you.

"You're not under arrest," Krämer repeated, looking Pabst in the face and smiling. Unless, of course, he thought, Hungermann had joined the party in the meantime. Then he would be powerless, then he could do nothing.

"That means, if I didn't come . . . " Pabst took off his glasses and cleaned them with the lapel of his jacket. "Then I would be . . . arrested?"

Krämer smiled. For a few seconds, he didn't answer, then he clapped his hands and stood up.

"I'm afraid I must decline," he said. "Urgent business. Have to get back."

"What must you decline?"

"Your invitation to lunch."

"I didn't invite you."

"Do you really have to say that out loud? No, esteemed maestro, indeed you didn't, and I headed off this mysteriously ill-mannered omission by gratefully declining the invitation you should have extended. Because at least one of us knows how to conduct himself."

Krämer held out his hand, and Pabst, evidently following a reflex more than a considered intention, grasped it and returned the handshake. Last time, thought Krämer, you called me a swine and threatened to hit me. We've made progress.

"Please sit back down," he said. "I see that your hip hurts. If you need good doctors, we can arrange that too."

Krämer waited a moment, but Pabst made no reply. So he left.

The corridor was empty. Krämer passed the kitchen. Two girls were sitting on the floor. Their hair was tied in bows, their faces seemed to have been molded out of dough. A shudder ran down Krämer's spine.

"What are your names?" he asked.

"Go away," said the bigger one.

Krämer wanted to take a breath and yell at them, but then he remembered that it was beneath his dignity to get into quarrels with peasant girls. Red-faced, he walked on. He pushed open the heavy door and stepped outside. Next to the portal, holding a shovel, stood the caretaker.

"From now on the Pabst family is to be treated with respect."

The man mumbled something, bowing and making subservient gestures of assent. But just as Krämer was about to add that he needed to teach his children better manners, the man preempted him by asking for his name.

Krämer was taken aback for a moment and then gave it.

The man asked for his first name.

Krämer gave it hesitantly.

The man asked for his department.

"Why do you want to know?"

"Just because," the man said in a language that was almost High German. "If I'm correctly informed and they didn't tell me anything wrong at the party meeting, the gracious gentleman is required to give his department on request."

"I don't have to do anything," said Krämer.

The man peered up at him crookedly.

"Reich Ministry of Public Enlightenment and Propaganda," said Krämer. "State Secretariat Two, Film Department, Film and Cinema Law Division."

"Film and Cinema Law Division," the man repeated as if trying to memorize it.

"Why?"

The man looked at him silently.

"Why do you want to know?"

The man remained silent. Krämer turned away brusquely and walked to the waiting car. When the driver saw him coming, he started the engine.

Krämer got in, took out his handkerchief, and wiped his bald head. Why had the fellow asked for his department?

But it didn't matter, he thought, as the car began to move and the castle receded—slowly at first, then faster—into the distance behind him. Just a runt in his cow village! And quite apart from that, thought Krämer, he had done nothing wrong, it had gone well, in a few days Pabst would be standing before the Minister!

Only why had he wanted to know the department?

"Pull over," he said.

They stopped, he got out, bent over, and vomited.

It took him a few seconds to collect himself. Then he got back in, slammed the door with all his might, and shouted: "Drive on!"

For a while they rode in silence. Gray-black forest passed by. Cows stood in a meadow chewing grass, then more forest.

"They invited me for a meal," Krämer explained. "Nice people. But terrible food. Made me quite ill."

The driver remained silent.

And even though he knew he was only making it all even more embarrassing, Krämer said: "Don't worry. I'm feeling better now."

Father of Lies

His friend and colleague Käutner had an apartment on Bleibtreustrasse. Pabst left his suitcase in the hotel and walked around Savignyplatz for half an hour, until he was sure no one was following him.

The swastika was everywhere. It flamed red from the facades, billowed in the wind, flapped from the roofs, its jagged black emblazoned on every wall. Three times he saw parades: drums and brown uniforms and sharp marching in lockstep. Passersby stopped and raised their right hand, and Pabst, not wanting to attract attention, hesitantly did the same—just for a second, with a jerk of his shoulder, after which he felt soiled to the core.

"It's bad," Käutner said softly as they sat in his living room, "and then again not so bad. Ufa has remained surprisingly apolitical, they let everyone do their work, even banned screenwriters continue to write under pseudonyms. Of course, you have to be extremely careful not to say anything wrong, even more so since the beginning of the war. But once you get used to it and know the rules, you feel almost free."

The doorbell rang. Outside stood a small pleasant-looking man, still panting from the climb to the third floor; he had brought two bottles of the finest red wine. It was the actor Heinz Rühmann.

He had come straight from Babelsberg, where they were shooting the movie *The Leghorn Hat*, based on a play by Labiche, directed by Liebeneiner. "Sparklingly cheerful and clever," he said, "one of the best movies I've ever acted in." He clapped his hands and recited several lines. Then he imitated Liebeneiner's way of snapping his fingers when ideas came to him, which, he said, was often: "Liebeneiner is full of ideas, a marvelous director! And not one Nazi, as far as the eye can see! You'd think you were in a different country! They tell jokes about Göring and Ribbentrop. Nothing is out of bounds!"

Käutner closed the window. "This isn't Babelsberg," he said. "I have new neighbors. The former residents are gone, now a married couple live there, both in the party."

"The lead character," Rühmann said, unmoved, "played by me, of course, constantly switches between action and commentary. The subjective camera is used in the most intelligent way. It's pure joy!"

Pabst drank and tried hard to listen, but his thoughts kept running ahead to what was coming the next day. So he drank more and opened the second bottle, nodding with interest when Käutner said: "You'll see, they need us more than we need them!"

"Germany is no longer importing films," said Rühmann. "And the cinemas still have to be filled, which can't be done with propaganda alone, so they have to rely on the few people who know how to make good films."

"Some made it to Hollywood," said Käutner, "Zinnemann, for example, and of course Fritz Lang! But the rest of us just have to do what we can. Stay clean, make as few compromises as possible. Just do our work."

"Of course, it can't be done with no compromises at all," said Rühmann. "I had to get a divorce from Maria, or else I would no longer be able to work. I then found her a fake husband myself: Rolf, a Swedish colleague. I wire them money every month; Göring approved the arrangement. So everyone benefits: I can shoot, Maria is safe, Rolf earns well."

Pabst asked where she was living, Maria.

"Well, with Rolf," said Rühmann. "Where else? He's her husband, after all!"

Then they drank in silence for a while. They took turns refilling their glasses, raising them, putting them down again, pouring until the bottle was empty.

"Yes indeed, you can work well," Rühmann finally repeated. "Now that Ufa is effectively nationalized, there's more money available than ever, and despite the war everything is amazingly well organized, because the decision-making process has become so streamlined. Everything goes through Reich Film Supervisor Hippler, who always consults the Minister."

"And what is the Minister like?" asked Pabst.

"You just have to stay on his good side," said Käutner.

"Tell him clearly what you're willing to do and what you're not," said Rühmann. "You can negotiate a lot. If you say, 'Herr Reich Minister, propaganda doesn't suit me, I'm an artist, I stay out of politics,' he accepts it!"

"There's nothing to negotiate," said Pabst. "I'm not willing to do anything!"

Rühmann and Käutner exchanged a glance.

"Maybe tell him you're in a crisis and only write poetry now," Rühmann suggested.

Käutner turned the empty bottles upside down, but unfortunately there was nothing to be done. They had no more wine.

"In the end, the Minister is just a film producer," said Rühmann.

"Albeit an unusually powerful one," said Käutner. "You have to imagine: Willi Forst absolutely wanted Theo Lingen for his last film. But Lingen didn't like the script, or maybe he didn't like Forst—anyway, he said no. He made excuses about other commitments. So Forst went to the Minister, who said: 'Dear Forst, I assure you, Lingen has no other commitments, and if he did, he no longer does!' Well, what was Lingen supposed to do then?"

Pabst stood up a little unsteadily, partly because his hip hurt and partly because after the last few months he was no longer used to wine.

"I have to go home too," said Rühmann. "It's getting awfully late!"

As softly as possible they went down the stairs. On tiptoe they stepped outside.

"Break a leg tomorrow," Rühmann said softly. And then, as suddenly as he had appeared, he was gone.

On the way to the hotel Pabst got lost, found his bearings, got lost again. It didn't help that he knew Berlin well, the streets seemed to have been treacherously rearranged; something about the way they met, formed corners, and curved was now so different and new that Pabst wondered whether he had somehow ended up in a distorted mirror world. Over in America he had so often dreamed of suddenly finding himself in this Berlin ruled by brutes, and now that he was there, it simply refused to seem real.

He stopped, walked on, and stopped again, feeling so weak that he had to lean against the wall of a house. As he looked around, the edges of the houses seemed askew; under the streetlamps fell sharply delineated shadows, darker than black; and while the street down below rolled away very straight into an endless distance, a chimney up above thrust itself into an oversize moon. This was how films had looked fifteen years earlier, and strangely enough this thought soothed him so much that he was able to walk on until at last he found his hotel.

He took the key from reception, climbed a staircase that seemed to stretch to an absurd length below and above him, even though he knew that the Savoy wasn't especially tall—farther and farther, so that he had to run to keep his floor from escaping him. Panting, he found his room, fell onto the bed, slipped off his shoes, wriggled out of his jacket, took off his pants, all while lying down, and closed his eyes—grateful that he was finally allowed to sleep.

There was a knock at the door.

"What?" shouted Pabst. "What is it, what do you want?"

A calm voice said that his car was here.

"My car?"

"Is here."

"Now?"

The voice didn't answer. Pabst stood up, opened the door, and shouted angrily that there must be a mistake. He wasn't being picked up in the middle of the night, but tomorrow morning, at ten o'clock, that was what had been arranged!

The liveried boy, who could hardly be older than Pabst's son, looked at him with a dull expression. "I apologize," he finally said, "but it's exactly ten."

Pabst groped to the window and flung open the curtains: light streamed in, cars were driving, people were walking on the sidewalks, the reflection of the sun flamed in a dozen window panes.

Breathlessly, he began to get dressed. He still had his shirt on, and his tie was hanging loosely around his neck, so he just had to tighten it again. His pants and jacket, however, were lying crumpled on the floor, and his socks were bunched up into little snails under the bed. I haven't slept, he thought, fastening all the fabric to his body, I just came in! But it was no use, the sun was shining, the car was waiting down below.

Sitting in the black car, which carried him soundlessly through the brightness of the morning, he wondered whether someone had slipped something into his wine. One of the bottles Rühmann had brought had already been opened, the cork inserted crookedly, and in truth he hardly knew this impish man. He winced. A woman pushing a baby carriage along the sidewalk had only one eye, and it was cyclopean, in the center of her head. But he must have been mistaken; the car was moving so fast that he had caught only a momentary glimpse of her. He rubbed his temples and stared at the broad nape of the uniformed driver's neck: a furrow ran straight through it, dividing it into two equal-size greasy fields.

They turned onto Wilhelmplatz. A long, stone-gray building stretched out in front of him; it must be the ministry. Someone opened the car door, Pabst got out, someone said: "Follow me."

It took a long time to get through the ministry. The building seemed larger on the inside than on the outside—it surprised him how reasonable a thought this seemed to be. A corridor led straight ahead for half an eternity, then a corridor branched off to the left and ran dead straight for at least as long: the uniformed man who had picked him up at the car walked in front of him without once turning around. They passed men in civilian clothes and men in uniform and occasionally even a woman moving in the opposite direction, almost all carrying briefcases. When the corridor finally ended and another corridor turned off at a right angle, not to the left, but now to the right, which made no geometric sense, Pabst was suddenly almost certain that they had at some point turned around and gone back and were in the first corridor again—a trick he himself had used repeatedly in long tracking shots.

Then the man in front of him opened a door. It had no number and looked exactly like all the others. How had he managed to find the right one? Briskly, he stepped aside, clearing the way.

Pabst had been expecting a large office, but not this large. The room could have held more than a hundred people; but all it contained was a huge carpet and, far away, a desk with a telephone and two chairs. On the wall behind it—so far away that you had to squint to make it out—hung a gold-framed portrait of the Führer.

Behind the desk sat the Minister.

This surprised Pabst. Because normally, if you were powerful, you made people wait. But the Minister sat there, looked up, made a beckoning hand gesture, and called out: "Pabst, Heil Hitler, come in!"

Pabst started to move. He had spent the whole train journey to Berlin pondering what he would say to the Minister. He had considered all the possibilities, thought through all the moves and countermoves, and finally developed a strategy that he couldn't even begin to remember now.

And he was still walking toward the desk. It was impossible to work in such a large room; station concourses were perhaps this large, but not offices.

"How was the trip?" the Minister called out. "How's your family? Your mother?"

"Fine, thank you," said Pabst. How was it possible that he still hadn't reached the desk?

"We've never met," said the famous high-pitched voice with the Rhenish accent. "Great admirer. *Palu*, magnificent! *Westfront*, masterpiece, despite everything! *Street*, politically not for me, but Garbo, God, Garbo!" He laughed sharply. "Delighted, delighted, delighted!"

Pabst was now close enough to get a better look at the gaunt, strangely youthful face: it was pale, slightly sweaty, with cheekbones protruding prominently under the deep eye sockets, as if he were trying to bite through something hard.

Pabst wondered whether a brief "Likewise" was too much of a concession; but before he had even given himself an answer, he heard himself saying: "Likewise!"

"I'm delighted you're delighted. Take a seat, let's be delighted together!"

And at last Pabst had reached the desk. He pulled up the visitor's chair and sat down.

The Minister smiled. His hands lay flat on the empty desktop. "The Red Pabst."

Pabst swallowed. He didn't know how to respond to that.

At that moment a door opened to Pabst's left, in the middle of the white wall, and the Minister entered. He raised his hand, said "Heil Hitler" and walked with brisk steps, not quite concealing a slight limp on his right side, toward the desk where Pabst and he himself were sitting.

"How was the trip," he called out as he walked. "How's your family? We've never met."

He reached the desk, where the Minister stood up to make room, and in a blur the two men became one man, who sat down and said, "I'm really delighted."

"Likewise," said Pabst. Since he had already said it, it came more easily to him now. It didn't matter anymore.

The Minister laid his hands flat on the desktop, smiled, and said: "The Red Pabst."

Pabst felt dizzy.

"I'm listening," said the Minister.

"Excuse me?"

"Well?"

Pabst rubbed his temples.

"Go ahead," said the Minister. "You wanted to speak to me. I'm listening."

"I didn't . . . You sent for *me*!"

"And?"

"Excuse me?"

"I'm listening."

Pabst didn't understand. What did this man mean, what did he want? This man, to whom once, in a life that was irrevocably over, he would never have spoken a word and whom he would have had chased off his set if he had dared to show up there.

"You're playing the innocent country boy," said the Minister. "Fine. Have it your way. There are things that are said, and things that are not said."

Pabst didn't understand.

"So what's said is that you came here to me. The Red Pabst. The Communist director. The left-wing hero."

"I'm not—"

"What's *not* said, please, is that I sent for you. Because it's better if you came of your own accord. A little better for me. But above all, better for you."

The Minister looked at him with a smile. Pabst, who couldn't think of anything else to do, nodded.

"So?" asked the Minister. "What do you want?"

Pabst furrowed his brow. "What do I want . . . ?"

"You wanted to see me, I received you. What do you want from me?"

"I don't want anything."

The Minister smiled. He closed his eyes. For a short while he sat motionless. It was completely silent; no sound from the street penetrated through the high windows. Pabst heard the air rushing. His throat was so dry that he couldn't swallow.

"Second try," said the Minister without opening his eyes. "Another word that should not be said, especially not by me, is: penance. You are here because you want to crawl to the cross. You are here to plead for peace and forgiveness. And of your own accord. Then we can talk further. About what I can do for you. What I can offer you. But without an act of penance, unfortunately, it won't be possible."

"That's a misunderstanding," said Pabst. "I came back to Austria—"

"Ostmark."

"I came home to look after my mother. I'm not a political person, and at the moment I have no intention of making . . . "

He fell silent. The Minister had vanished.

Pabst leaned forward. Indeed: he must have slipped under the desk in a flash. The massive desktop rested on three sturdy wooden panels, so Pabst couldn't see what was going on underneath. But he heard a creaking and squeaking, a tearing and scraping.

"Herr Doktor?"

The Minister reappeared. He heaved himself up into the leather chair, crossed his arms, and looked at Pabst expectantly.

"I have no intention of making any more films."

"Wrong answer," said the Minister. "Wrong answer, wrong answer, wrong answer, wrong answer, wrong answer."

Both were silent.

Pabst took a breath, but the Minister interrupted before he could speak: "Now it would be good if the right answer came."

Pabst opened his mouth.

"Consider what I can offer you," the Minister interrupted, "for example, a concentration camp. At any time. No problem. But that's not what I mean at all. I mean, consider what *else* I can offer you, namely: anything you want. Any budget, any actor. Any film you want to make, you can make. But you know that. That's why you came to see me. That's why you're going to do penance."

Pabst took a breath.

"Now it's your turn," the Minister interrupted.

Pabst nodded and tried again.

"I've spoken long enough," said the Minister. "Now you."

Pabst breathed out, breathed in again, opened his mouth.

"Or have you lost your tongue?" asked the Minister. "You wouldn't be the first."

Pabst took a breath. The Minister remained silent. Pabst was so taken aback that he forgot what he had been about to say. He cleared his throat, the Minister was still silent, and Pabst began: "For personal reasons, I currently have—"

The telephone on the desk rang.

"Holy shit," said the Minister, picking up the receiver. "I gave," he said into the telephone, "the most explicit instructions that I do *not* wish to be interrupted under any circumstances."

A howling came from the telephone. It rose and fell, it trembled and rattled, and no human sounds could be made out in it.

"Hold on!" The Minister lowered the receiver. "Pabst, just a moment, keep quiet for a minute, this is important." He pressed the receiver to his ear again and said: "Go on!"

For a while he listened to the whining sound. His strikingly white teeth were bared in a grin.

"Give him hell," he said. "Let him have it . . . yes, yes? What?" He listened again briefly, then let out a scream of rage and slammed the receiver so hard on the desktop, once, twice, a third time, that it shattered.

"Shit," said the Minister, lowering his head and feeling along the edge of the desk. Finally he found the button he'd been searching for, said "Shit" again, and pressed it.

At the same second, or actually even faster—so fast that Pabst would have sworn it happened not just simultaneously but even a moment before the button was pressed—the door opened, and a uniformed adjutant came in.

"New telephone!" shouted the Minister.

The adjutant saluted and whirled around, the door banged shut, and they were alone again.

"Pabst," said the Minister. "Sorry. I'm listening."

"For personal reasons, I have no intention of making any films for the foreseeable future. I believe I've said all I had to say as an artist. I'm no longer young, in September I had a bad fall. I am in pain. I feel unable to—"

The door opened, and four men brought a telephone. One of them disconnected the cable from the wall socket, another removed the damaged device, a third installed the new one, and the fourth held the toolbox.

"Are you looking at your watch?" asked the Minister.

"Why?"

All four stepped back and saluted.

"One minute fourteen," said one.

"One fourteen," the Minister said incredulously. "My goodness! Dismissed!"

The men raised their arms in silence; the next moment they were gone.

"I ask for your understanding that, for health reasons alone, I can no longer—"

"But you are sorry?"

"Pardon me?"

"You have engaged in Communist propaganda, you were an enemy of the German people, you have made common cause with other enemies of the people and with Jews. Actually, all that is unforgivable. And yet you're sitting in front of me, drinking coffee, and . . . " The Minister fell silent, picked up the phone, shouted, "Coffee!" and hung up. "Where was I? Yes, yet you're sitting in front of me and asking for forgiveness and saying that you were wrong and that you're sorry . . . Yes?"

The Minister looked at Pabst expectantly.

"I was never a Communist. And as for my movies—"

Two adjutants carried silver trays with cups, a porcelain coffee pot, a milk pitcher, and a sugar bowl. The pot was made of green and white Gmunden ceramic, as were the sugar bowl and cups, only the milk pitcher was made of stainless steel and had a small swastika engraved on it. The two poured coffee, saluted, strode to the door, and were gone.

To gain a little time, Pabst leaned forward, took his cup, and carefully brought it to his mouth. "I was never a Communist. With all due respect, I have also not engaged in—"

"You misjudge the situation. I'm not arguing. If you had just the slightest idea what could be in store for you, you wouldn't even try. It is what it is, and I say what it is, and all you say here is: I'm sorry! And you say: Now I know better! And: I have recognized my mistakes. And I want to do my part to build a new Germany. Well?"

Pabst slowly opened his mouth, but this time nothing happened, there was no interruption, they sat in complete silence.

Pabst cleared his throat again. He breathed out. He breathed in again.

The Minister looked at him.

"I'm sorry," said Pabst. "It was a misunderstanding. I never meant to help enemies—"

"Enemies of the people."

". . . to help enemies of the people."

"Now you know better?"

Pabst felt drained of all his vitality. He nodded.

"You've recognized your mistakes?"

Pabst nodded.

"I don't hear it."

"Yes."

"You have to *say* it."

"I know better, I have recognized my mistakes."

"And?"

Pabst rubbed his forehead. The words now came a little more easily. "I want to do my part. To build . . . Germany."

"Thank you," said the Minister. "I must confess, I wasn't prepared for this. That you would come here and in such a manner . . . I won't hide it, it moves me, and it just so happens, I have the perfect script." He picked up the receiver and shouted: "*Comedians*!" Instantly a new man entered, this time through a different door, bringing a stapled stack of paper.

"I deeply regret it," said Pabst. "For health reasons alone, I feel unable to—"

"Don't worry!" interrupted the Minister. "Pabst, my dear fellow, put your mind at rest! We accept your apology and are happy to take you in! It's never too late!"

"I'm not making films anymore!" cried Pabst.

"Tell it to someone who'll believe it. You've come home to the Reich. You want to make films. Not political films, but idealistic ones. Artistic films. Sublime films. Films that touch the German hearts of good, deep, metaphysical people. Deep films for deep people! And that's what we want too. To oppose the American cheap commercial trash with a resounding no. For example—with this." He pounded his fist on the stack of paper. "This." He hesitated, pounded again. "Caroline Neuber, Pabst! The inventor of German theater, Pabst! Lessing's patroness, Pabst! The script is by two *Weltbühne* writers, left-wing riffraff, people like you, who should be in a concentration camp, but who have recognized the truth and seen the light. Entirely apolitical material, Pabst. So it shall remain too. It is meant to be idealistic. Metaphysical, noble. A role for the great Käthe Dorsch. Acting opposite her as the duchess, I would say, will be Henny Porten. Pabst, the director of women. What could be more perfect?"

"Unfortunately, my health doesn't allow—"

"What's wrong? You can't really mean this business with the hip! Do you need a doctor? We'll arrange it."

"It's not just the hip, Herr Minister. I have all sorts of—"

The Minister tore the first sheet from the script, crumpled it into a ball, threw it away, and shouted: "Address me as Herr Doktor!"

"I'm sorry, Herr Doktor. It's not just the hip, I have all sorts of—"

"Oh, just read it! You're not committing to anything, read it, consider it, see what your heart says. There's no hurry. This one has your name on it! If you don't want it, no one will make it!" He looked at Pabst with an almost kindly smile, then tore out another sheet, crumpled it up, and threw it behind him. "Take this thing with you," he then said, "think it over, discuss it with your good wife." He shot up out of his chair and stretched out his arm—not diagonally upward but horizontally to shake hands.

Hesitantly, Pabst also stood up. The Minister's skin felt warm and as soft as rubber. Pabst wanted to let go immediately, but the Minister held on—for five seconds, and probably another five. Only then did he let go. At least, thought Pabst, he had been spared the Hitler salute.

"Heil Hitler!" said the Minister, slowly raising his arm.

Pabst hesitated for only a moment. Then he did the same.

The Minister looked questioningly into his face.

"Heil Hitler," said Pabst.

"Don't forget your script. And remember, you are valued here. What you want to do is made possible here."

Pabst mumbled something that might have sounded like thanks, took the script, and turned toward the door.

"We don't treat our great artists like lackeys," said the Minister. "We know what we have in them. And we don't forget it."

Pabst began to walk toward the nearest door.

"Let me know if you like it. And if you don't like it, and you want another one, tell me that too. Do you know how to reach me?"

Pabst stopped. "How?"

"You could call the ministry. You could write a letter. You could stand on the street, any street, and speak. Or you switch on the light at night and say out loud whatever you have to say. That works too. I'll find out."

Pabst looked at him. The Minister looked at Pabst.

"Ha," said the Minister. "Ha! Ha! Ha! Ha!" And then, after this buildup, he truly laughed—a high-pitched bleating that sent a shiver down Pabst's spine.

Pabst continued to walk toward the door, which seemed to recede before him. He walked faster, the door receded even faster, he walked even faster, but all at once the room had folded over so that he was suspended from the ceiling, walking upside down, or more correctly: He was walking downward, bracing himself against the slope of the carpeted floor, but before he could wonder whether now he was really losing his mind, he was at the door and out and down the long corridor, which behaved almost normally, lurching only a little, while the same uniformed man as before, who had apparently been waiting the whole time, silently led him to the exit.

Had it gone well? Apparently, because he was, after all, still free. He was not under arrest, not on the way to a concentration camp; rather, he was going home to the castle where he lived.

The high gates swung open; they stepped onto the street. Pabst greedily breathed in the fresh air. His car was waiting with the engine running.

"Straight to the station, please," said Pabst.

"Not to the hotel?" asked the driver.

"No, Lehrter station, right away!"

Yes, it had gone well, because he had gained time. He would read this script, in a few weeks he would send a vague letter with a few questions, then he would announce that he would revise it a little, and so the months would pass. Maybe the war would be over by then, and if not, sooner or later there would be an opportunity to flee to Switzerland. And Mama would go to a sanatorium. All he'd had to do was make a hand gesture and say a few words. It wasn't just producers who could delay a film forever. If necessary, he could do it too.

With trembling hands, he opened the script. The Minister had torn out the first two pages, so the scene began midsentence. Pabst cleaned his fogged-up glasses with his tie and began to read.

German Literature

Trude rang the doorbell. A blond woman in a flowered dress opened the door. "Dear Frau Pabst! Welcome to our circle!"

She led Trude into a room stuffed with end tables, blankets, and carpets. There were silver cups in a glass cabinet and gold-framed paintings of green hills and deer in clearings on the wall—so many that hardly a patch of wallpaper was left uncovered. On three sofas, grouped around a small marble coffee table, sat four women in strange rigidity, as if they were there to be painted. One of them was the actress Henny Porten.

"I'm Else Buchholz," said the hostess. "This is Maria Lotropf, the wife of Professor Alwin von Lotropf; this is Gritt Borger, the wife of Dr. Erwin Borger from the Ministry of Finance; this is Heidrun Hippler, of course you know who her husband is; and here is Henny Porten, whom you know, she's currently filming with your esteemed husband. Dear friends, this is Gertrude Pabst, the wife of the great Georg Wilhelm Pabst, she would like to get to know our reading circle. We are very glad to have you!"

"Very glad," said Maria Lotropf. She was the oldest and already going gray.

"Very glad indeed," said Gritt Borger. She was small and round and had close-set eyes and a furrowed brow that lent her a peevish expression.

"Good afternoon to you, dear Frau Pabst," said Heidrun Hippler. Her eyes shone as if she had to cry for a reason that only she knew. Trude wondered whether she should ask who the husband she was supposed to know about was, but decided against it. She had long since learned that any question could be a mistake, and that when in doubt, it was better to keep quiet.

All eyes were on her. Trude realized it was her turn to speak. "I'm very glad to be here too. I . . . enjoy reading. I've enjoyed it all my life. Henny, thank you so much for the invitation."

"We'll see whether we find common ground," said Else Buchholz. "Not everyone can read with everyone."

"You have to be in spiritual harmony," said Maria Lotropf. Of course Trude hadn't wanted to come there. But these were the wives of influential men, it could be vitally important to know them. "I asked Henny to invite you to her book club," Wilhelm had said, "I asked her very emphatically!" As always when he mentioned one of his lead actresses, she felt a momentary chill. But no, Henny was no Louise, Henny was happily married—very happily, in fact, because she refused to get a divorce from her Jewish husband. She was so popular, so important to Ufa and the ministry, so many viewers went to the movies because of her, that she was allowed to continue working and her husband so far had been left alone.

And in a way Trude had been looking forward to talking to other people about books. She felt very alone on the long days when Wilhelm worked in the studio in Geiselgasteig. Jakob came home from boarding school only on the weekends, and Erika was safe in her luxurious nursing home in Mödling near Vienna—a clean place with many nurses, where the parents of high-ranking party members lived. It was important to be in the right place, because her mind was deteriorating further every day, and everyone knew the rumors that feebleminded people sometimes just disappeared from the homes.

So Trude was alone all day in the Munich apartment they had moved into five weeks earlier. She sat at the dining table, she stood at the window, she looked down on Residenzstrasse, she tapped keys on the piano, she made tea, she lay on the sofa, she sometimes even listened to the radio, she sat in the armchair. She barely went outside, because there were flags everywhere, and there was always a parade going on with uniforms and marching music, so there was nothing to do but go home again quickly, lock the door, and draw the curtains so tightly that not even the thinnest sliver of light could penetrate. They didn't have a maid. They could have afforded one, but it was too dangerous to have someone in the apartment in whose presence you had to watch your every word.

When Wilhelm came home late in the evening, he was tired, but also restless and full of aimless agitation. It was always like this during a shoot. He would go on about the troubles he'd had that day: the theater actors constantly slipped into declaiming and couldn't handle the cold, staring eye of the camera, the young Hilde Krahl didn't know her lines, and the fat actor playing Hanswurst, a party member you had to be careful around, had an unbearable tendency to overact. When he recounted these things, Trude, out of old habit, pretended to listen with interest.

And the film was going to be good, he exclaimed. The equipment was excellent, the crew was experienced, he had the best theater actors in the country, and there wasn't a single line in the script that he had to be ashamed of! All his changes were accepted without discussion. Neither in France nor in America had he been able to work so unhindered!

At this point he usually gave a start and said that it was of course a great misfortune to be stuck here. Then he was silent for a while, switched the radio on and immediately off again—it was never set to an illegal frequency, because the walls to the neighboring apartment were thin—and very softly said something about the developments on the eastern front and the lies that shouldn't be believed; everything was going to collapse. But after a short while he came back to *The Comedians* and an argument he had with the foolish Borsody about how the sets for a theater that is the setting of a film should not look like real theater sets, because otherwise it would seem to viewers as if they were seeing poorly constructed film backdrops; stylization is everything, but that's just what Borsody wouldn't comprehend! He got going again and gesticulated, growing red in the face. Käthe Dorsch doesn't speak naturalistically, but neither does she speak as if she were onstage; without falling into the theatrical tone, she quotes it, as it were, for the camera. With such mastery even Garbo or . . . well, no one from over there could compete, it was truly great acting! And Trude was grateful that he had interrupted himself and not mentioned Louise's name after Greta's.

So this was what she had become—a jealous wife. The reliable butt of the joke in hundreds of comedies. She, who had once seemed capable of anything, who had written plays, one of which, *Mysterious Depths*, the story of a woman caught between two men, had almost been performed—"We'd have to do it under a pseudonym," Reinhardt had said, "under a man's name, we'd have to change a lot, but then it would work"—she, who had turned heads on the street and who, from the age of sixteen, had become accustomed to conversations falling silent when she entered a room; she, who at nineteen had married a rich and kind man, who had left that man only a few years later because he had become too boring for her—she, of all people, could no longer sleep peacefully because her own husband, while lying next to her, was thinking of someone else. How could she, of all people, have grown into this role?

Sometimes she set balls of paper on fire. Now and then, using a fine scalpel previously disinfected over a flame, she made a cut on her upper arm and watched intently as the blood ran over her skin, first in one, then in two, and finally in several thin rivulets. She kept a bottle of vodka well hidden behind the boiler. But only once did she let a man who had approached her in the English Garden take her, just like that and without any fuss, behind a shed. Standing, he pressed her against the wooden wall, his stubbly beard scratched her cheek, he gasped in her ear, her fingers clawed at his linen jacket, and when he asked whether they would meet again, she simply turned and walked away.

"We're talking today," said Else Buchholz, "about *The Star Violin* by Alfred Karrasch. Who would like to begin?"

"I think," said Heidrun Hippler, "that we can all call ourselves Karrasch connoisseurs by now. Ever since we read *Wave, Colorful Pennant* last year—"

"True literature!" exclaimed Gritt Borger.

"—and then his outstanding acclaimed novel *Party Comrade Schmiedecke* . . . so we have now decided to take a look at Karrasch's new book . . . Perhaps our dear newcomer would like to . . . ? Frau Gertrude?"

Trude cleared her throat to buy some time. What could she possibly say? The book was so insipid that it wasn't even bad. A young violin virtuoso played a major concert that instantly made him a star, but then he was accused of having forged and sold a Stradivarius. His sister, a girl of pure virtue, was engaged to a prosecutor driven solely by devotion to his betrothed and a sense of duty, and so naturally he was torn between love and duty. Ultimately, however, it was not he but his father, also a prosecutor, who solved the case. The complication was quite ridiculous—a violin maker had swapped the instrument for the fake during a minor repair. In the end everything was resolved, instantly forgotten. The language had no power, the characters had no life, no one ever said anything interesting.

"It's . . . " Trude thought about it. "It's exciting. Yes, exciting. That's what it is. An exciting book."

"Absolutely," said Henny Porten. "But is that all, Trude?"

"I like how the music critic writes his hymn to the violinist . . . his name is Fritz, isn't it? Well, how when he writes the hymn while still at the concert, Fritz's mother happens to be sitting next to him. The old lady looks over his shoulder and sees that her son is going to be famous and is so happy. That's . . . a bit silly. But if you will, it's also moving."

"Yes, it's moving," said Heidrun Hippler. "And it's truthful too, and powerful. And not silly at all."

"Alfred Karrasch," said Else Buchholz, "is Heidrun's favorite author."

"Indeed he is, and he has been ever since the magnificent novel that all of Germany has read. It was thanks to *Party Comrade Schmiedecke* that I truly understood the movement that was sweeping through our country."

"A very strong novel, of course," said Else Buchholz.

"One of a kind," said Gritt Borger.

"Outstanding," said Henny Porten.

"He really is an unforgettable character, Schmiedecke," said Maria Lotropf. "Have you read it yet, Gertrude? Schmiedecke is a National Socialist of the first hour. Out of deep conviction. A gentle person, but also a fighter. A factory worker who doesn't let the Communists ensnare him. You were still abroad at the time when *Schmiedecke* came out, weren't you?"

Trude remained silent.

"You must know, dear Gertrude," said Heidrun Hippler, "when the novel was published, book reviews hadn't been banned yet. So there was a hatchet job in some tabloid, but then Karrasch himself wrote a reply informing the hack that his book had a certification of approval from the Examining Commission for the Protection of National Socialist Literature and that an attack on the book was therefore also an attack on an office of the Reich leadership. The worm had to make a public apology!"

"I still stand by it," Maria Lotropf said softly. "I prefer *Wave, Colorful Pennant*. Perhaps the most beautiful literary work the Curonian Spit has produced."

"You're just an apolitical sort."

"Yes, that I am."

"But today," said Else Buchholz, "we wanted to talk about the great writer's new work, *The Star Violin*. Would you care to start, Gertrude?"

"Have you read all of Karrasch's books together?" asked Trude.

"Well," said Henny Porten, "there's always a new Karrasch."

"But have you ever tried another author?"

"Maria once suggested the new Fallada. But our dear Heidrun was insistent that we begin with the new Karrasch . . . We then read *Hans Krämer—at Home!* An amusing book!"

"Mischievous," said Maria Lotropf. "He's a master of that register too."

"Coffee?" asked Else Buchholz. "Cake?"

All the members of the reading circle declared that they very much wanted coffee and that although they didn't actually eat cake, they would make an exception in this case, because the cake at the Buchholz house was always extraordinarily delicious.

Else Buchholz brought a porcelain plate from the kitchen with a flat and somewhat lopsided quince cake on it. These were bad times, she said, hardly any fruit was available, and unfortunately, this was the best flour she could find. She distributed plates, cut the cake, served thin slices, and poured steaming coffee into the dainty cups. No coffee substitute, she said, it was still made from real beans. To get those, you needed connections.

"Dear Else always spoils us," said Maria Lotropf.

"Dear Gertrude," said Heidrun Hippler. "But now you have to tell us how you liked the book."

"It was exciting," said Trude.

"You've already said that."

"I agree," said Else Buchholz. "The story is exciting, the resolution completely . . . That the violin maker himself swapped the violin. That was unexpected."

"For me too," said Gritt Borger.

"Like an electric shock," said Heidrun Hippler.

"Well, you could see it coming," said Trude. "For no reason at all, he describes how the violin maker goes out with the violin and comes back. You can tell right away that he's up to something!"

For a few seconds everyone was silent.

"I liked the girl best," Gritt Borger then said. "How pure her love is. How she's prepared to renounce the prosecutor. So innocent and good! It reminded me of Eichendorff or Hesse."

For a moment everyone was silent.

"Right, Hesse!" Gritt Borger confirmed. "But is he . . . I mean, is he still . . . ?"

"Yes," said Henny Porten. "Of course. Hesse still is. He's been living in Switzerland for a long time. That is, not only now."

"Have you ever met him, dear Henny?" asked Maria Lotropf.

Henny Porten shook her head.

"But I saw a photo once," said Gritt Borger. "You're standing next to him, he's wearing a tailcoat. Some premiere."

"It must have been someone else," said Henny Porten.

"Thomas Mann!" exclaimed Gritt Borger.

Again there was a moment of silence.

"And what do you think of the character of the prosecutor?" asked Else Buchholz. "He's the real hero of the story, isn't he?"

"The old or the young prosecutor?" asked Heidrun Hippler.

"That's the crucial question. What do you think, dear Gertrude?"

Trude realized that she had spilled some coffee on the table. She mumbled an apology and wiped up the small puddle with the embroidered napkin.

"You think it's the son," she said. "But then it turns out to be the father who straightens everything out." She paused. That's not enough, said a voice inside her, you want them to have you back!

But all they read is this Karrasch, another voice replied. Who could have guessed? Every week?

It's not that bad, said the first voice, it's a quick read, the hour goes by. When you live in hell, you need friends and allies.

"That's probably the strongest part," said Trude. "That it's the father who ends up saving the son. And the girl with him. She comes to ask his help, to release the son and entrust him to his duty. He is about to send her away, but then he's so touched by her virtue . . . that he helps." She closed her eyes, took the cup, and drank the disgustingly bitter coffee. "That's moving."

"I think so too," said Heidrun Hippler. "Have you recommended the book to your esteemed husband?"

"He works so hard," said Trude. "He doesn't have much time to read."

"But that's what I mean! Your husband could make something wonderful out of *The Star Violin*. You, dear Henny, could play the violinist's mother. Oh, that would be something!"

"Yes, that would be something," Henny Porten said expressionlessly.

"Where did you get these beautiful porcelain cups?" asked Gritt Borger. "If I'm not mistaken, they weren't here last time."

"An antique shop on Feldmochinger Strasse," said Else Buchholz. "A whole set. Eighty-five reichsmarks."

Everyone fell silent. Outside on the street two men could be heard talking to each other. The coughing start of a car engine was audible, as well as the splashing of the coffee Maria Lotropf was pouring into her cup.

"Milk?" asked Else Buchholz.

"Please," said Maria Lotropf.

"Oh, where's my head," said Else Buchholz. "Now you've been drinking your coffee black all this time, and the milk is still in the kitchen. Why didn't you say anything!" She ran out.

"But I always drink it black," said Gritt Borger.

"You shouldn't," said Heidrun Hippler. "It's bad for your stomach."

"I'm actually very fond of tea," said Maria Lotropf. "Especially peppermint."

"I don't like peppermint," said Gritt Borger.

The hostess came back with a milk pitcher and a glittering sugar bowl.

"That's beautiful!" exclaimed Gritt Borger. "Bohemian?"

Trude leaned forward. The sugar bowl was impressive: a tiny reflection of the window hovered among finely engraved decorations. "It's really beautiful! Is this from the shop on Feldmochinger Strasse too?"

"To come back to Karrasch's style," said Else Buchholz, "don't you think his sentences have become simpler since *Schmiedecke*?"

"I've seen a bowl just like that," said Gritt Borger. "But not here, that was over at the . . . Anyway, that was one just like it!"

"I think he's very influenced by Fallada now," said Maria Lotropf. "But when Karrasch wrote about the Curonian Spit in *Pennant*, that was stronger, more vivid. Writers should write what they know."

"Shakespeare wasn't in Italy either," said Heidrun Hippler. "What do you think of the ending, dear Gertrude?"

Trude swallowed, looked briefly at the ceiling, and answered. "The ending is good."

"But what exactly about it?"

The previous night Trude had fallen asleep somewhere in the last chapter. So she had no idea how *The Star Violin* ended. "The composition. How he prepares everything and then . . . resolves it. It's a good ending." She hesitated for a moment before saying: "It's very nice how the young couple ends up together." That was no great risk. In this type of book, if there was a young couple, they definitely ended up together.

"But what do you think of the last sentence?" asked Gritt Borger.

Trude leaned forward, took a piece of cake, shoved it into her mouth, and gesticulated helplessly to show that she couldn't speak at the moment.

"Henny, would you read to us a little?" asked Else Buchholz.

Henny Porten opened the book, looked inside, leafed through it a little, reflected, leafed some more, leafed back again, and found a passage. She let a moment pass before she began to read with a delicate timbre. "'We have no right to drag someone else's life into our misfortune. You must break off your engagement to Hans so that he isn't ostracized too. He deserves it. We, however, are indeed poor—and in dire need—but we have not yet forgotten our pride . . . ' Here the girl lost her composure. She sought help and comfort and protection on her mother's breast: 'It's not pride, Mother—it's not pride . . . ' With a trembling hand, Frau Kestner stroked Elisabeth's hair: 'But you love him, child—but you love him, child.'"

Henny Porten fell silent. She had read well, in a high but full voice, pausing at unexpected points, and the sentence "you love him, child" had flowed out like a sigh.

"That was wonderful," said Else Buchholz.

"I will never forget," said Gritt Borger, "seeing our dear Frau Porten in Schnitzler's *The Lonely Way*. When was that again?"

The actress shrugged.

"In Vienna, in any case, at the Theater in der Josefstadt, staged by Otto Preminger, wasn't it?"

"Gritt, that's enough now!" cried Else Buchholz. "I really must ask you! You're always getting sidetracked, jumping from one topic to another, first some sugar bowl and now Schnitzler, always things that have absolutely nothing to do with . . . No, don't say anything, *for once* don't say anything!"

Gritt Borger sat there with her mouth open. Her cheeks were flushed, her eyes wandered from one woman to the other. None of them looked at her.

"A circle like this is based on agreement," said Else Buchholz. "On harmony. Where that is not the case . . . Dear Gritt, with all due respect, maybe we'll carry on without you for a while."

No one uttered a word as Gritt Borger picked up her purse with unsteady hands, pulled out an embroidered handkerchief, and dabbed away her tears.

Then she stood up. Her dress rustled, her nose was very small and pointed in her round face. She clutched the purse to her chest and walked out with small steps. While the others sat motionless, they heard her taking her coat off the hook in the hallway; they heard the apartment door open and close.

"I think the way Karrasch describes the violinist Fritz works very well," said Maria Lotropf. "The talented hothead. The beautiful relationship between his mother and him."

"That's right," said Else Buchholz. "Isn't it, dear Gertrude?"

Trude nodded.

"How nice that you're with us now! I'm looking forward to reading together."

"Me too," said Trude. Apparently she had passed the test.

"By the way, we still have to agree on which book we'll read next. Maybe this time we could—"

"I have a suggestion!"

"Glad to hear it, dear Heidrun, but maybe this time . . . a different writer?"

"Oh!" Heidrun Hippler raised her eyebrows. "I was actually going to suggest *The Undes*. A book for which Karrasch was praised by the leading authorities!"

"I understand," said Else Buchholz. "But we could . . . There are also others who are praised."

"Of course," Heidrun Hippler said sharply. "There are others! There always are!"

"As for Karrasch, you know how much we . . . And I'm sure *The Undes* . . . I have no doubt . . . "

Heidrun Hippler sighed impatiently.

"Well, it's not up to me. At least not me alone." Else Buchholz looked around the room with a fixed smile. She was pale. "Shall we put it to a vote?"

Abendruh

On Fridays there was always fish. "When you wake up on Friday," said Professor Stelzner, "you're in a bad mood right away, because you know you'll have that awful, overcooked fish again. On other days the food is fine—not good, of course, but not disgusting either! The problem is that those other days exist only in theory—whenever you try to remember where you are in the week, you end up back on a Friday here at the Abendruh Sanatorium in Mödling near Vienna, facing that disgusting fish, am I right?"

The woman sitting next to him, Frau Erika, nodded in vague agreement. She had just had a visit from her son, the director, but had mistaken him for her husband, and her grandson, who had been there, for her son. Both had tried to clear up the misunderstanding, but to no avail. If this was her grandson, she had asked, then why was he in uniform?

"The Hitler Youth," her son had said.

She had asked what that meant, the war was over, after all, and the Kaiser dead, but then she hadn't even waited for the answer and asked whether she could go home now, and when her son said, "Not yet, Mama, they're taking good care of you here," she got very angry, and then the two of them left, though not before Professor Stelzner asked for help: "You're a famous man, Herr Pabst, can you please lodge a complaint somewhere that in this sanatorium it's always Friday and there's always fish?"

The famous director had promised to help, kissed his mother on the cheek, and left with his son, whom his mother had mistaken for her son, that is, himself. They'd had to catch a train back to Munich, where he was shooting a film; he had tried to tell his mother the plot, something about an actress and the theater two hundred years ago. She had become very upset and angry and sad that he was involved with such sordid matters, and it took some time after the two of them had left for her to settle down.

Then the French nurses had led all the inmates of the sanatorium out of the lounge into the dining room, as they did every day. The dust from the construction site blew in through the open windows, and you could hear the same furious hammering as always. The nurse Françoise had a pleasantly gentle way of holding you by the elbow—loosely, but in such a way that you never lost your balance. Once Professor Stelzner had thanked her for it, but she had just shaken her head, because you weren't allowed to talk to her. Only recently, on a Friday, of course, Françoise had started crying, and when asked what was wrong, she had replied that she missed her children. Frau Erika, who didn't care for sentimentalities, had asked her to pull herself together and drink a glass of water, adding, "Drinking water almost always helps."

So now they were sitting in the dining room, which always smelled somewhat putrid, while the kitchen helpers Olga and Katka served fish. It was also possible that they were now called something other than Olga and Katka, because although they were always the same two women, every few weeks they had different faces, and with the new faces came new names too. Professor Stelzner knew it was hardly worth asking Frau Erika or any of the others whether they recalled a day that hadn't been a Friday: the two ladies next to Erika were even less responsive, one being a countess and the other a commercial councilor, and almost no one at the Abendruh Sanatorium still boasted a properly functioning memory.

You weren't allowed to talk to Françoise, but if you did, you were merely given a sharp warning. Olga and Katka, however, you really weren't allowed to talk to. Interaction with the Western workers was tolerated, but any conversation with the Eastern workers in the kitchen and cleaning service was forbidden, without exception. Violating this rule, the home director Wiesinger had said, would not only put the Eastern worker in question at risk of removal, but, above all, would also put the patient at risk of expulsion from the sanatorium, or worse. No one wanted that, of course, especially the worse consequence, and so even those who forgot everything else adhered to this rule so well that Olga and Katka moved across the room like unnoticed ghosts.

Professor Stelzner hummed a tune from *La Traviata* and heard Frau Erika talking to the countess about her husband's work: every morning he went to the Franz Joseph station to command the trains, and when the countess didn't respond, she suddenly started talking about her son's films, which she was ashamed of because unfortunately there was no way to make films without coming into contact with indecent women, but which she at the same time regarded as great works of art, without ever having seen one. Something about this account of the glory of Frau Erika's son offended the countess, who then turned to the commercial councilor, prompting Frau Erika to turn to him, Professor Stelzner, and nod in agreement when he remarked that under the emperor of India there had still been good dumplings on the moon. Dumplings made of clouds, he added, just like the cotton candy in the Prater, and she didn't contradict him. This is how we all talk here, thought the professor; having already discarded the world and its reason, we dream and fabricate and ramble and chat as if nothing concerned us anymore.

At that moment, the home director Wiesinger passed by. Frau Erika raised her hand and called his name. When he stood in front of her, she asked why there was war again.

"Well, because world Jewry wouldn't have it any other way."

"So that's why my son is back in uniform?"

"No, he isn't," said Wiesinger. "He was just here, your spotless son. It's obvious he's arranged things nicely for himself. After all, he's *not* in uniform."

"But the poor boy," she exclaimed. "He just came back from the prison camp and now he's supposed to go to war again? There must be—"

"And the fish," interrupted Professor Stelzner. "Otherwise I don't care what day of the week it is, but if it's always Friday, there's always fish, it's unbearable!"

"We have fish only on Fridays," Wiesinger said irritably.

Professor Stelzner asked what day of the week it was today.

"Friday," said Wiesinger.

"*Quod erat demonstrandum*!" cried Professor Stelzner.

"As for the matter of the war," said Erika, "I must say—"

"I was a genuine mathematician," cried Professor Stelzner. "I worked on the Goldbach conjecture. Please, don't always be so quick to contradict me!"

Wiesinger looked back and forth between them, then walked away without a word.

Erika started recounting how she had recently, just after her wedding, been on summer vacation with her husband in Spindlermühle in Bohemia. In the forest she had seen a large stag with a broken antler on the right side.

"You can't trust the deer anymore," Professor Stelzner remarked, "but you can trust the birds even less. They fly around as if there's nothing important to do. It's pure idiocy."

"Anyway, the stag," she said. "The antler. I was pregnant, and my husband saw it as a sign."

"Except the blackbirds," said Stelzner. "They don't waste time. They're good fellows."

"But then my son went into theater, and now he makes films or something like that."

"I went to the cinema once," said Stelzner. "That nonsense should be banned."

"Yes, exactly," said Erika, "absolutely right!"

"In that film there was a vampire," said Stelzner, "but there's no such thing as vampires; it was only an actor in makeup." He shook his head sadly and looked at his plate, around which small pieces of fish and potatoes were scattered on the table. Professor Stelzner was not a tidy eater.

But now he could no longer understand Frau Erika, because the hammering from the construction site was too loud. The construction site was a nuisance to them all. The noise started early in the morning and ended exactly at midnight when the workers were picked up. They weren't allowed to take a lunch break either—sometimes a scream and a loud crack could be heard when someone on the site was being disciplined. It was very unpleasant to live so close to it, but it was also impressive how quickly a building rose up when the workers couldn't do as they pleased, when there weren't constant breaks and questions and discussions, when the work was simply done.

When the hammering stopped for a moment, Frau Erika pushed her plate away—stray fish bones jutted out, white and twisted—and recounted again and in exactly the same words how she had been in Spindlermühle with her husband the previous year. On a walk—the bones had reminded her—she had seen a stag with a broken antler. Then she fell silent, gazed ahead with moist eyes, and asked softly when her husband would come to take her home. He had promised to take her, so why was she still here? Did it have to do with the war?

"Don't cry," Professor Stelzner said gently, "please, dear Frau Pabst."

But it didn't help; she continued to sob. "I have to complain to Wiesinger," she said, when the hammering briefly stopped again. "Right now. Also about the war!"

"Better not," said Professor Stelzner.

"But it's important!"

He hesitated for a few seconds. There was no nurse nearby, no other patient listening.

"Dear Frau Erika," he said. "We're safe here, our confusion is tolerated, but you mustn't take that for granted."

Now one of the orderlies walked past behind them with slow steps. Professor Stelzner sat up and shouted: "When numbers collide, smoke is produced. I know that, it was my profession."

He sat still, his eyes following the orderly until he was out of earshot.

"Accept that you are here," he then said. "Believe me, it's a great mercy. I had to do a great deal to be allowed here. Outside they would have come for me long ago. But no one is looking here. After all, we're very old. Our brains are fragile. Thankfully, we are the most uninteresting people."

Erika searched for her napkin, but it had apparently fallen on the floor and was lost; she hadn't been able to bend down for a long time.

"The most important thing is not to stand out," said Professor Stelzner. "Not to say anything about the war, for example. Do you understand?"

Erika stared unhappily at her napkin on the floor.

"Of course," Stelzner said as he picked it up for her, "the best would be already to be dead. Not to have to witness any of this anymore. But we can't choose that. Not everyone has the courage to die. I don't."

"The antler was broken," she said.

"I beg your pardon?"

"On the stag!"

She said more, but now he couldn't understand her at all. The hammering drowned out everything.

Highlands

Pabst had rarely seen such a spectacular sunrise. Solidified flames seemed to stretch across the horizon, glaciers sparkled, clouds hung in fiery filaments in the sky. Seconds later, glistening daylight lit up the dewy meadows.

So this was where she wanted to pretend it was Spain—in Krün, Bavaria. She'd had an entire village built out of plywood, sparing no expense: white walls, Moorish balconies, and above it all the cardboard silhouette of a seemingly distant, majestic castle. He would have done it all much more cheaply in the studio, but she wanted natural light, and she believed the Bavarian mountains looked just like the Sierra Nevada.

He had arrived yesterday, had slept fitfully, had been woken at half past four, and had then watched the cameramen and prop masters setting up. To his astonishment, the extras, who usually were the last to arrive, were already there: some thirty men blowing on their hands and shifting from one foot to the other to keep warm. They must have arrived in the dark.

From the shooting schedule he knew that the first scene was a dance sequence. That didn't surprise him. Her true calling, as she regularly repeated in all the magazines, was dance! Even back then, on the glacier, she had insisted on dancing. Fanck probably would have given in, but Pabst had managed to prevent it.

He didn't want to be there. His mind was entirely on *The Comedians*, the film he had finished shooting a few weeks earlier in the Geiselgasteig studio halls and now had to edit.

Griffith and Lang could compose images better than he could, and without a doubt Reinhardt was superior in working with actors, but no one could edit better. Ideally, a film was a single uninterrupted movement; every shot had to be connected with the next. If a ball rolled from left to right, the next shot had to continue the movement with a car, a hand gesture, or a person entering. Someone turning his head upward had to be followed by something rising. The camera should never turn without a reason; it always had to accompany a movement. This often meant sitting over the celluloid snippets for hours and racking your brain just to maintain the flow. Because sometimes you just didn't have it, the shot you needed; it was an endless puzzle. From the chaos of material you had gathered under the most absurd circumstances in many places over a long period, you pieced together something that in the end must seem a solid and necessary unity.

But instead he was here, in this miserable village, far away from his work. He looked around. Nearby sat a chubby young man with clever eyes and a half-bald head, thoughtfully blowing gray smoke into the air.

"Do you have one for me?"

The young man cast him an amused look. Then he stood up, came over, offered Pabst a brass cigarette case, and flicked open a lighter. Pabst pulled out a cigarette, held it to the small flame, and introduced himself.

"I know who you are, of course," said the young man. "I'm Franz Wilzek, camera assistant. Yesterday everyone was very excited about you: Pabst is coming, they said, she managed to get Pabst to help her direct."

"I'll do my best."

For a few seconds they smiled into the rising smoke. Neither had said anything dangerous, and yet they had understood each other.

"I've been working for Albert Benitz," said Wilzek. "For half a year. Fortunately for me, he threw out my predecessor. This way I'm at least learning something. The best cinematographer in Germany."

Pabst tilted his head.

"Not the worst, anyway."

Pabst smiled.

"Anyway, one who often changes his assistants. He throws a lot of tantrums. Lucky for me—and whoever ends up in my place. It's easy to get in, which is good, and easy to get out again, by which time you don't mind."

"Where were you before?"

"I studied film in Munich. Most recently with Harlan."

"Harlan is good," Pabst said reflectively. This time he didn't smile, because it was true: Harlan was a great talent.

"Professor Harlan recommended me to Benitz. What can I say, it's better than being on the front."

"Really?" asked Pabst.

They both smiled again. The whistling sound of dozens of spotlights hung trembling in the air. Despite the alpine morning brightness, the director had erected a battery of lights.

"You're from Vienna?" asked Pabst.

"You can tell?"

"Clearly. How's the filming going?"

"Wonderfully, of course. All the problems are being solved."

They looked at each other. Pabst waited, but Wilzek didn't change his expression.

"Well, that's why you're here," Wilzek finally said. "Because even the problems that of course aren't problems have to be solved in the best possible way. The greatest director in the Reich doesn't need any help, but she is prepared to listen to consultants when it comes to the question of what it is the actors should do with their faces. That's a difference between feature films and sports or party rallies—the faces count!"

"Yes, faces," said Pabst. "Film would be so much easier without them. Or hands, hands are tricky too . . . "

"Unless you're saluting!"

"Yes, in that case it's clear. Then you know where to put the hands. But otherwise you have to do something with them all the time. It's a problem."

At that moment everyone stood up, stubbed out their cigarettes, stood on tiptoe, and turned in the same direction, because the director was approaching, followed by four assistants. Since she was also playing the lead role, she was in costume.

"Georg," she said.

"Fräulein Riefenstahl."

She held out her hand to him without a Hitler salute—her handshake was firm, her hand cold to the touch.

"Thank you for being here!"

"Of course," said Pabst.

She had grown older since he had last seen her, her features were sharper and more angular, her neck thin, her nose strikingly pointed. Her face was colored light brown with thick makeup. She was wearing a low-cut flounced dress, because she was playing a very young Spanish dancer.

"Shall we start?" she asked.

Immediately everyone was in frantic motion. Franz Wilzek knelt next to the camera while his boss peered through the viewfinder above him. She spread her arms, bent her knees a little, stood in a pose.

"Roll film!" cried the first assistant. "Camera rolling!"

A second assistant clapped the clapperboard. Though no music could be heard, she began to click the castanets. With precision she turned her head, took steps forward and back, raised and lowered her hands, without the slightest misstep.

When she was finished, she paused. She was not out of breath. A makeup artist scurried over, dabbed some sweat from her face, reapplied brown makeup. A second makeup artist fixed her hair. Then they both backed away.

"And go!" she said.

"Rolling," cried the assistant. "Please dance!"

And again she made her moves. None of them differed in the slightest from the moves before. When she was finished, she paused. The makeup artists approached, did their work, and backed away again.

"One more time!" she said.

"Roll film!" cried the assistant. "Camera rolling!"

Pabst took off his glasses. Now his vision was blurred, which made it better: something brownish gray in a billowing dress was briskly jumping back and forth and clicking the castanets. There was only one solution, he thought. You had to move the camera, following the dancer's steps in short tracking shots, pointing it at the spectators as if seeing them from her perspective, and then you had to cut it in such a way that viewers mainly saw this very audience and details of the dancer only for seconds at a time: her hair flying back, her hand with the castanets, sometimes very briefly her face. If you set this exactly to the rhythm of the music, each cut a tenth of a second after the beat—never right on it!—it could work.

She paused. "Thank you!" she said. "That's a take."

The spotlights were turned, and the lighting was rearranged, aimed at the extras playing the spectators, the inhabitants of the Spanish village. Benitz and Wilzek changed the lens.

"Georg!" she said. "You take care of the faces! We need lustful eyes, everyone is overwhelmed by the dance."

Pabst looked at the extras. Where had she gotten so many men in times when almost all the young men were on the front? He cleared his throat and made a little speech. He knew they weren't listening to him, it was all about gaining time. They had to forget what they had just seen. They had to imagine a dancer, any dancer, just not this one, not this dour woman with her thick brown makeup.

So he spoke about the nature of music and the nature of dance. He quoted Schopenhauer. He made a few jokes and told an anecdote about an argument between two lighting technicians that had happened during the filming of *Don Quixote* in France, but he claimed it had been during the filming of *Westfront*.

"Look at the camera. Energy emanates from it. Warmth. Power. You're missing something and can feel it, there's an emptiness inside you. What you see is not just a beautiful woman. You see everything you don't have. Everything that makes life inadequate. You feel everything that is missing in life as you look at the camera—not into it, look just past it. The camera stands for everything you lack."

"We need a few spots shining from the front," said the director. "Into his and his and"—she pointed to an older man whose front teeth were missing—"his eyes."

"That would look artificial."

"I'll do the lighting," she said, "you do the faces."

Pabst closed his eyes, breathed in, breathed out, opened them again, and pointed to one of the extras.

"We'll start with him," he said to Wilzek, "then pan to the right over him and him and him and stop on him. What's your name?"

The man looked at him uncomprehendingly.

"Your name," said Pabst.

"Mario," said the man.

"You're looking just past the camera, Mario. You're completely spellbound. You're staring while the camera slowly pulls back."

"I'm thirsty," said Mario.

"Can someone bring him something to drink?"

"My legs hurt," said Mario. He had a strange accent, half Italian, half Slavic. Someone brought a glass of water. Mario drank greedily.

"I'm thirsty too," said the man next to him.

"Me too," said another. "Very thirsty."

"We'll shoot a take," said Pabst, "then you'll all get something, okay? Mario, the important thing is: don't blink. As the camera pulls back, you must not close your eyes. You're completely—"

"This one instead!" The director pointed to another man. "He's better looking."

"Maybe he is," said Pabst. "But we need someone to whom life has been unkind. It's about longing—"

"We'll take this one."

"Could we maybe try both?"

"No."

"I think the extras are all thirsty, is there anything we can do?"

"Filming time is expensive, Georg!"

Pabst closed his eyes again, breathed out and in, opened his eyes. Then he started shooting. He had the camera pointed at a man and said: "Open your mouth a little." To another: "Tilt your head!" And to the man next to him: "Look over there, imagine a woman. She doesn't know you exist, she'll never know, imagine that!"

"I'm thirsty too," said the man.

"In a minute!" Pabst exclaimed. "Imagine it, look over there!"

He could feel the director's impatient glances. After just under an hour he was finished.

"Not much of it will be seen," she said. "Only two or three seconds, cut in briefly. Mainly Martha will be seen dancing."

"Next take," said the assistant. "The marquis, strumming his guitar."

And there he was, in a frilled Spanish costume, Bernhard Minetti from the Prussian State Theater in Berlin.

"Dear Pabst," he said softly. "Such an honor finally to be working with you."

"The pleasure is all mine. We'll do a medium shot. You strum the strings a little harder than necessary. You're hiding a feverish excitement."

"Yes," said the director. "That's good. That's right. Feverish!"

"I dined with the Minister yesterday," said Minetti. "He's delighted that you're helping with *Lowlands*. The two greatest film artists in our nation together, he kept saying, what a momentous event, what a joyful occasion!"

Pabst knew the connections by now. Leni Riefenstahl's production company was the only one in the country that was not under the control of the ministry; she alone was allowed to make decisions about her films. She had actually wanted to make *Penthesilea*, based on Kleist's play, but without Kleist's text, a wild fantasy with Amazons on horses—and that was exactly what she had come up with, Amazons and horses and nothing else, and after a year she still hadn't written a script, and then the war had broken out and Libya, where she had wanted to shoot, was no longer accessible. So now she was making *Lowlands*, based on one of the Führer's favorite operas, with herself as a Spanish dancer and with an amateur actor, whom she had recruited from the military because she liked him, as a courageous shepherd from the mountains.

Even now it was the most expensive movie that had ever been made in Germany, and it wasn't getting anywhere. So the Minister sent people like Pabst and Minetti to prevent the worst from happening. Someone like Minetti could save almost any scene. He was playing a lecherous landowner, the enemy, the villain.

"Shall we try it out?" asked Pabst.

And indeed, Minetti strummed the guitar very well, and he knew how to stand, how to hold himself, how to look. The famous actor was a dangerous person, everyone suspected that he was reporting to the Gestapo, but as long as you were careful what you said around him, he was easy to work with.

"Wonderful!" said Pabst.

"I know," said Minetti.

Then a gong rang for the lunch break.

The food was inexplicably good. During *The Comedians* there had been potatoes every day, sometimes also semolina porridge and disgusting coffee substitute. That was just the way it was during the war, the production manager had explained, there was nothing to be done! But here there was pancake soup, there was beef with chopped carrots followed by apple strudel, and excellent beer. To Pabst's right sat Benitz; to his left the young camera assistant took a seat.

Opposite Pabst sat the director. She wasn't eating anything; in front of her there was a cup of steaming tea.

"Right now for the seduction scene between me and the marquis, I really need you, Georg."

"When we made *Palu*," he heard her telling the group, "he showed me everything. Listen inward, he said. Be completely still, Leni, be silent, listen to your soul. And only then, *not* before, not *before, not before*, do you speak! I've never forgotten."

Pabst finished his glass of beer. He felt the dull pressure that usually heralded a headache. He turned around, waved the man with the tray over, and took a second glass.

"Because I've been on both sides," she said, "I know how much we actors need good direction, and I also know how much we directors depend on good actors."

"Sarah Bernhardt," said Benitz, "supposedly once said to a director—"

"Benitz, I don't like it when people interrupt me. We depend, I was about to say, on actors who don't need everything explained to them. For whom one word is enough, or even"—she looked Pabst in the face with a skull-like smile—"a glance?"

Benitz had turned ashen.

"But it's important to remember," said Pabst, "that acting, as we understand it today—"

"Is it because I'm a woman? That no one is letting me finish today?"

Pabst fell silent, embarrassed.

"Well, I have things to do anyway." She stood up, took her cup, and walked away.

All three remained silent. Pabst knew that the other two knew that he would have liked to say something mocking now, and he also knew that they felt the same way, but they weren't well enough acquainted with each other. So he silently finished his second glass of beer and looked around through the descending fog of heaviness and headache for a third.

"Where are the extras anyway?" he asked.

"Already on their way back," said Benitz.

"They're not from Krün?"

"They come from Salzburg."

"They bring the extras all the way from Salzburg?"

The gong sounded, the lunch break was over.

Now the seduction scene between the innocent dancer and the evil marquis was on the schedule. They were filming in a studio that had been specially built next to the plywood village. The marquis had invited the beautiful woman to his estate, he played the guitar and seduced her with a mixture of charm and menace. They were shooting with two cameras—one pointed at the dancer, the other at the marquis.

"Do you like it here with me?" asked the marquis. "What's your name?"

"Martha."

"Tell me about yourself, Martha!"

"There's not much to tell, sir. We wander along the country roads, and where there's an inn, that's where I dance."

"Where did you learn to dance?"

"I never learned it."

"It's in the blood, isn't it? And do you have a lover?"

"No, sir."

"You, you're not fooling me."

"It's true, sir."

"Thank you!" shouted Pabst. "One more time." And softly he asked the director: "Who wrote this?"

"Me. Do you have any suggestions?"

"No, no."

"Improvements? Tell me, Georg! I'd be grateful."

"It's perfect as it . . . Only when . . . Fräulein Riefenstahl, when . . . May I call you Leni?"

"No."

"When the marquis talks to you, you have to listen to him. I mean, really hear what he says, take it in. You're afraid of him, every word could spell your doom. Do you understand?"

"I'm not deaf. I can hear. Back then you told me to listen inward, now suddenly outward?"

"Yes, now outward. You're very . . . present . . . when you speak your lines, but afterward it's, how should I . . . As if someone flips a switch. And you're no longer there until it's your turn again."

"A *switch*?"

"I mean—"

"Is this how you speak to me?"

"Dear Fräulein Riefenstahl, you brought me here so that I could—"

"Actually, it wasn't me. It was someone in the ministry. Do you really think I can't direct on my own? I'm *very* present. Don't worry, Georg. I'm present."

"But why are you putting spotlights on his face from below?"

"To make him look evil!"

"I know . . . a few evil people. And they're not usually sharply lit from below so you can tell."

"You don't say. What kind of evil people do you know, Georg?"

Let it go, he thought, remember that she can put you in a camp. And this time it worked, and he listened to himself and simply said: "If there's a light source down there, that is, if you spotlight him from below, then you have to do the same to yourself. You're in the same room."

"I don't have to do anything. Don't forget why you're here."

"And why is that?"

"Dialogue direction. Pronunciation. Speech tempo."

"All right, when you're trying to create intensity, you always speak so breathily. Every time. But you might want to vary it a little."

"Martha is afraid! She's confused! She's also fascinated by the marquis, the audience has to hear that!"

"Then let them hear it." Be quiet, he thought, don't say it out loud—but then, to his horror, he heard himself saying it: "If you want people to notice what she's feeling, why don't you try acting?"

Suddenly there was silence. All conversation had stopped. The director stood in front of him, her mouth half open, looking at him. I was wrong, he thought. You actually can recognize the truly evil people at a single glance.

"I'm sorry," he said.

"If you forget yourself again—"

"That was uncalled for."

"—there will be consequences."

And there it was, thought Pabst, her real voice.

"Let's do it again," he suggested. "And you, dear Minetti. It's enough if you play just one fiend. It doesn't have to be ten. Do a little less."

And again she looked stiff and automaton-like, and again she breathed: "Martha."

"Tell me about yourself, Martha."

"There's not much to tell, sir. We wander along the country roads, and where there's—"

"Stop!" shouted Pabst. "Martha is in distress, isn't she? She has to think, she's looking for the best response. You're trying to make yourself uninteresting here. You're still hoping he'll let you go. 'There's not much to tell'—that has to be full of hope. Maybe he'll believe you."

"I'd be obliged if you wouldn't interrupt again."

And they resumed their dialogue: What's your name, Martha, tell me about yourself, there's not much to tell, we wander along the country roads, and where there's an inn . . . Her features didn't move as she spoke. Back on the mountain she had been a better actress, alert and vital, but in the meantime something inside her had gone completely cold. Where did you learn to dance, I never learned it, it's in the blood, isn't it? And do you have a lover, no, sir. It couldn't have been said worse, that ridiculously chaste "No, sir!" but he wouldn't interrupt again.

"You, you're not fooling me." Minetti overacted in his turn, his eyes half-closed to look even more evil.

She breathed in a soft, high, false voice: "It's true, sir!"

And then they both paused for a moment and waited before Pabst called out "Thank you, cut!"

"So," he asked, "shall we do it again?"

"How should I know? That's what you're here for, Georg."

Pabst rubbed his aching temples. "I think it's fine as is."

"Are you sure we shouldn't do another take?"

"Well, all right, then let's do another one."

"But what would you like me to do differently, Georg?"

"Nothing. All very good." He hesitated. "Maybe a little slower with: 'It's true, sir.'"

"Why is that?"

"No?"

"I think it was perfect."

"Yes, that's right," said Pabst. "Perfect. Let's do it again anyway. Just perfect again."

And she spoke everything exactly as before, not a syllable was different, not a breath, not a movement, from the beginning of the scene to the end.

"Thank you!" shouted Pabst. "Now scene change please for the close-up of the marquis."

"So quickly?" she asked. "Wouldn't you rather do it again?"

"It won't get any better. But you decide. It's your movie."

"Our movie. Our movie together."

"Well, then," he said hoarsely. "One more time."

And when she finished and Pabst said that it had been perfect again, she had them do another take and then another and then another, and unbelievably she managed never to deviate in the slightest detail; her voice never sounded natural, she never emphasized a word differently, and not a single strand of her full, shiny black hair ever fell differently than before.

"One more time?" she asked. Pabst couldn't remember how many takes it had been. He shrugged and shouted "Roll film!" and he saw that the clapperboard already had the number 11 on it. And then the number 16. And now a 21.

"But that's enough for now," she said.

"Really?" Pabst asked incredulously.

"Perfectionism is good, but at some point it's time to move on, don't you think?"

While the lighting technicians were setting up for the next scene, Pabst sat leaning forward on a folding chair, resting his aching head in his hands, smoking. He heard someone sitting down on the floor next to him.

"Is it always like this here?" he asked.

"Every day is different," said Franz Wilzek's voice. "You can never predict it. Do you need an aspirin? The foehn is bothering me too. Bavaria is not for me. High mountains and no one has a sense of humor. How can anyone stand it!"

"Why are the extras being brought from Salzburg?"

"Maxglan, to be precise."

"Where?"

"The place is called Maxglan."

"But why from there?"

"I have nothing to do with it."

"What do you mean?"

"I mean, I have nothing to do with it."

"With what?"

Wilzek remained silent. Pabst opened his eyes. The sun had already disappeared behind the mountains in the west, the sky was a flickering dark red. He had missed a whole day because of this wretched movie, and it would be exactly the same the next day, and the day after; who knew how much longer. One of the assistants brought a glass of water and two aspirin tablets. Pabst threw them in his mouth and drank greedily.

"When you imagine," said Wilzek. "On top of everything else. That they then also have to stand there and stare at the boss. Lustfully. That they're ordered to do that. On top of everything else."

"Everything else?"

"Poor bastards."

Pabst put the glass down on the floor, but his hand was suddenly shaking so badly that it fell over.

"God," he said. "I didn't . . . "

"Where did you think we got the extras? You've never heard of Maxglan?"

Pabst rested his head in his hands. His vision had gone black.

"There's nothing we can do. We didn't make it happen. We can't keep it from happening. It has nothing to do with us."

Pabst wanted to say something, but his voice failed him. He saw the gaunt faces in front of him, the wide eyes, the mouths. He heard the instructions he had given: look over there, raise your head, things like that, and what else had he said? Suddenly it was unbearable to remember.

"We have to keep going."

Pabst didn't move.

"Come on," Wilzek said gently. He put his hand on Pabst's shoulder. Ordinarily, Pabst should not have tolerated such a gesture, but at that moment he was grateful.

"Nothing can be done," said Wilzek.

"No," said Pabst. "I guess not." He managed to stand up.

The director had made use of the scene-change break. She had had more dark makeup applied, her hair had been redone, her dress freshly pressed. Her eyes glowed coldly. She clapped her hands.

"We have to hurry. You've taken far too long. Twenty-one retakes, what nonsense!" She posed, stretched out her arms, and commanded: "Go!"

Everything fell silent, the spotlights shone, she made lunges, turned her upper body, threw her hair back, spun around, while Minetti strummed his guitar.

Pabst watched as attentively as he could. That helped him not to think about the so-called extras, the emaciated faces, the instructions he had given. She wasn't such a terrible dancer, he thought. People who had never been to Spain, or Mexico or California, might have believed that this was what flamenco looked like. She jerked her hips stiffly, twirled her arms stiffly as if shooing away a fly, backed away stiffly, her face probably meant to express fear as she stared at Minetti with his guitar.

"And—cut!" she shouted. Then she looked at Pabst and asked: "Satisfied?"

"Very."

"You didn't experience anything like that in Hollywood, did you?"

"Not like that."

"I was there too, shortly before the war, on a publicity tour with *Triumph of the Will*. And believe me, I was not impressed. But who am I telling? You came back too."

Pabst remained silent.

"For all our differences," she said with a smile, since the dancing had apparently put her in a better mood, "we do have that in common. That we gave up their so-called success to create art for our countrymen back home."

Pabst shrugged. The pain in his head had concentrated into a single throbbing point behind his left temple.

"One more time?" she asked.

He nodded.

"You're actually right with your twenty-one takes. The more you shoot, the more material you have for editing. And that's the most important thing. That's what you always said back then, on the mountain. I remembered that. That the cut is the most important thing! You see, I've been paying attention. After all, you're my teacher. Is everyone ready?"

The assistant clapped the clapperboard. The director looked at Pabst with a seductive smile, stretched out her arms, and danced.

Summer Vacation

Even on the train the air smells of summer. The locomotive emits a long-drawn-out whistle. The ball of the sun is so huge and glaring that they can't look directly at it—they try, squinting, peering upward, but none of them can manage for long.

All three have their feet up on the opposite bench. This is forbidden, but because they're wearing their Hitler Youth attire, the conductor will say nothing. That's exactly why they swapped their school suits, which are actually more comfortable, for the rough uniforms with the side caps and itchy neckerchiefs for the journey.

Jakob has opened his sketch pad. It's not the landscape that he's trying to draw, but the journey itself—the flow of one hill into the next, how their speed blends the colors. The movement through the blooming summer: a delicate ochre intensifying into a sharp yellow, below which lies a deep rich bulging blue with small white tips.

"You can't see a thing there," says Felix.

"No," says Jakob. "But at the same time you see everything."

"I see degenerate art," says Boris.

All three laugh. They know each other well, they share a room at Salem boarding school, Boris is the room leader.

"I'm curious to meet your old man," says Felix.

"Don't expect too much," says Jakob.

"Oh come on, he made that amazing vampire flick."

"That wasn't him."

"But *Metropolis*, that was him, right?"

The compartment door is flung open, a man with two suitcases, who must have boarded in Stainach-Irdning, looks questioningly at the empty bench where they've propped up their booted feet.

All three look at him. None of them move their feet.

The man closes the compartment door again and drags his suitcases away.

"He didn't do that one either," says Jakob.

"But *Pitz Palu* with Udet and—what is it they call the Riefenstahl woman?—the Crevasse, that was him, right?"

"Yes, that was him." Jakob decides to include the man with his suitcases in the picture, but him too, of course, since he's on the moving train, spread out along the route: an elongated line for the mustache, somewhere above it the solidified amber of his sad eyes, one here, the other a few kilometers away. Eyes are a challenge, very difficult to make with thick oil pastels. And unfortunately he's out of orange. It's always surprising which things are no longer available during the war and which are still easy to get.

"And that was how he was able to buy the castle?" asks Boris. "With the money from that film with the Crevasse?"

Jakob carefully smudges some blue pastel with his thumb and asks, "Have you seen it?"

"Of course. It was showing in Petershagen last year when I visited my folks over Easter. You wonder how they filmed the avalanches. There was a whole film series in Petershagen. Everything Riefenstahl ever made. *The Blue Light*, *Pitz Palu*, and of course the Olympics stuff and the rallies."

"He didn't shoot the avalanches. That was the other director. They worked together. I've never seen the film. Never had the chance. I've only . . ." Jakob falls silent. He almost mentioned having seen *A Modern Hero* at the premiere in Los Angeles, but that was in another world, one he no longer thinks about. "I've hardly seen any of his movies. I missed *The Comedians* too."

"I saw it," Boris says with his eyes closed. "A lot of theater."

"Well, it's about theater."

"Yes, but they all talk like they're onstage. It's a bit odd. The really young one is great, her name is Krahl. Have you ever met her? I'd like her."

Jakob adds a small stroke of green at the bottom edge. The compartment door opens, a woman with two small fat children stares at the seats where their feet are resting. Several long seconds pass, then she closes the door and moves on.

"You still owe me four marks," Felix says to Boris.

"Why?"

"I bought the tickets, Pabst paid, you didn't."

"You Jew."

"You're the Jew, never wanting to pay!"

Boris elbows Felix in the ribs, Felix puts Boris in a headlock, Jakob shouts: "Stop it, or the conductor will come!" To his surprise they actually stop. Boris takes out his wallet and, grinning, counts out four reichsmark bills.

"Any news on the summer offensive?" Boris asks.

"It's going great," says Felix. "Don't you listen to the radio?"

"Of course it's going great. Our tanks are at Voronezh. The Russian can only pray now."

"Russians don't pray," says Felix. "They're Bolshiks."

"Bolsheviks," corrects Boris. Felix puts him in a headlock again.

"Cut it out!" says Jakob. "The conductor!"

But this time no one listens.

Jerzabek hasn't come. No one is there to pick them up. They wait for half an hour on the square in front of the Leibnitz station, listening to the crickets. Then they set off on foot.

The road is in poor condition, cracked in many places. The grass in the meadow is tall, here and there a farmer swings a lazy scythe, a buzzard hovers high in the sky with outstretched wings. The sky dissolves in brightness.

Out of habit, they sing a marching song. The flag high, the ranks tightly closed, comrades who march in spirit in our ranks—Felix is singing slightly off-key, but there's nothing to be done about that, he's tone-deaf.

Jakob looks up pensively at the bird of prey. At the Hitler Youth camp, where they go almost every weekend, they've practiced hitting birds, first with air rifles, then with real shotguns, .44 caliber. Moving targets are incredibly difficult to hit, you don't aim at them but ahead of them; you make their movement your own, shooting where they will be in two seconds. Jakob has never hit a bird, but he did manage to hit a deer once. He'll never forget how the delicately tensed body suddenly tumbled over. And when he approached, heart pounding, he found the animal in the grass, foam at its bared teeth, blood gushing from its flank.

"Coup de grâce!" shouted Group Leader Warnike, a tall, gaunt man, a bicycle locksmith by trade, who had lost his leg in France, which spared him from returning to the front. It took Jakob some time to recall what the word actually meant: coup de grâce. Then he took aim, breathed out fully, and centered the deer's head in the crosshairs of the scope, which wasn't easy at all, because at such close range all you can see in the scope is bristled fur.

When you can't do something and at the same time have no choice but to do it, there's only one solution: have someone else do it. Someone who looks like you and who uses your body, but who has no difficulty shooting two bullets into the head of a small screaming deer. Someone who can raise the rifle, squint one eye, breathe out fully, then hold his breath, and who doesn't care at all that the moaning thing in front of him is breathing and suffering terrible pain and is so terrified that its fear is visible—it looks like a dark cloud, the fear.

Jakob realized that killing has something in common with painting—both work best when you forget that things are more than just color and shadow. Both are best done when you think away the inside.

And now the little whipcrack of the shot was released, and the deer whirled once around itself and then remained lying motionless, and Group Leader Warnike limped over and shouted: "Well done, maybe you'll manage with a bird next!" But Jakob never hit a bird after that either, and so never received the bronze marksman's badge. Because the deer doesn't count; deer are too easy.

So he feels longing and mild annoyance looking up at the buzzard on the way to Tillmitsch. He could probably hit that bird, hovering so calmly up there, so sharply defined against the blue. Unfortunately, however, they aren't soldiers yet and have no rifles with them.

Jakob later painted the deer, and it became one of his best pictures. Deep red, streaming, bubbling, flowing, streaked with black flashes of pain, and at the lower edge of the painting, impossible to miss once noticed, an eye widened with terror, moistly ringed with foam.

When Dreiturm Castle appears on the horizon, Jakob is surprised: it's so much smaller than in his memory, really just a large house.

"It doesn't have three towers," says Felix.

"Not even one," says Boris.

They cross the lawn, which is overgrown with weeds. The castle door is wide open. Next to it, smoking a cigar, leans the actor Werner Krauss.

"Oh," Krauss says in a musing tone. "Kids."

For a moment Jakob stands rooted to the spot, no sound coming from the two boys behind him. "I'm Jakob Pabst," he then says. "These are my school friends, Boris Glattweg and Felix Sprenger."

"Well, well. Nice. Very nice," says Krauss. "Are you here for the break? That's wonderful, really wonderful. Boys, yes. Your Herr Papa is upstairs. In the library."

"He's just my father," says Jakob. "These are schoolmates."

"Lovely," says Krauss.

Jakob looks for a moment into his angular, world-famous face, nods politely, and steps into the entrance hall, into the musty cool smell of his memory. He walks up the creaking stairs and along the corridor. At first they lived up here, then they had to move down to the caretaker's quarters because Papa had been an emigrant, a Jew-lover, and made Communist films, but then Papa was suddenly a good German again, and so they were allowed to move back to the second floor, and the Jerzabeks almost disappeared in their humility and eagerness to serve. Then Papa went to Munich to prepare the movie, and a month later Mama followed him, and he himself was sent to the boarding school in Salem, where he had to embark on another well-planned campaign for recognition, just as before at school here. This time, however, it was somewhat quicker, because now he knew how to go about it, whom to hurt and whom to take as an ally.

He knocks on the library door. A voice says, "Come in."

The room has changed. The same dusty books are still on the shelves, but now in the middle there are maps, pictures, and charts spread out on a table. On one of the bookshelves hangs a corkboard with photos of actors pinned to it. Among them is a photo of Werner Krauss.

Papa is sitting in an armchair with his feet up on a stool, smoking a large cigar. Bent over the table, a pen in one hand and a magnifying glass in the other, stands a young man with thinning hair and reddened skin. Another young man is sitting in a folding chair. A third man, in a tweed jacket, somewhat older, and with a broad, friendly face, is leaning against one of the shelves, smoking a pipe.

"Jakob! Welcome! This is my son. My dear, beautiful boy. Come here!"

Jakob goes to him, bends down, lets Papa pull him in, and gives him a kiss on the cheek. Papa's breath smells of smoke and a little of whisky.

"This is Franz Wilzek." Papa points to the young man with the reddish skin. "My assistant. This is Bruno Stephan, our cameraman, and this"—he points to the man in tweed—"is Kurt Heuser, the screenwriter. And over there is Krämer."

"Kuno Krämer," says a man sitting on one of the deep window ledges. He's sitting there so inconspicuously, so still, that Jakob actually overlooked him. "I'm pleased to meet you, Jakob."

Jakob nods uneasily. He noticed that his father explained everyone else's job to him, but not this man's.

"These are my roommates Boris and Felix."

"Welcome!" says Papa. "We're having a meeting here, the new film, very elaborate, set in the Middle Ages, *Paracelcus*. You can listen if you're interested in that sort of thing. But first bring your backpacks into the room!"

So the three of them head back out.

"It's quite lively around here," says Felix. His father works for the railroad, probably nothing interesting ever happened in his parents' house.

"It's always like this here," says Jakob. What luck, he thinks, that Werner Krauss was outside at just the right moment—nothing better could have happened. They'll be talking about it everywhere; it's almost as good as if he had hit the bird back then.

They go into his old room. There's a thick layer of dust on the desk, chair, and wardrobe. Liesl Jerzabek clearly never cleaned here. There's only one narrow bed, and it's not made.

"Where are we going to sleep?" asks Boris.

"The caretaker will handle it," says Jakob.

On the other side of the corridor a door opens and a woman comes out. It takes Jakob a moment to recognize her.

"Mama! This is Boris, this is Felix. This is my mother."

"Boris," she repeats. "Felix." But she doesn't look at the two of them. Jakob steps carefully toward her. He notices for the first time that he is taller than she is—he's grown, of course, but she also seems to have shrunk. Hesitantly, he gives her a kiss on the forehead. Her skin feels cool. Her breath smells of wine.

"Where are the Jerzabeks?" he asks. "Someone should make the bed. Boris and Felix need places to sleep."

She doesn't respond.

"Mama," he says. "The room. For the night. The Jerzabeks. Or we'll do it ourselves. But then you have to tell us where the bedding is. Do you hear me?"

"Yes."

"What's wrong with you?" he asks softly, nearly forgetting that he mustn't lose his composure in front of his companions.

She steps back, still not looking him in the face, instead looking at his collar, at the uniform buttons on his chest. She raises two fingers and first strokes his cheek, then the swastika on his armband. Then she turns around and goes back into her room. The door closes behind her.

"I think she's ill," says Jakob.

"You don't say," says Felix.

Jakob considers for a moment whether he has to hit him now, but he decides that it's not strictly necessary: it's common among Hitler Youth members to speak disdainfully about parents.

"Maybe she wasn't completely sober either," Jakob says, to be safe, because if he mocks his mother himself, he doesn't have to start a fight just because someone else does. "We have to find the caretaker."

To get into the cellar, you have to open a trapdoor in the entrance hall, then you're standing over a dark hole. There's a braided cord on the wall; if you pull it, an electric light comes on far below and you can see a wooden staircase leading straight into the depths, so steep that it's actually a ladder. You have to go down backward, holding on to the rough side planks.

But now the trapdoor is open and the light below is on. Jakob could swear it was closed just before. He kneels down and calls out: "Hello?" and "Herr Jerzabek" so loudly that he hears his voice echoing back from downstairs. And indeed there's an answer: a clattering and a human voice uttering something short and unintelligible.

So they descend.

The stairs are longer and plunge deeper than Jakob expected. He has never ventured down here before; he used to be too afraid of the cellar. They climb down carefully, setting one foot below the other—Jakob first, then Felix, then Boris. After some time has passed, they are still descending, and then, quite a while later, Jakob is overcome by a dizzying sense of unreality as he realizes that it's still going on, that they are still not at the bottom. Why on earth does such a small castle have such a deep cellar?

And finally his foot hits stone. He looks around. A single light bulb emits a yellowish light. They're standing in an empty vault. The smell of mold hangs in the air. At the other end of the vault is the black rectangle of a closed door.

"Herr Jerzabek?"

Again an answer, muffled, as if from far away, and strangely it seems not to be coming from ahead, but from below, from the solid ground. Jakob approaches the door. He joggles it, and it opens. In front of him is a small room, in the center of which is a vertical shaft.

They bend over it. Deep, smooth blackness. Jakob calls out the caretaker's name again.

Again they hear a voice.

Or do they? No, it's not entirely clear. But what else could it be? Once again no word can be understood—although not, it seems to Jakob, because the call is from too far away but because it's in a foreign language.

"I'm not going down there," says Boris.

"Are you scared?" asks Felix.

"No," says Boris, "not me! You're scared!"

"I'm not scared!"

"Well, then go down."

"Why me? You go!"

"Are you scared?"

The two of them look at each other helplessly. Neither knows what to do.

"Let's go back up," Jakob suggests. "We don't need him. We can make our own—"

"Scaredy-cat!" shouts Boris.

"Chicken!" shouts Felix.

The two of them start to cluck like chickens.

"But what's the point?" shouts Jakob. "Let's just drop it and—"

"He's wetting his pants!" Felix shouts in a high-pitched voice.

"Wetting his pants, wetting his pants!" shouts Boris.

So Jakob starts the descent. On the first five rungs he can still see, then darkness closes in around him. He feels his way step by step, grip by grip. This is ridiculous, he thinks, no one needs the caretaker, all the better if he hides himself away in the cellar and doesn't bother anyone. But now that it's come to this and since he absolutely can't let his companions think him a coward, he no longer has a choice.

Only then does he realize that they haven't followed him.

He stands motionless on the ladder. He listens. They're not coming. He squints. And listens. Below him he sees nothing, above him the distant square glimmer of the trapdoor.

He climbs up a few rungs, then pauses. No, he has to go farther down. It must not look as if he is afraid. Precisely because he is indeed afraid, it must not look that way at all. And yet there's no real reason to be afraid, except of course for the spiders that surely live in a cellar like this. Jakob can't stand spiders. He can't even draw a spiderweb, because he finds them so disgusting. But no one is allowed to know that. Just because Hans Krentz from his class is afraid of bugs, they put live cockroaches down his nightshirt while he was asleep, and then the whole dormitory delighted in his long, squealing girl screams. To this day, Hans is considered a laughable wimp. And Johann Megelwand, who fears heights, was overpowered, tied up, and hung from a thick rope out the window of the top floor. Even the teachers who found and freed him in the morning could barely suppress their laughter, and because Johann had pissed his pants while hanging up there, less out of fear than simply because it had been so many hours, he also spent four days in detention, because a German boy must not wet his pants, no matter what. When you're scared, the one important thing is that no one finds out.

So Jakob descends farther. Step by step, rung by rung, seeing nothing. Now he hears a distant humming. Is it an animal, a person, or a machine? He pauses again and listens, now he no longer hears it, perhaps he was mistaken. All he hears now is his own breathing and his heartbeat and the rush of blood in his ears.

He reaches the bottom, squints, and sees a faint glow ahead. As he slowly walks toward it, something sticky touches his face—he wipes his cheek and brushes off the spiderweb, a thread sticks to his eyelashes, he feels it on his lips, his fingers are sticky too, and he's not sure whether he's imagining it, or whether there really is something with many legs crawling over his arm. He shakes it off in panic.

The light ahead has grown brighter; he walks as fast as he can, which isn't very fast when you can't see anything. The corridor ends, Jakob sees the slanted crack of a door left ajar with light shining behind it; he pushes against it, the door is made of metal and creaks as it opens, and as he moves forward, squinting, he stops short, because at that moment he already sees what he can't actually see yet, because the door is still covering it, but then it is open and his breath catches, his heart skips a beat.

A bare, dirty, not very large room. A pale light bulb dangles from a cable. On one wall stands a nearly empty wooden shelf with tools in its lowest compartment—a hammer, a screwdriver, some twisted metal thing, and dirty crumpled paper.

Right in the center of the room crouches something. It takes him a moment to recognize Jerzabek.

Maybe it's the excitement, or maybe his eyes haven't yet adjusted to the light, but for a moment he saw a dark creature fall from the ceiling when he entered; but now he sees the caretaker with his blotchy skin, large pores, and shifty little eyes.

"What are you doing here?" asks Jakob.

"Jesus," Jerzabek says in a high-pitched voice, though stretching the name almost beyond recognition, and then immediately assures him that this reunion gives him such absurd joy that his heart can hardly bear it. As he repeatedly professes his joy in his heavy dialect, he is still crouching on the floor, legs and arms spread insect-like, looking at Jakob with bloodshot eyes. Such a fine uniform, he says, so dashing, so dignified, only just a child, and now already a man, it could bring tears to your eyes, and as proof he actually raises his index finger and tugs a lower lid with a yellow cracked fingernail, so that Jakob can see the tears that the sight of him has brought to the caretaker's face.

"But what are you doing down here?" asks Jakob, automatically mimicking Jerzabek's accent.

At his reply Jakob momentarily thinks he has slipped into a foreign language. Then he understands: There's work to be done here, says Jerzabek, there's always so much to do in a castle like this, day and night, always something to do. He straightens up to his full height, which still isn't very tall, with his crooked back, his left shoulder drooping so low that Jakob can't help but wonder whether he's exaggerating for effect.

Jakob clears his throat and asks about bedding. "I have two friends visiting who need places to sleep, in my room or elsewhere."

The caretaker asks what kind of friends they are.

Jakob frowns, not understanding.

The caretaker walks past Jakob, closes the metal door, and looks at him sharply and attentively. His hand rests on the door handle. "What kind of friends?" he repeats, his words slurred into a muddle.

Jakob stares at him, puzzled by the question.

The caretaker asks softly and almost unintelligibly whether they are vulgar, ugly, dirty friends, who do not love the Führer and who have to be dealt with deep in the cellar, in the deepest cellar, deep down below, where no one can hear them scream. Or are they rather good boys, German boys, decent boys? Jerzabek squints and looks into Jakob's face as if waiting for an answer.

Jakob looks around. There is no second door. The swinging light bulb makes their shadows grow and shrink, grow and shrink. He clears his throat, then says, "Good boys, Herr Jerzabek."

A long second passes. Another one. And another.

Then, as if Jakob had said exactly the right thing, Jerzabek steps back and opens the door. Jakob hurries out.

As he feels his way along the corridor toward the ladder, he hears the caretaker muttering behind him—this time completely incomprehensible, chewing up the hard sounds and stretching the soft ones until his dialect seems to have turned into a foreign language. Jakob hears him switch off the light in the small room. Now they're walking through darkness. Jakob feels his way along the brick wall, and suddenly, as he hears Jerzabek shuffling and muttering behind him, he is overcome by the feeling that he could be struck or stabbed at any moment, that anything is possible down here, where nothing needs a reason. He pushes himself forward, walking faster, and sees the glimmer of light from above; the next moment he bumps into the wall with its bars and starts to climb as fast as he can—one foot over the other, one hand over the other, and he himself couldn't say why he is so afraid. He climbs like a monkey, panting, feeling his pants leg catch on a nail jutting from a rung. He yanks on it, climbs even faster, reaches the trapdoor; hoisting himself up, he rolls over and lies on the floor, breathing heavily.

In front of him sit Boris and Felix, smirking. Between them crouches Jerzabek.

"What happened to you?" asks Boris.

"Did you shit yourself?" asks Felix.

The three of them laugh. Jerzabek has turned red with pleasure.

Jakob stares at him open-mouthed. Just a moment ago, down there, he was behind Jakob—how can he now be up here in front of him? For a moment, Jakob suspects that there must be more than one Jerzabek.

"Why are you here?" he asks.

"I'm the caretaker," says Jerzabek.

And again the three of them laugh so heartily that Jakob has no choice but to pretend he finds it funny too.

"Let's go upstairs," says Jerzabek, though only Jakob understands him because of how the words run together. "I'll make the young masters a bed." And his small eyes flash cunningly in Jakob's direction, as if they shared a secret.

At dinner everyone sits around the long table. The stag's head stares above them. At one end sits Papa, at the other Werner Krauss. To Papa's right sits his assistant Wilzek, to his left the screenwriter Heuser, next to him the cameraman Stephan. Next to Wilzek sit Jakob and Boris; opposite Boris, next to Stephan, sits Felix. Sitting next to Felix, silent, motionless, almost invisible, is the strange Kuno Krämer. Only Mama has not come.

Liesl Jerzabek and her daughters bring bowls of soup. The soup is completely colorless, with huge lumps of dough floating in it. There's a name for this dish, but no one understands it, not even when Liesl Jerzabek repeats it for the third time. Papa stands up and grandly pours white wine into all the glasses, including those of the boys.

Immediately Krauss raises his glass, thrusts his prominent chin toward the antlers, and exclaims: "I drink to the master!"

Since he obviously means Papa, the latter replies: "No, *I* drink to the master."

"No, no no!" exclaims Krauss. "*I* drink to the master."

And then they all drink and eat the very salty soup. Jakob looks furtively at the Jerzabek daughters, who have shot up tremendously since he last saw them: Gerti must be almost two meters tall, Mitzi is only slightly shorter. Their eyes are piercing, and curves are already starting to show under their blouses.

"She's pretty," Boris says in Jakob's ear.

"Which one?" asks Jakob, but before his friend can answer, the actor leaps to his feet and, oblivious to the general embarrassment, delivers a speech to the table about divine gifts, glorious heavenly power, quintessentially German struggle, and the blessed majesty of sublime art. The speech is long and sounds as well rehearsed as if he had delivered it word for word many times before. "May we together!" he exclaims. "Awaken! The great Paracelsus, the glorious! German doctor, to new! Life! To that! Master, friends! To that!" And he drains his drink, sits down, and starts spooning his soup.

"Thank you!" says Papa. "I'll remain seated, I just want to say: let's make a good film. Old Herr Hohenheim should not be ashamed of us."

"Who's that?" asks Krämer.

"Theophrastus Hohenheim is the real name of Paracelsus. If that's not in the script, it needs to go in immediately."

Kurt Heuser, the writer, opens the notepad that has been lying ready next to his plate and writes something down. Krämer has turned red.

"How many days do we actually have now for the Saint Vitus dance?" asks the cameraman.

"What's a Saint Vitus dance?" asks Jakob.

"Dancing like you're possessed by the devil," says Papa. "First people watch, then they join in. They can't help themselves."

"That could be seen as an allusion," says Wilzek.

"I didn't hear that," says Krämer.

"Hear what?" asks Werner Krauss.

"That's the right attitude," says Krämer. Everyone except the actor laughs.

"At the moment we only have one day for it," says Wilzek. "The shooting schedule is too tight."

"One day is enough," says Papa. "Have faith, boys. When I was shooting *Westfront*, they cut our budget on the fourth day of filming. A third less shooting time! We rewrote the script in two days and lo and behold, it worked, and in retrospect I'd say the film was better for it. Because we couldn't build a fortification, we had to shoot in a small destroyed bunker from the war. When you're making a movie, you're always in a bind. That's the normal state of affairs."

"Who was the producer?" asks Wilzek.

"Nebenzahl."

"Well then," says Stephan. "No wonder. A Yid."

"And those dark! Times!" says Krauss. "Over! Because now there are no more cuts! What our ministry promises you! You get! Even during the war. You can rely on that!"

Papa smiles vaguely and pours himself more wine.

"That's right," says Krämer. "What the ministry promises, you receive. Foreigners are surprised when they see our working conditions. I was just in Belgium. There we had an English writer, very famous over there, huge print runs, very superficial writing of course, no depth, far from true art, but a clever man. We'd arrested him at his villa in northern France. 'Look,' I said, 'all doors are open. You don't have to be in the prison camp. You're not a Jew, we have nothing against you, you could be in Berlin's finest hotel! We appreciate art!' I really said that, 'We appreciate art,' although his books are of course . . . Well, over there they're considered funny, but in Germany no one would laugh at that garbage, except maybe a few Jews in the old days. 'But what am I supposed to do?' he asks me. 'I can't write German books about weight lifters and horses.' He really said that. I don't know how he came up with that. Weight lifters and horses."

Krämer tilts his head and thinks for a moment. It seems to surprise him that everyone is listening and no one interrupting.

"'You could record a few radio programs,' I said. 'Nothing political. We would never demand that. Just lighthearted chats where you talk about how we Germans are also humans, not monsters. Or am

I a monster? Look at me! We are civilized people!' Of course, he was shocked at first and groaned and scratched his head . . . I know how it is. People always get nervous at first when you make them an offer. And sometimes"—he casts a quick glance at Papa—"they get downright aggressive. That's because they're not used to selflessness on the part of a state. Because they come from a world where only money counts. I knew I had to give him time. Three days later I came back to his barrack in the camp, and I sat down on one of the stools and offered him a good cigar, the kind that's almost impossible to get these days, and the very next day we were on our way to Berlin. Gentlemen, I've never seen anyone write so quickly! They can do that, these English professionals. They'll never understand German depth, but my God are they quick. So now the fellow is sitting in the Adlon, smoking good cigars, drinking cognac, and hammering away at the typewriter. And then he rides with our chauffeur to the radio studio and can't believe how good our microphones are, and the modern magnetic tapes and the soundproofing. 'Never seen anything like this at the BBC!' And of course I don't tell him that, if he likes the microphones, he ought to have a look at the antennas! Those giant antennas at Calais, aimed straight across the Channel so they'll hear him loud and clear. And it was really not bad, his broadcast! He talked about the prison camp as if it were a summer camp for boy scouts." Kuno Krämer sighs, then reaches for the wine bottle, and fills his glass.

"And you're paying for his stay at the Adlon all this time?" asks Heuser.

"No, that's the best part! He's earned so much with his plays! We froze the royalties immediately in thirty-three, and since then they've been yielding good interest at the Berliner Volksbank. The whole thing pays for itself." Krämer flushes with pride and pleasure.

"Shakespeare," says Krauss. "Would not have let himself be bought so cheaply."

"By whom, Herr State Actor?" asks Krämer. "By us?"

Krauss furrows his brow, confused by the question. "Well, of course. Of course, of course. Shakespeare certainly would . . . Shakespeare was at heart a German. The Bard. The Swan of Avon."

Everyone waits, but Krauss adds nothing.

Jakob watches as the two girls walk around the table a second time with the soup pot and ladle. Is he mistaken, or does Mitzi keep glancing over at Felix? And doesn't Gerti pass so close to Boris that her upper arm brushes the back of his head? No, he must be wrong. Jakob looks intently at Gerti, but she seems not to notice him. Now she ladles soup into Werner Krauss's bowl—"Thank you, my beautiful child!"—and for a moment looks right in Jakob's direction, looking through him as if he were invisible. She giggles sharply as the actor's hand, visible to everyone, strokes her back and behind, then she steps back, walks around the table, looks at Felix, and now it's definitely no mistake, she really does it, with narrow, attentive eyes. Mitzi goes out with the soup pot. Gerti follows her with the ladle.

"Oh, oh, the youth," says Krauss. "It warms the heart. Old age approaches swiftly. So seize the day. My father almost lived to be a hundred."

"My mother died last month," says Papa. "In the nursing home in Mödling near Vienna."

"My condolences," says Krauss. He closes his eyes, listening within, and says in a suddenly changed voice: "Only once did love soften the Ruler of Shadows, and still at the threshold, sternly, he called back his gift." He falls silent and makes small swinging motions with his right hand, apparently following verses that he doesn't speak but only thinks.

And then something strange happens: Jakob feels as if he too hears the verses—not as words, but as soft, sad music. But how is it possible for a person who can't form a thought or finish a sentence to achieve such a thing solely with his facial expression and a movement of his hand? You can't look anywhere else but at his soundlessly murmuring lips. Jakob realizes that he must remember this face, that he absolutely must draw it.

"The gods weep," Kraus says softly. "All the goddesses weep. That beauty fades, that perfection dies." He falls silent for a moment, then sighs, and continues spooning his soup.

Gerti brings in a loaf of bread. Again she looks at Boris, then turns her head toward the door. As she walks out, Boris pushes his chair back, stands up, and leaves the room. Outside a car approaches, gravel crunching under the brakes; a few seconds later the doorbell rings.

"Are we expecting anyone else?" asks Papa.

Jerzabek enters with two men in leather coats.

"Herr Pabst?" asks one.

"G. W. Pabst?" asks the other.

Jakob sees that Papa has turned chalk-white.

"Lost your voice?" asks the first.

"I am Wilhelm Pabst," says Papa.

"What's Garbo like? Compliant?"

"I'd sure like to meet her," says the other man.

"But excuse me," says the first. "Completely forgot my manners. Karsunke."

"I," says the other, "am Basler."

Papa takes off his glasses, clears his throat, puts them back on. "What can I do for you?"

"Take it easy, Pabst," says Basler. "Don't panic."

"Hey!" Karsunke exclaims, pointing at Krauss. "You're Jannings! Man, Emil Jannings, what a thing! Huge admirer!"

"I'm Werner Krauss," Krauss says softly.

"Ah, well—not your fault," says Karsunke.

Both laugh.

Jakob watches them intently. He wants to remember them so that he can draw them, they're both so lean and tall and healthy, and their faces are so blank, as if nothing at all were looking out of their eyes. He feels furtive envy. To be free of thoughts, while healthy and very strong. How wonderful that must feel.

"But seriously," says Karsunke. "Enough of the funny business."

"Yes, seriously," says Basler. "Which of the gentlemen here is . . . "

He falls silent and looks at his colleague. The other pulls a notepad out of his pocket, taps his finger on the tip of his tongue, and squints as he flips through the pages once, twice, three times.

"Just kidding," says Karsunke.

"Keeping it light," says Basler. "Keeping it carefree."

"Kurt Heuser," says Karsunke. "Which of you is that? Please no multiple responses."

"Lottery win for Kurt Heuser," says Basler.

Jakob sees Papa breathe a sigh of relief. Tension also falls away from Krauss, and Wilzek's hunched shoulders sink back down. But the screenwriter's face has become very narrow. He sucks in his cheeks, his eyes wide open.

"Me," says Heuser.

"Are you sure?" asks Karsunke. "You're him, without a doubt?"

"What's this about?" Heuser asks.

"Everyone asks that," says Karsunke.

"Always," says Basler.

"Always, always, always," says Karsunke.

"And yet we never answer that."

"We just say, 'Come with us!'"

"If you have nothing to hide, you don't need to be afraid."

"It can be quite harmless. That happens too."

"Not usually, though."

"No, not usually. Shall we go?"

"Now?" asks Heuser.

They both laugh.

"Everyone always asks that too," says Basler. "Well, if it's not a convenient time, we could come back next year." They laugh again. Now Boris and Felix are smiling too. Then the cameraman smiles. And finally Werner Krauss smiles too.

"So yes," says Karsunke. "Right now, immediately. And move quickly, or else we'll have to shift modes."

"Change keys," says Basler. "From major to minor."

"This man is from the ministry!" Heuser points at Kuno Krämer. "You can't just . . . You have to talk to him first!"

"Oh, really?" asks Karsunke. They both look at Krämer. He sits motionless, staring at the tabletop. "Which ministry?"

Krämer clears his throat, then says softly, "Propaganda."

"Oh," says Karsunke. "And you want to say something?"

"No, no," says Krämer, without looking up. "No."

"Are you sure? We could put that in our report."

"We're making a report?" asks Basler.

"There's always a first time."

"Not necessary," says Krämer. "Everything's fine."

"Thought so," says Karsunke.

"Heuser!" says Basler. "Shall we?"

Heuser stands up. "May I call my wife?"

"You know the answer," Karsunke says. "You little piece of shit. Come on now, and don't yap our ears off."

Dragging his feet, Heuser walks around the table toward the door. Basler puts a hand on his shoulder.

Jerzabek asks whether the gentlemen would like something to eat or drink.

"Huh?" asks Karsunke.

"Again," says Basler. "But slowly. You call that German?"

Jerzabek grins subserviently and repeats everything as clearly as he possibly can.

"That's nice," says Karsunke. "Something to drink. No one else here thought of that! To offer us something. After the long journey."

"And you are?" asks Basler.

"Local Group Leader Karl Jerzabek," says Jerzabek, standing at attention and then, quite unnecessarily, raising his hand in the German salute.

"You could give us some rolls," says Basler. "For the road."

"Yes, indeed," says Karsunke. "Wouldn't be a bad idea."

Jerzabek ducks to the side and shuffles off toward the kitchen.

"Well, then," says Basler. "Always best to leave on a high note."

And just like that the two of them are gone, having taken Heuser with them. Jakob rubs his eyes. He feels something strange happening: even now, although he usually never forgets a face, he can no longer remember what they looked like. He can no longer recall their voices either, and a moment later he can't even be sure which of them was Karsunke and which was Basler.

Everyone sits in silence. From outside they hear crunching steps on the gravel, they hear Jerzabek saying "Here you are, gentlemen, your rolls," they hear the slam of a car door three times, they hear the engine starting up, the tires crunching into motion. Then the engine grows softer. And finally they hear the birds and wind again.

"Back to the Saint Vitus dance," Stephan finally says. "I really don't think one day is enough for that scene."

"You'll see," says Papa. "I'll manage it."

"Why is . . . " Wilzek falls silent. He rubs his forehead. "I mean . . . Why did they . . . "

"Surely a misunderstanding," says Papa. "It'll be cleared up."

"Heuser has always had difficulties," says the cameraman. "But never anything really bad so far."

"I need him," says Papa. "Krämer, I can't let him . . . you'll make sure of that, right? That I don't lose him!"

"He's always had difficulties," the cameraman repeats.

"An insubordinate fellow," says Krauss. "He was supposed to write this film I was in, the Minister really wanted him, but he just didn't do it. I say, to each his own, but then he shouldn't be surprised."

"You mean *Jew Süss*?" asks Papa.

"Yes, exactly! You can always say no. But then you shouldn't be surprised."

"You could have said no," says Wilzek.

"Six Jews, all different, I played each one differently! Each one, completely! Different! That's not something an actor simply . . . ! Have you seen it?"

"I believe we've all seen *Jew Süss*, Herr State Actor."

"Probably there's a new job for him," says Krauss. "And they want to make sure he doesn't! Just say no again, that's all it! Will be!"

Papa claps his hands and stands up. "All right, boys, back to work! We still have to go through the second part."

"Without a writer?" asks Stephan.

"As I said, in filmmaking you're always in a bind. And yet we manage."

Everyone stands up.

"Where's Boris?" Felix whispers in Jakob's ear. Jakob shrugs, because he can guess, but he doesn't want to talk about it, doesn't want to know, and doesn't want to think about it either.

"Jakob," Papa calls over to him. He remains standing. Only once everyone has left does Papa ask softly: "Did it scare you?"

Jakob doesn't answer.

"It will be cleared up," says Papa. "They'll release him soon, you'll see. It must be a misunderstanding."

"Why would it scare me?"

His father looks at him, puzzled. Jakob notices that for the first time they are exactly the same height.

"I don't know anything about this man," says Jakob. "But there must be a reason. Otherwise they wouldn't have come."

His father silently folds his glasses and puts them into his breast pocket.

"They're the best men in the Reich. They know what they're doing."

His father looks at him, his eyebrows drawn together, his forehead creased, as if he were looking into a painfully bright light.

"How do you come to be writing a script with someone like that?"

"With someone like that?" Papa takes a step back. It is as if he wants to say something. But he says nothing. "Would you like to listen in on the meeting?" he finally asks. "It could be interesting, if you ever want to work in film."

"But I don't want that. I'd like to do something to help my people in their struggle. There are more important things than movies. Don't take it the wrong way."

Papa glances over Jakob's shoulder for a moment, as if to check whether someone is standing behind his son, speaking instead of him.

"We believe in sacrifice," says Jakob. "We no longer want to be famous or rich. We want to be there for the whole, we want to fight, and if it comes to it, then we also want to die for something greater than ourselves. For the Reich and for our Führer. If we're lucky, Felix and Boris and I, by the end of the year we'll be in uniform."

"But you're already in uniform."

"I mean the real one. The Wehrmacht."

Something has happened to Papa's face that Jakob has never seen before. The muscles around his mouth and eyes have slackened, his cheeks have sagged, his gaze has lost its strength. Suddenly Jakob can see what his father will look like when he's an old man.

"Don't get me wrong," says Jakob. "I have great respect. The people need movies. They must be entertained and educated."

Papa turns away and walks up the stairs. His shoulders are slumped as if he were carrying two heavy suitcases.

Trude wakes up with a start. Always such dreams. You doze off, yet sleep never protects you for long, and now you're back in the world of real people and solid things, where everything is much worse.

She looks up at the ceiling. A thin crack runs through the gray. How much time have you now spent staring at it? Then you lie there, looking up, feeling the pressure on your chest, the dull ache in your belly, and the stabbing pain in your right knee and left elbow, hearing the rattle of your own breathing and the whistling in your ears that never stops and is only sometimes forgotten for a while, and on your tongue lingers the bitter aftertaste of white wine, and you also hear all the noises from the building, including the voices from the dining room.

Often, when she lies like this and closes her eyes, she can even hear the distant hum of the squadrons. They're flying very far away—but they are so large and consist of so many engines and propellers that you can still perceive them here.

She found herself thinking of these machines when she was sitting next to Wilhelm at the premiere of *The Comedians*: Käthe Dorsch spoke so beautifully, Henny Porten spread her fingers so elegantly, and Hilde Krahl bowed her head so sweetly, gently, and naively and sighed with such deep modesty. At some point, Trude could no longer hold back: a sob welled up inside her, her shoulders shook, tears ran down her face, and Wilhelm, believing she was crying over the tragic fate of the theater manager in the movie, took her hand, and when she still couldn't stop after several minutes, he proudly handed her his silk handkerchief.

The day after the premiere they walked a path in the misty Grunewald forest. They came there not for the sake of nature—which near Berlin is generally gray, muddy, and oppressive, with pitifully patchy grass and bent trees—but to speak freely with each other. In the apartment, that's impossible, because the walls are thin and the neighbors attentive, and at home in the castle, under the caretaker's rule, it's utterly out of the question. Sometimes she even feels as if the caretaker is traveling with them, as if he is walking behind her on the street in Berlin, or standing in a corner of the staircase, as if there is never a moment when Jerzabek is not close by, watching with his caretaker's vigilance, lurking, breathing heavily.

Back then in Grunewald she said everything.

For a while he was silent. It hit him harder than she expected.

"You're right," he finally said. "But only half right. Because all this will pass. But art remains."

"Even if that's the case. Even if it remains, the . . . art. Doesn't it remain soiled? Doesn't it remain bloody and dirty?"

Yes, this once her words struck him deeply. He looked hurt, battered, downright wounded.

"And the Renaissance? What about the Borgias and their poisonings, what about Shakespeare, who had to make accommodations with Elizabeth. Poems can be written alone, pictures can be painted alone, but films? That always takes power and money. For every film, a vast machinery. You know I'm not here by choice, but—"

"Do I know that?"

"We came for Mama, suddenly the war broke out, and after my fall from the ladder, I was trapped!"

"That's the story you're telling now?"

"Isn't it true?"

"It's true as much as any story is true. Kuno Krämer said that over there he had already offered you—"

"And I chased him away. I threatened to hit him!"

"Have you ever hit anyone in your life?"

"What's that supposed to mean?"

"When we came to Austria, to the castle, to your mother, before you fell off the ladder. The ladder that Jerzabek supposedly shook. Before that happened, did you really want to go back to Hollywood? To the producers who don't know who Pabst is, to the people who give you only bad scripts, where you might end up working as an assistant for someone who was recently your assistant? Is that what you wanted?"

He remained silent for a while and rubbed his forehead, as he always does. Their breath rose in gray steam clouds into the autumn air.

"Maybe it's not so important what one wants. The important thing is to make art under the circumstances one finds oneself in. These are my circumstances now. And you know, they're not that bad! I have good scripts and high budgets and the best actors. *The Comedians* is my best film in a long time, *Paracelsus* will be better than anything Lang is making over there. *Paracelsus* will still be watched fifty years from now, when this nightmare is long forgotten!"

Believing he had convinced her, he placed his hand on her cheek with a grateful smile. There they stood facing each other as it began to drizzle, under crooked, rustling trees, looking into each other's eyes—he questioning, she rigid with despair.

She feels this rigidity even now on the bed, as if she were locked up inside her body. Her thoughts can't leave her body, can't get out, but are stuck to her aching joints, the stabbing pain behind her forehead, the whistling in her chest, the bitter taste in her mouth. Her ears pick up a car pulling up down below and men arriving. Their voices can be heard, speaking louder and more firmly than people do when they pay a friendly visit, which doesn't bode well. But if you don't move and just listen and think yourself away from everything, then it's as if you're not really there, as if the world is taking its course on its own, as if you don't exist.

The men are talking so loudly that you could now even understand what they're saying—but sounds right outside the bedroom door drown everything out: something is coming up the stairs, a giggle and a murmur, then a grim, lustful scuffle, one of the Jerzabek daughters and a young man she doesn't know. Or is it . . . ?

No, she thinks with relief, not Jakob's voice, thank God. Two bodies crash against the wall with force, the floorboards groaning, followed by a sharp cry, then a laugh. A door is pushed open and shut, then the voices from downstairs again, this time from the entrance hall.

"Can I write her a few lines?" asks a man. "My wife doesn't even know where I—" A thud, he falls silent. The door creaks, and just seconds later the engine starts up outside.

Open your eyes. The crack in the ceiling. The water pitcher on the bedside table, the empty glass. Get ready. You'll hear something again soon. It never stays quiet for long.

Yes, now they're talking again. First one, then another, then another, and here again is Wilhelm's voice, calm and confident. So he's still here. They've taken someone else.

Close your eyes. He's going to film it, his good movie. One more on his list of good movies. And when the movie is finished, he'll put on his tails and you'll tie his bow tie because he still can't do it himself, even after all the premieres.

You'll put on a dark dress, probably a new one, with silken pleats and a long train, and a makeup artist from the movie will come to the hotel and twist your hair around her curling iron, and then you'll walk down the carpet on his arm, past the pillars of light formed by upturned spotlights, so popular now, and if you forget, he'll whisper a reminder for you to smile.

As she imagines this, she feels part of her consciousness actually slipping back into slumber: They're walking through the cinema, past crimson curtains, a man in uniform weightily shakes Georg's hand, and now they're sitting, and the movie is playing, and on the screen a little man is swinging his arms and legs and sticking out his tongue and staring down at her with unrestrainable malice, and her fear ruptures her sleep, and with a pounding heart she's back in her room.

It's dark. It must be night. How long has she been asleep? This is happening more and more often now, you think it's been only seconds, but suddenly hours have passed. Maybe it's the headache, maybe the wine.

Snoring from several directions. You can even make out Wilhelm's snoring, coming from the room to the left, where he now sleeps alone. In the room on the right someone she doesn't know is snoring, as well as on the other side of the corridor.

She switches on the light, sits up, and with unsteady hands pours water from the pitcher into the empty glass. Just as she's about to drink, she notices a fly. With its wings outstretched, it floats in the water, its legs trembling, buzzing softly.

Disgusted, Trude puts the glass down. Sharp pain throbs behind her temple. Thirsty, she sinks back onto the pillow.

She knows she has a long night ahead of her. What time might it be? It's usually like this: you doze through the day, and at night, wide awake, you watch the hours crawl by. But at least another day is over.

You're still alive, Jakob is still alive, Wilhelm is still alive. That's not insignificant.

She switches off the light and feels for the glass, unable to shake the feeling that she's forgotten something.

Sighing, she sits up and drinks.

Jakob lies awake in his old nursery. On the floor are two makeshift sleeping spots—a thin mattress, two pillows, two blankets—but only one is occupied. Felix snores softly. The moon hangs pale at the edge of the window. Jakob wonders why he's so angry. He lies staring at the window, listening.

Eventually, the door opens again. Someone comes in quietly. It's Boris.

"So?" asks Jakob.

In a daze, Boris goes to the washstand. He takes off his shirt, grabs a cloth, dips it in the water, and starts to wipe himself down.

"Well?" asks Jakob.

He knows what has to happen now—there is a particular ritual for this moment. When you've been with a girl for the first time, you have to tell the other boys, you have to smile crudely, you have to say that she begged for it and that you gave her what she wanted, whatever that means. Jakob has never been with a girl.

"So?" Jakob asks again, disgusted by the ritual, especially knowing that it was for his benefit alone that Gerti took his school friend Boris with her—just to irk him. But how is he supposed to explain this to anyone! He doesn't understand it himself. He wouldn't want to get close to her for the life of him, and yet it deeply irks him.

Boris looks at him. The moonlight turns his face ghostly pale.

"She . . . " Boris falls silent, then tries again. "What's her name?"

"You don't know?"

"She didn't tell me."

"That was Gerti."

Boris sits down on the floor and starts to cry softly.

Felix mumbles in his sleep. For a moment it looks like he might wake up, but then he turns over and continues sleeping.

In the cold, white light Jakob clearly sees the tears running down Boris's face. He realizes Boris will never forgive him for seeing him like this. At this moment their friendship is over.

"What did she do to you?"

Like a beaten animal Boris crawls under the blanket next to Felix. Jakob waits, but Boris doesn't stir again.

So Jakob lets himself sink back into bed, into his old childhood bed, where he lay when he was just four years old. And though he doesn't want to, he falls asleep within minutes, because the day was long and the journey arduous, and above all because he is still young.

When he wakes up early in the morning, he remembers dreaming of a fly wriggling in a water glass, then of a movie premiere in a cinema full of people. On the mattress next to him, only Felix is sleeping. Boris is gone. That night he packed his backpack and headed back on foot, without a message, without a word of goodbye.

Shadow Play

When Krämer mentioned that our journey to Salzburg would coincide with a premiere, I must confess, my curiosity was piqued.

Not, I hasten to say, because I was to "witness the birth of a genuine Aryan cinema," as he rather ghoulishly put it, but because the father-director in question was none other than G. W. Pabst!

Naturally I'd seen *Pandora's Box*—three times, in as many days. I considered it then, and consider it still today, the last word in sexual raffinement, and Pabst a genius of the senses. I shouldn't have thought either the picture or its author should have appealed to the Roundheads of the Reich.

Nor did I see who should have wanted me there.

To what, I asked, did I owe this honor? Pabst and I had never crossed paths in Los Angeles. The invitation couldn't have come from him.

Krämer informed me that I would be a guest of the ministry, and that he would be honored to stand as my escort.

Surely, I said, he could do better than to bring a writer—especially one so hopelessly English.

"Is this not the sort of occasion that Mrs. Krämer might enjoy?" I had no idea whether there was a Mrs. Krämer.

"I need you there," he said, with some evident embarrassment. "It's a grand premiere. We need an international audience, international flair."

"What has that got to do with me?"

"We're not well stocked with personalities at the moment. Foreigners have stopped coming, and our own have left the country."

"Ah, yes . . . Marlene."

His gaze clouded as if he had a toothache. "For example."

I had met her once. At Sardi's, in the company of Noël and Erich Remarque. She was eating a cannellone with a spoon. I found her frightfully German, in the most endearing way. If one had had holes in one's socks, one felt she might have reached into her mink and pulled out a pair of darning needles. But glamorous, glamorous of course!

Even in her absence, I told poor Krämer, I felt sure they could do better than yours truly. Not relishing the thought of giving up my really quite comfortable room at the Adlon, or of the journey from Berlin to Salzburg, or of an evening shaking hands with Nationalist bigwigs who knew no more English than I knew German, I firmly declined.

"We would be deeply honored if you attended," came the reply.

The honor would be all mine, I assured him, but nevertheless, etc.

For its part the ministry, in the person of Krämer, gave me to understand that it would consider the entire evening less than a success if I were not among the attendees, etc., etc.

Things grew rather desperately polite before Krämer saw fit to remind me, in an apologetic tone, "But you are a prisoner of war."

In Los Angeles, it used to be said of Mary Dousey, then publicity chief at Metro-Goldwyn-Mayer, that in the humorless, bullying, bludgeoning manner so dreaded by her legions of enemies she was "like a German general." Having now some small experience of German generals, I consider this a slander. Among his cronies, at least, Krämer evidently had a sense of humor, though the language barrier constituted, in our case, a sort of no-man's-land where pleasantries went to die, and yet his courtesy was never anything but elaborate. Indeed, two days later, it was with an unexpected sense of obligation that I sat back in the ministerial Mercedes-Benz beside my host, admiring the craggy cliffs of Salzburg, its looming castle, and all the baroque abundance of its bell towers. I had never dreamed there could be so many.

"It is fairly bristling with churches," I remarked, in what must have sounded a slightly disparaging tone, for it led Krämer to assure me placidly that the National Socialist state was, of course, modern and anticlerical.

In fact, there was much to be said for Salzburg—to begin with, it hadn't been bombed, which lent the entire place an air of calm and unreality after the incessant sirens of Berlin. As we fetched up in front of the Golden Stag—for such was the inevitable name of our hotel—I felt almost grateful, especially after the strain of the first three broadcasts, about which my feelings were generally rather mixed. I had found them "heavy sledding," is the truth, for it was understood they must be amusing, with nothing to offend on either side, and yet one felt a duty that went beyond the obligation to play along with the ministry, a duty, that is, to be "characteristically" British, to show native pluck and something more, a sort of sunny vagueness rising to the level of defiance, never admitting, for example, the possibility of defeat (whatever one's private fears). And then, one wished to reassure dear friends of one's personal safety, and to raise the public morale, so badly in need of frivolity.

In my room I was surprised to find my own evening clothes, which evidently had been rescued from Le Touquet, hat and all, and transported across Europe, in the midst of the war, just for a premiere! One detested the Germans, their thuggery, their pogroms, their murderous lust for power, yet one could not fail to admire their attention to detail. Now, having taken a long bath, having shaved and dressed, I could not help casting an inquisitive eye over the figure in the mirror. The waistcoat, bib, and braces did their work, and although the trousers bagged slightly, and although one could feel a certain looseness across the shoulders, the coat was brushed, the pumps shone, and the distinguished gent with the child's face was plausibly, really rather remarkably, myself.

Krämer was waiting for me in the lobby, looking oddly disheveled despite his full-dress regalia. There was a dab of shaving cream behind one ear.

"We're running late!" he exclaimed.

I assured him that there was no danger of anyone arriving late to a film premiere, not even under the Thousand-Year Reich. In war and peace, in heaven and hell, where actors are involved, no curtain at any first night will ever rise on time.

We ambled through the old streets, a rather conspicuous pair—the lost foreigner and his Virgil—nearly dazzled by the streetlamps, accustomed as one was to the blackouts in Berlin. We trudged over cobblestones, through stone underpasses, past fountains and churches and more churches and still more churches, then turned a corner, and here, on a wide square, in all its stony opulence, was the so-called Festival Hall.

Outside the entrance someone had directed spotlights vertically into the sky, creating pillars of light, just as in the newsreels of a Nationalist rally, although there it had been a hundred and not merely three—or four, but one was broken, so that two pillars stood imposingly side by side, with the third looking rather disconsolate and abashed. On a giant billboard could be read the title *Paracelsus*, and beside it the face of the famous Werner Krauss glowered down with the serious frown of an actor on a poster. Beneath his gaze were all the usual accoutrements: crimson carpet, barriers, photographers. Enfin, it was a premiere. To the gentle *pop-pop-pop* of the cameras various persons in gala attire were stretching and posturing importantly—they must have been the performers. Werner Krauss, however, was not among them; no doubt he was off making another film.

"You too," said my companion. "In front of the cameras, please!"

I bridled. There had been no mention of cameras.

"It's not a suggestion."

So raising my chin and an eyebrow, with what I knew to be my most ironic smile, I sauntered before the barrage of the bulbs. None of those people had any inkling who I was. They merely assumed that, since I was standing unmolested on this side of the barrier, I must be of some importance, and snapped away. Two actors eyed me with envious displeasure. I endured it, counted slowly to twenty-four, then moved at a measured pace to the end of the carpet and into the foyer, which for the occasion had been lavishly decorated with the usual "medieval" nonsense, shields and suits of armor in the style of Henry VIII. I made my way toward the bar.

And as I collected my glass of Riesling, in the thick of the throng, I spotted the great man himself.

"Mr. Pabst!" I exclaimed. "May I introduce myself? I can't say what a tremendous admirer—"

His eyes grew wide behind his glasses, and he gazed at me in bewilderment. Clearly, by addressing him in English, I had committed a terrible faux pas; and now he was racking his brain as to whether he ought to have understood me.

Feeling my error acutely, I was just bowing myself out of the scrum when he rushed forward and seized my hand, smiling the most open and friendly, the most human, smile I had seen since my internment. I felt the pleasure, childish but not to be sneezed at, of having been seen by a well-known personality and greeted, as it were, as a member of the club.

"My dear sir!" he said, with a vigorous pump. "What for a surprise! I heard you were swept off in Berlin. How is it you come to Salzburg?"

It surprised me that someone as worldly as Pabst should speak such halting English. But then, I suppose, he had learned his English on the sound lots and the lawns of California.

"Well, you!" I exclaimed. "I'm here for your film!"

"Ah, such an honor, and this for all the shoelace rain!"

Having no clear idea what Pabst was trying to say, I made noises of assent. Now I was warmly introduced to his retinue: the assistant, the cameraman, the set designer—or, *per* Pabst, the "homemaker"—and the fellow who hung the lights, each with a differently unpronounceable name that I promptly forgot. And this, he said, pulling over a beautiful, rather vague-looking woman in an evening gown, was his wife! I bowed, she looked blankly in my direction and seemed to wobble. She was, if I was not mistaken, pickled.

For the first time that evening, Krämer laid a flat, soft, somewhat feeble, yet oddly sticky, hand on my arm. I was being steered in another direction. But before he could draw me away, I remarked to Mrs. Pabst, without any real expectation that she would understand me, something to the effect of how marvelous it was that films were still being produced at all, that one might almost believe the world hadn't come to an end.

"Yes, and what is more we are producing excellent films," she replied. "A state like this is perfectly suited for cinema. Perhaps more so than any other in history."

"Not counting Sparta," I ventured, more out of surprise than from any wish to provoke.

"Ah, Sparta, yes—but we have seen such improvements in equipment."

"To make the pictures move, I suppose, one had to turn the amphora."

"By hand."

"And every one a peplum!"

Feeble jokes, but we were joking, and she smiled.

"You speak such beautiful English," I told her. "You might give lessons."

With this she cast a glance at the back of her husband, who was busily accepting the congratulations of a very fat man bursting out of what seemed to be a frock coat, with a swastika in the lapel.

"Would you believe, I have tried."

"Ah."

"If only he had learned English, then maybe . . . " She looked around, with a gesture that encompassed the entire lobby, at which moment Krämer's gentle push came to shove, and he bowed a firm farewell to Mrs. Pabst. As he guided me to the other side of the lobby, he informed me that the ministry had in attendance the cream of Salzburg society.

All the same, I remarked, it seemed a long way from Berlin.

"We always have film premieres here. Or in Prague. No blackouts, no bombs."

"But, my dear fellow, sooner or later, as any writer or director can tell you, everybody bombs." He gave a look of blank mistrust. "I mean, lays an egg. Comes a cropper. Fails, you know—with the critics."

"Critics? We have no critics! Criticism is a Jewish genre that no one needs. Instead we have art appreciation! Look." He stopped a tall, bespectacled man and said: "May I introduce you? Guido Merwetz. Once a feared critic. Now one of our subtlest describers."

Clearly not understanding English, the man looked back and forth between us with friendly concern, shading into dismay.

Krämer, however, had found a subject he could warm to. "Merwetz describes the beginning, the middle, the end," he explained. "He describes what the actors look like, and sometimes he even describes the beautiful nature in which they stand around! Describes until his fingers bleed!" He placed his left hand, the one he wasn't using to clutch me, on the man's shoulder, prompting a pained, jovial smile. "He's not even allowed to write that an actor is good! For that would be criticism too, and would . . . include? Enclose . . . ?"

"Imply," I said.

"Thank you . . . it would imply that the actor *could* be bad. But how would that be possible? The films are produced by the ministry, so how could they be anything but excellent!" He turned to the art describer, and the two of them shared a short German burst of laughter, one cheerful, the other a trifle pinched.

"He'd imagined things differently," Krämer said. "On the first day after the annexation, he threw his boss, Dr. Kornsteiner, out of the office—literally, out the window. Didn't you, Merwetz? Ha! Then he tried to become just as sharp and nasty and feared as Kornsteiner himself, and for a few years he almost succeeded, until there came the new regulation: from now on, only description is allowed!" He said something else in German, the fellow paled and bowed himself out of our presence.

We were pushing our way through what was now quite a crowd. Some of the gowns were surprisingly tasteful, as compared with the dour uniforms and quaint Tyrolean garb of the men, and yet—compared with the broad laughter and grins of the men—there was a sort of coldness or fear in the faces of the women, a naked unease as if, beneath the long gloves, their arms might be covered in gooseflesh. The women frightened me.

Near the door to the cinema stood a peculiarly spine-chilling creature. She had evil eyes and bared frightfully white teeth. Her skin seemed to be cast from Bakelite.

"Yes, this is the one," said my companion, preempting my question. "The Directress."

"Even she has come all the way from Berlin?"

"She is filming *Lowlands* in Bavaria. She has built a Spanish village."

"Yes, I remember reading an item in *Variety*, but this must have been . . . years ago."

"It's a very great film she is making. Such a film requires time."

Eventually an usher led us to our quite good seats: fifth row, slightly left of center. Murmuring our apologies in the usual way, we shuffled past several dozen knees whose owners nodded briefly, smiled, and made those gestures that indicate a nuisance is forgiven and forgotten the moment it occurs. For a brief, eerie moment I felt that I had woken from a terrible dream, to find myself back in civilization. More specifically, the West End.

The last man I climbed over, however, did not smile. He emitted a deep growl, staring up with a beastly glare as I stepped over his pointed knees. He was short and bald, he wore round black glasses and, in his hunched position, he bore an astonishing resemblance to a Beatrix Potter frog. A malevolent Beatrix Potter frog.

"I would very much like to introduce you," said Krämer, once he had taken the seat between us. "This is a colleague of yours who is very highly esteemed in this country, the author of the acclaimed novel *Schmiedecke, Friend of the Party.*" He pondered for a moment. "Or *Member of the Party*, that's probably a better translation, *Schmiedecke, Member of the Party.*" He turned to the frog, who was looking at us in silent but unmistakable rage. To my surprise, the frog erupted. He was shouting at Krämer and looking at me, to the interest of our neighbors one row behind and much to Krämer's consternation.

It occurred to me then how alike they looked—both squat and hairless—and yet Krämer was by far the more appealing of the two.

"What's he saying?"

"He says he knows your name. But even when you weren't banned, he'd never have touched one of your books in his life."

"Tell him I understand perfectly. If I could write them without having to read them, I'd never go near them either."

Diplomatic, I thought, but Krämer wasn't given a chance to translate, as the writer continued his tirade, punctuating his words with emphatic little jabs. Deciding that these two could debate the merits of my work without my help, I scanned the auditorium.

The rows were now filled; over in the center aisle the director and his wife were slowly making their way to their seats, probably in the fourth row, where directors usually sit at their premieres. He nodded to right and left, and when a medal-laden officer raised his arm with a jerk, he carelessly and quickly did the same.

"Mr. Karrasch has just elaborated further on why he wouldn't read you, not only because you're an Englishman. He says he would never read an Englishman as a matter of principle, but even if there were Englishmen he might read, you would certainly not be one of them. It's important to him that I tell you that."

I nodded approvingly toward the Frog King; he swiftly turned away.

"Charming," I whispered.

"His *Schmiedecke* was praised by the Führer himself, and his *Violin of the Stars* is a marvelous suspense novel that was a great success. Pabst is going to make it into a movie. That's why Mr. Karrasch is here! He's come all the way from the Curonian Spit."

"Has he! Well, please tell him that I shall look forward to the adaptation."

At this the enraged little man wheeled toward me for the last time, and snapped in my direction.

"He says you won't fool him. Even if you're now publicly on our side. He knows you don't really mean it."

For a moment I was at a loss for words. "What does he mean? On his . . . on your . . . *side*?"

"To the world you are now one of us, he's saying. But not to him."

"I'm hardly one of . . . You said it yourself, I'm a prisoner of war!"

Krämer smiled. Then he gestured toward . . . Well, what was it? It took me a moment to realize that he was pointing at my tailcoat, at the plush red seat I was sitting in, at our entire sumptuous surroundings.

"You forced me!" I exclaimed so loudly that a couple of ancient dowagers spun around in disapproval.

"Yes, you know that, and I know that, but even here in this hall no one knows it, and do you think they'll believe it back home when they hear your amusing episodes?"

"Well, obviously those were written under duress."

"'Duress' is a strong word. You were requested to make them. I wouldn't have cut off your limbs. You would have just remained a normal prisoner. No Adlon, no cigars. Every man is the architect of his own fortune. The German Reich is your home now."

I actually did it: I stood up. I who am usually so frightfully averse to the grand gesture. But for a moment I lost my composure, my hands trembled, the whole colorful hall reeled around me; it was a near thing that I didn't run out screaming.

In fact, I should dearly have loved to storm out of the place, with great strides and billowing coattails, and vanished into the vast, black night. But that would have required me to squeeze past all the knees of the gentlemen and ladies in my row, considerably diminishing the effect of my tempestuous exit. And then, where in that vast, black night would I have gone?

So I paused, pretending to rummage for something in my trouser pocket, and looked around me. I shouldn't have done that, for it was then I saw the large newsreel camera positioned next to the screen in a side box, trained on the audience in the front rows, and, at that very moment, trained on the standing gentleman with the impeccably tailored tailcoat so unusual for these parts. In my shock the color drained from everything around me, so that for an instant I saw the entire theater as the world would see it, in black and white. My legs were trembling as I retook my seat.

"Krämer," I whispered, "the Reich shall never be my home."

By then Pabst had reached his row, indeed the one right in front of ours. Those seated rose to let him and his wife, now even paler than before, pass by. A slightly uplifting moment of confusion ensued, because just two seats away from his designated spot—and thus squarely in his path—sat the Directress herself, seemingly oblivious to his presence. Which was all the more implausible as she must have known whose premiere she was attending—a pretense even more astounding than his own, for he too acted as if wholly unaware of her being there. The result was that they now stood facing each other, far too close, in poorly played mutual surprise. He reached for her hand, apparently to deliver a kiss upon it, but she had already raised this very hand in a German salute, to which he instantly responded in kind, except that by then she had already lowered her arm again to receive his kiss; but the tomfoolery ceased when she left her hand down, he lowered his, grasped hers, and with a smile of deathly self-control, brought his lips to hover just above her alabaster skin. Then he straightened up, their eyes met for a horrified instant, and he moved on to his seat. His wife, trailing behind him, did not merit even the briefest glance.

"You should know, the two of them worked together," my well-informed cicerone remarked, having watched the scene unfold just like everyone else in the hall. "On her film, for about five days."

"That's not long."

"Supposedly it didn't go well, and because . . . " He trailed off, distracted. I followed his gaze: as the lights dimmed and the murmuring died away, a solitary fellow legged it down the center aisle, clearly in a hurry to find his seat without drawing attention. My guide muttered something in German.

"Who is that?" I inquired.

"The scriptwriter."

"You seem surprised to see him here?"

He didn't reply. The man reached his seat, squeezed into the row, bent forward with his shoulders hunched tight.

"But if he's the scriptwriter," I tried again, "one would expect him to attend the premiere, wouldn't one?"

But by now it was dark. The cone of light from the projector flared to life, as always revealing a shimmering flurry of bright dust, causing me, at the start of every motion picture, to wonder how it was possible that one could actually suck all this flotsam down into one's lungs with every breath; then, mercifully, came a fanfare of trumpets.

Brass rang out, German names scrolled across the screen—how sad, I mused, how sparse: an entire film's opening credits, and not a Levy, Cohn, or Fischer among them; surely, this could hardly bode well. Fade in, a bustling crowd in front of a cathedral. Immediately one could see how skillfully it was all done: first a wide shot, then a tracking shot following two noblemen down a stair, only to tilt forward into a close-up of a beggar clutching pleadingly at one of their legs. The reverse shot showed the beggar looking up, the camera intentionally positioned low and angled upward, so the noblemen loomed high above the beggar. The effect was feudal in the extreme.

It's always a pleasure to see professionals at work. No matter the setting or circumstances, be it plumbers, bus drivers, waiters, or a director—when people excel at their craft, it gives one the feeling that the world isn't such a vale of tears after all. So, strange to say, I forgot the nightmare of the preceding minutes, sank further back into my seat, and listened to the German sentences, whose gist was altogether clear, although of course I understood not a word.

It was a long while before the hero made his entrance. The director took his time, preparing the scene with deliberate care. Only after ten minutes did an old woman bang on a door and call out: "Paracelsus!" Apparently someone was ill, and the great doctor was urgently needed.

Then a room, the shutters half open. Werner Krauss stood, nearly inconspicuous in the shadows, facing a young woman, whose bare back was to us. Her arms were outstretched, he pressed his ear to her breast—not seen but undeniably present; one was distinctly aware of this breast as he stepped back and the woman slipped on her dress. Never would such an image have been allowed in Hollywood; not today, not tomorrow, not in ten years, not for this director or any other.

I was captivated. Was it the best film I'd ever seen? Perhaps not, but it was off to an awfully good start. Paracelsus was now speaking expressively, with a strange twist to his mouth, so that even I could grasp his anger, his wisdom, his peculiar forlornness.

Before I knew it, half an hour had passed. There were parts I didn't understand, but I could follow most of it. The doctors, all impostors, frauds, were against the wise man, wanting to rid themselves of him, but the young students were on his side. And then it seemed a disease came to town. We saw the townspeople sweating and coughing, gripped by a great fear, and then . . .

Then something incredible happened.

A tavern, people sitting at tables, while a slender juggler danced in the middle. The actor did it quite well, his movements at once jagged and fluid, the music old-fashioned yet with a modern edge trembling within.

The people in the tavern were engrossed in his dance. They tapped their feet, nodded their heads, shrugged along to the music. It all looked so normal and natural, and it remained so even as the first few stood up and mimicked some of his steps—but then more and more of them joined in, and then no one could resist, no one could sit, everyone in the room was dancing.

There was nothing joyful about it, neither mirth nor freedom: forward and back, to the right and to the left they jumped, their bodies twitching and writhing, seemingly unleashed, yet in perfect unison and with desperate faces. No one deviated in the slightest.

Paracelsus entered, a large sword in his hand. He watched them dance, with a diagnostic eye, then he gave a mighty shout.

And all at once, the dance came to an end. The madness drained from every face. More indifferent than alarmed they stood there, resumed their seats, reached for their tankards, were now back on their benches, still a trifle stiff, a shade sheepish, but, on the whole, behaving as if nothing much had happened.

I rubbed my eyes—and this is no cheap phrase, I raised my hands and squiggled my eyelids in disbelief.

But it wasn't over yet: Paracelsus now sat at one of the tavern tables, surrounded by his pupils, and spoke to the somewhat discomposed dancer perched above him in the rafters. Something about the fellow seemed to displease the doctor; with a furrowed brow he reached up and felt his hands—then he started and shouted something.

His words crackled through the room like fire. The juggler sprang away, but people stopped him. He bolted first for one door, then for the other, but someone always sprang into his path. They tried to hold him, but now Paracelsus shouted something else, louder than before, with a thunderous voice, and all shrank back from the dancer. In close-up a barrel fell and rolled across the floor, and the juggler suddenly collapsed, spent, while Paracelsus shouted once more and everyone fled to the doors.

"What did he say?" I whispered.

"He said: 'Don't touch him, he has the plague.'"

Now Paracelsus stood behind the fallen man, wrapped his arm around his shoulder, placed his hand on his heart, and, holding him close, raised his other arm with the sword. He stood there like a saint from a twelfth-century fresco.

One heard a loud rasping. Metal on metal. There, on a bench, sat a figure cloaked in black, sharpening something. When Paracelsus looked over, the figure was standing, without having been seen to rise. He raised what turned out to be a scythe. Paracelsus held his sword in front of the unconscious man, the scythe clashed against the blade of the sword, and for a moment, a close-up of a skull filled the screen, only to dissolve in thin air. Only now, after Death had vanished, did we hear his brief, otherworldly laughter.

Then the movie simply went on! In an entirely naturalistic style! Without transition, transformation, or explanation! The doctor healed the sick and argued with other doctors, who were, of course, ignorant and portrayed as such; then the story apparently moved to the closing of the city against the plague. Various merchant types opposed this, presumably for the usual reasons, but Paracelsus did not yield. His watchword, repeated again and again, was "Quarantine!" Soon he lost his sway over the town; only his young followers remained loyal. In the end, none other than the scrawny dancer he had saved from the plague smuggled him out of the city to freedom in his wagon.

And then it was over. The screen went black, the silver beam faded away, the lights came on, the audience clapped—not wildly, not stunned, not unrestrained and overwhelmed, as would have been fitting, but certainly not without pleasure and appreciation either.

"What the devil was that?" I asked Krämer. "The Dance of Death in the middle, the attack of the skeleton?"

He shrugged. For a moment I doubted whether this was something I had actually seen—could I have dreamed it? How dark it had been, how bizarre and masterly—how German, really. In a daze, I joined the crowd streaming toward the exits.

Suddenly I found myself beside the famed Directress. Her hair flowed as if with invisible electrical energy, her nose pointed sharply into the air. And as she stood before me, for reasons I cannot explain—although she is not the first woman to have done so—she stared at me, transfixed. I greeted her with a bow.

"Remarkable, no?" I asked.

Her stare grew quizzical.

"The film!" I said, and repeated: "The film!" I knew the German word sounded akin to the English; she had to understand.

"Do you speak German?"

"Alas, I do not. Nothing would afford me greater pleasure, mind you, but one never quite expects to find oneself a prisoner of war, at least not when one is on holiday."

She gave me what they call on Broadway "elevator eyes," before delivering her verdict: "This is a bad film."

"Do you think? I must confess, I found it all rather impressive. Particularly the Dance of Death and the business with the Grim Reaper. I've seen nothing like it since the days of your Expressionists. And besides"—here I felt, all at once, the strain of my situation—"I found it inexpressibly moving."

"This is a bad film. Without acting. Without camera energy, only talking, talking, talking."

"Talking?" I repeated.

"Without strong! Without talent! Without action!"

"It is short on javelins, I suppose."

"Ja, craftless!"

"I did wonder about that: Why no javelins? The whole dashed thing is set in the Middle Ages. Surely, there ought to be spears!"

"I am now making a film in Spain."

"In Spain! How extraordinary. I had thought—"

"No, no, we shoot in the south of Germany."

"Spain is overrated."

"Ja, ja," she said, nodding, and her hair shimmered in undulating waves. "Ja, ja, ja!"

"Are they much for javelins in Spain?"

A familiar hand clamped itself onto my shoulder, I yielded to its tug, and the Directress was no longer by my side. For a moment longer I saw her blond hair gleaming; then she was gone.

"May I introduce you?" He indicated, without waiting for my assent to the introduction, an officer with the usual impossible name and the face of a genial butcher. The officer and I nodded to each other, cozily united in our complete lack of reciprocal interest. Krämer said something in German, to which the officer replied with a smirk and a wink. I awaited a translation, but none came.

As the officer continued in German, and as Krämer apparently found it impossible either to interrupt or to abandon him, I seized the moment and drifted to the door.

Stepping outside, I took a deep breath of the clear, cool night air and set about cutting a cigar.

"Got a light?" a voice asked.

It was the director's wife with a cigarette held to her lips. I flicked my lighter open. I was surprised that she smoked so openly in public. Ladies didn't usually do such things in the German Reich. And without even a cigarette holder!

"Did you enjoy the film?" she asked.

"Madam, I am at a loss for words. Your husband's film is like nothing I have seen. If you will forgive the hackneyed phrase, it is—in my humble estimation—a masterpiece."

"Yes," she said. "Another one. I'm so pleased."

Hers was a voice of ice.

"You don't agree?"

"Indeed, I do!" She held her cigarette to the small, trembling flame shielded by my hand. "Only, I have seen enough of masterpieces. If there were one less in the world, I shouldn't miss a thing."

"I say, you do speak excellent English!"

"And because I do, and because no one else here does, I can speak my mind. You must have been impressed by the Saint Vitus dance and by Death suddenly appearing there, and then also by Ulrich von Hutten's last visit to Paracelsus! How Paracelsus bluntly tells him of his fatal illness, and how composed the knight remains, how resolute!"

Oddly, I had no recollection of that scene at all. Could I, in fact, have dozed off after all? With eyes narrowed and the corners of her mouth drawn back into the tiniest of smiles, she blew smoke in my face. "Yes, meeting death, dancing with death, all that deathly business—Wilhelm is quite adept at it now."

"The German expertise in these matters is indeed unparalleled," I conceded.

"And how do we get out?"

"I beg your pardon?"

She stared at me with eyes wide open. I felt the curious glances of other guests. We were starting to draw attention.

"How do we get away from here?" she asked, not lowering her voice. "We cannot simply stay, we have to leave! How do we do it? My son must come too, he must get out too!"

"And your husband?"

"My husband"—she sucked almost greedily on her cigarette—"is here by accident, a string of misfortunes, but now he makes one film after another, and you're quite right, they're very good, these movies! But yes, when I ask him, he says he cannot stand it either, so I think we all must leave together, what do you suggest?"

"That you lower your voice. English is not so rare a language as all that."

"Do you think then"—she made a sweeping motion with her glowing cigarette—"that all these people would find it scandalous that we want to leave?"

"They might not take kindly to it. They strike me as rather tender souls."

And once again it lay on my shoulder, his scrawny, sticky hand. I had half a mind to say, "Stop touching me in that overfamiliar way," but instead I remarked: "By the by, this chap speaks excellent English."

"I know Kuno," she said. "Wilhelm and I have known him some time. It is to him that we owe our presence in the Reich and this wonderful premiere."

"Too much credit," he said. "Without me, you'd be exactly where you are now, only someone else would be standing where I am. We humble servants of the party are interchangeable."

"Kuno?" I asked. "But who is Kuno?"

Krämer eyed me, trying to discern whether I was serious, as I realized my gaffe.

"Ah, you mean Herr Krämer of course. Our mutual friend Kuno Krämer."

On his otherwise rather expressionless face flashed genuine hurt. But at this delicate juncture, G. W. Pabst himself appeared, placing a hand on his wife's shoulder, so that the four of us made a mirror image. I saw her give the hint of an involuntary shudder.

"It gives me much joy that you are here," Pabst said to me.

"A Pabst film! I had no choice."

He said something to his wife. She shook her head; he repeated it, and pulled her along, his arm firmly around her and with a pressure that could no longer be described as gentle.

She turned back to me. "You haven't answered my question!"

For the second time that night, I found myself the center of attention.

"'Nuns fret not at their pensive citadels, and hermits are contented with their rooms,'" I said, smiling weakly. "'And bumblebees inside their foxglove bells.' And . . . that's not exactly it, but—you know what I mean."

"I have no idea what you mean."

"'The prison into which we doom Ourselves no prison is.' In his films, your husband has more freedom than any director I know. And for you, dear Mrs. Pabst, this freedom must be a source of great happiness, pride, and consolation. But as for your question, I'm afraid I haven't the slightest idea."

She gave me a long look filled with disappointment. Then she let her husband lead her away.

The square in front of the ornate theater had emptied, only a few stragglers still emerged, and the rain flickered in the three uneven pillars of light.

Silently, we set off side by side, in harmonious step. Old houses arranged themselves around us, painted gables warding off the night, statues leaning from their niches, fountains burbling away, as fountains are wont to do.

"Could we stay? Here in Salzburg, I mean? Or, do you think you might put me up here for a little while?"

"We need you in Berlin. The next episode of your broadcast has to be ready in four days. And we prefer that you speak about this excellent film."

"About the dark German masterpiece that I just had the honor of seeing?"

"Something like that, yes."

"And this is just a suggestion? You wouldn't force me?"

He didn't answer—partly owing to his habit of remaining silent when the only possible answer was one he did not want to give, and partly owing to the three rough characters who had stepped out of the darkness as if they'd been lying in wait, which they hardly could have done, since we had chosen our path so aimlessly that no one could have known which of the many nocturnal squares they might have met us at; unless, of course, they had followed us.

Which indeed they had. For one of them, who distinguished himself from the other two by looking exactly like them, said . . .

A name, but it wasn't mine.

My guide posed a question, the fellow repeated the name. And he confirmed, yes, that was he, that was his name, he was Kuno Krämer. Then he turned to me and said: "This is a misunderstanding, it will be cleared up." He addressed the trio again, but they didn't impress one as being interested in what he had to say. Instead, two of them planted themselves beside him, and the third gestured somewhere and uttered something that might have been a command or perhaps just a cough.

"But this is quite the worst possible moment," I protested. "I'm rather at sea here, being alone. You must kindly arrange to do this at another time, when I'm back—"

"Please!" Krämer interjected. "Quiet!"

"But why you? What have *you* done, old boy?"

"I really don't know," I heard him say as the four of them vanished into the baroque darkness.

And then I was alone.

I slowly turned in a circle. Only a few windows were lit; the night sky was low and black. As the rain slowly but insistently ruined my silk hat, I set off in search of my hotel.

Molander

Pabst found himself at a complete loss. Why on earth had he agreed to shoot a third-rate whodunit? He could have declined!

Now, declining an idea from the ministry for a nonpolitical film was inherently not without its dangers—because then they might come back with an idea for a less nonpolitical film, which would be harder to decline, and suddenly you might end up like Kurt Heuser, who had refused once too often. Though Heuser had returned, he was clearly not the same as before; something had happened to him, and of course you couldn't ask him what they had done to him or what he had said to be released. When he had appeared at the premiere in Salzburg, Pabst had scarcely dared to say hello, and he spent their brief, forced conversation wondering what he might once have said in Heuser's presence that could hurt him now. It was, of course, possible that Heuser hadn't told them anything, that he had merely agreed to write a political film, but even that he couldn't have shared with Pabst, since for all he knew, Pabst might inform the Gestapo himself.

So Pabst had retreated to Dreiturm with a copy of *The Star Violin*. The weather wasn't as bad as usual, there was still a little snow on the fields, you could feel the onset of spring, sometimes it didn't rain for two days at a time, and the caretaker was so occupied with air raid duties in Tillmitsch, Muggenau, and Lebring, all of which had already been bombed, that he had no time to make Pabst's life difficult. Jakob had recently written from school to announce that the day had come at last: he had been called up.

Trude had stayed in Berlin, supposedly so that he could work in peace. He missed her, yet he welcomed the respite from her air of silent reproach. When he had told her which book he was going to adapt, first she had stared at him, then she had started to laugh, loudly, hysterically, until tears were streaming down her face.

Yes, she had shouted, she knew all of Karrasch's works, *Schmiedecke*, *Pennant*, *Krämer*, *Undes*, you name it, *The Star Violin* too! And when he had asked her whether the other books were just as insipid as this one, she had merely pointed to the living room wall—their way of reminding each other that the neighbors could hear. Karrasch, she had said, was a true Goethe, and a true Schiller besides! Then she had walked out, still laughing, and he had packed his suitcases for the castle.

There had to be a way. *The Joyless Street* had been a potboiler, and look what he had made of it! But back then he had been younger, freer, less burdened, everything had come easily to him, and now everything seemed difficult; he felt ossified, as if immured in his own habits.

A few months earlier he had seen his friend Käutner's new film in the editing studio: a gentle love story set among people living on barges in Berlin. Everything happened slowly and quietly; you would never have guessed that the filming had taken place during breaks between bombings, in the middle of a capital sinking into destruction. If you had good ideas and knew your trade, anything was possible.

But the ideas wouldn't come. He was supposed to start shooting soon; the hall in Barrandov Studios in Prague was reserved, the actors were cast, the crew was in place. All they needed was a script.

The novel was about the young musician Fritz, whose Stradivarius is swapped for a fake by a deceitful violin maker after his first big, triumphantly successful concert. In his almost unheard-of purity of heart, Fritz tries to sell his violin to pay for the wedding of his sister,

Elisabeth, whose nobility and kindheartedness are equally unheard of, to the likewise very noble and decent young prosecutor Holk. But since the violin is a fake, Fritz is arrested for fraud. Prosecutor Holk now wants to resign his post immediately to avoid any conflict of interest, whereupon Elisabeth preemptively breaks off their engagement. Holk's father, however, an old and experienced chief prosecutor, a man of sterling character, starts investigating and quickly solves the case, allowing the brilliant Fritz, reunited with his instrument, to forge ahead on the path to fame and Elisabeth to marry.

My God, Pabst wondered as he trudged through the wet meadows, what was one supposed to do with this crap?

"What a load of shit," he said to a cow lazily chewing its cud. It looked at him amiably, blinking its long eyelashes. "Such wretched trash, what should I do?"

He couldn't hire a cowriter either. He no longer trusted Kurt Heuser. Erich Kästner might have been available—even though his novels had been publicly burned in Berlin, he was allowed to write screenplays under a pseudonym—but first of all, according to the unwritten rules, a former emigrant could not work with a banned writer, and secondly, Kästner wasn't his kind of writer; with him, everything was dialogue, fast and witty, like onstage. Kästner would have been right for Lubitsch, not for him. All the other good writers had been arrested or had emigrated, leaving only the bad ones and the party members. And they were to be steered clear of, because he knew that any writer who was a party member would turn the two noble prosecutors into party members too; the temptation would be too strong. Nor could there be any objection to such a suggestion; once it was made, it had to go in. Moreover, something inscrutable had happened at the ministry. Kuno Krämer had been unreachable since the Salzburg premiere. There was no hope to be found in Wilzek either. Franz was a reliable man with solid filmmaking skills, but he needed instructions and had no ideas of his own; he would never become a real director. Having arrived in Dreiturm the previous week, Franz followed Pabst on his walks, took copious notes, listened respectfully, and complained only quietly about Liesl Jerzabek's inedible food. It was pleasant to have him there, but he wasn't any help.

Something inside Pabst had grown constricted. In his youth, all he had to do was listen inward, and images and stories would rise from the darkness. Now, when he listened, he felt as if he were locked in a small room with the shutters closed. Nothing came forth, no image formed, no voice spoke to him, there was nothing but worry about Jakob, who would be sent east any day now.

But didn't he have much more experience than before? He had made so many movies, set up so many scenes, directed so many cameras, given instructions to so many actors—all this he had over the young man he once was!

And it changed nothing.

Perhaps it simply wasn't possible. Not every piece of crap could be turned into gold; perhaps this trite tale of the violinist, his sister, and the two prosecutors was simply beyond saving!

Reportedly, the Swiss border was still permeable in a few places. Maybe they could still get out of the country before everything collapsed. If Trude, Jakob, and he made it to Zurich, he could direct at the Schauspielhaus there—he hadn't done theater in a long time, but he would manage. Trude would be immensely relieved; the shadow would lift. Maybe they would even be happy again.

In the middle of the night he woke up with a start.

He hadn't dreamed of Louise in a long time. Sometimes he went whole days without thinking of her. But suddenly she was back. She had stood so close to him that he could feel her body.

He closed his eyes and tried to recall what she had said. He sensed the contours of the words—they had just been within reach. He held his breath, only to realize his mistake: what he could almost grasp a moment earlier was fading, dwindling, gone.

He got out of bed. It was hardly imaginable that he had sat across from Louise in that coffee shop not so long ago, utterly inconceivable that there had really been a moment in his life when he had felt her lips on his—his memory held only fragments, a streak of light slanting through the window across her forehead, her short hair on the pillow, a small dark spot below her very white shoulder, and the moment her hands had closed behind his neck. He felt a sharp envy toward the person he had been in those moments—why had time continued to unspool, why had his heart kept beating, stupidly and stubbornly, until now?

He went to the window and looked out, shivering, at the meadow bathed in moonlight. In the distance he heard antiaircraft guns, but that was almost every night now; he'd grown used to it. He knew, of course, that Louise had not magically spoken to him. What had just appeared to him in her form was that part of himself made up entirely of desire and longing.

And there, as he looked out at the grass illuminated by the moonlight, he saw the violinist Fritz before him, a silhouette against blazing spotlights, hundreds of faces watching as he struggled, for his playing was effortful and only somewhat better than mediocre. The camera rose weightlessly, looking down on the crowd—this is precisely what all art speaks of: the world is longing. Human life is unfulfilled. The deepest expression of this is music.

That was why Fritz played, but he didn't play as well as he wanted. Just as the violin maker wanted to create a violin as good as those of the old masters but lacked the skill and out of defiance had to steal one. The girl Elisabeth wanted to be loved, but above all she desperately wanted to love someone, because she had been taught that this was the way it should be; but since there was no one, she had gotten engaged to a stiff prosecutor, who in turn wanted to be like his father, which he would never achieve, while his father did not want to become weak and decrepit, for he already felt his mind slackening and his body decaying. The music knew all this, and the camera knew it too, as it circled the characters in constant motion; it was a gaze from nowhere, from beyond time, on all this helpless, desperate striving. Pabst paced back and forth in the moonlit room. This was exactly what it had to be about—that music only seemed to speak of beauty, but in reality it spoke of how nothing was ever enough, how everything always fell short. How so much would never be ours.

He had turned on the light and was sitting at the table. He wrote with a pencil stub on an old envelope: REICH CHAMBER OF FILM BERLIN was marked as the sender. Without looking up, he wrote until the envelope was full on both sides, and because he knew that even the best ideas at night are forgotten if not preserved, he tore it open and continued writing on the inside. Only when he had no more space to write and not a piece of paper left did he put on his slippers and the silk dressing gown he had once bought in Paris, and went next door to wake his assistant.

Louise did not return. He had hoped to encounter her again in his dreams, but she did not oblige him. Instead, from time to time his mother appeared, reproached him, and told him long stories that had no purpose or meaning other than to take away the freedom that had come over him. But she didn't succeed, the doors now stood open: as soon as he was awake, images and ideas came to him, and early in the morning he sat again at the long table under the antlers, dictating the script to Franz, barely noticing when Liesl Jerzabek or her two daughters peeked in, curious and with undefined anger, for just like Erika they disapproved of the transformation he had undergone, preferring him depressed, weak, and abstracted.

Then the caretaker appeared, in a stained uniform, sweating and stooped and peering up at him subserviently, but because Pabst had just had the idea for a tracking shot through the remand prison where Fritz was locked up, from one door to the next, so that at each one, through the recessed barred window, the viewer could see for a second an inmate forsaken by God and humanity, he didn't look up as Jerzabek complained about the dirty swine who hid their livestock and belongings, who no longer feared the camp, no longer feared being shot, no longer feared the local group leader, but he would show them! Now came the last levy, the Volkssturm was rising, the young and the old and those who had previously been exempt—he slapped himself on the crooked shoulder—would lead Germany to victory. When Pabst finally looked up to reply, Jerzabek had long since shuffled away.

The cinematographer Willi Kuhle arrived on the day Pabst finished the script. He was a wraith who had just emerged from the ruins of Hamburg, where he had spent three days trapped in an underground shelter.

"To think I get to work with Pabst," he said, "the great Pabst! What luck, what great luck!" To express his enthusiasm, he slapped himself on the forehead a few times, causing a thin trickle of blood to run down between his eyes over the prominent root of his nose. Pabst and his assistant exchanged a worried glance. The days underground had taken their toll.

Pabst called the ministry. He was put through multiple times, from one office to the next, until a brusque man informed him that resources were currently scarce; all available cinematographers were working under high pressure on morale-boosting films, a large quantity of which would be needed to steel the people's resolve until the final victory. So regrettably, damaged or not, Pabst would have to make do with the people he had.

For what must have been the tenth time he asked whether he could speak with Kuno Krämer.

"He has been transferred," the voice said, "but we will notify him. If he has time, he will get in touch."

* * *

"So, Pabst," Paul Wegener called out boisterously as he stepped off the train, "what are we doing? I haven't seen a script yet! I'm here because of you, you know!"

"You can read it on the way."

"I don't have to read it. I've had it explained to me. Prosecutor solves case and arrests forger. That's all I need. Just have cue cards held up next to the camera, I'll recite the stuff. Read it, say it. The deep secret of my profession." Wegener let out a booming laugh. Then he said to Jerzabek, who stood there giving a German salute, "Put your paw down!"

"I'm surprised you didn't cast that moron Krauss again," he said, as the donkey slowly pulled their cart toward the castle. "Was the idiot not available?"

"You're the right one for the part," said Pabst, who had of course previously approached Werner Krauss.

"But you would say that no matter what."

"That doesn't make it untrue."

"I always say what I think," said Wegener. "That's why I wasn't as good a director as you. But I live better."

"Perhaps shorter too."

"Maybe, but I'm already seventy. They can only kill me once." He leaned forward and asked the caretaker, who was sitting hunched over in his party uniform, "Right?"

Jerzabek didn't respond.

"One contorts oneself thousands of times, but dies only once," Wegener said cheerfully. "It's simply not worth it."

"About your role," Pabst said softly. "I'd like you to play the prosecutor as a Nazi."

Wegener laughed.

"Determined, stubborn, old. The fact that he finds the forger doesn't make him right."

"Who's playing the forger?"

"You."

"Oh!"

"You're playing both roles."

"Why am I only hearing about this now?"

"Because I only thought of it yesterday. Two old men, almost indistinguishable—who cares who's on which side!"

"I see it differently, Pabst. It makes all the difference in the world which side one stands on. But if you're paying for two roles, why not, I'll play them both."

The evening before his departure, Pabst called Trude in Berlin. "Are you sure you don't want to come to Prague?"

"To watch you make Karrasch into a movie?"

"It won't have much to do with him, I promise."

"What about Jakob?"

"I don't know. No letters are getting through."

He listened to the receiver for a moment. A high-pitched hiss, and a distant deep electric creak. There was so much he wanted to say, and none of it could be spoken over the phone.

"The film," he said. "I know you don't believe it, but I'm going to make something of—"

"Yes, Wilhelm! I do believe it. You'll make another good film. Another masterpiece."

They fell silent. Antiaircraft guns could be heard in the distance.

"I love you," he finally said. He waited, but there was only silence, and then the connection was cut.

The journey to Prague, which just recently had taken four hours, now lasted three days. The train moved at a crawl and kept stopping to give way to military transports. Pabst sat by the window, the script on his lap, a pencil in his hand.

"What if Meyendorff plays the young Molander with a touch of madness?" he asked. "She could bite her nails, and every now and then her voice suddenly breaks!"

"That would be interesting," Wilzek said distractedly. He had just been telling Willi Kuhle about his childhood home in Döbling, his school days at the Schottengymnasium, and his parents, whom he missed a great deal. His father was a gardener. The most apolitical of professions; no one ever demanded that a gardener join a party. Then, for some reason, he spoke of his cousin Barbara, with whom he had once been very much in love, but she had married and now lived in Wels on the Traun, which seemed so important to him that he repeated it twice—probably he liked the sound of it: "She now lives in Wels on the Traun, married, in Wels on the Traun."

"If the renunciation of her fiancé does not come across as magnanimous but confused, excited, and self-satisfied," Pabst said, "only then will something interesting come of it, and the situation will gain its own authenticity."

"Can Meyendorff play that?"

"I'll teach her."

In Wiener Neustadt they were caught in a bombing raid. The squadron's target was probably Linz, but a few bombs were dropped too early. Suddenly their inn shook under a noise like nothing Pabst had ever heard before. Glasses jumped from the racks, books from the shelves, plates from the tables, and the air raid sirens could not drown out the thunder.

Just when Pabst truly thought he was going to die, it stopped. The sirens wailed a moment longer, then they too fell silent.

He opened the shutters and recoiled. The night was lit up as bright as day. The house next to them was ablaze, as was the one across the street. Whirling flames hissed, sparks fell like snow. He threw on his silk dressing gown, slipped into his shoes, and ran out of his room, along the corridor, down the stairs. On the bottom step, hunched over with his head in his hands, howling like a dog, sat a man.

"Calm down," said Pabst. "Herr Kuhle, pull yourself together. We've been lucky."

But Kuhle was beyond the reach of any words. Howls erupted from him, tremors seized him and would not stop. Pabst flung open the front door.

He felt the heavy wave of heat. The innkeeper was already outside. Behind Pabst, Wegener appeared in a fluttering nightshirt and with bare feet.

"Holy crap," he said. "What an unbelievable mess!"

Behind him came Franz, who had somehow managed to get fully dressed and even button up his vest. They stood side by side, hands over their faces, watching helplessly as people staggered out of one of the burning houses: a man and three women, two of whom were holding screaming infants.

The innkeeper crossed himself, declaring that without the Blessed Virgin, his inn too would have been destroyed, it was the rosaries his wife prayed daily! No one felt like contradicting. A single fire truck rolled up. From inside they could hear Willi Kuhle howling.

The train stopped for five hours outside Brünn. Clay-gray fields stretched around them. Several times, low-flying planes streaked through the sky; at first, everyone in the compartment threw themselves to the floor, by the fourth time they barely glanced out the window.

"A word about the camerawork," said Pabst. "We're going to be constantly jumping the line—intentionally!"

"I'm always scared in Prague," said Kuhle. "That the statues will come to life again."

"Again?"

"Yes," said Kuhle. "It has happened before." He scratched his head, looked around thoughtfully, and began to cry.

"Please focus. We used to jump the line in the twenties, and back then the audience wasn't bothered. I think if we do it deliberately now, it creates . . . What's the matter, Herr Kuhle? I beg you, pull yourself together!"

Kuhle obediently stopped crying and looked ahead seriously and sheepishly.

"For instance, during the big concert," said Pabst. "Fritz Molander, when he looks into the audience, glances past the camera to the right—but the audience, when it looks at Fritz, does the same!"

"When I was buried," said Kuhle.

Pabst waited, but he didn't continue.

"Well, what then?" asked Franz. "What happened there?"

"Happened where?"

"When you were buried."

"No air," said Kuhle.

"These are going to be difficult shoots," said Franz.

"It'll be fine," said Pabst. "When you're making movies, you're always in a bind. There are always problems, you always need a plan B and then a plan C. The important thing is not to lose your nerve."

Kuhle began to sing. He had a beautiful voice. It was an aria from *The Barber of Seville* and astonishingly he knew the libretto by heart. At that moment the train started moving again.

"The concert," said Pabst, but then he fell silent. In the distance a wall with barbed wire had appeared. Everyone turned their heads; Kuhle stopped singing. The wall was so long that it stood on the horizon for minutes. A narrow tower, on it the motionless silhouette of a man.

"The concert is the most important scene," Pabst said after a while. "It's right in the middle, but beforehand we see it in flash-forwards, afterward in flashbacks. I envision an oversized hall, we fill it with more people than a concert hall can possibly hold."

"But an overly large hall," asks Wilzek, "won't that look strange?"

"Only if the hall isn't big enough! One-third too big looks like a mistake, five times too big, that's style!"

Beyond a small town whose name they couldn't pronounce, they had to spend the night on the train. Tanks had blocked the tracks, the commander couldn't let them through; he himself didn't know why, but an order was an order. From a distance, where Brünn was, they could hear airplanes, artillery, and explosions.

That night his fear for Jakob kept him awake.

But if they had gone to England—who was to say they wouldn't have met their fate there, amid all the bombing raids? Had they stayed in France, they would now be just as much under German rule! If he were in the United States, Jakob would now be in the American army and equally in danger, perhaps in Europe, perhaps in the Pacific. The time was out of joint, everywhere, and you had to find a way to do your work.

At that moment the earth shook. A pulling sensation ran through their limbs, as if they were falling.

"Good Lord," said Franz. "Was that the wonder weapon?"

"Earthquake," said Wegener. "Those still happen. Or did you hear a bang? Sometimes when the earth shakes, it's not a bomb but an earthquake."

They waited in silence, but it did not occur again. As the sun rose, airplanes flew past. An hour later the tanks rolled aside; they had received orders to clear the tracks.

In Prague there was hardly any destruction. Which was why films were now being shot there: in the Protectorate, you could still work without being disturbed by air raids. There was even enough food to go around.

At the inn, a telegraph from Jakob was waiting for him: he was very proud; tomorrow he would join the tanks, then head to the eastern front.

In hall seven of Barrandov Studios the prop master had built the apartment of the Kestner family, now called Molander in Pabst's version. A bourgeois living room had been constructed, the girl's bedroom, a chamber where the young violinist practiced his instrument under the picture of his stern father. Everything was excellently crafted, believable down to the smallest detail.

"Tear it down," said Pabst.

It happened faster than he'd ever experienced: the modifications were carried out by over a hundred French prisoners of war, who were friendly and compliant, all happy to be assigned to light work. Pabst had the walls put at a slant and the paintings redone: above the dining table hung a withered steppe with tree skeletons looming like corpses, and the deceased father in the painting turned into a gnome of malice. The dining table itself had to be slanted and had only three legs; the surrounding chairs were all too high, forcing those seated to lean forward to reach their plates.

"No one really does this sort of thing anymore," said the set designer. "Twenty-five years ago, they did this sort of thing!"

"I know," said Pabst. "I was there."

He had the shadows of the family seated at the table painted: sharp, elongated, and with thin limbs, they stretched across the floor and up the slanted wall. "If the actors sit still and only move their mouths, no one will see that the shadows are painted on! And at the empty place at the head of the table, we'll paint the father's shadow!"

On the other side of the hall he had the prison built: slanted walls here too, and behind each window, only a brick wall. Through barred holes in the doors, you could see the crouching prisoners, which he had the craftsmen of the Prague puppet theater make out of papier-mâché—distorted grimaces, some laughing, some dozing in half sleep, others with their eyes wide open.

He asked Elisabeth Markus to speak as Mother Molander with a brittle voice, "a broken woman, dissatisfied to the core, filled with hatred for life, even for her own daughter."

"But that's terrible!" she said. "I don't want to do that."

"That's why you got the part," said Pabst, who had found her name on the ministry's casting list and had never heard of her before. "That's why I insisted on your involvement! Because you can do it, because no one else can! I implore you, grant me, grant us all your gift!"

As always, he spoke differently with each actor. To one he gave commands; with another he pleaded; to a third he gave explanations in a dryly serious tone; with another he laughed until they could no longer stand upright and fell into each other's arms. To Werner Hinz, who played the young prosecutor, he spoke in the tone of a strict father; to Irene von Meyendorff he whispered that Elisabeth was actually mentally ill, on the verge of collapse, consumed by a despair she herself could not comprehend, but no one must know. And to Wegener he said: "Don't act at all, just speak the lines."

"But don't you find it strange, Pabst, that we're making a movie like this in the middle of the apocalypse? Such a . . . work of art?"

"You say that as if it's a bad thing."

"More like a strange thing."

"Times are always strange. Art is always out of place. Always unnecessary when it's made. And later, when you look back, it's the only thing that mattered."

Pabst wrote down instructions for the actors. Small slips of paper told them how to act out the next scene: *She's lying* was the instruction for Irene von Meyendorff, who had to explain to the old prosecutor why she could no longer marry his son. *He believes every word* was written on Wegener's note. In the next shot, after the lighting had been reset and the camera repositioned, her note read: *She's telling the truth*, and his: *He believes nothing*.

Wegener nodded with a smile. Irene von Meyendorff looked at Pabst in confusion.

"I know," he said. "It's contradictory. Just do it."

Because Willi Kuhle was barely responsive anymore, Pabst and his assistant operated the camera themselves, one taking over for the other. It worked better than expected and shortened the shooting time.

Pabst had lost weight. He was poorly shaved, and a crack ran across the right lens of his glasses. Everyone noticed that he always wore the same suit; there was a joke going around that he probably slept in it too.

Werner Hinz was stiff and wooden and very conscious of his appearance: he stood in front of reflective surfaces for a conspicuously long time and after saying a sentence, he seemed to listen to his own voice, concerned with its effect and sound. While delivering his lines, he ran his fingers with pleasure through his full hair.

Pabst spoke softly to him. He stood leaning forward next to him, one hand on Hinz's back, his lips near the actor's ear, and he spoke with such concentration that it seemed he wanted to hypnotize him.

On the next attempt, Hinz was less wooden, but he remained stiff and superficial.

Pabst stopped filming and took him outside the hall. They sat smoking on the grass. Everyone was waiting, but the two seemed in no hurry. Hinz smoked and listened, while Pabst spoke.

The day passed. In the evening, everyone went home, and Pabst canceled the next day of shooting. This was possible only because the production manager, a scrawny and serious man named Hänel, was bedridden with the flu.

On their day off, Pabst and Hinz strolled along the Old Town Square. Most of the time, Pabst spoke and Hinz listened. At times, the actor also talked. He gesticulated with both hands and looked very serious, while Pabst nodded thoughtfully, seeming to give him his full attention. They stood on the Charles Bridge: the Moldau flowed dark and slow, boats occasionally drifted by, and the windows sparkled in the sun.

As evening fell, they wandered into a tavern. Pabst ordered beer and soup, and they ate and drank until the evening curfew forced them back to the inn, where they said goodbye with a long embrace. They were now on a first-name basis.

The next morning Hinz delivered his lines as if for the first time. He spoke as if each word came to him the second he said it; he spoke as if he weren't an actor but actually a prosecutor among colleagues, slightly distracted, friendly, without any pretense. He spoke softly and seriously, as one does to another person in a small room, personal and sincere.

In hall seven the concert hall was built: a stage and twenty-five rows of chairs. Since that wasn't enough for him, however, Pabst had sections of the walls covered with mirrors, set at an angle to each other, just as Lang had done in *Metropolis*.

"You're already way over budget," said the production manager Hänel, who had just recovered from his flu.

"I have the full backing of the Minister."

"This is supposed to be a whodunit. A small, exciting film for a million reichsmarks. What you're doing—"

"Dear Hänel! Think about it! The Minister called me the most important representative of German filmmaking."

"Where did he say that? That's Harlan."

"When this war is won, dear Herr Hänel, and you know it will be soon . . . or don't you?"

Hänel straightened up as if someone had ordered him to salute. "Of course."

"So, when this war is won—soon, very soon—people will ask what cultural achievements the Reich has made in the meantime, and they'll ask who supported those achievements and who stood in their way."

"But Herr Pabst—"

"I'm just making a point!"

"But a budget beyond a million is simply not—"

"Hänel, it's war, it's chaos, we have to help each other, everyone improvises as best they can, flexibility is the watchword! Should we be on a first-name basis? I'm Wilhelm."

"Adolf."

Pabst hesitated for a second. "Dear . . . Adolf, flexible and united toward victory, that's the motto, and if the budget has to be increased, I know it will happen. And I know that because I trust Germany!"

"Yes, but who exactly is 'Germany,' if—"

"We all are! Together! Now, go talk to the people at Prague Film, Adolf. There's surely a special fund for war-related expenses, there always is. Usually, Ufa gets the money, but not this time! You can make it happen!"

"The special fund is for morale-boosting films!"

"If there ever was one, *The Molander Case* is a morale-boosting film!"

While Hänel worked to secure money from the special fund, Franz set up the lighting. Everything was meticulously planned, nothing could go wrong: 750 extras would fill the hall for a day. Since all of them had to wear elegant evening attire, the city's costume rental shops had been cleared out and fourteen tailors had been brought in to fit the costumes. Hänel had arranged for four Wehrmacht companies. The women had been harder to organize; they had gotten only thirty antiaircraft auxiliaries, forty cleaning assistants, and ten radio operators. To keep the excess number of men from standing out, the women would have to be placed at the front, and some men disguised as women would have to sit far in the back—thirty-seven wigs in different hair colors had been obtained for this purpose. They would have to work very quickly and precisely; both the extras and the large hall were available for only a day. After that, Barrandov Studios would be used to film a major Ufa comedy with a budget of two million, directed by Liebeneiner, who was so influential that there was no chance of delaying his production.

The next day there was one of the rare air raids: first the alarm wailed, then the antiaircraft guns could be heard, then an apartment building on the Lesser Town side went up in gray smoke, and quite a while later a hail of small stones pelted the surrounding streets.

In the studio, where Pabst was filming the fingers of the violinist Jan Worzack playing on the strings, none of this was noticed. Pabst stood on a scaffolding above the concert stage; the camera was pointed straight down at the violinist's hands so that only the fingers and the violin and a piece of the floor could be seen. It was important that Worzack played well, but not perfectly. To the majority of the audience he had to sound like a virtuoso, but those who really knew something about it should recognize the truth.

When Pabst and Wilzek stepped out of the studio at noon, Hänel came toward them. "Good news and bad news. They have retroactively approved our existing budget overruns. Two hundred and four thousand reichsmarks. It must not go any higher, but we're balanced."

"I knew it!" exclaimed Pabst. "And what's the bad news?"

"They're not coming."

"Who?"

"Apparently because of the air raid. There have been new orders. And a misunderstanding with the army group leadership. They had agreed to help us . . . But Colonel Wintrich has been relieved of his command. There's nothing I can do!"

Pabst grabbed Hänel by the lapel. He had never done that to anyone before. It was a gesture so silly and hackneyed that he would never have let an actor get away with it.

"Talk!" he shouted—and out of habit he thought: This isn't good dialogue. "Talk, Hänel! What happened?"

"They're not coming, Herr Pabst. Let go of me."

Both men had forgotten that they were on a first-name basis.

"Who's not coming?"

"Let go, or I'll break your nose. I used to be a boxer in the regiment."

Pabst let go of Hänel.

"They've been called up for duty, the soldiers, but also the antiaircraft auxiliaries and the radio operators. Only the cleaning women are left." He straightened his rumpled collar. "But there aren't many of them."

Franz and Hänel looked at Pabst. They waited.

Pabst remained silent. He slowly took off his glasses and turned them between his fingers.

Some time passed. Pabst still said nothing. He stood hunched forward, shoulders drooping, and turned the glasses between his fingers. It bothered Franz that he kept touching the lenses.

When he still hadn't spoken after a while, Franz asked, "We'll manage, right? When you're making a movie, you're always in a bind!"

"Yes," said Hänel. "That's what you always say. 'Don't worry,' you say, 'we'll manage.'"

"We can't shoot the concert later," Pabst said softly. "We only have three days left, then we won't have the studio anymore, and the actors' contracts will expire. We can't reshoot. We can't shoot in front of an empty auditorium either. And we can't make do without the concert. The film would make no sense."

"Then we just show the violinist," Franz suggested. "And the audience in the front row. That's how it's often done."

"That would ruin the film."

"Well," said Hänel, "there's no other way. Like you said, we can't just collect eight hundred extras off the street."

"No," said Pabst. "Not off the street."

They both looked at him questioningly.

"Not off the street," Pabst repeated. Then he slowly put his glasses on. He had to squint, because the lenses were covered with fingerprints. He took the glasses off again and looked Hänel in the face; Hänel too was squinting now and took a step back, confused, bewildered, gradually comprehending.

"We can wait one day," Pabst said. "But the day after tomorrow we have to shoot."

"But you know . . . " said Hänel. "I mean, you know . . . I could do it. But . . . you know, if I—"

"I know that we have to shoot."

"I'd have to appeal directly to the Reich Protector's office . . . "

"That's your responsibility. Where you make appeals, what you discuss with whom—that's your job. My job is to shoot the day after tomorrow."

"I don't understand," said Franz.

"I think I do," said Hänel. "But I need to be sure if you really—"

"*I* need to be sure," said Pabst, "that I can do my work!"

"So first I'll call the Reich Protector's office, and then of course I'll need the help—"

"Spare me the details, and don't waste my time!" Pabst brusquely turned away, opened the steel studio door, went inside, and let it slam shut.

"I think," said Franz, "I'm a little slow on the uptake right now."

"Yes," said Hänel, "you are." He had turned pale, muttered that he had to make a phone call, and left.

Franz stood for a while with his head bowed, watching the small blades of grass that had grown through the cracks in the asphalt tremble in the wind. It occurred to him that he could go to the station and take the next train to Vienna. That wasn't forbidden. It would probably have consequences—his exemption from the military would be revoked, and he would be sent to France or even Russia. But he could do it.

Then he sighed, marveling at his own thoughts, and followed Pabst into the studio, where they continued to shoot footage of the violinist's fingers.

That night Franz Wilzek slept little. He was weighed down by an oppressive feeling he couldn't name. In the morning he felt dizzy and run-down. He took the tram to the studio, rubbing his aching head and squinting gloomily at the glittering reflections of the sun on the Moldau, which now seemed harsh and intrusive to him.

First he had to film details of the concert hall: a columned portal from which a tiny piece of marble had been chipped off, the velvet covering on a box balustrade, the glint of a doorknob, all crafted from cardboard. Then it was time for close-ups of the main characters at the concert: the mother, the sister, and her fiancé, listening intently to the music. They did well and looked attentive and moved; no one ever would have guessed that they weren't hearing a violin playing but the sawing and hammering of the workers assembling the last missing pieces of the set.

"No," said Pabst. "That's boring. No one wants to see actors at work." He thought for a moment, then said to Hinz: "Laugh!"

Hinz did so, laughing into the lens hovering just centimeters from his face. He laughed cheerfully and enthusiastically, because by now he did anything Pabst wanted without hesitation.

"Pull the corners of your mouth back," said Pabst. "Bare your teeth. As if you're about to bite."

Hinz did so, and Pabst brought the camera even closer to his face. Then he filmed Meyendorff, who had to bite her lip as if in anger, again and again until there was blood. Finally, he had Elisabeth Markus squeeze her eyes shut as if something terrible was threatening her.

"What's all that for?" asked Franz.

"We'll use the shots where they're smiling. We'll splice in the other ones for half a second each."

"But then people won't even notice them."

"Yes, they will, but they won't be sure. They won't know that they noticed them."

When they stepped outside at noon, soldiers had marched up in the parking lot. The men were smoking, laughing, eating, sitting on the ground, and waiting for something.

"What are they doing?" asked Franz.

"I don't know. We can't attend to everything."

In the afternoon, the concert hall had to be finished. The last mirrors were mounted, the last chairs were covered with felt, which would look like velvet on camera, and ten painters applied marble veining to the floor.

From outside they occasionally heard shots. The bored soldiers were trying their hand at target shooting.

"But what do they want?" asked Franz.

"You really are too easily distracted. My God, it's war, soldiers turn up all the time, what does it matter to us!"

Franz was about to ask another question, but a strange numbness filled him. Silent and thoughtless, he knelt, completely focused on taping down a piece of electrical wire under the floor covering. That much, at least, he could do, and so he didn't call one of the many workers over, but did it himself because there was nothing like having a task.

Only when they got into the car that was supposed to take them back to the inn did he ask again: "Do you really think we can shoot tomorrow?"

The large entrance gates had just been pulled open, and two open troop carriers filled with soldiers drove in.

"I'm Wilhelm," said Pabst.

Franz looked at him in bewilderment.

"If it's all right with you, we can use first names. You've always been a good student. An acolyte I could trust. A good assistant."

Franz looked in confusion at the back of the Czech chauffeur's head. The man had patches of gray hair, dandruff on his shoulders. On the rearview mirror a small cross swung on a string of pearls. Why was everything so unreal? And yet he knew that he had just received a great honor.

"A great honor," he said hoarsely.

"Not at all," said Pabst.

They shook hands. Franz noticed how exhausted Pabst looked: his cheeks were sunken, there were deep circles under his eyes. Franz wanted to ask whether he was ill, but then he was once again overcome by such confusion that for a moment he felt as if he weren't there but back home, on his way somewhere in Vienna. Three, four, five, seven, nine, ten, eleven, twelve, and even more large trucks drove past in the opposite direction. Franz turned his head, wanting to follow them, but couldn't because the convoy still hadn't passed.

A moment later he found himself in his hotel room without knowing how he got there. He sat on the edge of the bed and thought about something he couldn't put into words.

There was a knock at the door.

He had met Daša a month earlier at the inn where she worked as a waitress. The next evening he had come back, and the one after that too. He'd never had much confidence with women, but her simple friendliness and the fact that she had a long nose and a very thin chin, which most wouldn't have considered pretty, had given him courage. He had told her about his life, and it had impressed her that he worked for Pabst, because she had seen *Pandora's Box*. "Louise Brooks," she had exclaimed in her strong accent, "my God, what a beautiful woman!" The following week she had visited him in the hotel at night despite the curfew. They couldn't go to her place, because she still lived with her parents.

But this time Franz was just confused. She sat on the edge of the bed, brushed back her long hair, and tried to cheer him up with stories from the inn, where of course no one could know she was meeting with a German.

With a compassionate smile she took off her blouse; he ran his hand over her forehead before they slipped under the blanket, but his mind was elsewhere and his spirit felt numb. She kissed him on the cheek and said it didn't matter, then fell asleep while he lay in the darkness, listening to her breathing and thinking about the train to Vienna that was departing in a few hours; it was still possible to leave everything behind. But then, when it seemed to him he was up and on the way to the station in the pale morning light with a suitcase that was much too heavy, he had in reality fallen asleep and it was only a dream.

When he woke up, Daša was long gone, for her parents mustn't suspect anything. It felt like a dream that she had been there, and like a dream again when he sat next to Pabst in the same car as the day before, in the same seat, and behind the same driver. They didn't speak a word. Pabst had his arms crossed over his chest, didn't look at him, and was more distant and brusque than Franz had seen him since the start of the shoot.

Ten minutes before reaching Barrandov, they passed the field-gray trucks parked in a long row on the roadside. Again Franz couldn't manage to count them; something about them blurred, as if they didn't quite belong in the world of things. The gates stood open, an armored vehicle with a machine gun blocking the entrance. As they approached, it rolled aside to let their car in. Behind them came the two buses that always brought the actors and crew in the morning.

In the courtyard stood soldiers—mostly Wehrmacht, but among them were some with the double jagged rune of the SS. Franz wanted to ask a question, but his throat had constricted, and all he could think about was that he had missed the moment when he still could have taken the train.

They got out and crossed the courtyard in silence. Franz realized that he didn't want to know what he knew, so much so that his thoughts had ceased. Where he usually talked to himself in his head, there was only a dull silence. Silently, he walked through the line of guards to the door of the hall, someone opened it, and he entered without a word.

The extras were there.

They sat motionless, row after row, multiplied by the mirrors so that they seemed innumerable. They were gaunt, their faces emaciated, a heavy smell hung over them, but they wore their costumes, even though the collars were too wide and the jackets baggy. Franz closed the car door behind him and walked silently through the line of guards, silently followed by Pabst, toward the studio door, wondering whether he had actually already been inside just then, whether he could really have already seen what he knew he was about to see. Someone opened the door for him; he stepped inside.

There they were, motionless because they had been ordered to be, silent because they were not allowed to speak, row after row, some there in the room and some beyond the mirrors, trying to sit upright because they had to, but many could not, and some were coughing, which they were not allowed to do but could not suppress either. The smell was terrible. Franz involuntarily stepped back, closed the car door, walked toward the studio through the line of guards, but he knew that he was actually already inside; time had become tangled like a film reel so that, as he was still walking toward the door, he was also already inside staring at Pabst, finding no words and nothing to reply when Pabst, pale-faced, gave him the instruction to film from the stage down, from the musician's perspective: the long-prepared, most important shot of the film.

What surprised Franz most was that they were already in costumes. The work must have gone on all night with immense efficiency, but where were the tailors who had fitted the clothing? Now Franz found himself on the stage, where the camera was already set up. A command rang out from somewhere, and the soldiers who had been standing at the edge of the hall ducked down and disappeared behind the cardboard walls simulating heavy marble; only from up there were they still visible, on the scaffolding among the spotlights.

Through the viewfinder there was only a hall full of spectators staring forward, sitting as if spellbound, not moving, because a voice shouted through a megaphone, "Stare, spellbound, don't move!"

Then he realized that he wasn't behind the camera after all; he was at the side of the room next to Pabst, and the voice shouting "Stare, don't move!" was coming from the other side, or was it from above, where the spotlights were hanging? At last Franz managed to speak, his voice hoarse. "No!" he blurted out. "This can't be. It can't be! Wilhelm, this just can't be!"

Pabst looked at him. The beams of the spotlights were reflected in his glasses.

"No one," he said softly. "Not a single person. Will be harmed because of us. No one has been . . . The film must be finished."

Franz shook his head. He wanted to reply, explain, say something, but all he could muster was the word: "No!" And again: "No!" And: "Not this."

"What do you mean?" asked the set designer Ladinger, a broad and friendly man Franz had always liked. Pabst, on the other hand, couldn't have heard him, since he was standing elsewhere, on the other side of the hall, talking to the chief lighting technician. The gaffer shook his head, just as Franz had done a moment earlier but as Pabst continued to speak, he said something into a telephone receiver. Immediately, the light changed its temperature, the gold around the chandelier gleaming even more golden.

"What do I mean?" said Franz. He pointed to the full rows and the surrounding soldiers.

"Why?" asked Ladinger.

Franz didn't know what to respond, what he could say out loud; he didn't know whether it was possible that Ladinger truly didn't understand him—but it seemed so, because when Franz said nothing, the set designer shrugged and turned his attention in complete indifference to taping up a tear in a cardboard wall.

And Franz himself, before he knew it, found himself back on the concert stage behind the camera, ready to film the frontal view of the audience. Pabst was nowhere to be seen, but he remembered what he had just said to him in the gently hypnotic tone Franz had heard him use with actors: "All this madness, Franz, this diabolical madness, gives us the chance to make a great film. Without us, everything would be the same, no one would be saved, no one would be better off. And the film wouldn't exist."

Franz looked through the viewfinder: an old man with shrewd, piercing eyes, next to him a woman of indeterminate age wearing a silk headscarf, probably to cover a shaved head. Here too the costume people had done what was necessary; all the women wore scarves or hats, and a few wore wigs. As ordered, they looked toward the camera, which meant they all saw him, Franz, standing there and knowing what he was doing: as he saw them, they saw him, and so he found himself the next moment stepping out of the car again and walking toward the metal studio door, through the line of guards, not yet knowing what he knew, and the hope rose in him that he had merely lost his mind, but a second later he found himself inside again, rolling the camera along with three workers down the center aisle between the rows of chairs.

"To the front, only to the front!" commanded the voice through the megaphone, "no one stare into the lens," and they all adhered to it, which extras otherwise never did the first time, and just as they had planned, the camera now rotated around its axis, angled upward to the crystal chandelier and then back downward to the stage, where the actor Robert Tessen pretended to play the violin, which he didn't quite manage, apparently having for the moment completely forgotten the violin lessons he had been given for weeks, and because Franz saw that there was no one else, he himself called out: "Please stand up straight, remember, you don't actually have to play, don't listen to yourself, it doesn't need to sound good, only the movements have to be right," and he was surprised to notice that Tessen listened to him and immediately improved.

Then came the next shot: the violin-playing actor from behind, in front of him the hall blurring into the distance. Very slowly, as if the music made it weightless, the camera rose—just as Pabst had imagined in the bedroom in Dreiturm. They stood on a hydraulic lift, and up it went, and higher, and just as the camera did not quite focus on the people in the hall, but kept the focus on the back of the actor's head, so too did Franz's eyes not focus.

There was no time for a lunch break. This pace was possible only because everything had been meticulously planned, because Pabst had mastered his craft so well, and because none of the extras ever went outside or asked for water or food. They now took a wide shot of Irene von Meyendorff, Werner Hinz, and Elisabeth Markus sitting at the edge of the first row. All three looked spellbound and enthusiastic, for they were actors and knew how to do that, and one would have had to look very closely to realize how heavily it weighed on the young actress that a pale man in a tuxedo that was too wide was sitting next to her, so close that his elbow touched hers. When they had finished, Pabst called out: "Markus, Meyendorff, Hinz, that's a wrap, you're done, have a safe journey home!" Normally, as always when actors finished their roles, there would have been applause. But not this time.

Then the most complicated shot. The tracking shot began on the concert stage, moved down into the hall, past the rows of seats on the right side, and then up. The camera was on a platform on the long arm of a crane, and as it rose, it turned back to the stage, where Tessen receded farther and farther into the distance, because the cameraman, who of course had to be Franz because Pabst was afraid of heights, continuously shortened the focal length. It was very difficult to execute, and the first attempt was unsuccessful: Franz missed the focus, and Tessen blurred.

"Again!" shouted Pabst, now among the soldiers on the scaffolding. Next to him were Hänel and the set designer Ladinger. Franz had enough time to observe them standing there awkwardly, not exchanging a word, because it took a while for the crane to lower again.

On the second attempt, it worked, the turn was achieved without the camera shaking, and Franz kept the focus sharp: the maneuver had been so difficult that he felt a brief surge of pride. Not everyone could do that, he thought against his will; no, almost no one could.

The next time, it failed because Franz couldn't get the violinist in focus, but the fourth attempt was successful again. As Franz was slowly lowered to the ground, he saw his former pediatrician.

Dr. Sämann was sitting in the middle of the fifth row, looking just like a normal concertgoer. He had always come in the early afternoon, back home in Vienna, after his consultation hours, making house calls between two and four—what could have brought him to Bohemia?

Franz stepped off the platform and stood there feebly. Dr. Sämann turned his head. He had recognized Franz long ago. He smiled as he had once done when he stood by Franz's bed and placed his cool hand on his forehead. With feigned bafflement he shrugged.

Franz opened his mouth. He wanted to speak, to shout something, but he was not allowed, and indeed Dr. Sämann shook his head as if it were up to him to calm Franz down. Then it was all over.

Colors emerged, shapes came together, Franz had been in a garden, and his grandmother had asked him something. But before he could answer, he was looking at faces and took a while to recognize them: Hänel, Ladinger, now Pabst too.

Someone helped him up. There was Dr. Sämann, looking at him in a way that could almost have been called pitying, and it was too much, Franz could take no more. He went to the door, the soldiers stepped aside, he pushed it open and staggered into the light.

He stood outside, breathing heavily. He felt dizzy. The surrounding soldiers smirked. The door opened; he heard someone come out. He didn't have to turn around to know who it was.

"We don't have to do it again," said Pabst. "We have what we need. It's understandable to feel sick when you're spun around in the air like that."

Franz slowly sat down on the wildly swaying ground.

"I can take care of the rest without you," said Pabst. "Go lie down." Then he was gone.

Franz propped his head in his hands and didn't move.

"You movie bastards are all the same," said a soldier. He had a mustache and small eyes set at an angle.

"The brave little tailors," said another. He looked like a child, no older than sixteen. "The ones who had to fit the costumes. They fell over, they puked, they wanted to run away."

"They tried, the Czech scum," said a third. "They didn't get far."

"Who gives a shit," the first one said. "Where they come from, they get luxury treatment anyway. They could be doing worse."

They all laughed.

Franz stood up slowly. With unsteady steps he walked to the first of the two waiting cars. When he got in and said, "Drive!" the driver actually started the engine. The gates opened, and they drove along the long line of gray trucks, which still couldn't be counted, but after a while they had passed, and it seemed to Franz that he would soon be able to breathe again.

He closed his eyes. "Last day of shooting! Tomorrow Liebeneiner will be here already. You have to adapt to the . . . Those who make movies are always in a . . . But I don't have to go back. Last day of shooting!"

Always a good student, Pabst had said. An acolyte he could trust. For some reason Franz thought of Paul Wegener. Lucky that he was already back in Hamburg and hadn't had to witness this.

"Lucky!" Franz murmured, opened his eyes, and was standing in the forecourt of the studio, surrounded by grinning soldiers, and for some reason the air smelled of gasoline. He was hardly surprised. He hadn't expected it to be easy to get away from there. He walked to the first of the two cars, sat down in it, and said: "Drive!"

The driver obeyed, but this time it took longer for the gate to open. Two men in uniform peered through the open windows and asked to see his ID and the driver's; they also opened the trunk to make sure no one was hiding inside. Only then were they allowed to leave. Franz kept his eyes closed until they stopped in front of the inn.

He fell onto the bed. He lay motionless, not sleeping, while the sky in the window turned first gray and then black.

At some point, Daša knocked. As he sat up and went to the door, he wondered how to tell her that he needed to be alone now. But when he opened it, she backed away, looked him in the face, and asked: "What happened?"

He didn't answer. She said that she would come another time, gestured quickly with her hand that he shouldn't follow her, and hurried away.

By the time Franz looked for her three days later, she was no longer working at the inn where they had met. Only then did he realize that she had never told him her last name.

He hadn't had time for it before, but now Pabst took long walks—preferably after dark, when the city was so empty that you thought it had been built just for you. And because his imagination, after so many decades, could function no other way, he envisioned films: a crime of passion on the great bridge, a golem rising from a deep cellar, the fiery sign on its forehead, a strange star in the sky heralding the arrival of a new era of deceit, the execution of noblemen on the great square before a mob crying for blood, the old Kaiser Rudolf, half-mad in his cabinet of curiosities, with a long beard and flickering eyes. They would have been somewhat old-fashioned, these films, but the city of Prague conjured such images of its own accord.

The Molander Case, on the other hand, would be sparklingly modern. The war would be over in a few weeks, and then the world would marvel at his work: his position among the foremost directors would be reestablished, and if he were to make movies in America, they could no longer impose any script or bad actors on him, and no producer would deny him the right to edit his own film.

Now all he had left was to succeed in the cutting room.

He noticed things he hadn't planned. Mother Molander held her head and hands in a way that reminded him of the late Erika, although he had never instructed Elisabeth Markus to do so! During the scenes between the two prosecutors, he observed Paul Wegener placing his hand on his son's head in a manner at once lovingly paternal and anxious, reminding him of how he had often stood before Jakob—and Werner Hinz, in turn, looked at his father with a gaze—childlike, yet sharp, scrutinizing, and concealing anger—that reminded him of his own son's gaze, and indeed he saw Wegener recoil the next moment as if overcome by a strange timidity, half guilt and half concern; and this reminded him that he still had no news of Jakob. In a scene where Irene von Meyendorff walked down a gravel path between her brother and her fiancé, holding hands with one and arm in arm with the other, for some reason no image of familial love emerged. Meyendorff's eyes darted excitedly between the two, but it was her brother she looked at with passion and her fiancé with sisterly gentleness, and when Robert Tessen briefly and mockingly returned her gaze, Pabst felt a chill—it reminded him of his own situation between a woman he loved with calm affection and one he desired with all his might. How had all this found its way into the movie?

Next to the studio halls was the film laboratory; on the second floor were the editing rooms. In one of them there was a telephone. He called Trude. Normally you couldn't get a connection, but this time it worked on the first try.

"No word of Jakob," he said.

They were silent for a moment, because with that the most important thing had been said, and everything else seemed trivial.

"You wanted to write plays," he suddenly said. "In the past."

"I wanted all sorts of things. I also wanted to be an actress. That was before I married you. You said, not in your movies!"

He nodded. There had been good reasons for that. He could no longer remember them all.

"Do you remember my play about the cave explorer, *Mysterious Depths?*"

"Of course!" He had no idea what she was talking about.

"He loves this woman, but he has to go down again, and she can't come with him. Reinhardt said it could be staged, but it would be better as a film. The deep caves, he said. Well lit, it could be something never seen before. But it shouldn't be built in a studio, he said, it needs real caves."

"The front is getting closer. I have to leave here, but I have to finish editing the film first. It will be my best."

She remained silent.

"I've been summoned to the conscription office for an examination."

"God."

"I would, of course, like to serve!" he exclaimed, to preempt her. Unthinkable if she now said something wrong. "It would be an honor for me to . . . But the ministry has made sure that I'll be deferred. Don't worry!"

"Yes, but if you—"

He waited, but again he heard nothing, and then the connection was cut once more. When he tried again, all he heard was a deep rattle, a whistle, then echoing silence.

Two or three times a day the power went out: the screens went dark, the reels froze, and all they could do was go outside and smoke. In the cutting room this was of course unthinkable; the slightest spark could ignite the nitrate film.

While they waited, they spoke little, but as soon as the power returned, they worked even better together than before. "Back," said Pabst. "When he looks there, see, we need a shot of the window as a transition to the reverse shot, do we have something?"

But before Franz could make a suggestion, a small bald man flung open the door and shouted something in a foreign language.

"German?" Pabst asked, perplexed. "French?"

The man shouted again, and only then did Pabst realize who it was. He had indeed met him once, at the premiere in Salzburg. And the shout had simply been his name.

"Herr Karrasch! What are you doing here?"

"Heil Hitler. Seeing my film."

For a moment Pabst was at a loss. He had to remind himself that there was a novel, which this poor man had written.

"Later, gladly. We're just editing now."

"I will take this to the party!"

"But why?"

"Karrasch is a distinguished, multiple award–winning member of the Reich Chamber of Literature. The Führer has praised my *Schmiedecke.*"

"Certainly."

"Karrasch was not invited to the filming, where he could have been of much use. But now Karrasch is here and demands to see his film."

"It will be an honor, but—"

"Alfred Karrasch will take this to the party and the chamber because he will not tolerate his work not being shown to him!" The small man had bared his teeth, and his eyes hung huge and moist, like little dirty moons, in his glasses.

Pabst pushed a stool toward him and said in his gentlest voice: "Please sit down, dear Herr Karrasch. No one intended—"

"You address me as Herr Doktor Karrasch! Why is there no cutter here? I have been involved in film before, isn't there always one in the editing room?"

Pabst and his assistant exchanged a quick glance. Pabst had sent the cutter home on the first day, but no one was supposed to know that, because if the man didn't receive his full fee, he would lodge a complaint in Berlin.

"He's off today," said Franz.

"Works very hard," said Pabst.

"Well-deserved day off," said Franz.

"In the middle of the movie? Well, show it already!"

"The first reel," Pabst said softly.

The film began slowly. The first ten minutes followed Elisabeth Molander's face on her way to work. She crossed streets, waited at intersections, boarded a tram, held on to the handle, rode one stop, got off, crossed another street, finally entered the office building where she worked, and ascended a long staircase with echoing footsteps. Only her face could be seen, sometimes reacting to people she passed. At first, the sounds of her surroundings could be heard; these soon receded into the background, and the flickering cadenzas of Paganini, which her brother would later play at the concert, rose up, only to mingle again after a while, so unobtrusively that it was barely noticeable, with the returning street sounds and finally to be drowned out by them. They had shot the entire sequence in the studio: Irene von Meyendorff had walked on a rolling treadmill; sound engineers and lighting technicians had created the noise and reflections of the city. The result looked as if a weightless camera had been carried through a peaceful Berlin morning, years earlier, long before the war.

Franz ran the reel with the already-edited beginning. Pabst laid a friendly hand on Karrasch's shoulder, but he shrugged it off with a scowl. Franz and Pabst stepped outside.

"What do we do if he wants changes?" asked Franz.

"That's the least of our problems. Yesterday I saw Czechs with rifles. Something is brewing."

"But don't you think that we—"

The door flew open, and Karrasch stood in front of them, breathing heavily. "Utter trash! Filthy, Bolshevik, Jewish, vulgar, pornographic, vile trash!"

On the screen in the cutting room was a close-up of the young woman smiling at someone. Streaks of light moved across her face.

"But you've only seen one minute!"

"Karrasch knew it! When they came to me, Hippler and Liebeneiner: 'We've found the right one,' and his stupid wife with her idiotic reading group!" He fell silent, bit his lips, stamped his foot.

"But you haven't even—"

Karrasch stood on tiptoe and whispered, "To the concentration camp. Both of you. Karrasch will make sure of it now."

Franz knew it was a dangerous situation. But he couldn't help it—he had to smile.

In his rage the small man seemed to go into rigor mortis. His mouth fell open, his face turned gray.

"I must apologize for my assistant," said Pabst. He paused to compose himself but failed. He smiled too.

Karrasch's eyes widened and became vacant. "Just you wait!" he hissed. He actually articulated the sounds so deep in his throat that words barely formed. You had to listen closely to discern that he was speaking and not merely wheezing. "You—wait! You!" Then he ran off with small, waddling steps.

"Another reason why we have to hurry," said Pabst.

"But what was . . . He hasn't even seen anything yet!"

"It was probably enough. He has an instinct for quality."

In the white-tiled rooms of the film laboratory below them, where a dozen women in white protective suits worked, positive prints were made. Pabst and Franz then cut the film from these, after which the original negative was in turn cut and respliced downstairs according to the resulting template.

"Almost anyone can shoot," said Pabst. "It's in editing that you make a film."

The footage of the concert had just come up. The violinist was clearly visible, his fingers playing, his bow jumping across the strings. And then there were the shots from the crane ride: a whirl through the radiant hall, the heads of the crowd far below. And so Pabst assembled the sequence of images: each cut a beat, faster, faster, slower, take a breath, here the faces of mother and sister, and now time hurled itself into acceleration, and the camera shot upward—so breathtaking that they barely heard the explosion. Lights flickered, the window glass rattled.

They looked at each other in surprise. There had been no air raid warning.

Then came another bang, and for the next twenty minutes they heard gunfire crackling in the distance. But because the power didn't go out, they continued working until the night turned pale and the sun rose. Only when it grew dark again did they have to stop.

They took the tram into the city. Since the end of the shoot, they no longer had a car at their disposal; those were all for Liebeneiner, who was shooting his morale-boosting comedy in the studios. On the way they saw soldiers stacking sandbags. At an intersection there was a tank. The tram stopped three stations too early. Instructions were given in Czech; apparently everyone had to get off. As they walked to their inn, they heard a gunshot from somewhere.

"Five hours," said Pabst. "We don't sleep any longer than that. Then back to work."

The receptionist explained to them that the radio was to blame for everything. The day before it had suddenly stopped broadcasting in German and started broadcasting in Czech, and since that was forbidden, it was understood as a signal. People had torn down the German street signs, and there had been shooting.

"And what happens now?"

"Only God knows, sir!"

But when they stood outside the hotel at dawn, the street looked the same as always: people walking in no particular hurry, cars passing by.

Pabst had a huge empty army rucksack under his arm. "I don't think we'll be coming back here."

They boarded the tram, but it stopped after just three stations, and they had to continue on foot. On a nearby square, angry voices shouted in Czech. They hurried away.

"We should take the train to Vienna," said Franz.

"That's what we'll do. With the film. Once it's finished."

They turned onto a path along the river. They walked as quickly as they could, even before they heard shots again. Then they heard other shots that seemed to respond.

"Those who make films—"

"Yes, I know!" Franz exclaimed. "Always in a bind!"

"If we don't finish editing *Molander*, it was all for nothing." Pabst stopped and looked at Franz through his reflective glasses. "Everything!"

"You mean, the extras? Even that was for nothing?"

"Those weren't extras, those were soldiers."

"What?"

"Franz, you were there, you saw it!"

Suddenly all of Franz's memories seemed blurry. Was it possible that none of it had happened? Could one decide it hadn't happened? Could one have been mistaken, imagined it, could one decide to have imagined it, could the memories be false, or could one decide they were false, simply because one wanted them to be?

"But I remember."

"Remember what?" Pabst looked at Franz intently, seemingly serious with his question.

Franz gave no answer; they hurried on, stooping low. No more shots were fired. Half an hour later they had reached the studio.

"We have to finish," said Pabst. "Then we go downstairs, have the original cut, and take it to Vienna."

So the day passed; so the night passed, and another day. They ate sandwiches that Franz stole from the hall where Liebeneiner was filming, they drank copious amounts of black coffee, and the film came together, shot by shot, and Franz noticed with nearly indescribable relief that Dr. Sämann was visible in none of them, so maybe he had been mistaken. At one point the ground shook from an explosion, but the power went out only briefly.

The next time Franz brought down the positive prints, cut and spliced, he found the laboratory empty. The women in the white coats who had been sitting there just the day before were gone.

"Then you'll have to do it yourself," said Pabst. "I'll finish the editing upstairs, you adjust the negative downstairs."

"I can't do that."

"In the days of silent films, the first assistant was always the master editor. You can do it, you just have to concentrate. And you must never take off the gloves, there must not be the slightest scratch."

So now Franz sat at the rewinder, in front of him the counter, with large film reels to his right and left, cranking meter by meter, cutting, splicing. No wrong cut could be made on the negative; each mistake would have cost a frame, making for a jerky transition. He felt slightly dizzy from the sharp smell of the adhesive. Deep silence surrounded him. Even the hall next door was empty, Liebeneiner's people having disappeared; pieces of the set lay on the floor, among them a harp and a broken porch swing. Only a solitary janitor wandered through the hall, listlessly dragging his broom.

The next time Franz came upstairs, Pabst had fallen asleep at the editing table. Franz let two hours pass before waking him.

"You shouldn't have let me sleep," said Pabst. "We don't have time!"

By the time Franz himself had to pause, another day had passed. He slept on the hard floor of the laboratory. After half an hour, Pabst came down and woke him. Explosions could be heard from the city, regular like hammer blows.

And because now they really had no time left, they cut the last reel, the last ten minutes of the movie, together in the laboratory, directly on the original negative. At the end came the scene where the violin forger, played by Wegener as a gentle, loving person, a poetic lost soul, was arrested by the police: large men in leather coats took him between them and dragged him away. Then the old prosecutor, who was also Wegener, delivered a brief and horrifying monologue in praise of the law, and then the betrothed couple fell hesitantly into each other's arms; the shock at the fate that condemned them to a life together was clearly visible on their faces. In the last shot, Fritz Molander left the prison. The walls towered gigantically behind the slender man. Inside, his hands had been broken; he cradled his fingers against his body. He would never play the violin again. Then, to Paganini's music, the credits would have started, but the titles had not yet been painted, so the film broke off after the last frame.

Franz spliced the final piece. Then he carefully removed the reel.

"Now," said Pabst, "to the train station."

It was early morning. Trams were no longer running, cars were scarcely to be seen. They walked as fast as they could, Franz groaning under the weight of the army rucksack, which held five stacked reels of film, each in its metal can. Pabst carried a burlap sack with two reels. He was so tired that it seemed to him as if the asphalt were slightly undulating; then also as if they were walking upside down and the sky was an endless abyss. A military boat chugged lazily by, appearing to hover, and he wondered whether the heavy gray clouds over the city were from fires.

"I can't go on," said Franz.

"You must."

"It's too heavy. I can't do it."

"But it must be done."

"I have to rest a moment."

"Rest on the train."

"Do you think a train is still running?"

"It must."

"Why?"

"Because we need it."

Pabst had become so attuned to film editing that it seemed to him he could continue out here, as if everything he saw were up for manipulation. It struck him as odd that he couldn't simply shorten the long way along the river on that street—which was now no longer called Passauer, because the German signs had been torn down—by showing their walking feet, then for a moment the meaningfully crooked tree over there, and then already the moment when they triumphantly crossed the bridge into the city; so much useless time, so much empty trudging, it could be done better! And when he concentrated, he actually succeeded in making a nearly seamless cut: feet, tree, sky, and there they were already, on the New Bridge, which was now also no longer called that, because the sign with its name was smeared with red. Pabst had to lean against the stone railing for a moment; even the sack with the two reels was very heavy. Beside him stood Franz, drenched in sweat and bent over the rucksack with the five reels.

"Don't give up," said Pabst. "We're almost at the station."

It was then that he saw five men with rifles standing across the way. They aimed; one of them shouted something in Czech. They apparently took Franz and him for Germans, which was on the one hand not quite right, but on the other hand not so wrong that it could easily have been cleared up.

Pabst pondered, an absurd lightness, composed of fatigue and confusion, having taken hold of him; you just have to change the perspective, he thought, imagining a camera behind the men, looking over their shoulders, along the gun barrels, at the two distant, heavy-laden figures on the other side of the bridge. And now a pan, he thought—the camera turned, streets passing by; to the left on Potskaler, which was no longer called that, someone had erected a barricade of chairs, garbage cans, and a piano; it kept turning until it reached the small street leading toward Wenzelsgasse, and now, by means of a double exposure, the two men appeared there and continued slowly on their way, unable to make swift progress due to their load.

"Don't turn around!" Pabst said, since it would have ruined the effect, and at the same time he wondered: Can it really be done this way, why does this work? But he knew without looking: The bridge behind them, at which the men were still aiming their rifles, was now empty.

They made their way toward the train station. Franz was gasping, his shirt and jacket completely soaked through. But as they came to the wider street, whose now-erased German name Pabst didn't know despite having often crossed it on his walks, something erupted: there was an explosion on a roof, glass shards rained down, they instinctively ducked into a doorway, and then part of the wall broke, stones rumbled, whitish gray mist rose and covered everything.

Pabst saw that Franz was staggering and white in the face, not from shock but from the dust. Before they could take deeper cover, there was a hail of shots—it was impossible to tell from where and at whom, but someone had evidently been hit, since a high-pitched whimper filled the air, and then Pabst heard a noise that sounded familiar, the boom of a howitzer, followed by the crash of surrounding masonry, not directly overhead, but nearby. They walked faster. Pabst would have liked to run, but neither of them was capable of it.

"Don't go left!" shouted Pabst.

"Why not? The station is to the left!"

"Because it's wrong," said Pabst. "In the last shot we went from right to left. If we go the other way now . . . it won't work!"

So they went right, and apparently that was correct, because a passage took them in, a small staircase leading down into a musty-smelling cellar, and Pabst thought: difficult to light, from daylight through the cloud of dust into darkness. At that moment, they heard the roaring and grinding of heavy chains above. The tank that had fired passed by; they had escaped it by seconds.

Groaning, Franz put down the rucksack. As their eyes adjusted to the dark, they saw that others were crouching in the cellar: men, women, and children, motionless, waiting, but most of them didn't look frightened, they looked determined. Good faces, thought Pabst, you had to search a while for those; casting agencies rarely managed it. He was so tired that he had to sit down on a crate for a moment.

"You're G. W. Pabst!" a man said in German.

"Yes, have you seen my films?"

"Some."

"Did you like them?"

The man laughed. It was a strange laugh, not malicious, not disparaging, but not approving either; it was enigmatic.

"What's going on here?" asked Franz.

"The uprising," said the man. "At some point, you can't take it anymore. When you fear the life you're living more than death."

Another man said something in Czech. He spoke quickly and at length, then spat.

"He says," the man translated, "that the utmost filth, the lowest of the low, the worst wickedness and baseness, should not exist, after all. Maybe for a while, but then no longer. A lot is possible, but not everything."

Pabst looked at the ground. He felt as if he had dozed off for a moment. He quickly raised his head again.

A woman said something in Czech.

"She asked where you're going."

Pabst pondered for a moment whether he should lie but saw no point in it and said, "Station."

"That's good," said the man. "There might still be trains running. Don't take the direct route. Go around back there." He then mentioned some Czech street names, but it was immediately clear to Pabst that he wouldn't remember them.

"Thank you," he said.

Where the man was pointing, there was a staircase. It seemed to Pabst as if it hadn't been there just before, but that was impossible; such major continuity errors didn't occur. He lifted the sack, which for a moment felt heavier than before, but then he heard a buzzing sound: The burlap tore, the two cans clattered to the ground.

"Into the rucksack," said Pabst.

"Too heavy," said Franz.

"It must happen."

Pabst opened the rucksack and placed the two tin cans with the five that were already inside. For a moment he feared it wouldn't close, but when he pulled with all his might on the leather straps, it did.

"Too heavy," said Franz. "I can't. I can't go on!"

Pabst lifted the rucksack. It was indeed immensely heavy. He threaded his arms through the straps, briefly felt unable to keep his balance under the weight, but somehow he managed: carefully he took one step and then another, there was the staircase, he grasped the steel railing and pulled himself up step by step.

When they reached the street, a massive crowd scene was unfolding there, so elaborate that he couldn't help thinking of the cost: not since Griffith had there been such a display. People streamed by, continuously joined by more from the adjacent squares and streets. It was a pity that he didn't have a crane, for such a procession should have been filmed from above; the camera had to follow the motion of the people while continuing to rise, so that the viewer would hold his breath as the multitude grew.

Every step seemed an almost impossible effort for Pabst, his shoulders hurting, his knees threatening to buckle. This scene would have required a moving camera, shifting from an aerial view to the perspective of someone hurrying ahead, shaky, chaotic, headlong. As he stumbled along, step by step, he saw that the streets to the right, leading to the Old Town Square, were all blocked off, and there stood men in uniforms adorned with the double rune—no one wanted to get close to them, and from the snatches of conversation exchanged by the passersby he could tell they were speaking German. All the Germans in the city suddenly seemed to be running to the train station.

"I need a break." Franz leaned against a wall, breathing heavily. "I can't go on. The rucksack was so heavy."

"No time," Pabst gasped.

"But I can't go on!"

Then so be it, thought Pabst, let him stay behind. The film was edited, Franz had fulfilled his task. He continued walking.

But soon everything halted, people crowded together, apparently there was an obstacle farther ahead—Pabst stumbled to the right, where a narrow street opened up, one he knew from his walks. A few meters farther on, there was a passage to an inner courtyard. He crossed it, stumbling once, the weight of the rucksack pulling him sideways, but he held on to a wheelbarrow, didn't fall, and kept going. He pushed a clothesline away; on the other side of the courtyard was another passage, probably only a meter wide. He squeezed through with all his might, the heavy load on his back dragging him down, but he didn't fall; soon he was back on the street, and there was the train station just across the road. He wiped his face. His clothes were so soaked with sweat, it was as if he had fallen into the water.

Staggering, he crossed the street. Cars honked, someone yelled something in German, brakes screeched, then he had reached the other side.

The entrances to the station were blocked, a tank barred access to the hall, heavily armed soldiers checked IDs, people screamed and protested, but it was no use, they were not allowed in.

Pabst pushed his way to the front and showed his passport. Someone behind him also handed forward his passport; turning around, he was surprised to see Franz; without the burden, he had apparently followed him the whole way after all.

"Special permit?" asked the soldier.

"I am G. W. Pabst. I am a well-known director, traveling at the Minister's behest."

"Then you have a special permit?"

"Not in writing, but—"

"Without a special permit I cannot let you through."

"Don't you understand who I—"

"Good man," said the soldier, "everyone here is someone, everyone wants through, everyone is a friend of some big shot, but I have orders!"

Pabst didn't move. He couldn't think of anything more to say, but he knew how it worked: now something surprising had to happen, a miracle, something enormously unlikely that nonetheless somehow only just made sense. It was always so in films, so it had to be this time too.

He closed his eyes. He could no longer hold the rucksack. His shoulders ached as if his arms were about to fall off. He felt he was seconds away from fainting. Maybe like this, he thought: I collapse, someone takes pity, and when I wake up, I'm already on the train. He wanted to give in, to let himself sink. Simply to lie down, he thought, without this weight . . .

"Is that you, Ferdl?" he heard Franz saying.

"Yes, my God, Franzl," the soldier exclaimed. "I can't believe it!"

"Ferdl, you're alive!"

Pabst heard them embracing and thumping each other on the back.

"This is Ferdl Graspurek," said Franz, "we grew up together!"

"Pleased to meet you," said Pabst. He opened his eyes, almost regretting that he didn't get to collapse yet after all.

"How's your papa?" asked the soldier.

"In his last letter he wrote he's fine, it's a bad time to be a gardener, of course, but he gets by! And your mama?"

"Well, listen, get a move on," said the soldier. "There's your train!"

"Ferdl, I don't even know how to—"

"We'll talk later on. Now run!"

They heard the locomotive whistle. Pabst couldn't run with the rucksack, but he moved as fast as he could. A sign read: VIENNA. There was no time for tickets, they would simply bribe the conductor, if one appeared. The train doors were still open, people stood packed inside, faces pressed against the windows, there was hardly any room left, but they climbed aboard, forcing their way in. The doors began to close. Pabst let the rucksack slide to the floor and sat on it.

At that moment they heard the crack of gunfire, and now it was no longer individual shots, but volleys, more and more, a clatter that escalated into a roar.

"The Vlasov army," said a man next to Pabst. "It's unbelievable. First they betrayed Stalin, now they're betraying us."

"Who?"

"The Russian Liberation Army is intervening, but on the side of the Czechs!"

Pabst didn't know who Vlasov was, and had never heard of the Russian Liberation Army. Only one thing mattered, that the train begin to move.

It began to move.

Pabst closed his eyes. He had never been so tired in his life. The train swaying under him, the air so stifling that it was hard to inhale, he felt himself sinking, but just before he lost consciousness, a disturbing thought came to him, something he couldn't quite grasp, which took no clear form yet wouldn't be dispelled: if he was this tired now because he had been cutting the film for days without sleep, if he could no longer think clearly now, had he been thinking clearly before? Was it possible that the film too was the product of a weakened mind? He could no longer remember anything, everything was a blur; he had made so many decisions, but could not recall a single one, he saw only the flickering monitor, heard the rattling of the reels, smelled the musty scent of the nitrate. He had to watch the whole thing as soon as possible, right after the film was copied in Vienna, hopefully the Rosenhügel laboratory still existed, one didn't know where the bombs had struck, one didn't know what one didn't know, that was the problem, and therefore one also didn't really know what one did know, and the next moment he knew nothing more and felt the glass of the train window against the back of his head.

* * *

He came to because the train had stopped. It was early evening. In fright he groped for the rucksack with the film reels. It was there.

"We're almost in Brünn," said Franz. "If we're lucky, a lot of people will get off."

"I'm getting off," said a huge man, "my seat will be free! You gentlemen are heading to Vienna?" He had a broad, good-natured face and a thick black beard.

"Yes," said Pabst. "Vienna." He rubbed his eyes and tried to remember, but looking back, there was only a chaos of colors and noise, and he could recall only vaguely what had happened in the past few days. Had he really just experienced an uprising in Prague?

"Incredible that we made it out," he said.

"You can say that again," said the large man. "I'm a farrier, I managed to find metal, no one cares about it anymore, all those horses, the poor animals! There aren't enough vehicles for the Wehrmacht, so they're using horses. Those poor, poor animals, I feel so sorry for them!"

"What are you implying?" a man with a gap in his teeth asked sharply from the front. "Are you criticizing the army command?"

"Sir," said the farrier. "I'm not blaming anyone, I'm just saying that so many horses have died, and all that good iron is lying around! It's needed for vehicles, they say, but because there weren't enough vehicles, they used horses. And when peace comes again, what will I use to shoe the horses?" He paused and listened, but no one offered a suggestion. So he said: "What are you doing in Vienna?"

He had asked Pabst, but it was Franz who answered. "I'm going to see my parents. I haven't seen them for so long."

"Which district? I have a friend in the ninth. Hannes Schilbacher. Do you know him?"

"No, never met him."

"Strange," said the farrier. "He's lived there for ten years. And you, which district?"

"Döbling. Cottage Quarter. My father has a nursery."

At that moment the train started moving.

"Wilzek Nursery," said Franz, apparently too tired to really know what he was saying. "If you ever need tulip bulbs, there's nowhere better."

"I don't need tulips," said the farrier. "I need more horseshoes. And I need a wife. I want to get married, and I need peace too."

"What are you implying?" asked the man with the gap in his teeth. "There will be peace when the war is won, certainly not before!"

"Sir, I know, but that will be soon, won't it?"

The man was silent for a moment before saying: "Yes, of course, soon! Very soon!"

The farrier looked at Pabst with curiosity, his head slightly tilted in a way that reminded Pabst what a questionable appearance he presented: he hadn't shaved or changed his clothes for many days, and his glasses were cracked in several places. Also, his entire body ached. His old hip injury burned like fire; his shoulders and knee joints throbbed with dull pain.

"Care for a game of cards?" asked the farrier.

"Always," said Franz.

There was now a bit more space than at the beginning of their journey; apparently people had spread out better through the train. The two sat down on the floor and began to play cards. Next to the farrier was an army rucksack, just like the one Pabst had.

"Who's dealing?" asked Franz.

"You," Pabst heard the farrier say. "I go first."

"Then play," said Franz.

"Trick," called the farrier.

"It won't do you any good," said Franz.

"I'll win, even if the world falls apart!"

"What do you mean by 'if the world falls apart'?" asks the man with the gap in his teeth. "You doubt the final victory?"

Pabst heard the farrier reply that he was a simple man and would of course never presume to doubt the final victory, and he heard Franz call "Trump!" and heard the farrier's reply. Then he slept again.

He woke up as the train came to a stop in Vienna. He heard the doors opening, a voice on the loudspeaker saying "Vienna South Station," and thought for a moment of that station, very close to here, that his father had commanded, a long time ago, when a Kaiser had still reigned and had named that station after himself.

It was probably early morning; the sun had already risen. His hip hurt as if something inside it had shattered, his mouth tasted sharp and bitter. Next to him Franz was rubbing his eyes. Pabst clung to the rucksack, somehow got to his knees, then to his feet, and straightened up. There wasn't a bone in his body that didn't ache.

"We made it," he said. "Now straight to the film laboratory, then we'll see what's really going on with *Molander*."

A strange worry had started to gnaw at him. Shortly before waking up, he had dreamed of a film he had to make. That wasn't unusual, it happened often, but with this film he hadn't been able to decide how it ended: Was it a comedy, or was it the kind of story where something crucial interfered at the last minute? In this dream, which also involved Franz and a beautiful actress whose face he couldn't recognize—even though he of course knew who she was—he had then made a decision and given an instruction, but which had it been, which one? He bent down to pick up the rucksack—and immediately noticed that something was wrong. It was very heavy, but the weight was distributed differently. Something was not as before.

With trembling hands, he unbuckled the straps.

At first he did not understand the meaning of what he saw. He did not understand that the decision about the kind of story had been made; he also did not yet understand that he was now condemned to that future he had just thought he could escape, a future of narrow limits and meager circumstances, a future of small and dispensable movies. He understood only that the two army rucksacks, which looked exactly the same and exactly like all other army rucksacks, had been switched, and that a kind man whose name he didn't know was now walking through Brünn with his. Because this rucksack here, standing silent and heavy and hideously stupid in front of him, contained horseshoes, perhaps a hundred or more, in neat bundles.

And although there was no longer any doubt, he pulled them out, all the bundles of horseshoes, one after the other, as if his film could be hidden among them, threw each onto the floor of the car, and then he picked up the rucksack and shook it, finding no note inside, no card that might have revealed the man's name; only a few horseshoe nails were still to be found at the very bottom and a hammer and nothing else.

"Maybe he'll get in touch," said Franz, as he searched the empty rucksack a second time. "He might find out what the movie is, he might have it shown to him in some cinema, and then he might find you."

"Yes," said Pabst. "He might."

And numb, almost senseless with horror, he let the rucksack drop and carefully stepped onto the platform, where people were stretching, squinting into the light, embracing each other, and laughing with joy.

AFTER

Depths

David Bass arrived shortly after midnight. It was pouring rain. The last few kilometers he had driven at a crawl, fearing that the small used Citroën he had bought the week before might skid. He had also gotten lost several times. The light inside the car had been so weak that he had barely been able to see the road map lying on his lap; the night landscape melting away in the rain looked nothing like the drawing on the paper. Now and then the headlights of oncoming vehicles flared up, each time causing him to slam on the brakes. Wouldn't it be an unspeakable irony, he thought, one of God's typical acts of impertinence, if one had escaped war and mass murder only to die in a ditch in Lower Austria? Occasionally he saw the outlines of ruins: destroyed farmsteads next to bomb craters that had yet to be refilled, but the road itself was already in good condition.

The inn was in the middle of the village, a squat house with thick walls and small windows. A sign above the front door read INN, a name apparently being unnecessary, just as the bakery across the street was labeled BAKERY and the butcher shop next door BUTCHER. David Bass parked, ran through the rain, pushed open the door. On one wall hung deer antlers, there must have been more than two dozen. He pressed the bell at reception.

He waited. From next door he heard the buzz of voices and the clink of glasses, the unmistakable sounds of every village inn. He pressed the bell again. And indeed a fat woman appeared and gruffly asked his name.

"David Bass. I have a room reserved."

She sized him up with a rustic heavy gaze, and he was quite certain he knew what she was thinking: Yet another returnee, what are you doing here?

"Making movies," he answered the question she hadn't asked. "It's all I can do."

Without the slightest curiosity as to why he had said that, she handed him the key.

Before going upstairs, he opened the door to the taproom for a moment. There they sat, all men, their faces angular and full of red blotches, glasses in front of them, all seeming to yell at each other, except for a few sitting there dully staring, too drunk to raise their voices. He quickly closed the door. He still couldn't quite believe that they would no longer do him any harm.

His room smelled of mold. A Savior hung heavily on a crucifix. The wardrobe had no door. There was also a bed, a table, a chair, nothing else. The rain pattered so loudly against the window that sleep was hardly conceivable.

But it didn't come to that anyway, because a moment later there was a knock. Outside stood a gaunt man, crooked and aging, with red-veined eyes, a typically devious party member's face.

"Are you the new production manager?"

David Bass hesitated before confirming. It still felt strange to him. He had had to take over this job literally overnight two days earlier when his predecessor, the universally well-liked Gerd Metzler, had suffered a heart attack. He knew almost nothing about the film *Mysterious Depths*; he had just managed to read through the script the night before.

"At this hour?" asked David.

"Crisis meeting, room twenty-five. The shooting schedule has to be changed. The rain has flooded the cave."

David tried to look as competent as he always did when he heard something he didn't understand and didn't know how to respond to. He had no idea what one did when a cave was flooded.

"Sorry," said the gaunt man. "Where are my manners? But it's so late. I should be sleeping. I'm Paul Levy, I do the sound."

"Levy?"

"I've been back from Mexico for a year."

"Why?"

"I still can't speak Spanish, and I kept craving goulash and apricot dumplings. You?"

"Boston. I went over there with my parents, then I was in the army, then I interrogated mass murderers. From there it wasn't much of a leap to film."

"Mass murderers?"

"None of the stars. Well, Dönitz, at least. He said to me, 'I shouldn't even be here, Herr Bass! But the Jews are persecuting me, they won't let up.'—'Well, maybe,' I said, 'it's because you started it?'"

Paul Levy laughed melancholically. He felt faint envy: this young man had his life ahead of him, he would find his way. For himself it was too late. He was almost sixty. His wife had died in a camp, as had his parents and sister. His daughter had disappeared, and it had been so many years now that he no longer had the strength to keep hoping. It was a mystery to him why he had never stopped fighting for his survival.

They walked down the hotel corridor, around a corner, straight again, around another corner. More antlers hung on the walls at irregular intervals, without any discernible pattern.

"What kind of films were you allowed to make back home?" asked David Bass.

Paul Levy made a dismissive gesture. He was too exhausted to talk about it. His first job had been on *The Singing House*, a ludicrously stupid movie directed by a man named Antel, who had been a member of the Nazi Party long before the annexation of Austria. The film was supposedly about a jazz band, but the music passed off to the audience as jazz was tripe, and the dialogue was so unbearable that you could mix the soundtracks only while drunk. His second film, *Peter Dances with Everyone*, had even worse music, a director with no experience, and a young lead actor of preposterously oily professionalism.

Paul Levy had vivid memories of Hugo von Hofmannsthal, who had frequently dined with his parents. He had met Rilke twice in his youth, and once had the privilege of sitting at Joseph Roth's regular table in Berlin. On his return he had braced himself for criminals, brutalized people, and escaped Nazis. What he hadn't anticipated were all the mischievous girls, slick-haired young men, eccentric uncles, and deeply unfunny jokers who suddenly populated German films, as if the whole country had gone mad. It was buried in silence everywhere, but in the movies it was plain to see.

"And what's he like?" asked David Bass. "The great man?"

"Pabst? Hard to describe. I'd imagined him differently. You'll see for yourself. How is Herr Metzler doing, is he out of the woods?"

"He'll probably survive," said David Bass. "It would just be too cruel. A man survives the eastern front and then dies of a heart attack on set? After all the executions he's carried out? Don't forget, these people are as hard as Krupp steel and as nimble as greyhounds."

"He was on the eastern front?"

"Waffen-SS."

"I didn't know that."

"He doesn't like to talk about it."

"Such a polite person!"

"They're all polite again now," said David Bass. "And why not! You must have seen Pabst's *Trial*, his big statement against anti-Semitism. It's all mixed up now. When you knocked on my door earlier, I actually thought . . . I took you for . . . But how is one to know!"

"But was he really a Nazi?" asked Paul Levy. "Before the war they called him the Red Pabst."

"What do I know? People were many things before the war, and then they were something completely different. I'm telling you, it's all mixed-up and jumbled."

They turned another corner, walked past more antlers, and there at last was the right door. Paul Levy knocked, and they entered.

The hotel room was full of people. A tall, somewhat pale, very beautiful woman sat on the bed. A burly man sat on a stool, two men leaned against the wall, and a woman with a tired face crouched on the floor. Behind the table sat another man, bent over and as if half asleep, wearing thick glasses. Everyone was smoking, the smoke billowing through the air and hanging like gray fog on the ceiling.

"A pleasure," said the tall woman, standing up and holding out her hand to him. "You're Herr Bass? I'm Trude Pabst. I wrote the script. It's good that you're here. It's the perfect storm—first the production manager has a heart attack, now the rain floods the cave!"

"The perfect storm?" repeated David Bass.

"An American expression."

"I know, I last heard it at Omaha Beach."

"Where is that?"

"I'll tell you another time."

"I'm sorry you don't have more time to get oriented. This is Herr Schneeberger, the cinematographer; Herr Schlichting, who handles the sets; this is Herr Gurnbichler, who's responsible for the equipment; and Frau Schrewitz, the assistant director. You've already met Herr Levy. And this is my husband, the director."

David's gaze wandered around the room for a moment before settling on the man sitting at the table, who looked detached, as if none of this concerned him.

"The large chamber in Hermann's Cave is underwater," said Gurnbichler. "It certainly won't be usable tomorrow, even if the rain stops."

"The weather report says it won't stop," said the assistant director.

"Either way we have to pump it out first. And that can only be done at night. The occupying authority won't let us use too much electricity during the day."

Just at that moment, the men downstairs in the taproom began to sing. The words were unintelligible; only the muffled rise and fall of their voices could be heard.

"But the stream is navigable," said Schneeberger. "We have to rewrite the script so that the rescuers try to get into the cave by boat. We dealt with worse on Pitz Palu, didn't we, G. W.?"

Pabst raised his head. He looked at Schneeberger as if he had been roused from deep thought.

"Does anyone have a cigarette?" asked David Bass. No one moved. He looked at Gurnbichler and extended his hand. With provocative slowness, the man took out a pack of Marlboros, pulled out a cigarette, and handed it to him.

"What do you suggest?" David Bass asked the director.

"Weak actors," said Pabst. "A nice little film. It's not important."

Everyone was silent for a moment.

"But if it must be done," said Pabst, "then we'll do it like this. Schneeberger gets in the boat. We need a double for Skodler. If Skodler drowns, it helps no one. Though it would be no loss to the art of acting. We have to add a scene: the rescuers stand in front of the cave, leaning over maps, and discover the river as a means of access." He fell silent for a moment, so the rain and the voices from below could be heard. Then he added: "Or something, it doesn't really matter."

"I can write the scene at the map table by tomorrow," Trude said.

Pabst didn't respond; he seemed already to be thinking of something else.

"Herr Gurnbichler would have to procure boats," said Trude.

"What am I supposed to get?"

"Boats."

"Now?"

"Please!"

"At night?"

"Since we'd need them tomorrow, yes. Please."

"How am I supposed to get boats in the middle of the night?"

"I don't know, dear Herr Gurnbichler," said Trude, "but if there is a way, I know you will find it."

Alois Gurnbichler dropped his cigarette on the floor and ground it out. Singing could be heard from the taproom. He knew the song, of course. Good thing he was the only one, he thought. In times like these, you couldn't even sing the old songs without someone starting to whine. He had actually intended to complain to the new production manager about how the shoot was going. They were constantly being bossed around by this woman, who apparently had that fool, the Communist, her husband, completely under her control. And now the new production manager was a Jew, from whom, of course, no help was to be expected!

"Would you please pick that up?" asked Trude.

Alois Gurnbichler looked at her and weighed his options. She couldn't throw him out. She needed him. He didn't move.

"Pick it up!" said David Bass.

With people like you, we didn't mess around, thought Gurnbichler. We made you dig trenches, then it went quickly, if you were lucky. You would have begged. Wouldn't have done any good.

"Now," said David Bass.

Gurnbichler bent down and picked up the cigarette butt.

"Can you manage that with the boats?" asked David Bass.

"There are boats everywhere," said Gurnbichler, looking at the butt in his open hand.

"A question," said Schlichting, who had been silent until then. He had a soft, pleasantly melodious voice. "I still don't understand why the rescuers don't get dynamite right away."

"We really don't have time to discuss the script now," Trude said.

"But if it isn't explained, the people in the cinema might laugh. They try everything to save those trapped, they give up, death seems certain, and only *then* does someone come up with the idea of using the most obvious thing?"

"Not now," said Trude.

"G. W.," said Schlichting, "it wouldn't be hard to change that and—"

"Doesn't matter," said Pabst.

"On the contrary," said Schlichting. "The whole movie stands or falls—"

"This movie doesn't stand, and it doesn't fall either."

Schlichting sighed. He had once worked with Lang and Murnau, later he had built a Spanish village in Bavaria for Riefenstahl, now he mainly constructed salons and stuffy living rooms for the little comedies that the audience apparently wanted to see after all those nights of bombing—he was proud that he could work with all directors and on all types of films. But they really should have listened to him. The ending could have been effortlessly improved.

"Fine," he said, offended. "Then I can go to bed." He stepped over the assistant director, pushed past Paul Levy, and paused once more to give someone the chance to ask him to stay. No one did, so he left.

"Can I go too?" asked Paul Levy.

"The lower cave chamber needs better lighting," said Pabst. "The stalactite isn't coming out properly. And we're only doing it because of the stalactite. Otherwise, we might as well go into the studio. Where's the lighting technician, where's Kampits?"

"He's asleep," Trude said gently. "And it's not Kampits, he was the lighting technician on the last film."

"Stronger lighting on the cave ceiling," said Pabst.

Everyone waited, but he added nothing more.

"Good night then!" said Paul Levy, who could hardly bear the tingling in his mouth and the twitching of his lips any longer, he was so craving a sip of schnapps. He hurried out.

"At least they're not singing anymore," said David Bass.

"What do you have against singing?" asked Schneeberger.

"Well, what do you think?"

"I don't think anything, you tell me."

"We're all tired," said Trude. "And we have to get to work. I'll write the new scene, you get the boats?"

Everyone started moving. The assistant director stood up and left, Gurnbichler followed her, and David Bass also went to bed, relieved.

Trude locked the door and opened the window. Cold night air flowed in.

"Go to sleep now. You're tired."

"And you?" asked Pabst.

"I have to write the new scene."

"At this hour?"

"You know, in filmmaking you're always in a bind."

He stood up and went to the window. "Do you think there's still a chance?"

And because she knew what he meant, she replied: "There might be!"

"That someone will bring the film cans back to me? You think it's possible?"

"Why not."

"If only Kuno Krämer hadn't disappeared. He could have helped. He would have known what to do."

Trude had slowly grown into her new role. The man who had returned to Dreiturm from Prague was no longer the one she had known. He had spoken of nothing but the lost film, brooding day and night over where it might be, whether it still existed, what had happened to it. He had even asked the caretaker—who had been working with other local men to find prisoners who had escaped from one of the nearby camps—for his opinion: the film reels had to be somewhere, at some location, a point, a place that could consequently be reached, found, and visited. He had repeated this over and over, even the nagging worry about Jakob seemingly forgotten.

Then he had practically stopped speaking. He had sat for hours in the library, in his old armchair, not smoking because there was no more tobacco, holding the empty cigarette case with Griffith's initials, and replaying that film, which he could still see before him, frame by frame, scene by scene.

Dreiturm had largely been spared the consequences of the collapse; the tanks and streams of refugees had passed by at a distance. At some point, they learned that Jerzabek had been arrested, but no one knew any details. Once, Soviet officers turned up to investigate a report: someone had anonymously informed the occupying forces that the lord of Dreiturm Castle had been a creator of Nazi films, member of the Reich Chamber of Film, and a favorite of the Propaganda Minister. But then, for an hour, his old personality had returned. He had regaled the men with vodka, and told them that he had once been called "the Red Pabst" and that he had made film adaptations of the Soviet author Ehrenburg and the Communist Brecht. He had been so charming and convincing that he and the officers had parted with warm embraces.

Shortly thereafter, a letter arrived from the film producer Hübler, who had just received his license from the occupying authorities.

Trude called him. She was herself surprised when she heard herself say: "My husband has lost his voice. A bad flu. I'm speaking for him. But of course he's interested. He can hardly wait. Please come; we have many guest rooms."

That had worked immediately. As long as Pabst was in the room, she could negotiate on his behalf, could accept or decline things; no one minded if he didn't talk. Soon his old colleague Kurt Heuser had shown up with a script about a trial against a Jew in 1860, written quickly, not a masterpiece, but solid, and suddenly there had been production meetings in the library again as before, and then the great actor Ernst Deutsch, just back from Hollywood, had taken on the lead role of the persecuted man.

"I know," Deutsch had said, "it's crazy. Someone is playing a Jew, and it's not Werner Krauss with a fake voice or Ferdinand Marian looking as dangerous as if he eats children; it's a real Jew."

"Why did you come back?" asked Trude. "Doesn't it hurt to be here again?"

"More than one can say. But it's my country too."

Pabst's lack of interest in this movie wasn't really a problem. The people on set knew what they were doing. Now and then someone would quietly ask what was wrong with Herr Pabst, but then she would simply say that the last year of the war had been very hard on him, and that was enough; no one wanted to know more.

Occasionally, unexpectedly, he would say something helpful. Sometimes he would give an actor good advice or indicate with a hand gesture where the camera should be positioned or where a spotlight should be aimed. Then he lost interest again, fell into brooding, or asked someone whether he had heard anything about the lost film reels.

He still knew *The Molander Case* by heart, but individual scenes were already fading, and he could recall the faces of some supporting characters only with difficulty. The movie still existed in his head, so he could keep it from disappearing for good by replaying it over and over within himself. That was why he couldn't devote himself to any other task, let alone concentrate on the much less important movie being shot here in his name.

Only once had he come back to life. When his former assistant had visited the set, Pabst had run up to him and embraced him, but Franz had had little time because he was directing a first film of his own, and so Pabst had only briefly been able to talk to him about *The Molander Case*: Did he remember how they hadn't had a usable reaction shot of the young man listening in the big scene between Wegener and Tessen? And so they had instead cut in a shot of a bird sitting on the windowsill, then back to Wegener, then the empty windowsill without the bird; and precisely because it had been such a minor, easily overlooked detail, Pabst was particularly proud of it.

But Franz had behaved strangely. He hadn't wanted to talk about the movie, had kept changing the subject, and then he had suddenly spoken about a concert hall in Barrandov, looking at Pabst with strangely shimmering eyes. Pabst and Trude had exchanged uncomprehending glances; perhaps it was because Franz was now a director himself, perhaps there were other reasons, but after this halting conversation, Franz had quickly said goodbye, and then Pabst had become lost again in his thoughts.

He had been absent-minded when he attended the premiere in Vienna, bowing with Deutsch, Heuser, and Hübler while Trude sat clapping in the first row, and when he accepted his prize at the Venice Film Festival, where he had recently been honored under swastika and fasces flags for *The Comedians*.

"But it makes no difference," he had told Trude on the way home. "An award like that changes nothing. The only thing that matters is whether you've made a film that endures."

"And, did we?"

"I'm afraid not."

When another letter from Hübler had arrived, she had replied that there was a project G. W. had always wanted to film: a play she herself had once written about a woman caught between two men, one of whom was a speleologist, lost in the depths of the earth, living only for his profession.

Hübler had come from Vienna again. Liesl Jerzabek had cooked tough roast pork with especially hard dumplings, and at lunch Pabst briefly broke his silence and said yes, in a cave, why not, and then he excused himself and left the room, saying he needed his afternoon nap.

"You know, madam," said Hübler. "It's still quite difficult to finance a movie, but it's getting easier. A destroyed country has hardly any tax revenue, but if you act wisely and have connections, there are opportunities again. A cave film, for example, could be funded by the tourism board! But for that, you need connections, and not the wrong ones. You know, madam, I was banned from working under the Nazis. I am not one of them! But I have to live here, I have to work here, I have to make do with what's available. And Pabst has a special position. He isn't clearly implicated . . . " Hübler emphasized the word "clearly" in an indulgently dismissive manner, as if it were an almost amusing quirk of the current administration. "On the other hand, he did stay in the country, while the other famous film artists of the prewar era were far away, in safe places with beautiful weather, madam, that's just the way it is, with magnificent weather, and only very gradually are they showing up in our poor, destroyed country, and they have no connections anymore. One must understand that those who held out in the homeland in dark times, who didn't just escape to comfortable foreign . . . that they meet them with a certain mistrust. It's unfortunate, madam, but is it incomprehensible? All right then, don't look at me like that, call it incomprehensible! But it doesn't change the fact that a G. W. Pabst is now in a good situation."

A week after the waters had drained away, they shot the last scene in the cave. As she did every time she descended, Trude had to push back an attack of cold panic. When writing, she had imagined the cave as a deep, symbolically rich place, but not as something that felt so oppressively real. Walking on the muddy floor, through the smell of mold and moss, and seeing the mineral formations sprouting from the walls like a stony premonition of life, while at the same time realizing that the mountain above consisted of a hundred million tons of heavy stone, she found it all far from symbolic. Farther down, deep below the chamber where they were filming, there were prehistoric cave paintings, but no one on the shoot had ever climbed down there.

What Trude had been least prepared for was how many creatures lived in such a cave. You only had to shine a light anywhere to see beetles crawling over the walls like a flicker of vision, which wasn't even as unsettling as the moths that kept flying out of the darkness into your face, or all the sticky spiderwebs. Moreover, the moisture constantly caused short circuits, so that Alois Gurnbichler's painstakingly installed ceiling lamps all failed at least once a day.

In the last scene, the speleologist, Ben, and his great love, Cornelia, trapped together, awaited death. Cornelia had previously left this man, who had insisted on repeatedly descending into the depths without her, for the wealthy industrialist Roy, but she had never been able to forget the man to whom her heart truly belonged—whom she had followed on his final cave expedition and with whom she had been buried alive. They sat closely entwined, without hope, without a way out, yet united.

While the lights were being set up, the lead actors, Ilse Werner and Paul Hubschmid, sat next to each other on wool blankets, their costumes artfully speckled with mud and dust.

"I'll thank God when I don't have to come down here anymore," said Ilse Werner. She had an enchantingly beautiful face and great charisma, and besides being a passable actress, was a notable whistler. "How deep are we?"

"About seventy meters," said Trude.

"You shouldn't have told me that. Now I feel sick."

"If you had spent the war down here," said Hubschmid, "maybe you wouldn't have had to perform for the troops all the time."

"I don't have to take that," said Ilse Werner, whose ban by the occupying authorities had only recently been lifted. "Not from a Swiss man who was milking his cows while the bombs were falling on us."

"Better to milk cows than to whistle for the SS."

"They wouldn't have wanted to listen to you whistle, the SS! They had taste!"

"Please," said Trude. "Ilse, Paul! Not now!"

She looked around. Pabst was standing next to her. Schneeberger was kneeling behind the camera, Gurnbichler was attaching a power cable, the assistant director, Ilse Schrewitz, was crouching with the clapperboard in front of the two actors. No one looked at her. The small, gray-haired woman had been treated with a strange awkwardness by everyone ever since it had become known that she had hidden a Jewish family in her cellar throughout the entire war. It wasn't that anyone held it against her. It was just that no one knew what to make of the fact that she was a completely different person than anyone had suspected. Paul Levy held the boom microphone. David Bass leaned, smoking, behind the entrance to the chamber, which was already too crowded for anyone else.

"Would you like to explain the scene to them?" asked Trude.

"You do it," said Pabst.

"You're alone," Trude said. "Trapped. The way out is blocked. But you're together. For you, Ilse, there was briefly another man, but he was a mistake, an illusion, a mere reflection, nothing more. Now you are trapped, but you're in the truth because you're with your companion—no matter what labyrinths you've fallen into."

She fell silent for a moment. It must have been the air down there, but her voice had briefly faltered.

"When two people belong together—that's what the story is really about. That you can lose your way. Because of his mission, he loses himself and is suddenly in a place from which he can't find his way back to the light on his own. And it's about how you can be caught between two people, but only one of them is the truth. Now they understand. Now they're together. Until death."

"But not quite," said David Bass. "Because someone's already coming up with the idea of the dynamite."

The boom microphone swayed because Paul Levy had to suppress a laugh. Ilse Schrewitz also smiled.

"But you know nothing of that," said Trude. "You firmly believe there's no escape." And sensing that the moment was precarious and her authority needed support, she asked, "Isn't that right, Wilhelm?"

"Yes," said Pabst.

But since she felt that this time that wasn't enough, she continued: "Should they be more composed or more desperate?"

"Actors," said Pabst.

"Excuse me?"

"They are actors. You can tell at a glance, and that can't be changed."

Schneeberger rolled the camera, the assistant clapped the clapperboard, the two actors clung to each other and spoke their lines. Trude thought it went well, but she knew that each scene had to be shot multiple times; that was the custom and expectation. They did it again, and then again, and then again, and then again, and then again. Over and over, the two actors, who couldn't stand each other, cuddled up and professed how much they loved each other. Finally together, finally united, finally without the man who had stood between them.

"Thank you," said Trude. "That was good. We have it now." She turned around and asked: "Right?"

"One more time," said Pabst.

And they did it one more time, and indeed, now both were better than before. How had he known?

"Thank you," she said. "Finished?"

"Finished," said Pabst.

"Well, then, let's get out of here," said Ilse Werner.

"Is the Wehrmacht calling?" asked Hubschmid.

"Better the Wehrmacht than your cowshed."

Trude leaned against the damp wall and watched as the cave emptied. The actors left, the spotlights were dismantled, Schneeberger took the camera away.

"Come on," she said. "It's the last day. Let's go deeper. We haven't seen the paintings yet."

She took her husband by the hand and led him. He followed without hesitation. When they had left the chamber, walking through the semidarkness with fewer and fewer lamps above them, she switched on the flashlight. One last light bulb dangled from a wire, then there was only the flashlight beam.

They had to walk carefully; the floor was wet and uneven, and now it was becoming increasingly steep. They came to a fork, with a small wooden arrow, possibly set up by a speleologist from the previous century, pointing to the right.

"I can hardly see anything," said Pabst.

"Just follow me. I've always followed you."

The passage forked again. An arrow pointed to the left.

"I'm sorry," she heard Pabst say.

"For what?"

"Everything."

And here was a three-way fork. A wooden arrow directed them to the middle shaft, which curved to the left.

So they walked for a long time. Or perhaps it was only minutes—it was hard to say; time seemed no longer to exist down there. When you lifted the flashlight, you saw stalactite formations hanging down, jagged and bizarre. Beside them, the stone wall folded, rippled, curved, and creased.

The passageway opened up a bit, and they entered a low chamber. Trude shined the flashlight on the wall. It flickered, making her suddenly worry about the battery. She turned around and illuminated the opposite wall.

Buffalo, drawn with only a few strokes, their legs and horns clearly recognizable. Among them ran little men with spears. Closer inspection revealed how artfully each of them was executed; one threw his spear, another held an ax over his head. From above, where the sky must have been, yellowish lines fell, snow or rain or falling stars. Trude shined the light along the herd. Pabst had stepped beside her.

And there, in front of the charging animals, surrounded by other men bowing before him, falling to their knees, holding out offerings to him, stood a twisted creature. Its back was crooked, one shoulder higher than the other. Where its head should have been were a few red spots, above which hovered two staring eyes. Whatever it was, it didn't seem to belong among these people; it looked as if it came from far away or an even more ancient time. A being from eons past, a brutal and evil creature they tried to appease with offerings.

"Do you recognize him?" asked Pabst.

"Of course."

"Did he speak such a strong dialect even back then?"

"He's still in prison, isn't he?"

"He'll be out soon. The younger daughter, what's her name . . . ?"

"Mitzi."

"She's marrying the deputy governor."

"Well then," said Trude. With mild horror she looked at the small picture, painted so many thousands of years ago, that mockingly returned her gaze. "It wasn't really Hitler who ruled. Not Goebbels or Göring or any of them. It was always him."

"And nothing will happen to him."

"I never asked you what you thought of my script."

"That's right, you didn't."

"Then I'm asking now."

"It has a few good lines."

She was silent for a while, then said, "*Molander* is lost. You won't get it back."

"I know." In the suddenly flickering glow of the flashlight, she saw him take off his glasses. A bat darted through the beam. The light flickered, flared once more, then went out. Trude shook it, to no avail. The battery was dead. They listened. Somewhere water dripped. The silence was complete.

"Like in your movie," he said.

"It's your movie."

He put his arm around her shoulder. She took his hand, feeling his fingers between hers, and he squeezed her hand in return. So they stood, nestled together, listening, not moving.

"I've hurt you so much," he said. "I loved another woman, and I brought you and Jakob back into hell."

"One can be forgiven, but the other . . . Do you remember? The letter he wrote at night when he was sixteen and couldn't sleep from excitement because the whole class would be joining the party the next day? That can't be forgiven."

"Never?"

"It doesn't matter. I stopped loving you long ago."

He was silent for a while before asking: "You don't know the way, do you?"

"Not in the dark."

"Maybe someone will come looking for us."

"It's Friday afternoon. No one will come before Monday, if at all. It was the last day of shooting; everyone's leaving now. They'll think we've left too. It might take a very long time before anyone thinks to look for us here."

"Maybe someone rescues us with dynamite. Or a door opens that no one knew was there. Or we're suddenly outside, without anyone ever finding out how."

"Or we die," she said. "That wouldn't be so bad. So many have died. It hardly matters."

"Yes," he said. "Or we die."

So they stood, holding on to each other and waiting.

Lulu

Jakob was expecting an old lady. Although the woman who opens the door for him, beckons him in, leads him through a messy hallway into an even messier living room, and takes a dirty plate from a chair, indicating that he should sit down, is really no longer young, something about her makes it impossible to call her old.

Jakob sits down. She must be in her midsixties, her face is pale from too much makeup, and the smell of strong perfume fills the room. The apartment is incredibly messy, with magazines and books and clothes and glasses filled with cigarette butts everywhere. It smells of stale smoke. Once, Jakob would have wanted to draw this apartment: the jumble of lines and shapes, the disorder that reflects a life gone off course.

"How old are you?"

"Forty-five."

"My God, only just a baby, now such an old, tired guy. What's with your face?"

Jakob freezes. Normally, no one asks. Everyone always pretends not to see the scar. It's not proper for her to bring it up.

"War injury."

"How?"

"I was in a tank."

"What happened?"

"What happens to every tank. It got hit."

"Does that really happen to every tank?"

"Our tanks had an average lifespan of four days."

"But aren't they . . . armored?"

"Doesn't help much."

Jakob closes his eyes for a moment; he can't stop the memories from flooding in with such force: Arnold and Hubert next to him, behind them Lieutenant Kraneck, still shouting a command that no one understands anymore because now a crash is tearing the world in two. Somehow Jakob crawls up through the pain, clings to glowing metal, doesn't let go, reaches daylight, beside him Hubert's melted face and a messy mixture that was once the lieutenant. He falls to the ground and thinks, as he's falling, that he should be losing consciousness now, but it doesn't happen. He hears his bones break and sees everything, remembers everything afterward, even though he usually manages to push it away, just as he remembers the executions he witnessed, the screams and pleas, the flashing muzzles. He himself didn't shoot, but only because he wasn't ordered to.

"And your hands? Can you use them?"

What gives her the right to ask such questions?

"In general, yes. I'm not a pianist."

"It would be nice if you were a pianist. He would have liked that. Did he have a good death? I always called him Mr. Pabst, you know. I can't imagine him dead. It doesn't suit him. There was surely a wake, and many people came?"

"It was a big funeral. Very respectful obituaries. The governor was there, the president wrote Mama a letter. But it was actually coming to an end for years. The doctors said it was old age, but he never really seemed demented to us. When he said something, we always understood him perfectly. Only in the last few years he hardly wanted to say anything. At the end of the war he lost his best film, it dealt him a blow, he was never the same again."

"That wasn't his best film."

"No?"

"That was of course *Pandora's Box*, and because of me. Besides, his mastery was in editing, so he wasn't the same when sound came along. The talkies were a blessing for Lubitsch, but not for Mr. Pabst. Where did you learn English so well?"

"I went to school in Los Angeles."

"Of course! That's when Mr. Pabst made that bad picture here. And your English just comes back like that?"

Jakob nods. And with the language come the memories. The corridor with the lockers, Mr. Halliway's classroom with a skeleton in it, the baseball field with the chewing gum stuck under the benches, the icy sweet taste of Coca-Cola. "I was an American kid before I became a French kid, and then briefly a Swiss kid, then . . . "

"Yes?"

"A German."

"You were about to say, 'then a Nazi.'"

Jakob remains silent.

"That Mr. Pabst went back, that's one thing. A strange, confusing thing. But—"

"It was a string of misfortunes. He wanted to take his mother to a sanatorium, then there was an accident in the library, and then—"

"No one has to justify himself to me, Jakob. I'm a simple woman, with very few opinions. I know life is complicated. Everyone has to get by somehow. But there's something else I know. It's one thing that he went back. That he took you with him is another. He shouldn't have done that. Just look at you. They broke you."

Jakob stares at her. He feels hot all over.

"Some people make it through life unbroken, but we're not among them. I was already completely at my wit's end in my hellish apartment in New York when Kodak suddenly called me on the phone. They have a motion picture museum here in Rochester. Kodak is insanely rich. Do you know why?"

"Because they invented color film?"

"They didn't. It's from Germany. A small, nice company, and our soldiers went in and searched it, and that's why the good people at Kodak could give me this apartment. Because I am film history. You wouldn't believe it, but for a short time I was as famous as Greta or Marlene. I was also better than both. But I made bad decisions. I would never have suspected what awful things could happen to a star. You think that once you're world famous, you've insured yourself against ever being unable to buy food or becoming homeless."

"You were homeless?"

"No, but to avoid it, I had to do things I won't tell you about. I don't want to make you blush. Yes, just like that! That's what I mean. Like a tomato! Like your poor Papa. He would always blush too and think no one noticed. Want a drink?"

"No thanks."

"Oh, come on." She reaches between old magazines and pulls out a glass. She bends down, finds a bottle under the table, pours, drains the glass, looks around for a second glass, doesn't find one, fills the same glass again and hands it to him. Hesitantly, Jakob brings himself to take a sip.

"Oh, come on," she says again. And because it doesn't matter anymore, he drinks the glass empty. She refills it. "How's Trudy?"

"She's writing. And doing many other things. Do you know her?"

"Oh yes, she once translated for me in Berlin. Such a devoted woman. I always thought he was very lucky with his dear, devoted wife!"

He eyes her in confusion. Why the mocking tone? She drains the glass, refills it, hands it to him, he drinks it down immediately.

"It's true. When I was called up, I happily went off to fight. And when I was wounded in the military hospital, I mainly thought I had to get well quickly to keep fighting. I had a friend in school named Boris, he once came with me to my parents' castle during vacation, but then he left early because . . . He was in my unit, I saw him bleed to death—even that seemed completely normal to me. That's just how the world is, I thought. You always have to fight. That's what they taught me."

She looks at him intently, her head slightly tilted, her mouth a little open, her eyes even brighter than before, perhaps because of the gin, which now also fills his head with a soft, pleasant dizziness.

"I take it you never talked to him about it."

"It wasn't so easy to talk to him. When he wasn't working, he wasn't quite . . . present. It's all in his films. The anger and the ambition and the cunning and the violence. When he was directing, he always knew what people had to do. But he himself never really knew what he was supposed to do." Now Jakob would like another glass, but she doesn't pour any more. "Anyway, he gave me three gifts years ago. 'If you ever go to America,' he said. 'I won't be going there again.' For Louise Brooks, for Seymour Nebenzahl, that was his producer, and for Marc Sorkin, his assistant on the great silent pictures."

"Have you seen Marc?"

"Yes, yesterday. In Brooklyn. He got Papa's meerschaum pipe. He only said nice things about him."

"That doesn't surprise me. He was always servile. The ideal assistant. Just as Trudy is the ideal wife. But you won't have any luck with Nebenzahl. He's moved on to better things."

"Excuse me?"

"Died. A few years ago, in Germany, by the way."

"That explains why I couldn't find him."

"What do you have for me?"

Jakob took out a small, hard object wrapped in newspaper.

"Did you really come all the way across the ocean to bring offerings to old ghosts?"

"No, I'm doing that on the side. I'm here on business."

"Where do you work, Jakob?"

"At the Theater Museum in Munich. I'm here to collect two estates."

"Estates?"

"Sketches, documents. Two set designers. They emigrated here, worked on Broadway, and left their estates to us."

"You're lugging around dusty folders? That's your job?"

"I assume they're folders, and they may well be dusty."

"Why do you do such a thing?"

"I have many tasks at the museum! For example, I also get to help with exhibitions and—"

"Jakob, poor boy. Sorry for calling you that, but I really could be your mother, if . . . " She laughs. "If the world were even crazier. What happened to you? Such a dead museum! Such a dull, lifeless grave for the living! Mr. Pabst once told me that you painted all the time! He said he was almost afraid because you were so clever."

"I used to paint a lot. But then . . . " Jakob raises his hands. His disfigured, damaged hands, his painful hands: the skin blackened on the right one, the pinkie and ring finger no longer able to bend, the left missing the tip of the thumb, the index finger always curved and unable to straighten. You can live quite well with it; it hurts only in damp weather.

"I don't believe you."

"Excuse me?"

"That it's because of your hands. I don't believe it."

He stands up slowly. "I have to go!"

"A soul is quite sensitive. Today I couldn't act as . . . freely and lightly in movies as I used to, because of the things that happened to me. Life bends everyone, but it breaks some brutally and early. You and me, for example." She begins unwrapping the newspaper. Inside is a flat silver object. She holds it up to the light, flips the lid open, reads the engraved letters: "D. W. G.?"

"D. W. Griffith."

"Why?"

"My father got it from Griffith."

"What would Nebenzahl have gotten?"

"A manuscript of *The Joyless Street*."

"I'd rather have that."

"I'm not sure I can . . . just do that."

"But what am I supposed to do with this?"

"Griffith gave Papa the case as a sign of appreciation. The thing is actually to blame for the accident that befell him in . . . "

"A real pig."

"What?"

"Griffith. I knew him well. Take it back, I don't want it." She fills the glass again and pushes it toward him. "Have you seen *Pandora*?"

"No, only *Mysterious Depths*." He reluctantly recalls how the film was booed in Venice, how Mama slumped down next to him, deeper and deeper into her seat, while people snickered. The explosion that effortlessly freed the trapped lovers from the cave chamber provoked an outburst of malicious hilarity in the auditorium. Mama never recovered from that. And Papa, who had probably seen it all coming, wasn't even there; he stayed home in Dreiturm as if it didn't concern him.

In the years that followed, he made his two films about the Nazis, *It Happened on July 20th* and *The Last Act*: Bernhard Wicki with an eye patch as Stauffenberg, the shouting Albin Skoda with Hitler's mustache, the young soldier putting his hands around his neck to kill him—all competently filmed and not particularly interesting. It's not hard to make a mediocre film; you just need to gather some experienced people, and everything runs itself. Only good films are difficult. Recently, he happened to see his father's last work on television, *Through the Woods, Through the Meadows*. He held out for ten minutes before he couldn't take it anymore.

"I have to go."

"Stand by the window. I can't really see you. My eyes . . . ! I don't have glasses because I'm too vain. Or because I don't have the money. One or the other, take your pick. If you stand there in the light, I can see your face."

So he stands by the window. Down below lies a sleepy small-town street, trees swaying in the wind, a woman walking a poodle. A man in uniform unhurriedly empties a mailbox.

"You're as old now as he was when I played Lulu. When he taught me what acting is. You look like him. You're slimmer, of course, and taller too. That comes from your beautiful mother." She takes a step closer, then another. Then she stretches out her hands toward him. He wants to back away, but holds still to avoid being rude.

"I won't hurt you. You know, when I said I could be your mother . . ." She places her hands on his cheeks, takes a final step forward, gently pulls his head down, stands on tiptoe, and kisses him—not on the cheek, but on the mouth. Her lips taste warm and salty.

He backs away. He hears himself mumbling that he's in a hurry, that he has no time, that he really has to go.

He also hears her say something, but he no longer understands; he takes flight. He runs through the hallway, down the stairs, past the mailman, who is still standing in the same spot, past the woman with the poodle, past a child who has appeared out of nowhere, balancing on a rolling board. Only when he stops at a safe distance, gasping for air and reaching into his jacket pocket, does he realize that he has left the cigarette case with her after all.

Tulips

The TV is broken.

I can't believe it. There are no words. This isn't just bad luck, it's fate mocking me. I'm picked up by a car, I'm taken to the studio, Heinz Conrads interviews me about my life, and that very morning the TV in the Abendruh Sanatorium stops working! I can't even tell them, because they won't believe me. Anyone could say: "I was on TV." If no one saw it, it didn't happen.

When Zdenek tells me not to get worked up, that the technician is unavailable on Sunday but will come tomorrow morning, it's all I can do not to scream. I was on TV *today*, tomorrow there will be other people who don't live here in the sanatorium!

I try anyway: at lunch I tell Franz Kahler that I was just at the Austrian Broadcasting Corporation, but he doesn't listen.

With Frau Einzinger I get a bit further. "Really?" she asks. "On the radio?"

"On television."

"Which program?"

I want to tell her, I can clearly see the presenter with the snow-white hair and the angry face, but I can't think of his name.

"On Sunday morning the only thing on is Heinz Conrads," she says.

"Yes!" I exclaim. "On Heinz Conrads!"

She laughs. She doesn't seem to believe me.

"What's so funny? He asked me about my life. My work with Pabst. About Peter Alexander."

"You know Peter Alexander?"

I must have told her this many times, and I don't mind telling it again, but now it's pointless. I leave the dining room before the cake, walk through the corridor, take the elevator up to my room.

Maybe there will be a rerun. Sometime at night. Which won't do me any good either, because no one is in the lounge at night, the TV is off, no one will see.

I sit in the armchair. I kick off my shoes and put on my slippers. Everything feels instantly better. What a difference slippers make! Out the window the trees sway in the wind. Earlier it was raining, or was that yesterday? Now the sky has cleared.

Why am I so upset? Of course, there's the disaster with the broken TV, but I feel like something else unpleasant has happened.

Rosenzweig.

Someone had that name. But who? And something didn't go well in the program. I was asked about something I don't want to talk about. Minna maybe? We were only married for fourteen months, she drank, emptied our bank account twice, and gambled everything away. The thought that she's still alive somewhere and, if I'm very unlucky, will one day move into the Abendruh Sanatorium sometimes keeps me awake.

But no, why would they ask about her? No one cares. And she won't move in here. They must have asked about Pabst.

I close my eyes. Fragments come back, gray areas fill with color. I remember something without quite knowing what. So I open the closet and sink to my knees. It's difficult, I have to hold on, the pressure on my kneecap hurts terribly, and if I didn't hold on to the door with my left hand, I'd lose my balance.

An army rucksack. At the back of the closet, behind my suit jackets and pants on their hooks, it's dirty and old. Every time I take my jacket out of the closet, I see it, but because it's always there, I haven't thought about it in a long time.

I pull at it. It's hard to believe I once carried it on my back. I tug it into the light, then work at the two buckles. They resist, the leather is stiff, but then they open. I feel metal. Seven film cans. Without counting, I know how many there are.

A man has come in. He's tall and has a full beard, and although he's clearly standing before me, I know that this is all happening a long time ago, just like the filming in Prague or my school days, which seem so close that often when I get up in the morning I think I have to hurry or I'll be late. He stands before me, just as he did back then in the nursery. I'm kneeling in a peat bed, just as I'm on my knees now too, here on the carpet, and even then my back hurts, although I'm still young. I'm kneeling in boots and a thick jacket, and the smell of damp earth makes me strangely happy.

He lowers the rucksack to the ground, a rucksack like this one, that is: this rucksack. He groans. Even this huge man could evidently just barely carry it. He tells me his name, but I don't remember it. I think I forgot it immediately back then.

How did you find me?

Wilzek Nursery! That's what you said, last week, on the train! You said if I needed tulip bulbs, I should come to your father. No one has better ones, you said.

Do you need tulip bulbs?

I don't need tulip bulbs, but I have your rucksack. I lugged it all the way to Lischin, fool that I am. They all look the same, the army rucksacks.

You came all the way to Vienna?

I need the shoes!

They were left on the train.

He rants for a while, stamping his foot, grinding his teeth, and saying words you wouldn't want to remember. But it doesn't take long for him to recall that he's actually a gentle person. He calms down, we even shake hands, here on the carpet, me kneeling, him standing, the rucksack next to us, and he pats me on the shoulder and asks about the tin cans, and I say: Oh, your horseshoes were more valuable, and then he says goodbye to my dear old father, who is grafting a fruit tree, wishing him health and a long life, which sadly didn't help, because Papa died the following year, and then the farrier is gone, and I'm standing next to the rucksack thinking: I have to tell him! He'll be so happy. He has to hear it immediately.

And don't move.

I have to call his castle, and if the call doesn't go through, I have to take the train. I have to tell him his film is here!

And I don't move.

A good student, he said, an acolyte I can trust. Maybe not so good after all. Maybe not so trustworthy. In any case, I'm kneeling there in the garden with the rucksack, doing nothing. Just as I'm not moving now on the carpet.

I put it off. Weeks passed, months. When I visit him on the set of *The Trial*, everything feels awkward—how can I explain that I've already had the film for a year? I'm supposed to be the good student, the acolyte, so how do I explain it? I mention the concert hall in Prague, mention the extras, but he doesn't pursue it, he doesn't seem to know what I'm talking about.

Later I was in Dreiturm, three or four times, maybe more. At some point he always starts talking about the lost masterpiece. The great film that might be found again, that might still turn up. If only we knew, he says, who the farrier was.

Yes, I reply. If only we knew. And I think: Maybe later. And I think: I still have time.

And the years pass, and suddenly Pabst is dead. A good student, an acolyte. What is someone like that to do?

There's a knock, someone's coming again, but this time it's not the farrier, but the caregiver Zdenek.

"Are you all right, Herr Wilzek? You didn't eat your cake."

"My cake?"

"There's cake on Sundays. You like it so much."

"You gave me a bad shave."

He looks at me calmly and uncomprehendingly. I'm angry, and I know exactly what I wanted to tell him—my memory isn't that bad.

"I was on TV. How often does it happen that someone goes on TV from the sanatorium? And I had a bad shave!"

"You were on TV, Herr Wilzek?"

"You know that."

He looks at me indifferently, uninterested. He's never interested in anything, so nothing can surprise him.

"A car picked me up! Do you have no memory at all?"

He shrugs and repeats, "A car." Maybe it's a question, maybe an exclamation, maybe just sounds. "Shall I bring the cake to your room?"

I really don't want to eat anything now, but on the other hand, I know myself well enough to know that I almost always want cake, so I say: "Well, bring it then."

"What's with the rucksack?"

He always has to distract from the main issue. "You gave me a bad shave!"

"I'm sorry, Herr Wilzek. It won't happen again. Shall I put the rucksack in the closet? So you can close the door again?"

Then he really goes to the closet and fumbles with the rucksack, pushing and pulling and groaning, and says, "My God, Herr Wilzek, what do you have in here?"

And because right now I'm not sure myself, I say: "None of your business!"

He finally manages it and closes the closet door. "Should we have that picked up for you? It's just in the way. That heavy thing. Surely, you don't need it anymore."

"Can you imagine that I could lift that once?"

"Really, Herr Wilzek? You must have been a strong guy. When was that?"

I would tell him, but I can't remember. I carried it, the rucksack, I know that. It was very heavy. But I was young.

"Be careful," I say. "When Frau Kraninger died, she had no relatives either; everything was thrown away."

"But Herr Wilzek." He is embarrassed. You don't mention the dead in the Abendruh Sanatorium, and certainly not those whose possessions are carried down and carted away immediately after their death because no one wants their things.

"I'm just saying. I have no relatives either. Only an ex-wife, but she . . . !"

"Herr Wilzek! What do you mean?"

"By what?"

"Should we take it to someone? I mean, if you . . . if you're . . . What do you mean?"

"If I'm—what?"

"If . . . " He shrugs helplessly. What does he want from me?

"Leave me alone now. I haven't had a nap yet."

"So no cake?"

"Yes, cake."

And so he leaves. I look around the room. The closet is firmly closed. Wasn't it open just a moment ago, wasn't there something there?

I sit down. Rain is pattering against the window. My back hurts. I'm very exhausted. At the same time, I feel hot. I think I have a fever. It's been a strenuous day.

There's a knock.

"Not now!"

From outside Zdenek's voice says something about cake. I don't know what he wants.

"Not now!" I shout again.

I hear him saying something else, but I ignore it, and so he leaves again. I'm tired. The warmth on my face feels pleasant, like when I was sick as a child. Then the doctor would come. "Franzl, are we sick?" His cool hand on my forehead. And then I thought, he's not sick, Dr. Sämann, so why does he say we? Only I am sick.

Author's Note

The author thanks the German Federal Archives, the Deutsche Kinemathek, and the Austrian Film Archive.

The chapter "Shadow Play" has been substantially revised for the present English translation.

Although this novel is largely inspired by the life stories of the historical G. W. Pabst and his family, it is a work of fiction; for instance, there was no son named Jakob. Pabst's films are still accessible today; only *The Molander Case*, filmed in the last months of the war in Prague, is considered lost. Practically nothing is known about the circumstances of its shooting.

About the Author

Daniel Kehlmann was born in Munich in 1975 and lives in Berlin and New York. His novels and plays have won numerous prizes, including the Candide Prize, the Heimito von Doderer Prize, the Kleist Prize, the Nestroy Prize, and the Thomas Mann Prize. His novel *Tyll* was shortlisted for the 2020 International Booker Prize, and *Measuring the World* has been translated into more than forty languages and is one of the biggest successes in postwar German literature.

About the Translator

Ross Benjamin is the translator of numerous works of German-language literature, including Franz Kafka's *Diaries*, Clemens J. Setz's *Indigo*, Joseph Roth's *Job*, Kevin Vennemann's *Close to Jedenew*, Friedrich Hölderlin's *Hyperion*, and Daniel Kehlmann's *Tyll* and *You Should Have Left*. The recipient of a 2015 Guggenheim Fellowship, Benjamin was also awarded the 2010 Helen and Kurt Wolff Translator's Prize for his rendering of Michael Maar's *Speak, Nabokov*. His translation of *Tyll* was shortlisted for the 2020 International Booker Prize.